AMBUS

Movement to his right caused McConnell to spin in that direction and drop to a crouch. He could dimly see men with automatic weapons moving in the mangrove. He took the moving shadows under fire—two- and three-round bursts to conserve ammunition. Some of the shapes were going down but more were filtering out of the mist.

He looked around for the rest of his SEALs and found they were not there. My God, he thought, I'm alone!

Holding the Stoner with his left hand, he ripped the radio handset off the velcro carrier on his right lapel. "Mainstay, Mainstay, this is Swamp Rat, come in, over!" Nothing. "Mainstay, this is Swamp Rat, I am hot! Request air support priority one, how copy, over?" Again silence.

Fear and frustration produced the familiar nausea and burning lump in his stomach. First Cribbs, then the rest of the squad. No communications and lots of bad guys.

Sweet Jesus, they took my men and now they're coming for me!

SEAL TEAM ONE

DICK COUCH

AVON BOOKS 🔷 NEW YORK

SEAL TEAM ONE is an original publication of Avon Books. This work has never before appeared in book form. This work is a novel. Any similarity to actual persons or events is purely coincidental.

AVON BOOKS
A division of
The Hearst Corporation
1350 Avenue of the Americas
New York, New York 10019

Copyright © 1991 by H.R. Couch
Published by arrangement with the author
Library of Congress Catalog Card Number: 90-93614
ISBN: 0-380-76115-7

First Avon Books Printing: June 1991

AVON TRADEMARK REG. U.S. PAT. OFF. AND IN OTHER COUNTRIES, MARCA REGISTRADA, HECHO EN CANADA

Printed in Canada

UNV 10 9 8 7 6 5

For my friend Gene,
who I miss.

The Staff Officer plans,
The Logistician provides,
And the General says when to begin.

But the killing is done,
And the battle decided,
By the work of much younger men.

Foreword

UNDERSTANDING THE VIETNAM War is not easy for it was not a single place or event. It was a long war, fought with different levels of intensity under three presidents. One's Vietnam and personal slice of the war depended on your duties, your branch of service, and when you were there.

I think most people remember Vietnam through the eyes of the draftee—adolescent, naive, terrified, and often courageous. For them, a tour in Vietnam was like a harsh prison term. For some of them it was a life sentence. But there were others, the volunteers, whom you could find in all branches of the service and in every outfit. Many were senior enlisted men who went back on multiple tours. The fliers were mostly volunteers, as were the Navy Riverine Forces. The Army Special Forces, the Rangers, the Marines, and the Military Advisory Groups were all-volunteer outfits. Some were volunteers just a step ahead of the draft. Others, once drafted, wanted to serve in the best way they could and joined a special unit.

Some volunteers had no more choice than the draftees. It was their time to go and there happened to be a war in progress at the time. Some volunteered for adventure and challenge. For others, Vietnam was a place to find out how good they really were. Some of those volunteers were closet patriots—not an easy thing to be in Vietnam. And some were professionals—craftsmen in their own way, whose chosen profession and commitment to their trade required that they be there.

Vietnam was the first public conflict for a unique vol-

1

SEAL TEAM ONE

unteer, the Navy SEAL. A Navy man has to volunteer to be a SEAL, and a rigorous training program tests the level of that voluntary commitment. It is unique among the service elite in that at any time, during or after training, a man can walk away by merely saying, "I quit." He is no longer a SEAL and he no longer has to do what is asked of Navy SEALs. It sounds easy—"I quit"—but some men cannot say those two words. *SEAL Team One* is the story of those volunteers in Vietnam. It is a novel and the characters and events are fiction. However, the SEALs and their operations in Vietnam were very much like those described, and on occasion, certain episodes in this book come very close to the truth.

I was a SEAL platoon commander in Vietnam and that experience helped me to write this book. It is very comfortable and convenient for us old-timers to talk about the old days and what great operators we were. I probably suffer from the ex-warrior's affliction: "The older we get, the better we were." The combat record of the SEAL platoons in Vietnam is a proud one and I share that pride. But I'm even more proud of what the Navy SEAL teams are today. My observations are that they don't make them like they used to—they make them a lot better. Today's Navy SEALs have to be. The current world political climate may demand a rapid response in the arenas of low-intensity conflict and terrorism, as well as conventional fighting. These requirements demand a much higher degree of military skill and professionalism on the part of our military special operators.

I'd like to thank my teammates who contributed a few anecdotes and much encouragement to this project. And my special thanks to Boat Support Unit One-Det Charlie, the Solid Anchor HAL-5 Seawolf Det, and my fellow SEALs from Whiskey Platoon who contributed so much more, way back when. I've heard more than one Navy SEAL say, "Why can't someone tell it like it is?" Well, guys, I hope you're not disappointed.

Chapter One

THE TRIBE

McCONNELL WAS EXHAUSTED, struggling, both mentally and physically. His clothes, equipment, and body were wet and covered with mud. The swamp's brackish water mingled with sweat and stale urine. He smelled like a sewer. The patrol had pushed through the elephant grass and nipa palm most of the night, and the foliage had removed much of his dark camouflage face paint. What remained served only to mark the lines in his face and make him look dirty. It was the face of a young man, but the eyes were older, almost out of place, and they shifted continuously, combing the foliage ahead and to either side. They would be out of it in an hour if nothing happened. He now had to force himself to concentrate and move carefully.

McConnell was in a hurry to get the patrol safely out of Viet Cong territory. They were moving along a trail near the edge of the Nam Can Forest while the dawn cautiously filtered through the mangrove trees. There were several things wrong. The boat was late getting them to the insertion point. He had allowed for an hour and a half to get to the ambush site, but it had taken longer. They had made no enemy contact and now they were late in returning to the pickup point on the canal—still another two klicks away. He hoped the boat would wait. The next sixty minutes or so would be the most dangerous for the

SEALs as they traveled over semi-open country in the early dawn. Just like the VC, the SEALs were much safer moving at night.

Cribbs walked ahead of McConnell on point, some fifteen meters up the trail. Periodically he halted the squad file to listen for a few moments before signaling them to continue. During these stops he would cock his head to one side and seem to sniff the air. McConnell wished he would move the patrol along more quickly but said nothing. Cribbs was a pro and knew the risks of moving too fast. After one such stop he disappeared from McConnell's view around a bend in the trail.

The squad file had passed into a marshy area sparsely populated by mangrove trees—some dead, some alive. Waist-high grass and low scrub brush clung to the firmer ground along the edges of the trail, parting the mist that rose from the swamp on either side.

McConnell listened but could detect only the normal morning bog sounds filtering through the high-pitched hum of his personal swarm of mosquitoes. He negotiated the bend in the trail expecting to see the hawk-eyed Cribbs crouched on the trail, waiting for the rest of them to catch up. Instead he saw a small Vietnamese boy in the middle of the trail, flanked by a Viet Cong guerrilla and an NVA regular. The VC was dressed in customary black pajamas while his comrade wore the tan field uniform and pith-type helmet of the North Vietnamese Army. The boy was barefoot and wore a shabby T-shirt and shorts, typical of the children of Vietnam. Both men held AK-47 assault rifles across their chests, like sentries posted to protect their small charge.

When they saw McConnell, the men moved to bring their weapons to a firing position. As McConnell thought, almost bemusedly, Now where the hell is Cribbs and what are these guys doing on the trail?, the rest of him was reacting swiftly to the deadly threat before him. He knew he had them if he moved quickly and didn't make a mistake. He didn't really raise his rifle. The butt stock was tucked in his left armpit, so his dropping to one knee had the effect of leveling the weapon along his extended right arm. Experience had taught him that the enemy, and most of the Americans for that matter, fired high when snap-shooting, so lower was safer. The Stoner Rifle tended to ride up and to the right, so he began firing at the knees of the man to his left. Fiery red tracers leapt from the long barrel, each escorting four invisible and lethal bullets as they slammed into the trio blocking the path. He raked them left to right and back again on full automatic, and their bodies jumped and twitched as if they were suddenly given life by a nervous puppeteer.

Earlier in his tour, McConnell would have been tempted to cut the two armed men away from the child. But that would have allowed one of the enemy an even chance to return fire, and he could not allow that. The boy was blown straight back up the trail while the two men jerked and spun off to either side. McConnell again looked up the trail for Cribbs. Only his training and the anchor of responsibility for the rest of his team kept him from hurtling up the trail in search of his point man. The two fallen enemy were partially concealed lumps in the tall grass while the boy lay awkwardly on his back with his limbs fixed at odd angles. What was the kid doing here in the middle of this, and where was Cribbs?

Movement to his right caused McConnell to spin in that direction and again drop to a crouch. He could dimly see men with automatic weapons were moving in the mangrove. "Ambush right!" he called as he took the moving shadows under fire. Two- and three-round bursts this time to conserve ammunition. Some of the shapes were going down but more were filtering out of the mist. Suddenly aware that he was the only one firing, he looked to his right for the rest of his SEALs and found they were not there. *My God*, he thought, *I'm alone! I've lost my men.* Holding the Stoner with his left hand, he ripped the radio handset off the velcro carrier on his right lapel, "Mainstay, Mainstay this is Swamp Rat, come in over!" Nothing. "Mainstay, this is Swamp Rat, I am hot! Request air support priority one, how copy over?" Again silence. McConnell sent a few more short bursts at the shadowy figures. They seemed to fade away when he fired and reappeared between bursts, methodically draining his ammunition and will to resist. Fear and frustration produced the familiar nausea and burning lump in his stomach. First Cribbs, then the rest of the squad. No communications and lots of bad guys. Sweet Jesus, they took my men and now they're coming for me!

"Hey, sir."

Commo! I got commo! "Mainstay, Mainstay, this is Swamp Rat, over!"

"Sir?"

"Roger Mainstay, go ahead."

"Hey, Mr. McConnell, wake up. You okay, sir?"

"Roger—huh?" A man wearing clear-framed military glasses and a faded blue flight suit hovered over him.

"We're almost home, sir. Catalina Island is in sight, dead ahead."

"Wha . . . Where?"

"We're almost home. We'll be at the North Island terminal in fifteen minutes." McConnell's rescuer then moved down the cabin waking other sleeping passengers.

McConnell brought his hand to his chin and wiped it clean. He glanced down at the small puddle of spittle on the front of his jungle greens. A thin sweat chilled him as the aircraft descended. McConnell closed his eyes again and then snapped them open, not wanting to return to the scene in the mangrove. The fear and the nausea subsided as he came more fully awake. Relax, he told himself, and in a few moments his heart began to beat normally.

The dreams were set in different places but the plot was always the same—he had lost his men, he had no radio communications and the enemy was closing in around him. The child was a new player and McConnell hoped he was not a permanent member of the cast. The dreams disturbed him and left the same unanswered questions when he awoke: Where did I make a mistake? How did I get out of radio range? Why did I let the men get separated? How could I have been so irresponsible!

"Hey, Chief, you got a smoke?"

The man across the aisle fished into the blouse pocket of his jungle greens and tossed the pack to McConnell. He shook one free of the box and returned it to its owner.

The man produced a match and McConnell leaned across the aisle to accept the light. He nodded his thanks as he drew the smoke deeply into his lungs. He'd smoked for a short time during his freshman year in college but had given it up. Six weeks into the tour he had started again.

Lieutenant (junior grade) James W. McConnell was a coming-home sailor and he found that hard to believe. It was a warm, comforting thought, one he allowed to linger. He looked out the window at the whitecaps sliding off the dark blue Pacific swells. It was over and he was almost back.

McConnell was a slender man, just over six feet tall and rather undistinguished except for the occasional boyish smile and wide-set, deep green eyes. His thick, wavy brown hair might have been an asset but for the poor work of an Army barber in Saigon. He hadn't been lean when he left San Diego, but he had lost fifteen pounds since and had aged more than the passing time would indicate. SEALs train as a team and deploy to Vietnam as a combat platoon. Seven months was the normal rotation for a SEAL platoon "in-country." Now McConnell and Foxtrot Platoon, SEAL Team One, were finally coming home.

It was the second week in April and they were scheduled to arrive in San Diego late Friday morning. The old C-54, a military version of the DC-4 that was queen of the skies in the late forties and early fifties, had made refueling stops in the Philippines, Guam, Wake Island, and Hawaii. She was now on the final leg of her journey. McConnell's men shared the plane with the platoon equipment boxes and spare aircraft parts being shipped back to the States. The flight had taken thirty-nine air hours with an overnight crew rest on Guam. But it was a freedom bird and the liberated quietly passed the hours sleeping, playing cards, or pawing through the stale sandwiches and dried chicken wings from the steady flow of box lunches. The old gal finally settled onto the tarmac at North Island Naval Air Station just after midday.

The reception at North Island was a low-key and somewhat tacky affair. The aircraft was parked at the terminal for about ten minutes before the ground crew was able to get the boarding stairs rolled into place. Five members of the brass section of the Navy band gamely played and replayed "Anchors Aweigh." The few wives on hand belonged to the air crew who had only been away from home for about a week. Their homecoming too was cause for a celebration. Two transpacific crossings in those old crates could definitely be classified as cheating death. Only one of McConnell's men was married and his wife had waited out the tour with her parents somewhere in the Midwest. When they'd left on deployment seven months before there had been two wives, but one was now a widow. A small group of SEALs, easily distinguished in their green fatigues, milled around a step van and a stake truck that would take Foxtrot Platoon and their equipment back across Coronado to the team area. God, I've dreamed about his, thought McConnell. But he noticed that his hands were shaking slightly as he retrieved his cap from under the seat.

He descended the stairs and stepped back into "the World," and was immediately greeted by Lieutenant Commander Sam Green, commanding officer of SEAL Team One. Around the team he was known as Daddy Sam, but he was always addressed in person as "Captain." Green was one of the few original frogmen still on active duty. As an eighteen-year-old enlisted man he had crawled ashore on Omaha Beach to tie demolition charges on the steel obstacles that the German's had spread like a giant child's toy jacks on the French beaches. As a chief petty officer he had radioed hydrographic data to McArthur's landing forces at Inchon. He was an officer now, a Mustang, as the Navy called the officers who came up through the ranks. Now he sent younger men off to fight. Green's lined face held watery blue eyes, guarded by bushy eyebrows that swept up in the middle like the sides of a loosely erected pup tent.

"Welcome back, Mr. McConnell." Green stood at attention and saluted his platoon officer. "You did a job over there and I'm proud of you." McConnell returned the salute and then shook Green's hand, knowing he had just received high praise from his commanding officer. Mc-

Connell remembered his CO as being stern and authoritarian. This was a very different Daddy Sam who now treated him as more of an equal.

"Thanks, Captain," McConnell replied. "It's sure good to be home. I wish a few more of us could have been on the plane."

"So do I, Mr. McConnell." Green's eyebrows drooped a bit lower. He looked carefully at McConnell for a moment before placing a hand on McConnell's shoulder and guiding him away from the boarding stairs. "Son, don't try to second-guess what might have been. A lot of your men wouldn't have made it without you. You know that, I know that, and your platoon knows it. You were in a hot area and damned lucky not to have had more casualties."

McConnell was surprised that Green seemed to know what he had been thinking about during those hours over the Pacific. McConnell knew he had done a good job with the platoon and, by most accounts, an exceptional one. He also knew that he could have saved a few purple hearts and maybe a life if he had been a little better or a little quicker.

Green excused himself and joined the other SEALs in the welcoming party as they circulated among the members of Foxtrot Platoon, shaking hands and offering congratulations. He made it a point to say a few words to each one of them. There were several cases of beer iced down in the back of the step van and most of the SEALs were enjoying a cold one.

"Beer, sir?"

"Thanks, Senior Chief, don't mind if I do," replied McConnell. Senior Chief Petty Officer Maynard Johnson was the Platoon Chief of Foxtrot Platoon. At first glance he looked very little like an authority figure. He was fortyish with an almost sloppy bulge pushing behind his belt buckle. But there was a sharp strength to his features and an awareness of everything around him. The Foxtrot SEALs could fool the Navy and the platoon officers, but they could never fool Senior Chief Johnson. Johnson ruled the platoon with an informal, seemingly casual brand of discipline. But everyone knew where the Chief drew the line, and no one wanted to be on the bad side of Senior Chief Maynard Johnson.

McConnell noted that the Chief wore freshly pressed greens and polished jungle boots, and he knew that under the starched fatigue cap, the Chief's 1950s vintage close-cut flat top was waxed into place, just like his short handlebar mustache. McConnell looked on his platoon chief with equal measures of respect, affection and trust. Johnson regarded McConnell as would a grateful father-in-law for the solid, doting husband who had married his much-loved, but unattractive daughter.

"Here's to you, Chief, and thanks again. We wouldn't be here without you."

"Easy day, sir," replied Johnson, lifting his can in return. "It's been a pleasure serving with you." They watched as Green finished his rounds and rejoined them.

"Afternoon, Captain," said the chief as he saluted the commanding officer.

"Well, good afternoon, Senior Chief!" Green returned the salute and warmly grasped the Chief's outstretched hand with both of his own. "And Maynard, thank you for bringing another platoon back." McConnell sensed there was something special between his CO and his platoon chief. The three of them watched the repatriated Foxtrot SEALs enjoy their homecoming. In differing ways for the three of them, these SEALs were "their men."

"Jim, my car's just behind the terminal; why don't you ride back to the team area with me."

"Fine by me, Captain," responded McConnell. He glanced at Johnson. "Chief, see that the men get liberty as soon as they check in back at the team. We'll break down the equipment boxes on Monday. Muster at thirteen hundred." Then, turning to Green, "No problem with a late muster for us on Monday, is there, sir?"

"None whatsoever," said Green.

Senior Chief Johnson then surprised both officers by snapping to attention and rendering a parade-ground salute: "Mr. McConnell, request permission to shove off with the platoon and to secure the men from this deployment."

McConnell hesitated and smiled before coming to attention to return Johnson's salute. "Very well, Senior Chief, permission granted."

Johnson spun on his heel and headed over to the van, where the platoon was still working on the beer. McConnell watched him all the way, then turned back to Green. "Ready when you are, Captain."

McConnell thoroughly enjoyed the ride across Coronado. Green cut through residential neighborhoods as they drove south to the SEAL compound located on the Silver Strand, the long sand spit that connected Coronado to Imperial Beach and Tiajuana. The neat wide streets and manicured lawns were a shocking contrast to the mud, swamp, and palm-thatched hootches of the lower Delta. The world he left had been one of dark green and dirty brown while this one was in Technicolor. It was all so *clean.* While Green drove he talked quietly about the team and the difficult deployment schedule that Team One was having to deal with.

"Jim, we're losing a lot of our experienced men and we're having to deploy too many first-tour SEALs with platoons I'm committed to send to Vietnam. Next week I'd like you to take a look at our training cycle and make recommendations as you think appropriate."

McConnell was flattered at being taken into the CO's confidence. He felt like a young brave back from an extended raid on an enemy village, and the chief, having found him worthy, was seeking his counsel. This was a different commanding officer from the stern, reserved Lieutenant Commander Green he remembered. The platoon officers had a tough job, but their commander's task was not an easy one, either.

McConnell sighed, thinking back to the beginning of the deployment. "Captain, I'll do my best. But the veterans are the key. I was lucky to have Cribbs and Reed and especially Chief Johnson." Our training's fine, he thought, and basically I knew what to do. But how do you train for the way combat operations make you *feel*? Then to change the subject, "You and the Chief go back a ways, don't you, sir?"

A soft smile worked across Green's lips. "He was my

leading petty officer when I took the first platoon to Vietnam. We were in the Rung Sat Special Zone in sixty-four. Jim, I know it's hard to prepare for what you went through, but if there's some way we can better train the outbound platoons, I want to know about it. Men like you are my best source of information. Talk it over with Chief Johnson and let me know." McConnell agreed and then Green added after some hesitation, "You know Hotel Platoon got hit a few days ago."

McConnell didn't know. How could he, having been in transit for the better part of a week? For McConnell, hearing that a platoon had been hit was like hearing that your brother was in a car wreck. The only question was how bad was it, and you were almost afraid to ask.

"And?" said McConnell, unable to better phrase it.

"They got caught by a VC ambush team. Jancavich and Waters took two rounds each, but they'll make it. They're at the Third Surgical Hospital in Binh Thuy. Lieutenant Bartholomew got some shrapnel and was at the Third Surg for a day or two but he's back at Rach Gia. The platoon's standing down now but they'll be back up in a few days."

VC ambush teams. The thought sent a wave of fear through him. McConnell had met all three of the Hotel SEALs when he had gone to Rach Gia for a visit shortly after the platoon had come in-country. They were all good men and McConnell had particularly liked Bart. Bartholomew and the other two were second-tour SEALs. Losing Jancavich and Waters was going to hurt Hotel Platoon.

"Will you send them replacements, Captain?" It sounded like an indictment, which McConnell had not intended.

"No. No, I won't be sending anyone over," said Green softly. "My experienced people on the Strand are committed to platoons in training, and I can't put new guys in an operational platoon. It's not fair to the platoon or the new men." Both men were silent for the remainder of the trip.

The war, reflected McConnell, was still there; it's going on without me. Was it supposed to end just because I left?

For a moment, residential Coronado now seemed like a foreign land.

McConnell had not spent all that much time at SEAL Team One between basic training and the deployment of Foxtrot Platoon. Nonetheless, driving up to the team area was something of a homecoming. The team area, or Naval Special Warfare complex, was a segregated series of compounds on the west side of the Strand Highway fronting the Pacific Ocean, while the rest of the naval amphibious base was on the east side of the highway, on San Diego Bay. The team complex housed SEAL Team One and the three West Coast Underwater Demolition Teams. The teams shared adjoining administration and office spaces, but each team had its own compound and entrance. The complex itself was a series of drab, modern, one-story buildings with open areas enclosed by eight-foot chain link. The most conspicuous feature was a parachute loft that rose some five stories above the sand and was shared by all four teams. The training unit, where tribal initiation rituals were performed, was located just south of the SEAL team compound.

At the team area, McConnell felt like a star football player entering his old fraternity house the year after graduation. *Welcome Back Foxtrot* was chalked on the board by the quarterdeck. Several of the officers greeted him with a handshake and congratulations. A few of the senior enlisted men saluted him with a semiformal "Welcome back, Mr. McConnell." This was formal tribute, as the SEAL team compound was very relaxed. Most of the men wore tan UDT swim trunks, blue T-shirts, blocked fatigue caps, and polished combat boots. There were furtive and respectful glances from the new officers and enlisted men when they learned he was with Foxtrot Platoon. McConnell remembered when Alpha Platoon had returned, just after he arrived at Team One. He and the other new men had watched silently as the veterans were welcomed back by their teammates. Now, he was a proven warrior and shown respect by the untested. He had taken a few scalps and counted much coup, and he was worthy to be in the company of warriors. He was even considered wise enough to give counsel to his chief. Lieutenant Commander Green watched this welcome, while his yeoman stood by patiently with a clipboard full of message traffic.

"Let's get together next week for a formal debriefing. Have Operations schedule it and include the outbound platoon officers. Have you completed your end-of-tour report?"

"Not yet, Captain," said McConnell. "It's done but I have to get it typed up. It'll be on your desk by next Wednesday."

"That'll be fine," replied Green. "I know the admiral will want to see it as soon as possible. Have a good weekend." With that, Green, the yeoman, and the clipboard were gone before McConnell could reply. McConnell headed for the operations office to check in and see about scheduling his debriefing. What I really want, thought McConnell, is to not be the Foxtrot Platoon officer of SEAL Team One for a while, and have some time to adjust to being back in the old US of A.

"Hey, Dude, welcome the fuck back," yelled the tall SEAL behind the desk in the ops shop when McConnell entered. Lieutenant Tom Harper was the team operations officer and a veteran of several combat tours. "Understand you really kicked some Viet Cong ass down there in the lower Delta."

Harper's sun-bleached hair and dark tan made him look like a beach boy, but his tailored tropical khaki uniform and rows of combat decorations made him look like a naval officer on a recruiting poster. He had the reputation of being a good operator, both in combat and in the San Diego bars. McConnell had known him casually before he deployed, having seen him at parties and around the team. Now he charged from behind the desk to shake his hand and clap him on the back.

"Sit down, man," said Harper. "Can I get you a cup of coffee?"

"Thanks, Tom, I had plenty on the plane."

"I'll bet you did," replied Harper. "My last trip back on the freedom bird I killed a fifth of Wild Turkey between

Hawaii and North Island. Fell down the fucking ramp and took out three guys in the band.''

Harper yelled for the personnel man to take Mc-Connell's service jacket and orders for processing, and filled his own coffee cup. He kicked a chair around in front of McConnell and sat on it backwards, cowboy fashion.

"Well, partner, I been following your after-action reports and you did one shit-hot job over there. Nice body count. And the word is out that you're some kind of a surgeon with that Stoner.''

McConnell was exceptionally proficient with an automatic weapon, and some accounts of his shooting had been magnified in the retelling. Apparently he was becoming something of a cult hero around the team as a result. A part of him enjoyed the attention his shooting skills had brought him, but he felt awkward about Harper's compliment.

"Yeah, we got our share of indians all right, but then we paid for it. On that score I probably could have done better.''

"Bull fucking roar,'' scoffed Harper. "There's damn few people that can do what you did over there. Running a SEAL platoon in combat ain't easy. Half this chicken-shit country thinks we're criminals 'cause we go to Vietnam—'cause we're a volunteer outfit. But the guys around here know what it takes to be a good operator.''

And as if he sensed some of McConnell's concern, he added in a quieter tone, "Sure, you're going to think about the guys who didn't make it back, but don't get down on yourself. Don't replay the bad operations and try to give them a happier ending. It isn't healthy—I know. Your tour's over and you did just fine.'' Then shifting gears like Mario Andretti, "Want to get laid tonight by a roundeye? I got a couple of schoolteachers up in La Jolla, sort of team groupies. Guaranteed they'll blow your socks off.''

"I'm fucking beat. Thanks, but I think I'll check into the BOQ and crash. Chief Johnson and the platoon will be along soon. Would you see they get in and out as quickly as possible?''

"Not to worry, mother, we'll take care of them. Have

a good weekend, and I'll see you at the Downwinds on Sunday if not before.''

McConnell went out to the parking lot behind the team area and took the cover off his old MGB. He hooked up the battery and, miraculously, it started on the second try. The truck had arrived with the platoon gear so he located his kit bag and tossed it in the passenger's seat of the little car.

McConnell checked into a room at the bachelor officers' quarters on the naval amphibious base and rescued his civilian clothes from the BOQ storage facility. He set up housekeeping, such as it was for a bachelor SEAL, and realized that he was starving. He chased down a burger and fries with a beer at the BOQ snack bar, then ordered a second. McConnell was not sure what time zone or combination of time zones his body was in, but he was beginning to tire. Sitting in the greasy military spoon, he realized that for the first time in longer than he could remember, he had no responsibilities—absolutely none. No warning orders, no mission briefings, no fire support requests—nothing. That realization and the two beers brought on a surprising euphoria, and he seriously considered cleaning up and driving over to Mission Beach where the crowd would be gathering to start the weekend drinking. But weariness tightened its grip and he was dragging by the time he got back to the room. He pulled off his boots and turned on the television. He hadn't seen a TV for over six months, but it was as familiar as going to the bathroom. He propped the pillow behind his head and watched the Roadrunner screw around with Wily Coyote. That was the last thing McConnell remembered on his first day back from Vietnam.

McConnell snapped awake just after nine on Saturday morning, disoriented and wary. There was a faint smell of disinfectant and the quiet hum of the central air-conditioning. The muffled beat of helicopter blades gave him a start, but they were different—steady and even, not from a machine that was flying low and hard. He dropped his head back to the pillow and exhaled sharply. Jesus, I'm not there! He lay there awhile contemplating his return home, feeling content and a bit strange. There was nothing he absolutely had to do that day, and he was a bit lost without the familiar tug of responsibility. The platoon was back and it was like the kids had gone off to college.

Rather than eating at the BOQ mess, he drove into Coronado to have breakfast at a coffee shop that had been his favorite. The place was filled with the usual mix of locals who nursed cups of coffee as they talked politics, sports, and general gossip. McConnell found an empty booth and settled in behind a cup of coffee. In the next booth three men in their mid-sixties were quietly arguing about Vietnam. McConnell couldn't quite follow the conversation, other than a phrase here and there: "shit or get off the pot . . . ain't our war . . . can't quit now . . . jest like Korea." Had McConnell been asked for an opinion he would have been hard pressed to give one. Before the deployment he had followed the course of the war in the papers and on TV news. They reported it like the sports or the elections; the casualty figures were much like the box score or the pre-election opinion polls. Americans needed to know whether their teams or candidates were winning or loosing. But as soon as he arrived in-country, he lost the big picture. Now he found that he was still digesting his combat tour, and it was hard to relate what happened in his little corner of the war to the general Vietnam conflict. On the flight back one of the pilots had sought him out about the war because he had "been there." McConnell had dodged most of his questions, saying that running SEAL operations and trying to stay in one piece didn't give him much time to think about it or form much of an opinion. This was partly true, but McConnell also realized that he, perhaps like most Americans, was seldom able to form an opinion without a steady diet of the American media. McConnell tried to find something profound in this but could only conclude that firsthand experience was no substitute for Walter Cronkite.

After breakfast, McConnell decided to take a walk around town and headed east on Orange Avenue. A light morning mist was starting to lift and the community was coming awake. McConnell drifted along looking in windows and at the people, who were mostly elderly and affluent, typical of Coronado. It was all familiar yet so very new. McConnell felt out of touch and caught himself wondering if things had changed at all or had his absence given him a different perspective. After a half hour of wandering he bought a couple of newspapers and headed back to the amphibious base.

He dropped into an easy chair in the back of the large TV room in the BOQ and went to work on the *San Diego Tribune*. Three or four other junior officers were in the front of the room watching a cowboy movie and drinking beer. He read the news on Vietnam in both the *Tribune* and the L.A. *Times,* again surprised at how little he knew about the war. McConnell closed his eyes and thought about the world he had just left, his own patch of swamp in the lower MeKong Delta—an area considered of little importance to the U.S. and of no importance to the Saigon government. It's like my war and the Vietnam War were two different conflicts, he thought. It bothered him that Americans at home who watched TV and read the newspaper had a far better idea of the general conduct of the war than he did. Or maybe it was just the media's version of how the war was going. And it angered him to think that Foxtrot Platoon's efforts during the tour seemingly had no effect on the outcome.

Later that afternoon he went for a run on the beach, heading south along the Strand toward the Mexican border. He was out of shape, but the clean sand and cool sea breeze made him feel wonderful. For a while he was able to purge himself of Vietnam and the coming home from it.

Sunday morning was a replay of Saturday, only there were comics with the papers. McConnell noted that you could pick up and follow the exploits of Prince Valiant just about as easily as you could the course of the war. About noon he again ran on the beach, only this time he went north to the Coronado public beach. Southern California was a crowded, wacky place but the beaches were great. McConnell went body surfing for a while and then joined in a few games of volleyball in the soft sand. He capped the afternoon off with a game of over-the-line soft-

ball, a three-man beach adaption of street stickball. He'd
have stayed longer but running in the soft sand was taking
its toll on him. He had to shower and change before heading off to the Downwinds.

McConnell arrived about five-thirty, well ahead of the
rest of the crowd. The Downwinds was a back room and
patio area behind the North Island Officer's Club, and it
was *the* place on Sunday evening for junior officers and
single women in San Diego. The singles ritual was enacted
at different base clubs on other days of the week. They
gathered at Mirmar Naval Air Station on Thursday and at
the Marine Corps Recruit Depot on Friday. But the best
was Sunday night at the Downwinds. The "Winds" usually got going about six-thirty. Most came directly from
the beach or the bull fights in Tijuana unless there was a
Chargers game. The uniform was tank top or T-shirt, ber-
mudas, and shower shoes. The informality, and that it was
the last gasp of the weekend, made the Downwinds the
wildest spot on the tour. It was one of the items on
McConnell's list of *Things I'm Going to Do When I Get
Back.*

McConnell found a table and ordered a beer. While he
waited for the crowd to arrive, he thought about the last
two days. Things hadn't quite gone as he had mentally
rehearsed them. Oh, he'd done pretty much what he'd
planned—a run on the beach, sleep late, eat restaurant
food—but it didn't feel right. In some ways it was like
he had never left the States and in other ways it was like he
had yet to come home. What's wrong with me? he thought.
I've been dreaming about this. Why do I feel so out of
place? He hadn't allowed himself to think about going
home until the end of his tour was in sight. But when he
realized he was going to make it, the anticipation of it and
his expectations had risen exponentially. Now those expectations, however ambiguous, were in conflict with reality. There was no one specific thing or event that
McConnell could put his finger on, but his life was out of
sync. He had seen a slogan on the side of a bunker a few
months back: *Life has a flavor the protected will never
know.* McConnell would have reworded it: Anticipation of

life is sweetest among those in mortal danger. Remove the danger and the reality is like a stale Coke—sweet but flat.

The crowd that gathered on Sunday evenings at the Winds was a social powwow of the various tribes that dwelled in San Diego. There was the Marine tribe, easily recognized by their short hair and the emblems or slogans on their shirts. The pilots wore gold-rimmed sunglasses and talked with their hands. The shipboard officers, perhaps the largest tribe, were hard to spot until you got close enough to hear the continuous flow of nautical jargon. There were some mixed breeds like Marine aviators. And there were the smaller tribes like the medical officers, supply officers, and the SEALs. Collectively they were a boisterous and hedonistic group, and the worst of the bunch were the SEALs. The pilots might have bigger egos, and a group of rowdy Navy dentists would have gotten a crudeness award in any theater of operations. And nobody's louder than marines when they get a few beers under their belts.

But the SEALs were consistently the wildest and probably the raunchiest of the bunch. What tied this collection of officers and hooligans together was a seemingly inexhaustible supply of women. McConnell could never figure out where they all came from. He saw more familiar faces among the camp followers than among the men. The officers came and went but many of the same women came back week after week, year after year.

He was on his third beer and second cigarette by the time the bar began to reach its normal standing-room-only capacity. He watched the various groups form and the girls move among them. Feeling like an old alum who had arrived early at a homecoming football game, he saw a few familiar faces but he could not attach the names. The crowd was mostly strangers and it seemed a lot younger than he remembered. He hadn't seen any of the guys from the teams yet but it was just a matter of time. McConnell noticed one particularly attractive girl as she walked in. She was short and rather athletic-looking. Her cropped dark hair and a terrific tan set off her white, even teeth. She and her two girlfriends joined a group of pilots near his table. McConnell caught her eye and smiled, but she seemed not to notice and turned back to the aviators. The crowd continued to swell in their tribal enclaves, standing and drinking beer. The few tables near the walls were occupied by lone Indians like McConnell and girls too timid to join one of the groups. It was all very clicky and ritualistic. His quiet, detached assessment was shattered when he was recognized by his tribe.

"Hey, asshole, you gonna sit there like a bottle of urine or you gonna come over and have a drink with your ship-mates!" Tom Harper was in fine form and glowed from the sun and beer of a long San Diego Sunday afternoon. He collared McConnell and dragged him to the middle of the room where he and three or four other SEALs had circled up. Harper wore a tank top that said *Peace Through Fire Superiority* on the front. On the back was inscribed *SEAL Team One—When You Care Enough to Send the Very Best*, superimposed on a map of Vietnam. He introduced McConnell to the other guys and filled McConnell's glass with the pitcher from which he was drinking, spilling some on both of them.

"Well, gunfighter," Harper said with his arm around McConnell's shoulder, "welcome the fuck back."

"Good weekend, Tom?" McConnell inquired as he drew down on his beer.

"I'll tell you something, pardner, I did enough screwing this weekend that I think I'm gonna have to have wheels attached to my knees and elbows. How about yourself—any action?"

"Nope, I just kind of dinked around and took it easy."

"Yeah, I know what you mean," Harper said in a more sober voice. "You're back but it takes a little while to really get here. Just relax and you'll get caught up. I find that a lot of beer speeds up the process." He topped off McConnell's glass and headed to the bar for a refill.

McConnell turned and surveyed the group. There were two girls, a tall redhead Harper called Coppercrotch and a sweet-faced blonde who answered to the name of Heavy Duty Sue. Both were sun-ripened beach products and McConnell had seen them at team parties before he de-ployed. They were joined by two more SEALs and inter-mittently by other girls as they worked the crowd. One of the SEALs, a tall, affable officer named Bill, sought McConnell out and began questioning him.

"Jim, welcome back. I hear you did a great job. I hope I can do half as well. I, uh, hope you don't mind me asking, but do you have any advice you could pass on? I go over with Juliett Platoon next week."

"Keep your head down," replied McConnell, "and listen to your second-tour guys. They know what it's about."

"What was it like, I mean your first firefight?" pressed Bill. "I hear you're something else with a Stoner rifle."

McConnell tried not to be flip or sarcastic. He didn't know quite how to deal with questions like this, even from a SEAL, though he could tell Bill was serious. McConnell remembered having the same questions, and looking for the same answers, ages ago on the eve of his deployment. He put his hand on the taller man's shoulder.

"Bill, I'm about half shit-faced, and I'm just not up to it right now. Let's have a cup of coffee at the team area tomorrow and I'll help you any way I can, okay?"

"Hey, thanks—tomorrow'll be great."

McConnell noticed two girls had joined the group and one of them was the dark-haired beauty he had seen arrive earlier. She was a knockout. This time she smiled back. McConnell walked over to her and was about to introduce himself when Harper appeared on the other side and put his arm around her waist.

"I saw you making eyes at this asshole. Does this mean our relationship is over?"

"Now, Tom, I saw a new face and I was just being sociable," the girl replied. "And what's this 'our relationship' business anyway?"

"Come on, Amy," said Harper. "You know—when we meet at the Chula Vista No-Tell Motel and you screw my brains out."

"Tom, you're such a potty mouth," laughed Amy as she squirmed away from Harper's grasp. "Gad, you smell like you've been drinking all day."

"Is the bear a Catholic"—*burp*—"does the Pope shit in the woods? Yeah, I've had a few brews. It's fucking Sunday, ain't it?" Harper had the ability to be gross, roguishly charming, outrageous, and relatively nonthreatening, all at the same time. McConnell wondered how he got away with it.

"Amy Brown, meet Jim McConnell, one of the badest dudes at Team One. But be careful—he just got back from a deployment and he probably has the galloping Asian crud from diddling those slant-eyed whores. You'd best stay away from him and keep yourself pure for me."

Amy Brown giggled and stepped behind McConnell, placing him between herself and Harper in mock terror.

"Okay, pilgrim, I guess you win this one," said Harper, running his index finger along the side of his mouth in a poor John Wayne imitation. "But I'll be back." He stumbled off in a Duke-like rolling shuffle and accosted a nearby groupie who squealed with delight.

"Can I get you a beer, Amy?" said McConnell as he guided her away from the group toward the bar.

"A glass of white wine would be fine."

"Right. One white wine, comin' up." Christ, she's good-looking, thought McConnell as he left her and dove into the crowd at the edge of the bar to order drinks. He returned in a few minutes and found Amy talking to another guy who quickly retreated when he saw McConnell.

"Thanks," she said as he handed her the wine. "From what Tommy said you must have been in Vietnam. How long have you been gone?"

"About seven months," replied McConnell. "We just got back on Friday."

"Oh, really," she said looking at him anew. "You're the one with Foxtrot Platoon. I've heard a lot about you. The guys from the team say you're really something special."

Now that's just great, thought McConnell. Even the camp followers know who counts coup. I wonder if she knows our body count. I'll bet she doesn't know how many of my guys got busted up along the way.

McConnell caught himself and took a deep breath. He realized he was being maudlin and Amy Brown didn't deserve to be a focal point for his bitterness. She was fresh and neat and cheerful, and as welcome a sight to him as the streets of Coronado.

"Well, I don't know if I'm special, but I did make it back. I even brought some of my platoon back with me."

The Winds was now in full swing and they had to stand very close to hear each other. She smelled terrific. McConnell learned that she was from Evanston, Illinois, and had gone to nearby Northwestern to study journalism. A degree, that smile, and those great legs had landed her a job as a stewardess with PSA. She was also a little out of his league. McConnell had always done "just okay" with the ladies, but Amy Brown was one of the classiest girls at the Winds. The beer had him pretty loose so he stepped up to the plate and swung the bat.

"Amy, I'm hungry and I probably don't need another beer. Let's go over to the Mexican Village for a taco and a margarita."

"I'd like that," she said. "Let me tell my girlfriend I'm leaving."

She quickly returned and they headed for the door. McConnell did his best to skirt the group of SEALs, but they couldn't avoid a grinning Tom Harper with both hands extended over his head signaling "touchdown."

As they drove, Amy put her hand on his arm. "Jim, the Village is a madhouse on Sunday night and you look tired. This may be a little forward, but why don't you take me home and let me fix you something. If you don't mind my saying, you look like you could use a little TLC."

Well, thought McConnell. Amy Brown is probably going to haul my ashes tonight. Only it isn't me she wants to screw—it's Foxtrot Platoon, SEAL Team One. I wonder if she'd be this easy if I wasn't fresh back from a combat tour. To hell with it—didn't the successful braves from the war party get the choicest horses and the fairest maidens? It's not like I'm a fucking charity case, right?

McConnell knew he was half in the bag and feeling a little sorry for himself. Why fight it, he told himself, if anyone's fully paid up on their tribal dues, I am.

"You've been reading my mail," he offered, trying to be casual about it. "Where do you live?"

"Over by Balboa Park. Just head for the bridge and I'll give you directions from there."

McConnell drove across the tall sweeping arc of the Coronado Bridge toward San Diego, trying to keep his anticipation and the speed of the MG under control. His thoughts were mostly on the slice of heaven sitting next to him, but he couldn't help remembering the first time he crossed this bridge over a year ago and entered the world of the teams.

Chapter Two

THE SEDUCTION

OFFICER CANDIDATE JIM McCONNELL was in the second rank of the outside row of C Company as they marched from Nimitz Hall to the auditorium. It was a crisp, sunny March day on the Newport campus of the Naval Officer Candidate School, best appreciated by those who had endured the damp, biting New England coastal winter. Just a month earlier they had marched through wind and snow, collars of the huge coats turned up around their ears and looking more like a Soviet naval contingent marching on the Winter Palace than future ensigns in the United States Navy. From his position in the formation, McConnell could enjoy the sailboats as they danced around a destroyer that was cautiously making its way in from Narragansett Sound to the naval station piers.

"Com-pan-eeee HALT!" barked the formation commander. "Fall out and fall in the auditorium."

The soon-to-be-commissioned officers filed into the auditorium, taking the rear seats first. These coveted seats in the back where you couldn't be seen, collectively known as Sleepy Hollow, had been prized by the tired, sleep-starved candidates during the last few months of sea power and leadership lectures held there. Today's agenda was service selection. The various warfare specialties within the Navy would make presentations to the candidates, hoping to lure the top talent. There would be presentations on

Navy air, surface warfare, the submarine service, and the Supply and Civil Engineering Corps. It was fraternity rush, military style. The candidates were excited about service selection, but they automatically took the rear seats first.

"What are you gonna try for?" said the candidate seated next to McConnell in Sleepy Hollow.

"I haven't made up my mind just yet," replied McConnell. "My dad was on a destroyer in World War II—I might just put in for a tin can."

"Not me, man. I got sick on the yard patrol craft—I'd die if I had to go to sea on a small ship. Give me a fast plane and a big, stable ship to land it on."

McConnell had arrived in Newport late October, five months after graduating college. The transition to military life and the demanding schedule of officer candidate school had been an easy one for him. He didn't stand at the top of his class or close to it, but he was better than average at his academic, physical, and military subjects. He stood solidly in the middle of the upper half of the class. He quickly learned what those few perceptive and observant new military inductees know: stay squared away, keep performance just slightly better than average, and no one will know you're there. He was never far behind the leaders, but his military evaluations said he had leadership potential. His classmates would recall McConnell as an okay, middle-of-the-road type of guy, and his instructors would barely remember him.

Jim McConnell was born and raised in Mattoon, Illinois, with all the advantages offered a boy in a small Midwest town in the fifties and early sixties. Jim's dad made a comfortable living in the insurance business. When he wasn't writing policies or working around the house, he loved to hunt.

The senior McConnell passed his passion for hunting to his son. Bill McConnell was well liked in the community and had standing invitations to hunt on most of the large parcels of private land around Mattoon. He and Jim enjoyed the best shooting in central Illinois. Young McConnell loved the fast-paced action of bird hunting as well as the patient stalking of deer, where you could spend days in the field waiting for that one perfect shot. Sometimes by himself, he would hunt squirrel and rabbit with his .22, and his skill at stalking game grew as did his shooting ability.

Bill McConnell was a good hunter and a superb shot, but his was a relaxed competence, derived from years in the field and an hour or so each week at the skeet club. Jim was different. His deliberate movements and his total concentration were almost primitive, and his shooting, especially with a shotgun, was incredible. The gun became an extension of his will. Sometimes the father would just watch his son rather than look for a shot. As the bird broke, so did his Jim—instinctively swinging the gun to his shoulder and firing as soon as the gun was in position, taking almost no time to lead the bird. When two birds broke in different directions, Jim would drop the one nearest to him and swing his gun around to the other bird, looking to see if his father was in firing position. If his father wasn't shooting, he would glance down the vented rib of his .16 gauge and pull the second bird out of the air. He missed so seldom that his dog would refuse to believe it when he did, and would have to be ordered off the false retrieve.

"Dad, that was your bird."

"There's plenty of birds, Son. We don't have to get them all."

"I know, Dad. I just don't want to miss a shot."

"Seats, gentlemen," barked the tall, white-haired captain, who then went on for fifteen minutes exhorting Officer Candidate Class 68-01 to serve their Navy and their country to the best of their ability.

It was time to choose tribes. The next hour and a half were a series of well-rehearsed recruiting pitches from the various communities within the Navy. The presentation teams had polished their act on the road, playing to naval ROTC audiences at colleges across the country. The naval aviators were the flashiest. The surface line recruiters came out heavy with travel and adventure, while the submariners talked about the educational opportunities in nuclear power. There were dazzling slides of ships and airplanes. The candidates loved it.

"Right *on*!"

"Navy air, all the way!"

"Surface line is mighty fine!"

"We're fuckin' outta here!"

After the supply corps presentation, a tall muscular officer, whose starched tropical white uniform provided a flattering contrast to his deep tan, walked to the center of the stage.

"Good afternoon, men," he began. "I'm Lieutenant Nick Van Patton and I'm with Underwater Demolition Team Twenty-two. Sorry to be in the wrong uniform, but I just flew in from Puerto Rico this morning. The team spends part of the winter in the Caribbean. The water's a lot warmer down there, and we have a terrific training facility on St. Thomas. I've been allowed fifteen minutes on the program to tell you about Navy special warfare and the Navy underwater demolition and SEAL teams."

"I remember that guy," the fellow next to McConnell whispered. "He was a fullback at Princeton and a real animal. Made all–Ivy League a few years back."

Van Patton ambled over to the podium just off center stage. He casually draped his left arm over the podium and handled the slide projector control with his right hand. He spoke without the use of the microphone.

"The opportunities in special warfare are different from those in the traditional naval callings, but I've personally enjoyed being in UDT. After an intensive four-month basic training course conducted at Little Creek, Virginia, or Coronado, California, you'll join one of the teams on the East or West Coast for some rather interesting duty."

Click. The slide projector produced a neatly spaced line of swimmers just outside the surf zone of a beautiful tropical beach.

"You may serve with one of the amphibious ready groups and conduct beach reconnaissance prior to amphibious landings."

Click, Click. Small group of husky, tanned men in swim trunks watch heavily equipped Marines with rifles running from the landing craft through the surf to the beautiful tropical beach.

"Amphibious operations also require beach clearance and then lifeguard duty. When the Marines hit the beach we've already been there."

Click, Click. Small mini-submarine escorted by two scuba divers, all suspended in a clear blue-green sea.

"UDT platoons deploy with a full complement of diving gear and our swimmer delivery vehicles."

Click, Click. Scuba diver, blond hair and air hoses streaming in the current, totes a satchel charge through the same blue-green sea.

"We also conduct training in demolitions and limpeteer attacks on enemy shipping."

Click, Click. Fatigue-clad skydiver in free-fall looking into the camera with a wind pasted smile. The sky is much like the sea only less green.

"Everyone in the teams is parachute-qualified and many go on to become proficient in HALO or military skydiving."

And so it went for the next ten minutes. Groups of young, well-conditioned athletes doing all kinds of quasimilitary things in sunny warm places. The military slides occasionally gave way to these same young men on liberty in Europe or the Caribbean, usually in the company of young, well-conditioned women. This kind of Navy looked mighty good to the winter-weary candidates of Class 68-01.

"Some of our UDT personnel go on to serve in the Navy SEAL, or sea-air-land teams."

Click, Click. Squad file of camouflage-painted faces patrolling through dense foliage.

"We have deployed platoons to the Republic of Vietnam and these teams have performed their special warfare missions with uncommon skill and valor."

Click, Click. Navy lieutenant at an awards ceremony receiving a medal, flanked by proud parents and a very attractive young lady.

"Not all of our duties are of a military nature," continued Van Patton. "We are heavily involved in the space program, both in underwater weightless simulation and capsule recovery operations." He then flipped through several slides showing frogmen leaping from hovering helicopters and helping grateful astronauts out of space capsules. The final slide was a shot of Van Patton in a wetsuit shaking hands with Alan Sheppard in a spacesuit.

"This has been a general overview of naval special warfare," he concluded. "If you'd like to do something special in the Navy, then give us some consideration. It's not easy and it's not for everyone. The training is tough and the work is demanding. But it's your opportunity to be someone special and to serve with one of the most elite units in this or any other Navy. Chief Petty Officer Williams and I will be at the Flagpole Grinder at zero eight hundred tomorrow morning for physical aptitude tests. Special warfare has been allowed up to six billets from Class 68-01 and we will be looking for the best qualified candidates. I hope to see at least a few volunteers out there tomorrow. Thanks for your time, gentlemen. And good luck to all of you."

Van Patton left the podium and was followed out by a short, sober-faced chief petty officer with five rows of combat decorations. This was the last item of the program. The class leader called the assembly to attention and dismissed them. The candidates were free until the following afternoon when service selection would take place. As McConnell's company marched back to Nimitz Hall, he saw Van Patton being driven away by a gorgeous blonde in a late-model Mercedes.

That evening McConnell and several of his friends went out for dinner at one of the pricey restaurants along the Newport city waterfront. There was a lot of animated talk about ships, planes, and duty stations. Most of them had made up their minds about choice of duty, but wanted confirmation from their classmates. The subject of Vietnam came up, but it was not an issue. Those aboard ship would only sail near Vietnam and those going to flight school faced two years of training before they saw an operational squadron. And after all, it wasn't like they were in the Army. DiNardo was seated across from McConnell and poured the wine. He noticed that McConnell had hardly touched his meal, and he was still nursing his first glass of wine while the group was on their third bottle.

"Hey, Mac. You want I should order you a glass of birdseed or a cup of tea," he chided. "Sailors are supposed to eat hearty and drink when they're in port."

"Yeah, well I guess I'm just not up to it. Anyway, Nardo, I know you'll cover my share of the vino."

"Horseshit, McConnell! You're gonna be out on the grinder tomorrow for frogman tryouts and you're just saving yourself, right?"

McConnell shook his head and smiled. It was that obvious. He had thought about little else since the assembly. He hadn't the engineering background for submarines. He had seriously considered flying but he wasn't sure it was right for him. Maybe knocking down so many ducks over the years had instilled in him a phobia of being shot at in the air. Naval aviation was the hot topic around the table and most of the group wanted to fly. He had just about decided to be a destroyer man like his dad when Van Patton cast his spell. It was not something McConnell would readily admit, even to himself, but the opportunity to be something different—somebody special—was very compelling.

"Nardo, you must be a psychic," he acknowledged. "I'm going to give it a shot."

"Did you see the medals on some of those SEALS?" said the man next to McConnell. "They don't give those out for Apollo space capsule recoveries."

"I hear the training is really the shits. They make you eat snakes and crawl around in the mud."

"And, Jimmy," added DiNardo, "those guys jump outta perfectly good airplanes. You gotta be some kinda fucked-up to do that."

"Well, maybe so," conceded McConnell, "maybe so." But his mind was drifting through a blue-green sea just offshore of a beautiful tropical beach.

Van Patton had set the hook in more bodies than just Officer Candidate McConnell. The following morning some thirty-five members of the class assembled on the Flagpole Grinder. After determining the number of push-ups, pull-ups and sit-ups they could do, the hopefuls were timed on a three-mile run and then taken to the pool for a 400-yard swim. McConnell was not first in any of these tests, but in none did he finish lower than eighth. Van Patton conducted the testing with a lot of enthusiasm— part coach, part cheerleader. The chief petty officer sto- ically called out the times and counted repetitions, mechanically recording the results on his clipboard. There was a sense of melancholy, even pity, emanating from this man as he watched the candidates go through their paces.

That afternoon when McConnell's turn came for service selection he wrote by his name:

1. Underwater Demolition, East Coast
2. Surface Line, Destroyers, East Coast
3. Navy Air

That next morning after he was commissioned as ensign in the United States Navy, he received his first set of Navy orders:

FROM: BUREAU OF NAVAL PERSONNEL
TO: ENSIGN JAMES WILLIAM MCCONNELL, USNR,
       313-44-6889
SUBJ: DUTY ASSIGNMENT

1. UPON DETACHMENT OFFICER CANDIDATE SCHOOL, NEWPORT, RHODE ISLAND, YOU ARE DIRECTED TO RE- PORT NOT LATER THAN 0800, 18 MARCH, 1968 TO THE US NAVAL AMPHIBIOUS BASE, CORONADO, CALIFORNIA, FOR BASIC UNDERWATER DEMOLITION/SEAL TRAINING.
2. UPON COMPLETION OF BASIC UNDERWATER DEMOLI- TION/SEAL TRAINING YOU ARE DIRECTED TO REPORT TO COMMANDING OFFICER, SEAL TEAM ONE FOR PERMA- NENT DUTY ASSIGNMENT.

Chapter Three

THE INITIATION

IT TOOK MCCONNELL a full day to check out of Officer Candidate School and get his MGB loaded for the trip across country. The secondhand sports car had been a present from his parents after his junior year in college. He drove it hard, but the little car responded well, even loaded with all his books, uniforms, and civilian clothes. Before he left Newport, he had asked about his orders to report to SEAL team after training rather than to underwater demolition. The OCS personnel officer had said that the training for both UDT and SEAL team was the same and to let them know that his choice was UDT when he arrived at the training unit in Coronado. It was McConnell's first set of orders and he had no reason to believe he couldn't correct things there. He wanted to have a few days in San Diego to get settled before the training started, so he made the drive to Mattoon in a day and a half.

The two days at home raced by. His mother served him huge plates of beef and starch, and he spent one afternoon bird shooting with his dad. Most of his high school friends were married and working. His mother thought being a Navy frogman sounded exciting, and she loved his uniform; but his dad, having been in the Navy, questioned him closer.

"Jim, what's the chance of you becoming mixed up in this Vietnam business?"

"Not much, Dad. There are five underwater demolition teams and only two SEAL teams, so I shouldn't have too much trouble going UDT. It's mostly the SEALs that are in Vietnam." He avoided mentioning his orders to SEAL Team One. "Besides, I have a lot of training ahead of me and maybe it'll be over by then. From what I've been reading in the papers, the Viet Cong really took a beating during their Tet Offensive."

"But they didn't quit and that kind of bothers me. I'd feel a lot better if you were shipping out on a destroyer."

"I'd probably get seasick. And I want to give UDT a try."

"You really want to do this, Son? You really want to be a UDT man?"

"Yeah, Dad. I really do."

"Well, I hope so, because I understand that the training is designed to see if you have any doubts about it."

McConnell had never been west of St. Louis, so the drive to California was an adventure. He drove into San Diego, and was enchanted by the broad bays and the blue Pacific. This was a different kind of Navy town. Newport was beautiful, but it was very staid and traditional. San Diego was fresh, sprawling, and young. He drove over the Coronado Bridge and down Orange Avenue past the Hotel Del Coronado to the naval amphibious base. It took him a half hour to check in at the BOQ and unload the car. That evening as he sat by the window in his room drinking a beer, he watched his first Pacific sunset and the lights along the Silver Strand, south toward Imperial Beach, come alive. If this is Navy life, thought McConnell, I'll have some.

The next day he slept in late and then did the San Diego tour—Balboa Park, the zoo, La Jolla and Mission Beach. San Diego was made for convertibles and the MG was never more at home. Late that Sunday afternoon he drove back to Coronado and took a drive past the training unit. BASIC UDT/SEAL TRAINING read the sign on the building. Over the door was an inscription, *Through These*

Doors Pass the Bravest Men in the World. A sailor came out of the building, a second class petty officer with several rows of ribbons on his chest.

"Can I help you, sir?" he asked as he came abreast of the car and saw the officer's decal on the bumper.

"Thanks, just looking," replied McConnell. "I don't report until tomorrow."

"You gonna be a frogman, sir?" he asked, a sly grin working across his face.

"Well, I sure hope so, sailor."

"My name's Wilson, SEAL Team One. Let me wish you luck sir, lots o' luck."

Wilson headed down the street, still draped in a grin, and McConnell headed back to the BOQ for the last night of normal sleep he would know for a while.

"Good morning, sir, what can I do for you?" The thin, balding yeoman didn't look like one of the club members as he leaned across the counter on his elbows.

"Uh, good morning, I'm Ensign McConnell, reporting for training duty." He slid the envelope containing his orders and medical records across the counter and waited at a relaxed parade rest.

"Very good, sir. I'm Knudson, yeoman first, and I'm the administration and personnel department here. I'll sign you in and get started on your travel claim. You'll want to check back here at the end of the day. The class is forming up out on the grinder, just through the main doors to your right."

"Thanks. Oh, one more thing. I was supposed to see about changing my orders from SEAL team to UDT. Can you take care of that for me?"

"Sir, this is a training command and we have no authority to modify Navy orders. I'll attach a note on them that there's a question about team assignment. Base Admin can take it up with Team One since you will officially belong to them. But with all due respect, sir, that's a long four months away."

"Thanks again, Knudson. Let me know what Base Admin has to say about the change."

McConnell was becoming a little uneasy about the

SEAL team orders. As far as he knew, the SEALs didn't see too much of tropical beaches or blue-green water.

The grinder was a large blacktop area surrounded on three sides by one-story cinder-block buildings. The buildings formed a U shape with the open end toward the ocean. A concrete sidewalk connected the buildings to the grinder and provided contrast to the smooth black asphalt of the open area. The area was clear except for a few connex boxes used for storage and a tall metal A-frame with three thick climbing ropes dangling from the cross bar. A square two-foot-high wooden platform was located on the seaward side of the grinder. The vertical portion of the platform was painted blue with large yellow lettering: THE ONLY EASY DAY WAS YESTERDAY. A large group of new trainees milled about near the platform. McConnell estimated there were well over seventy of them, including some ten officers. As he watched he could feel the nervous anticipation that emanated from the group. McConnell was so engrossed in watching the men on the grinder he failed to notice a man appear behind him.

"You got a ticket to this game, Ensign?" He was a stocky man wearing swim trunks, a blue T-shirt, and spit-shined combat boots. His starched fatigue cap had a chief petty officer's emblem on the front and his partially unzipped nylon windbreaker had *God* stitched into the left breast. The man had the largest thighs McConnell had ever seen. He was obviously a club member.

"I beg your pardon, Chief."

"You don't call me 'Chief' here, sir. You call me 'Instructor.' Are you a member of the new class or are you just here to observe?" He had one hand in his jacket pocket and the other supported a mug of black coffee.

"I guess I'm part of the new class, Instructor."

"Well, if the ensign would kindly fall in with his class, school is about to begin."

McConnell joined the rest of the group on the grinder, feeling something was terribly wrong about the instructor's polite smile and cordial manner. A clone of the first instructor without the windbreaker mounted the platform. He ordered them into ranks and called them to attention. He gave them their barracks assignments and plowed through a litany of housekeeping items—gear issue, meal chits, parking, etc.

"Now for the serious part. Today we begin with Phase One of your training, which is the Conditioning Phase. Hell Week begins five weeks from today and, gentlemen, you'd better be ready. Following Hell Week we will begin the Diving Phase for those few of you that are still here. The Land Warfare Phase on San Clemente island is the final phase of training. The survivors then go to Jump School at Fort Benning. We don't flunk people out of here, gentlemen. They quit. Anytime you think you will be happier going to sea on one of those big gray ghosts tied up over at the pier, you just ring that bell by the main entrance to the grinder and put your helmet on the line. You're outta here—no questions asked.

"Now you'll be excused until ten hundred. At that time you're to fall in here in fatigues, combat boots, and helmets. Instructor Molina would like to take you on a little beach orientation excursion. I suggest you use the time to settle into the barracks and square away your gear. Time is going to be in short supply come ten hundred. And remember, gentlemen, you *are* volunteers. That's it, DISMISSED!"

The trainees were required to live in barracks next to the training unit while they were in training. McConnell kept his BOQ room and brought only what he needed in the way of personal effects with him as he settled into the officer's wing of the trainee barracks. They were issued green fatigues, boots, helmets, and a field jacket. For swim gear each man was given tan canvas UDT trunks, large duck-type swim fins, face mask, inflatable life jacket, and a K-bar commando knife. At ten o'clock the class formed back up on the grinder. The ranks were straight but the rumpled fatigues and Army helmets, blue for the officers and red for enlisted, made them a ragged, almost comical lot. Instructor Molina turned out to be the chief petty officer McConnell had met earlier that morning. He ordered the class to attention and addressed the formation.

"All right, girls, my name is Instructor Molina and I'm in charge of Phase One training. This is the Conditioning Phase and you *will* be conditioned. Is that clear?"

"Yes, Instructor," came the collective response.

"I said, IS THAT CLEAR!"

"YES, INSTRUCTOR!"

"One or two of you might be frogman material but the rest of you are just a bunch of sea-lawyers and slipknots. Half of you will be back aboard ship by the end of the week. The teams are special. They are the most elite military units in the world. If you want to be in the teams, then you goddamn well better cut this program. Is that clear?"

"YES, INSTRUCTOR!"

"We'll see about that. Formation: LEEEFFT HACE! FAH-WAAAD HARCH!"

Molina marched the class out across the soft sand behind the training unit and into the Pacific Ocean. The water off Southern California is about fifty-eight degrees in late March, not what would be considered freezing cold. If, however, you stand in it for an hour you do get cold—teeth rattling, scrotum shriveling cold. After they came out of the water they did calisthenics in the soft sand amid yelling, cursing instructors who kicked sand on them. The bell rang twice before the class mustered for the afternoon's training. Molina took them back out into the water, but not as long this time. The balance of the afternoon they spent running, crawling, and rolling in the soft sand with periodic plunges into the surf. The bell rang four more times before they secured late that afternoon.

The next five weeks were a constant diet of cold water and physical pounding. The days began with inspection on the grinder. The trainees were now required to muster in starched greens. If an instructor found fault with the shine on a boot, belt buckle, or K-bar, or any part of a uniform was out of order, the trainee went into the surf. Often Molina found them to be collectively such a disgusting lot, he put them all in the water. Then followed calisthenics and a run in the soft sand and a tour of the obstacle course. They endured log training, where six trainees were teamed with a 250-pound log for a beach run or calisthenics. There was surf training that required them to paddle inflatable rubber boats through the breakers, often launching and landing over steep rocky areas with plunging surf. This drill cost the class one broken arm and a host of cuts and bruises.

McConnell gradually grew numb to it all. The various parts of his body that hurt became one dull ache after the first week and he stopped thinking about how bad he hurt the second. The trainees didn't really get stronger or faster. If anything they became slower, but they became almost impervious to pain and cold. To watch them running, even on hard ground, it looked as if they were in slow motion—as if the air were a more dense fluid for them. They acquired the gaunt, haunted look of World War II concentration camp inmates. The bell continued to toll and the line of helmets grew. One man fell off the cargo net on the obstacle course and broke his leg. He would be allowed back in the next class if he mended in time. Just a few days before Hell Week there were thirty-seven trainees left, about half of what they had started with.

McConnell was being pushed further than he ever had been before, but he was getting by far better than most of the trainees. He settled into his middle-of-the-pack routine, doing only what he had to and conserving his strength when he could. Intellectually, he was fascinated at the selection process and how the class responded to the training. Actually, it had been more of a testing or screening process than a training program. Some of the muscular, ex-jocks in the class rang the bell early on while some of the smaller, nonathletic men hung in there. It was a game of mental toughness, reasoned McConnell, and more a factor of the fight in the dog than the dog in the fight. He also knew that in spite of what the instructors said and the daily physical pounding, it took a lot of courage to walk over and ring that bell.

Toward the last week before Hell Week, McConnell noticed that a short, rather quiet instructor seemed to be observing him closely. Instructor Kanaka, or "Pineapple" as the other instructors called him, was a bandy-legged Hawaiian with a barrel of a chest. Large arms sprouted from his shoulders and hung well away from his hips. He had that Polynesian trait of always seeming to smile when he spoke, even when there was nothing to smile about. On the Friday afternoon before Hell Week, Instructor Molina mustered the survivors and gave them their final instructions.

"Motivation Week begins at twenty-four hundred, day after tomorrow. It used to be called Hell Week, but that was changed so as not to offend some of you hippies who stumbled into the Navy. That's Sunday midnight, girls, and you better not be late. Many of you should avoid the rush and ring the bell right now. The rest of you be standing tall in starched fatigues at twenty-four hundred sharp. And take a good look around, girls. There's gonna be a lot fewer of you here one week from today. Class DISMISSED!"

McConnell broke from formation and was making for the barracks when he was stopped by Instructor Kanaka.

"Meesta McConnell."

"Yes, Instructor Kanaka?"

"I want you wait for me over by da connex box, I be right back."

"Instructor Kanaka?"

"What is it, sir?"

"Instructor, may I ask what this is about?"

"Yes, Mr. McConnell. I wanna fuck wid you. Now you stand by and I be right back."

The grinder was soon deserted and while McConnell waited, his mind raced. What did Kanaka want? What have I done to cause me to be singled out? Being kept back alone, without the comforting cushion of others around, violated McConnell's herd instincts. Fifteen minutes later Kanaka returned. He walked past McConnell toward the beach, motioning him to follow. When they had crossed the soft sand and approached the water's edge he turned and faced the anxious trainee.

"Okay, Meesta McConnell, into da watah."

"Me, Instructor?"

"Ain't nobody else on dis fuckin' beech but you an' me, Meesta McConnell. You want I should spell it out fo' you? You tink maybe I speek funny? GET IN THE FUCKING WATER, SIR!" The smile was there but the eyes were deadly serious.

After a half hour in the water, Kanaka called him out and put him through forty minutes of torture.

"On you back! On you belly! On you feet! On you belly! Fifty push-ups, Meesta McConnell! I can't hear you, Meesta McConnell, you bettah start over! Into da watah, Meesta McConnell. Move you dead ass, sir! Get back out here on da double, sir! Give me another fifty, Meesta McConnell! On you back! On you left side! You other left fuckin' side, sir! On you belly! On you feet! On you back! Faster, sir! Into da watah, Meesta McConnell . . ."

He was racked with fatigue and his movements were becoming clumsy and disjoined when Kanaka called him to attention by the water's edge. His chest almost touched McConnell's so their faces were six inches apart, the shorter man's eyes level with McConnell's chin.

"You know why we here, Meesta McConnell?"

"No, Instructor Kan"—*gasp*—"Kanaka." In the back of his mind, McConnell was beginning to understand what Kanaka wanted, but he didn't want to admit it.

"I tink you do, Meesta McConnell. You smart college boy and I tink mebbe you do. But we work on it some mo' 'til you sure."

Kanaka went back to work on McConnell with the precise, consistent repetition of a Las Vegas blackjack dealer until McConnell passed out on the sand. Before McConnell lost consciousness, a realization burned through the falling curtain that for the first time in his life, he was not in control, and nothing short of unqualified mental and physical effort would regain that control.

When he woke up he was aware that he had sand in his mouth and nose. It was almost dusk and the clammy wet fatigues were making him very cold. With a sense of confusion and anger he realized where he was and what had brought him there. Coughing and snorting he looked up and saw the outline of the blocky Hawaiian standing over him.

"On you feet, Meesta McConnell."

McConnell struggled to one knee and fell down again. A few moments later he managed to balance himself unsteadily on rubbery legs.

"You unnerstan' why we here, Meesta McConnell?"

"I think so, Instructor."

"Why we here, sir?"

"Because I haven't been putting out in training?"

"Mebbe. Tell me, sir, why haven't you been puttin' out?"

McConnell hesitated, then let it pour out: "The object is not to quit, isn't it, Instructor? To get through? I thought that if I just did enough to get by, my chances would be better. That's the game here, isn't it, Instructor Kanaka, to make it through?"

The honesty and the physical effort of this declaration caused McConnell to drop his hands to his knees to keep from falling over. Kanaka stared at him for a full thirty seconds. Then he walked about five yards toward the water. With his back to McConnell he gazed out to sea as the red-running-to-purple sky chased the last daylight into the Pacific. He stood there for two or three minutes before returning to the still wobbly trainee. He stood in front of McConnell, close enough for McConnell to see the coldness in his eyes.

"Sir, what they teach you in college? What you learn at dat knife-an'-fork school in Newport? How to get by? You gonna lead you men from da middle of da pack? When you in combat you gonna jus' hope you fire team make it through? Why da fuck you tink you draw officer's pay, sir, so you can be da last man to quit? Meesta McConnell, them men need their officers to give a hundred percent or they won' follow. And they rate mo' bettah than some shitbird with a bar on his collar bringin' up da fuckin' rear." Kanaka paused for a moment, breathing heavily, staring at McConnell with his hands on his hips. Then he spoke in a quieter voice.

"Forget da hairy frogman shit, sir—do you unnerstan' what I'm talkin' 'bout?"

A sense of shame flooded over McConnell, driving out most of his anger and some of his exhaustion. And while he couldn't have put it into words just then, deep inside he knew he would never again have the luxury of looking out for only himself.

"Yes, Instructor Kanaka, I understand."

"I hope so, Meesta McConnell, 'cause if you don', we gonna be back out here every night. That clear, sir?"

"That's clear, Instructor."

Kanaka turned and walked back to the training area and McConnell slowly made his way to the barracks. He stripped off his wet fatigues while he stood in the hot shower, wondering who it was who dreamed up a system—a system unlike any other in the armed forces—that would allow an enlisted man to do to an officer what Kanaka had just done to him. The Navy had already spent a great deal of time and money trying to teach him to lead men, but it had been nowhere near as effective as this stumpy instructor had been using nothing more than a few hours on a beach. The thinking stopped the minute he hit the bed where he slept like a dead man for the next ten hours.

At midnight on Sunday, the trainees were driven out of the barracks with smoke grenades, flares, and automatic weapon fire. McConnell knew the instructors were firing blanks but it was still terrifying. They were in and out of the water until the sun came up. Then the class formed up and headed out on a ten-mile beach run. McConnell normally ran in the first or second rank. This time he dropped back toward the rear.

"How yuh doin', Smitty?"

"Okay, sir"—*gasp*—"only my fuckin' crotch is raw."

"Hang in there. How 'bout you, Watson—you're lookin' good."

"Feel like shit, sir, but thanks."

The rest of Hell Week was much like the previous six weeks of training, only the trainees were worked twice as hard and denied sleep. They went through the same training evolutions but they were often done in the mud flats south of Coronado. One evening they started running in the sand and were still running when the sun came up. The instructors drilled them in shifts so the harassment was constant. The bell rang and the class became smaller.

McConnell worked like he never had. Sometimes he was out front, but most often he was back in the pack trying to help someone. He found that as he tried to help the others, the cold and the fatigue took less of a toll on him. Many in the class began to look to him for guidance. When the class was divided into seven-man crews for surf passage in the rubber boats, there was a scramble to be in his boat crew. The instructors kept the pressure on him, but they began to treat him with a grudging measure of respect. By the end of the week he had become the class leader. He had not only earned it, but he was the only officer standing among the thirteen trainees who mustered on the grinder that Friday afternoon.

"Well done, men," said Molina to the ragged baker's dozen. It was the first time he had called them anything but "shitbirds," "assholes," or "girls." "Since you decided to stick around for a while, we'll now try to teach you how to be frogmen. Mr. McConnell, have the class mustered at zero six thirty on Monday for PT. You're dismissed." Just like that, it was over. They were elated, relieved, and dead on their feet. McConnell numbly moved among them, shaking each man's hand.

"Hey, Mr. McConnell," said one, "thanks for the help on that last run."

"Yeah, sir, thanks," added another. "Wouldn't have made it without you."

"Nice goin', sir. Ah figured if'n you could make it, so could Ah."

"I 'bout went for the bell last night, sir—thanks for the boost."

McConnell never felt better—or worse. *I made it and I even helped some of the other guys!* He limped slightly as he ran over to the barracks. Hell Week was over, but they were never allowed to walk in the training area. He fell onto his bunk without removing his wet, soiled fatigues. Before sleep smothered him, he savored the victory as only those can who suffer mightily to achieve a difficult goal.

The Diving Phase of training was a little less intense than the Conditioning Phase because the classroom work associated with diver training precluded constant physical harassment. That is not to say the trainees were totally neglected in that regard. Every morning they ran to the pool and spent two hours in the water, swimming laps with towels in each hand, treading water while holding buckets or treading water with their hands and feet tied. There were relay races hopping along the bottom with thirty-pound weights and any other sadistic games the instructors could come up with to place the trainees on the brink of drowning. The balance of the day was taken with the serious business of learning diving. They initially trained on open circuit scuba, and then moved on to the more advanced mixed-gas equipment and oxygen rebreathers, the latter leaving no telltale bubbles. The transition to open water was a milestone in that they had to pass the pool scuba harassment. Two trainees would swim to the bottom of the pool and wait while the instructors, like a school of sharks, would attack the pair and their equipment. Face masks were ripped off, mouthpieces torn away, air turned off, and the swim pair knocked around. The beleaguered trainees had to work together, repairing the damage and trying to keep at least one scuba unit operable so they wouldn't be driven to the surface. This usually resulted in a successful pair of trainees clinging to a single cylinder, no breathing regulator, each man defending his buddy as they alternated breathing directly off the tank valve. This often made for a few chipped teeth, but avoided being forced to the surface to face additional harassment. All but one of the trainees made it through pool harassment to the open water. There the class swam endless day-and-night compass courses with the various diving apparatus, methodically boring holes in the murky non-blue-green waters of San Diego Bay until they matriculated to the final phase of training.

The Land Warfare Phase of the training was held on San Clemente Island, a barren rock some seventy-five miles west of San Diego and thirty miles south of Santa Catalina. The training unit maintained a base camp facility there, and the trainees lived in field conditions while they learned small-unit tactics, weapons, infiltrations, exfiltrations, ambushes, and a host of military and paramilitary skills. The training was evenly divided between classroom and practical work. This phase of the training was the favorite because after morning calisthenics and an eight-mile run, the trainees were treated like students. The Third Phase senior instructor was a tough, wiry, no-nonsense chief petty officer who was a multitour Vietnam veteran from SEAL Team Two.

"Gentlemen, this is your final phase of training," began Chief Sweeney. "Most of the bullshit is behind you. Not all of it, but most of it. Many, if not all of you, are going to see duty in Vietnam. Even you slackers with orders to UDT. What you learn here can make the difference whether or not you become a statistic. The odds say that at least one of you here today will be dead within the year. Killed in action—KIA—and added to the list of those team members who gave that last full measure of devotion.

"I've given this little talk to future deadmen in previous classes. All of your Third Phase instructors are combat veterans. Most of us have seen our friends and teammates shot up or shipped home in body bags. Learn your craft well, gentlemen—your life depends on it. In a few months it may be a Viet Cong who jumps into your shit rather than one of my instructors. A few push-ups is a small price compared to a few rounds from an AK-47. Pay attention to detail, people. Think! Most of our casualties in Vietnam are the result of mistakes. We play the odds in combat. You can do everything wrong and get away with it—for a while. You can do everything right and get dead. There are no guarantees. But here, we learn how to stack the deck in our favor. It's our training, supported by our conditioning, that makes us superior. Back on the Strand at the training unit—you fuck up, you get your ass run. We're a long way from Coronado out here, gents. You fuck up here and I'll personally take you out behind the camp and beat the shit out of you. Is that clear?"

"YES, INSTRUCTOR!"

"Fair enough. Let's have good training."

It was good training. The class worked hard at mastering the skills of cover and concealment, patrolling, communication, and night movement. They practiced hasty-action procedures, where they simulated being caught in an ambush, and how to break contact. They did body snatches and learned prisoner handling techniques. There were support boats for maritime insertion and exfiltration training. McConnell had not lost his ambition to become a UDT frogman, but the Third Phase training on San Clemente was his natural element. His movement in the field was quiet and smooth, and he had superb night vision. Neither his classmates nor the instructors missed the ease with which he mastered "the combat game."

In many respects, it was just that—a game. The class played "catch-me, fuck-me" with the instructors. On night infiltrations against practice targets, the trainees tried to slip past the instructor-sentries. If they were caught, the instructors made them do push-ups or added a few extra miles to the morning run. McConnell had successfully guided the class on several occasions without detection. Then he was caught three straight times and the whole class had to pay with extra PT. The following night he changed his route to the target after they had begun the night problem, and they evaded the sentries. The next morning he sought out the head instructor.

"Yes, Mr. McConnell, what is it?"

"Instructor, recently we've been getting caught on the night problems, but last night we were able to get through to the target."

"Well, congratulations, sir."

"We didn't go in the way I said we would at the briefing. I changed the route after we were in the field."

"So?"

"Instructor Sweeney, you're always the proctor at the briefings. I think word's been leaking out to the other instructors."

"Maybe some of your classmates have been talking."

"They don't like extra PT any more than I do. Have you been telling them about our route to the target?"

"Ensign McConnell, are you accusing me of spying on you?"

"Well, I know nobody in the class let anything slip. I guess I am." Sweeney folded his arms across his chest and regarded McConnell with a poker face. "How about it, Instructor, did you let anything slip?"

"Okay, sir. I told them how you were comin' in."

"Doesn't seem right or fair, Instructor. You're the proctor."

"And if I was a Vietnamese hootch maid, or a guide, or an interpreter, you'd be dead."

"Yes, but—"

"No buts, mister. It's not right and it's not fair. And I know, this is training. But you're the leader and those men will follow you—to their death if you make a mistake. Trust nobody! Don't let *anyone* know where you're going or your patrol route unless you trust them with your life. Understand?"

"Yes, Instructor." McConnell was hot but he tried not to show it. *They bagged us three times!*

"It's okay, Mr. McConnell—I don't blame you for being pissed. But this is one lesson you won't forget. Catch-me, fuck-me is a lot better than catch-me, kill-me. And don't feel too bad—we nailed one class officer for three weeks before he caught on."

The beginning of the legend of McConnell's shooting ability came on the weapons range during Third Phase training on San Clemente. The trainees all scored well on the target range. They fired a standard Navy qualification course with their M16 rifles, and most of them qualified as expert. McConnell registered a near perfect score and would probably have had no hits outside the bull's-eye had there not been a strong cross wind blowing in from the ocean. The real difference came on the pop-up range. Here, the trainees walked down a trail, and spring-loaded silhouette targets snapped up on either side of their route. The men had a split second to engage the targets before they were retracted. The drill was to fire two rounds at each fleeting silhouette, using snap-shooting techniques. The targets appeared too briefly for anyone to aim. The shooter had to fire on the move, with only enough time to point at them with his gun. When his turn came, McConnell walked steadily through the course, the butt of his weapon in his left armpit and his left hand firmly holding the rifle's pistol grip—his index finger taking up the slack on the trigger. He grasped the forestock with his right hand, arm straight and pointing along the barrel with his right index finger. When a target appeared, he dropped to a crouch as he swung the rifle into position, looking down the barrel with both eyes. The movement and handling of a weapon were second nature to McConnell so he had only to concentrate on seeing the target. Two .223 caliber bullets raced for each target a fraction of a second after it appeared. He squeezed the rounds off so quickly the instructors thought he was on full automatic fire. He moved with the swift grace of a natural hunter.

"Mr. McConnell, would you please get your weapon and go through the course one more time."

"Be glad to, Instructor Sweeney."

Again McConnell stalked through the course, smoothly sending two rounds at each target. He cleared the weapon and rejoined the group of trainees. Sweeney stood with two other instructors, arms folded across his chest, regarding McConnell like a spinster schoolteacher would a potential spelling-bee champ.

"How'd he do, Jimmy?" Sweeney asked his head weapons instructor who joined them from down range.

"The same, Sween—fourteen targets, twenty-eight hits."

"And the groups?"

"His second shot tended to ride high and to the right but that's natural for a southpaw. None of the rounds were off center more than six inches. I ain't seen nothin' like it, Sween. He's so fuckin' quick!"

"Mr. McConnell," Sweeney called to the group of students, "get over here."

"Yes, Instructor Sweeney," replied McConnell, jogging over to the group of instructors.

"You done this before?"

"Not on a range like this. I've shot skeet and trap, and I've done a lot of bird hunting."

"What's 'a lot,' Mr. McConnell?"

"I've been hunting with my father since I was six. It's not that hard, Instructor. The targets don't move."

"Sir, you think you could shoot a man like you shot those targets?"

McConnell paused for a moment before replying. He'd never seriously thought about shooting a man.

"I suppose so, Instructor, but I hope I'll be going to a UDT team."

"That's all, sir, you can rejoin your classmates."

Having dismissed McConnell, Sweeney turned to his staff. "Jimmy, how many times you fire a perfect score on this range?"

"I only done it three times in the two years I been out here."

Sweeney scratched his head and thought about the smooth, mechanical way McConnell had gone through the pop-up range. It was nothing short of incredible.

"Hey, Sween."

"Yeah, Jimmy?"

"That kid don't belong in no UDT. Puttin' fins on him would be like givin' Babe Ruth a tennis racket."

"I know, Jimmy, I know."

The twelve remaining trainees returned to Coronado virtually assured of graduating from the Basic UDT/SEAL Training or "Frog School." All that remained was the formality of Army airborne training. The day after they arrived back on the Strand from San Clemente they left for Fort Benning, Georgia, and jump school.

Jump school was a world unto itself. Formations of fatigue-clad soldiers jogged from one part of the base to another, shouting, singing, and cadence calling. Sergeant instructors in black baseball caps buzzed around their student charges like fighters harassing formations of bombers. It was orchestrated, carefully choreographed mayhem on a scale McConnell found hard to believe. Several hundred airborne-qualified troopers graduated each week from the continuously convening three-week course. They began as lowly, earthbound "legs" and in three magical weeks they were transformed into hard-core, fearless airborne fighting men. Most of the students were recent draftees slated to join units already in Vietnam or were assigned to outfits that were scheduled for rotation to combat duty. McConnell wasn't sure whether it was the aging process at Frog School, but the Army guys seemed a lot younger than his men. He really thought of the Navy men as "his men." They all marched and jogged around the base during the first few days of training singing Army songs:

"I wanna go to Ve-it-na-am,
I wanna kill ole Char-lie-Co-ong."

I wonder if these kids really want to go to Vietnam or actually want to kill anybody? thought McConnell. I'm not sure I do. But who am I to criticize how another service brainwashes their men after what I've just been through. Maybe if these guys believe they're devil-soldiers from the sky, they might actually kill Charlie Cong before Charlie Cong kills them.

It was a long-standing tradition that the fledgling frogmen did what they could to make life miserable for the Army instructors. For the most part the sergeant instructors—or blackhats—took it well. They were professionals in their own right and tolerated, to some extent, the rowdiness of the young frogs. A blackhat would drop one of them for twenty-five push-ups for an infraction and all of them would drop. The guilty frogman would invariably lose count when he was just about finished and shout: "I lost count, Sergeant. We better all start over. One—two—three . . ." And so it went. They sang their frog school training songs and generally made a nuisance of themselves. The Navy men were in superb physical condition, far more so than their Army counterparts at jump school, and they reveled in it. It was the first time many of them had experienced the feeling of being special or elite, and it was like a new and powerful drug.

One afternoon toward the end of the first week, McConnell saw a blackhat take Watson, one of his men, up on a ten-foot-high observation platform while the rest of the formation watched. Watson was a baby-faced kid from Iowa who surprised everyone by making it through Frog School. He had straw-brown hair and a face that belonged on a box of cornflakes. At five-feet-eight and 150 pounds, he didn't look like a frogman. He always was in the back of the pack in training, but as the pack had grown smaller, he was still there. A few of the instructors on the Strand had tried to make him quit, but he would just smile and keep going. "I quit a few things before," he had confided to McConnell, "but I ain't gonna quit this. They want me to ring that fuckin' bell, they're gonna have to beat me over the head with it after I'm dead.''

''What are you doing, Sergeant?'' McConnell called to the platform.

''This wise-mouth sailor thinks he's hot shit. I thought he might like to show how really hot he is with a few parachute landing falls from up here.''

''Sergeant, could I have a word with you?''

''What's the matter, Lieutenant, don't you think he can handle it?''

McConnell paused and looked around. Everyone in the immediate vicinity had ceased training and was looking at him. A part of him still wanted to melt back into the crowd, but it was too late for that. McConnell glanced from the hopeful look on Watson's face to the stern features of the blackhat.

''Watson, you take the stairs back down and, Sergeant, I want a word with you.''

The sergeant stomped down from the platform followed meekly by Watson. He planted his spit-shined Corcoran jump boots in front of McConnell and tilted his head back so he could look up at the taller officer from under the bill of his ball cap, which rode just an inch off the bridge of his nose.

''Sir, does the Lieutenant have a problem with the way we conduct airborne training around here?''

''I have a problem with the way you conduct training, Sergeant. Putting a man off a ten-foot tower is unauthorized and you know it. It's unnecessary, dangerous, and I won't stand for it. And it's Ensign, not Lieutenant. I'm not in the Army.''

''Begging the Ensign's pardon, sir, but I thought you Navy guys were indestructible. If you don't think you can hack a little modification of our training program here, I guess that's okay, sir.''

McConnell again felt like he was on a stage and the silence of the green-clad audience around him was deafening. The young frogmen were prone to pop off to the Army instructors and they paid for it in push-ups and additional harassment. For the most part it was a good give-and-take. But this sergeant's attitude, and what he was trying to do to one of his men, made McConnell rage inside. Struggling to maintain control, he addressed the sergeant in a cold, measured tone:

"Sergeant, we've been to hack-it school and this man doesn't need to break a leg to prove it to you. You were deliberately trying to hurt one of my men and that really pisses me off. You pull that shit again, and you and I will be up talking to the colonel about it. Or you can take it up with me personally, right here and now. What'll it be, Sergeant?"

The sergeant had been in the Army long enough to know when he had pushed a man too far, as well as when he was wrong. And this officer was not like the shavetails that normally came through airborne training.

"Okay, Ensign, fall in and we'll begin the next evolution."

McConnell's stock with his men was high, and this confrontation with the blackhat added to it significantly. That evening they asked him to join them at the enlisted men's club on post for a beer after training. They began drinking right after the training was over, and by nine o'clock, they were collectively wasted.

"Yuh know, Lootenant," slurred Watson, "yer not such a bad guy fer an ossifer."

"Well thanks, Private Watson, you're not such a bad guy yourself." They had taken to calling him "Lieutenant," so McConnell had responded by addressing them as "Privates."

"Hey, Boss, when da yuh think we'll get sent over to 'Nam? I hear half the last class is in-country rat now. Ray said that one of them already done bought the farm." The speaker was a tall, reedy-thin boy from El Paso named Barnett. He was over six-feet-three and had long hard muscles from working on the family ranch. He looked awkward and even fragile, but he had tremendous stamina. The instructors had tried to harass him, calling him the "Asshole from El Paso," but it served only to kindle his determination. During Hell Week he greeted each day saying, "Well, shee-it; they fuck with me t'day and Ahm gonna jus' chuck it." But he was a tough kid, and quitting wasn't in him.

"Just rumors, Tex," replied McConnell, having to concentrate to get the words out. "Anyway, maybe you can put in for Ranger School at Fort Bragg. Hell, you could sit the war out in the U.S. Army if you play your cards right."

"Shee-it, sir. Ah cain't take much more o' them Doggies. Ah'd rather be in 'Nam than in the Are-mee—Ah swear Ah would."

"What do yuh think of the Army, Mr. McConnell?" said Watson a little too loudly. "Are they fucked up or what?"

"What do I think of the Army?" said McConnell, glancing around the club and noticing the cold, hostile stares directed at their table. The club had suddenly become quiet and it was if he were on stage. "By God, what I think is that we ought to drink to the sons-a-bitches." Pushing himself to his feet with both arms, he raised his glass: "To the U-nited States Army; our honored senior service, our hosts at this paradise, and our comrades in arms. We're proud an' honored to serve with 'em."

"Hear, hear."

"Goddamn straight "

"Fuckin' A."

The frogs all stood and joined McConnell in the toast to the Army. This gesture met with spontaneous applause, several toasts to the Navy, and more than a few pitchers of beer sent to their table.

"Yuh know, Tex," confided Watson, "Mr. Mc-Connell's a fuckin' prophet."

"What the hail you talkin' 'bout?" replied the tall sailor. "He's an officer, but he ain't no damn prophet."

"Now, hold on a fuckin' minute," continued Watson. "You know in the Bible, the Lord made wine outta water."

"Yeah, so?"

"Well, the boss made the Doggies buy us beer. Now, it ain't wine, but I reckon that makes him at leas' a prophet. Jus' look at all that friggin' beer."

Barnett stared at his glassy-eyed shipmate and then surveyed all the beer on the table. He started to argue, but thought better of it.

"Amen, Brother Watson," he said belching loudly. "Pour me some more of that there nectar from heaven."

By midnight they were knee-walking, commode-hugging drunk. McConnell staggered back from the rest-room as the men were pouring out the last pitcher of beer. Two of them were facedown on the table.

"Here's to the Doggies."

"Aw right!"

"Fuckin' A!"

"This beer's terrible!" exclaimed McConnell, drinking half his glass. "It tastes like weasel piss."

"Ah beg yer pardon, sir," replied Tex Barnett indignantly.

"We was outta money, Boss," explained Watson. "So we jus' passed the pitcher under the table. What the fuck, sir, you only rent beer anyway."

McConnell looked around the table at the slack-faced, smiling drunken sailors, all glasses empty. This was a long way from Wabash College and Newport, Rhode Island.

"I don' care what the blackhats say," declared McConnell draining his glass, "you guys are aw-fucking right."

The little band of drunks, leaning on each other and dragging their two inert shipmates, made their way out of the club and headed for the barracks.

"Reckon we can sleep in tomorrow, Boss?"

"Sorry, guys. Yuh can hoot with the owls but yuh still gotta scream with the eagles. We gotta be standin' tall in the mornin'."

The following morning they were in fact all standing tall, and they took all that the hot Georgia summer and the blackhats had to dish out. Except for an occasional breaking of ranks to run off to the side and throw up, it was just another day at jump school. By that evening, McConnell was feeling a lot less macho and more than a little hung over, so he stopped at the officer's club for a Bloody Mary before dinner. He was concentrating on his drink when a stocky, crew-cut Army captain got up from a table and stepped up to the bar next to him.

"Your name McConnell." It was not a question. He

was dressed in the Army green short-sleeve Class B uniform with multiple rows of combat ribbons. McConnell noticed two Purple Hearts and a Silver Star among the decorations as well as a Ranger tab.

"Yessir."

"I'm Captain Altschuler, officer-in-charge of Ground Week here at airborne school." He didn't offer his hand. "Understand you had a problem with one of my blackhats yesterday?"

"Just a miscommunication, Captain. I think we got it straightened out."

"Fair enough, McConnell. How's the rest of the training going?"

"Pretty well, sir. It was a little warm out there today, and," he confessed, "we had a few too many last night."

"That's what I heard. Your men doing okay?"

"They'll be fine, Captain. They're a pretty tough lot."

"I've heard that too. They remind me of some of my Special Forces troopers. Drink all night, run all day." The man was being cordial to McConnell but not really friendly, almost like he was consciously trying not to be too familiar. He ordered a beer for himself and another Bloody Mary for McConnell. Then he turned to the younger officer.

"McConnell, I'm going to give you some advice about this man's Army. I've been with Special Forces most of my short career. I think I know what it is to be special and to command men who are a cut above the straight-leg Army troop. I used to think the regulars were a bunch of candy-asses, and beneath the elite brand of soldiering we practiced in the SF. Maybe you feel the same way.

"But let me tell you something, McConnell, it's those candy-ass, green recruits, like the ones we get here at jump school, that win wars. Special units like yours and mine, we contribute, and our contribution may be far greater than our numbers; but it's that line Army unit that will take the ground and hold the ground they take. They win the battles and they win the wars. It's the same with the current shit-throw in Vietnam. If they can't take the ground and hold it, then people like us don't count for much."

He drained half his beer and continued. "I'll tell you another thing, McConnell, you and I have it pretty soft. We lead a well-trained bunch of volunteers, many of them veterans. A lot of the time we can choose our method, if not our objective. How'd you like to be in an outfit where the major tells you to take a group of these eighteen-year-old draftees up a hill to an exposed position, and orders you to dig in and hold off the North Vietnamese Army? Gives leadership a whole new meaning, doesn't it?"

"I see what you mean, sir."

"Do you?" he said skeptically. "Well, maybe you do. At any rate, these kids here training with you have a job to do, and when the goin' gets tough, they'll do it. Believe me they will. And your counterparts, those green second lieutenants, they'll grow up in one helluva hurry." Altschuler seemed to drift off in his own thoughts for a moment and McConnell didn't disturb him. He finished his beer and turned away from the bar. "You take a little bit of a strain here, McConnell, and maybe you might learn something."

"Uh, yes, sir, and thanks for the drink."

"Don't mention it." Altschuler left McConnell alone with his hangover and a bit of insight into the U.S. Army.

On Monday of the next week, McConnell and his men were saddled up for their first parachute jump. No matter how well prepared or how hyped up you are—and the blackhats did a good job of both—the first parachute jump is a terrifying experience. They were jumping out of the old C-119 Flying Boxcars. The aircraft held about thirty jumpers divided into two "sticks," each stick filing down opposite sides of the aircraft and out the two doors at the rear on each side of the plane. As they approached the drop zone, the Army stick on one side of the aircraft began to chant, "Airborne—Airborne, AIRBORNE—AIRBORNE!" as they shuffled back to the exit door. Behind McConnell the Navy men in his stick began to chant, "Fuck God—Fuck God, FUCK GOD—FUCK GOD!" The Army jumpers fell silent in fear and amazement, and the blackhats rolled their eyes in mock horror.

"Where do you get these animals, Lieutenant?" yelled the jumpmaster in McConnell's ear.

"Bars in San Diego are full of 'em, Sergeant," McConnell shouted back.

"Green light, sir—GO!"

McConnell led his men out of the Boxcar into the noisy, turbulent slip stream followed by a bone-crunching opening shock as the twenty-four-ton aircraft pulled the parachute off his back.

"ONE thou-san, TWO thou-san THREE thou-SOOOSHIIITT!!"

A week later they were back in San Diego. They marched off the airplane proudly wearing their Army jump wings and singing their own version of the Green Beret song:

> *"Fighting Frogmen, from the sky,*
> *We'd rather swim, than jump and die,*
> *Give me a ship, far out to sea,*
> *Than one more day, in the Armee!"*

The graduation ceremony from Basic UDT/SEAL Training was brief and with an imposed importance. The trainees formed up on the grinder in dress whites on the morning after they returned from jump school. A small contingent from the Navy Band played Sousa marches before and after the amphibious base commander tendered some remarks about the new graduates taking their place as members of the Navy–Marine Corps team. He seemed disappointed there weren't more of them and in a hurry to be someplace else. Following the ceremony, McConnell removed his gear from the barracks and was on his way over to SEAL Team One, which was located just north of the training unit. His feelings about the past four months were mixed. He was still savoring the thrill of having made it, but he couldn't wait to get out of there.

I'll bet convicts who do a stretch of time at a particularly nasty prison feel the same way, thought McConnell. On his way to his car he ran into Instructor Kanaka.

"I see you leaving us, Meesta McConnell," said the blocky Hawaiian. "Where you go now?"

"I've got orders to SEAL Team, but I was hoping to get them changed to UDT."

"That may not be so easy, sir. Team One, dey need men."

"Uh . . . Instructor Kanaka, I guess I should thank you for taking . . . well, a special interest in me."

"Dat's my job, Meesta McConnell. You a good officer, sir. You do okay. And I no mo' instructor now—you call me 'Chief Kanaka.'"

"Very well, Chief Kanaka," replied McConnell. "Thanks."

"Meesta McConnell," said Kanaka, coming to attention and saluting him, "you take care of you men."

"I'll do that, Chief." McConnell returned his salute. He was almost sure that he detected a trace of a genuine smile buried within Kanaka's ever-present grin.

Chapter Four

FOXTROT PLATOON

MCCONNELL CHECKED in at the SEAL Team One quarter-deck and asked to see the administrative officer. He was directed to the desk of a large, overweight chief petty officer with a well-used cigar clamped between his teeth.

"G'morning, sîr, what can I do for ya?" His jaw showed a five-o'clock shadow and it was only late morning.

"Good morning, Chief. I'm Ensign McConnell and I'm just reporting aboard. I had a question about my orders to SEAL Team. You see I—"

"Don't tell me, sir," interrupted the chief. "Let me guess—you want orders to UDT."

"Well, yes," replied McConnell. "You see I—"

"Sir, I'm sorry to keep buttin' in, but you're gonna have to talk to the executive officer. I got no authority to modify orders. And I wouldn't get your hopes up, sir, 'cause we're awful short of officers here at Team One."

"Thanks, Chief," mumbled McConnell. He felt like he was shoveling shit against the proverbial tide, but the blue-green waters and the space-capsule recoveries continued to beckon him. He was wandering down the hall in search of the XO when he ran into Watson, Tex Barnett, and a third former trainee, a short stocky man named Ray Bono. The four of them had orders to SEAL Team while the other eight graduates had been sent to the three West Coast UDT teams.

61

"Hey, Boss," cried Watson, "looks like we're back together again."

"That's right, sir," seconded Barnett. "Come on an' we'll show you."

They dragged McConnell into the operations office and pointed to a huge status board that covered most of one wall. Beside the simple heading *Platoon Status,* some wit had written *Who's Who in the Zoo.* Below this the operating platoons were listed: Alpha Platoon, Sa Dec; Bravo Platoon, Dong Tam; Charlie Platoon, Rach Gia; Delta Platoon, Soc Trang; Echo Platoon, Bac Lieu; Foxtrot Platoon, unassigned. Under each platoon, written in grease pencil, was a list of names of those assigned to the platoon. All but Echo and Foxtrot Platoons had at least one name with a line through it. Whiskey Platoon and X-ray Platoon were completely crossed out and "tour complete" written in the space.

"There we are, sir," said Bono, "Foxtrot Platoon."
McConnell walked over and studied the board:

FOXTROT PLATOON
Deployment:	Unassigned
Platoon Cdr:	Lt. France
Asst. Plt. Cdr:	Ens. McConnell
Platoon Chief:	HTCS Johnson
LPO:	RD1 Rawls
	HM1 Young
	BM2 Cribbs
	SM3 Bono
	QM3 Barnett
	SN Watson

There were five additional lines for the fourteen-man platoon with "to be assigned" written on each line.

"Sir," Bono interrupted, "me an' Watson an' Tex feel pretty good about being assigned to your platoon, and we was wondering if we could be in your fire team? Since we had to carry you through training, we thought it'd be only right if we help you with the fire team." Ray Bono had been the class clown in training, but he was a tough, street-smart New York kid. He had thick dark hair and olive skin, and classic features marred only by a straight vertical scar on his right cheek. He was only five-nine but he weighed over 170. He'd had few problems making it through frog school.

Before McConnell could answer, a Navy lieutenant with a brisk manner and a diplomatic smile joined them and held out his hand.

"Morning men, I'm Lieutenant Taylor, the executive officer. Welcome to SEAL Team One." He shook each of their hands and turned to McConnell.

"Mr. McConnell, Chief Schwartz in Admin said you wanted to see me."

McConnell glanced at the other ex-trainees and then at the XO. For an instant he wondered if this had all been staged—it was too well set up. But it didn't matter. He was trapped and he knew it.

"It was nothing, sir," replied McConnell. "Can you tell me where I can find Lieutenant France?"

McConnell found his lieutenant in one of the small offices set aside for the platoon officers.

"I'll bet you're my new ensign," he said, rising and offering his hand.

"That's right, sir, Ensign Jim McConnell."

"It's 'Dave,' and welcome to Foxtrot Platoon. Let's get some coffee and talk business." He had light brown hair that was beginning to thin at the front and his hands, which pulled unconsciously at the corners of his muskratlike mustache, were those of a laborer, rough and dirty.

They walked down the hall to the operations office to get coffee and France introduced McConnell to Tom Harper, the operations officer.

"You found us a home yet, Tom?" asked France.

"Well, Echo Platoon has been keeping a fire team at Firebase Delta and the admiral in Saigon would like to have a full platoon there. There's plenty of bad guys in the Nam Can forest so you won't have to go far to find work. You going to be ready for a September deployment?"

"September!" cried McConnell before he could check himself.

Harper and France had a good laugh at the new guy's

expense. They didn't call them rookies in the team. They were "new guys" until they made their first deployment.

"Easy, tiger," said Harper. "I can't get you there any faster. It's tourist season and all the flights are booked."

France and McConnell walked back toward the platoon office. "Jim, we've got a busy two months ahead of us to get the platoon ready for this deployment. It's going to be especially busy for you and the other new guys. They're all vets except for the four of you, so you're going to have to bust ass to come up to speed. We might as well get started right now with the fire team assignments and pre-deployment training schedule."

While they drank their coffee, France briefed McConnell. They would spend the next few days at the team area for issue of weapons and personal operational gear, and to get the platoon equipment boxes ready for deployment. The following week they would take their weapons and operational gear to the SEAL training camp in the desert east of San Diego near Niland, California. During the five weeks at this camp, they would complete most of their pre-deployment training. The last few weeks would be devoted to final preparation and leave time. France had also scheduled a week of night operations on the border. The border patrol welcomed any help they could get in stemming the tide of illegals coming across from Mexico, and the SEALs needed the practice of interdicting people at night. Their plane was due to leave North Island Naval Air Station sometime during the last week of September.

"What's the setup as far as fire teams?" asked McConnell.

"I've tried to split up the talent and experience," explained France. "I've assigned Chief Johnson and Cribbs to your fire team, plus another one of the new guys out of training. We'll be getting three men from Whiskey Platoon and two that are coming over from UDT."

"It's your call, Dave, but the three guys from my training class are good men. I'd like to have them with me if that's not a problem."

France considered this for a moment. It certainly wouldn't bother him to have all veterans in his fire team. "No problem here, but let's run it past the Chief first. By the way, we got a solid man in Chief Johnson. Our leading petty officer is Bill Rawls and he's a good one. He was with Harper on his last trip, and Tom says he's one hot-shit operator. They ran up a pretty tall body count on their deployment."

As they discussed the details of the deployment and the pre-deployment training, McConnell learned more about his platoon commander. France had graduated from the Naval Academy in 1964 and had a year in the fleet before he came to the teams. This was his first full SEAL deployment but he had spent a tour in Vietnam with UDT. He'd also relieved one of the platoon officers from Victor Platoon after the officer had been wounded, and he had finished the last three months of Victor's tour. He acquired the nickname "make-'em-dance France" around the team, because he always referred to killing VC as "making them dance." France made it very clear to McConnell that he intended for the little brown people in black pajamas to be doing a little soft shoe during Foxtrot's deployment. He had married his high school sweetheart right after gradu-ating from the Academy, but a long Western Pacific cruise on a destroyer and his volunteering for duty in the teams had encouraged her to return to her family back in Syra-cuse. France didn't make it clear whether he was separated or divorced. McConnell found himself liking France in a tentative sort of way. He sensed his platoon commander was very competitive and just a little too eager to get back to the fighting. He begged off when France asked him to join him for a beach run. He needed some time to himself to digest being in a SEAL team and that he was actually going to Vietnam. France was not gone more than five minutes when an older, stern-looking man stepped into the office.

"Good afternoon, sir, I'm Senior Chief Johnson. Glad to have you aboard."

"Thanks, Senior Chief," replied McConnell. "Glad to be aboard, I think. I wasn't sure I'd be permanently as-signed to Team One, and I just found out we deploy in two months. I'm still getting used to the idea."

"I understand you were looking for an assignment to UDT, Mr. McConnell," said Johnson, coming right to the point. "I'm sorry it didn't work out for you. The instructors over at the training unit say you're a pretty good officer."

McConnell was surprised at Johnson's frankness as well as his comment about the UDT assignment. But it stood to reason that the team chief petty officers and the training unit CPOs talked among themselves.

"What can I say, Chief? I wanted UDT, but I'll go anywhere except back through Hell Week." Then changing the subject, "Sit down and tell me something about our fire team." The chief smiled and took a chair.

"Well, sir, we have one hell of a point man in Cribbs," Johnson began. "He thinks like a VC. From what I know of those being assigned from UDT and Whiskey Platoon, they're a solid bunch."

"Chief, there are three men assigned to the platoon from my training class, and they're all good men. I'd like to see them in our fire team unless you think the experience factor would be too much of a negative."

Johnson paused to think before replying. "Not if they're good men, sir. I'd like to meet them first. Experience is a great thing, but it can sometimes work against you. Some of these veterans think they know it all because they've been there once or twice. New guys will do it our way rather than ask too many questions or complain that this wasn't the way they did it in their last platoon. If we take on the three new men—four counting yourself, sir—let's talk with Mr. France about assigning Reed to our team. He's a first-rate heavy weapons man."

They talked for about an hour about the deployment, Firebase Delta, and the platoon training that would be done before they left. McConnell learned that this would be Johnson's fifth tour in Vietnam with Team One. The chief came from a small town in northern Minnesota and had been in the Navy when McConnell was born. McConnell felt complimented that the chief talked with him as an equal, referring to "our tactics" and "our fire team." He explained the platoon structure to McConnell. They trained and deployed as a platoon, but operationally they functioned as two fire teams. As platoon chief, Johnson was responsible for platoon equipment and administration. As the senior enlisted man and most experienced SEAL, his advice was sought on all operational matters. The leading petty officer, or next senior enlisted man, was tasked with scheduling their training and enlisted personnel matters. The platoon chief and the LPO acted as assistant patrol leader in their respective fire teams. Johnson seemed comfortable with the way Foxtrot Platoon was manning up. Midafternoon, they were interrupted by a tall, blond-haired man who stuck his head in the door.

"Hey, Senior Chief, I'm goin' over to base supply and see about our vehicle request for next week. Well, howdy, sir—you must be the new ensign. Bill Rawls here."

"Glad to meet you, Rawls," said McConnell, rising to shake his hand. "I'm Ensign McConnell."

"Maynard, you got the ensign measured for a body bag yet?"

"I'll take care of Mr. McConnell, Rawls—you just see about the vehicles."

McConnell left the team area late that afternoon and drove back to the BOQ. To some degree, he had gone through the motions with France and Chief Johnson, and avoided confronting himself with the reality that he was going to Vietnam. On the way up to his room, he stopped at the BOQ bar for a beer, and for the first time, he really thought about it.

Christ, I'm a Navy SEAL and I'm on my way to Vietnam! Why did I let this happen to me? Was I too proud or too taken up with the program to admit that I didn't want to do this? Or do I?

McConnell had no clear opinions about the war, but he vaguely felt that America should help the South Vietnamese fight communism. When his place in SEAL team had been resolved by being thrust into Foxtrot Platoon, he'd felt relieved—along with being excited, resigned, and a little scared. It was easy to rationalize to himself that he really didn't have a choice. I do have a choice, he admitted—I'm still a volunteer. Every SEAL who goes to Vietnam is a volunteer, all the way. There was no bell on the SEAL team grinder that had to be rung if you wanted out.

But you still had to quit, and the act of quitting would be known to all.

It seemed there was a part of him that wanted to be in SEAL team, and wanted to go off to Vietnam. And there was a very real and rational part of him that knew he should have a better reason—a stronger conviction for doing this. McConnell's dilemma was not a new one. He was a typical American male being pulled by the magnet of combat—the ultimate test. It beckons everyone in the military, from the lowliest draftee to the career West Pointer. But if you shined a light down into the far reaches of the military man's soul, you would find that he didn't really want to be in combat so much as he wanted to *have been* in combat. The status afforded a combat veteran, both in and out of the military, causes better men than Ensign Jim McConnell to rally to the bugle.

"Hey, buddy," said an officer who sat down next to McConnell at the bar, "what's that insignia you're wearing?"

"I'm in SEAL team," said McConnell.

"No kiddin'," he replied. "I hear that's really tough. I've never met a SEAL before—let me buy you a beer."

"Sure," said McConnell pushing his empty glass across the bar. "Why not?"

"You been to 'Nam yet?"

"Not yet. My platoon deploys in a couple of months."

"Where they going to put you?"

"Looks like it's going to be a place called Firebase Delta, near the Nam Can Forest."

"No kiddin'. I hear the Nam Can is crawling with VC."

"That's what I hear, too."

"I just got back—Ops boss on an LST. It got a little hairy on some of the rivers, but not nothing like what you guys do. Is it true that you cut off their ears?"

"Their what!?"

"Their ears. I heard there was a bounty paid on VC ears and that you guys had a corner on the market."

"Do I look like the kind of a guy that collects ears?" McConnell's gaze made the officer squirm in his seat.

"Uh, well no, I guess not." The conversation moved to safer ground as McConnell learned about how his LST handled in the shallow rivers of Vietnam. The man quickly finished his beer and McConnell was again alone at the bar.

Two more beers didn't make him feel any better about his situation—or any worse, for that matter. He figured he could live with it, and the excitement and status of being a SEAL partially offset his apprehension. But there was the matter of his parents. Except for the few words with his father when he was last home, the prospect of his going to Vietnam had been an ever-present but untalked-about possibility. It was ten o'clock their time when McConnell telephoned them in Mattoon.

"Yeah, that's right, Dad, training's over. We just got back from jump school."

"Were you able to change your orders to underwater demolition?"

"No, I couldn't. There's a shortage of officers at SEAL team so I guess I'm stuck there for a while."

"Do you know what you'll be doing next?"

"That's why I called. I've been assigned to a platoon that's going to Vietnam in about two months." There was a pause before his father replied.

"That's pretty quick, Son. But I guess if you're on that team, you have to go, right?"

"Yes, sir, I guess I do."

They talked for a while but the conversation was awkward. He spoke briefly with his mother, who was shocked but supportive. She said they were both very proud of him, but he felt that in accepting their approval he had enlisted them in an affair that was less than honest. Before he called he had been concerned with his Mom's reaction, but he sensed that his Dad was working the hardest to remain positive. He rang off and went back to the bar.

During the next few days the platoon came up to strength, and the fire team assignments were finalized. They were a platoon unit in all respects except in the field where they operated independently in two squad elements or fire teams. They also drew weapons and personal gear that week. Each man was issued an M16 rifle or a CAR-15, which was just a shortened version of the M16. Some

of the SEALs had M-203 40mm grenade launchers fitted
to their M16s so the weapon became a combination automatic rifle and grenade launcher. All of them received
Browning 9mm automatics as side arms. The two heavy
weapons men were both veterans and assigned their own
special M60 machine guns. They were a shortened and
highly modified version of the standard issue. Reed,
McConnell's M60 man, had a flex tube that connected his
M60 with the 400-round magazine he carried on his back.
Cribbs's personal weapon was a Klashnakov AK-47. There
were a variety of other weapons available to the platoon—
several makes and nationalities of 9mm "grease guns,"
shot guns with duckbill chokes, even a fully automatic
shotgun. McConnell inspected the shotguns and winced at
the thought of what the 12 gauge, 00-buckshot would do
to a man at close range. There was an M14 sniper rifle, a
variety of silenced weapons and the deadly Stoner rifles.
He handled the Stoner for the first time, admiring the finely
machined weapon. He ran his hand lightly over the receiver group and carefully tested the action, cycling the
bolt back with the charging handle that was fitted to a slide
on the forestock.

"Made by the Cadillac Gauge Company in limited
numbers," said the old gunner's mate who appeared at
McConnell's elbow. He sounded like a combination of an
evangelist and a funeral director as he extolled the fatal
capabilities of his wares. It was clear he loved his work
with a morbid delight and harbored an unveiled loathing
for the SEAL operators who failed to care properly for *his*
weapons.

"She's a belt-fed, gas-operated machine gun and can
fire up to eleven hundred rounds per minute. Operates a
lot like the M60 but fires the lighter 5.56mm rounds—like
an M16." McConnell brought the weapon to his shoulder,
swinging it to track an imaginary target. It had a tight,
well-balanced feel. "Fine weapon, sir, but you gotta take
care of her—a lot more than the other machine guns."

"Accurate?" McConnell handled the weapon like a
woman handles an infant. The old gunner sensed that
McConnell was a man who appreciated a fine rifle.

"Oh, you bet, sir, and she won't ride up or walk around

on you. She's a real Thoroughbred.'' McConnell again carefully inspected the gun, then wiped it down with a rag before he placed it in the rack.

"Gunner, find me one of these, preferably a newer one that's nice and tight, and assign it to Foxtrot Platoon. Tag it with my name.''

"Aye, sir—I'll take care of it for you.''

There was also an assortment of Claymore mines, LAW (light antitank weapon) rockets, hand grenades, and booby traps that would serve individual mission requirements and fire team needs. The Team One armory was a smorgasbord of lethality.

The SEALs were fastidious in selecting their operational clothing and equipment, much the same as a woman shopping for just the right dress. They started with the standard issue camouflage jungle shirts, and then modified them for individual fit and to accommodate the special inflatable life jackets worn under the shirt necessary for some of their special missions. There were special pockets, loops, and snaps sewn on to meet individual needs and equipment load. The industrial sewing machines at the team parachute loft allowed them to construct special "web gear" harnesses adapted to handle their individual weapons and ammunition load. McConnell and the other new guys followed the veterans' lead and bought blue jeans for operational wear. Much of their work would be at night in the mosquito-infested mangrove swamp and Levi's wore better and were quieter for walking than the baggy jungle trousers, especially when wet. They were a very fashion-conscious lot and any new idea was quickly copied. The new guys were well caught up in the designer combat wardrobe fad, and finally Chief Johnson took them aside for a talk.

"Now, look men, I want you to have confidence in your equipment and carry your load as comfortably as possible, but the name of the game is rifles and radios. You've got to be able to hit what you're aiming at and be able to communicate if you've got the radio. What you wear doesn't have that much to do with it.'' Chief Johnson practiced just what he preached. In the field he pretty much stuck to the standard camouflage jungle greens and Army issue web gear and he usually preferred the standard M16, although he would occasionally carry a shotgun.

The SEAL training camp in the desert near Niland was a dilapidated collection of single-wide mobile homes. Most of the old trailers were used as sleeping quarters with one for storage and one for a field kitchen. They were located in the middle of a deserted government reservation. There was nothing for miles but scrub brush and dry washes, so the SEALs could shoot at anything except each other. The nights were cool and the days were upwards of 110 degrees with very little shade. They set up ranges for sighting in their weapons and snap-shooting practice. Each man tried to get at least 500 rounds through his personal weapon each day, as well as some work with the special weapons. There was a separate range for grenades and the bazooka-like LAW rockets. The fire teams had separate sectors well away from the camp where they worked on team reaction drills and practiced fire-and-movement. They rehearsed squad tactics for assaulting various target objectives and emergency procedures for breaking contact. And it was all done with live fire.

Chief Johnson set up plywood hootches for assault practice. The fire team would patrol in a single file to the objective hootch, and on McConnell's signal, the squad file became a skirmish line. They moved forward like the offensive unit of a football team approaching the line of scrimmage. Another signal and they broke formation, racing to their assignments. Two SEALs moved like wide receivers to cover the flanks on either side of the hootch and gain a firing position to take down anyone fleeing out the back door. The M60 man led the assault from the front like a fullback going up the middle on a draw play. He laid down a pattern of fire supported by two riflemen. On McConnell's whistle, all firing on the hootch ceased. The M60 covered the point man as he dived through the front door, a rifleman coming in right behind him. McConnell stayed out front in a control position while Chief Johnson acted as rear security, alert for an attack from the rear. McConnell soon began to feel the team as an extension of himself, like his rifle, only with a much greater range and firepower.

They did this over and over with Chief Johnson holding periodic critique sessions. Each man took a turn as the fire team leader and directed an assault. The Foxtrot SEALs, normally a relaxed and informal group, recognized the seriousness of what they were doing. The live fire made it dangerous business, even in a noncombat situation. McConnell felt good about the fire team's progress and so did the chief. He and France swapped members of their squads so the men could be freely substituted on either fire team. Occasionally they operated as a platoon. McConnell could see the control problems with twice as many people and guns moving about. As their procedures became proficient by day, they began doing them at night. Toward the end of their desert stay they were doing all of their work at night.

During their free time, they sat around the camp trying to stay cool or fired weapons on the range near the camp. It was there McConnell began to work with his weapon of choice—the Stoner rifle. The rifle looked something like the old Thompson submachine gun used by gangsters, but there was no pistol grip on the forestock and the barrel was much longer. The rounds were fed by a disintegrating-link belt into the weapon from a drum slung under the gun and just forward of the trigger housing.

McConnell learned that by increasing the tension on the recoil springs and enlarging the gas port that drove the bolt back to cycle the rounds, he could get a higher rate of fire. After these adjustments, he found he could nurse his Stoner up close to fourteen hundred rounds per minute. This twenty-two rounds per second could make the barrel glow in the shade. With the attached hundred-fifty-round drum, he had almost eight full seconds of continuous automatic fire without reloading. Paid out in four- to six-round bursts with good fire discipline, it lasted a long time.

The Stoner and a full drum weighed fifteen pounds, light enough to easily be shoulder-fired and heavy enough to be stable. The long barrel made it very accurate and partially avoided the tendency to ''walk'' or ride up in automatic fire. The M60s with their heavier 7.62mm rounds and the Stoners were normally used as area fire weapons. Their job was fire suppression while the real work was done by the riflemen. The automatic weapons laid down a blanket of fire to engage the enemy and keep their heads down—almost a defensive tactic—while the riflemen picked out individual targets and did the killing. And nobody but the M60 men ever fired from the hip. The SEALs learned that if the buttstock wasn't in your shoulder, you were just boring holes in the air and wasting ammunition.

McConnell was very good with the Stoner and with practice he became phenomenal. The Foxtrot SEALs would watch him snap up and knock holes in a pie plate at forty yards with two- and three-round bursts. Just like a gunslinger in the western movies, he would chase a tin can across the desert with the same short bursts, hitting it again and again, never allowing it to stop moving. He could group two or three rounds as accurately as the riflemen firing single rounds from their M16s. The Stoner was a delicate and somewhat temperamental weapon that required constant attention. Each evening, McConnell could be found at the cleaning table with his Stoner. The unassembled parts would be laid out on a clean towel after they had been thoroughly washed in solvent and dried. His father had taught him the ritual of cleaning firearms as soon as you came out of the field. The smell of cleaning solvents and gun oil always reminded him of his dad.

"You take pretty good care of that thing, don't you, Ensign?" Rawls sat down across the table and began to break down his M16.

"You have to take care of a weapon, especially a Stoner," he replied. McConnell was carefully scraping the carbon buildup from the near invisible groove inside the gas chamber. He used a specially designed tool for this called a Smith Scribe. It was not named for the designer of the tool, but for a SEAL who was killed when his Stoner jammed from carbon buildup.

Rawls was a narrow man. At first glance he appeared too thin, but the whipcordlike muscles in his forearms suggested he was both strong and quick. He wore his sun-bleached blond hair as long as Navy regulations would allow and then some, and combed it slick-straight back over his head. He always carried a pack of cigarettes in his right sock.

"I been watching you on the range and you're one helluva fine shot. But there's a difference in the range and the jungle. Tell me, sir, you about ready to go over there and really get it on?" His angular features became more pronounced when he smiled, and his broad grin gave others absolutely no clue to the degree of his sincerity. There was something eerie about Rawls. McConnell knew that all SEALs had to kill, but Rawls was the only one who actually looked like a killer.

"Rawls, just what do you mean?" McConnell ceased working on his Stoner to give the man his full attention.

"What I mean, Ensign, is are you about ready to stop shooting tin cans and bag a few gooks?"

"I'm ready to do my job. Is there some reason for you to think that I can't?" His voice was a little louder than he had intended.

"Hey, relax," Rawls replied from behind the smile. "I'm on your side. An' if you want my opinion, I think you're gonna do just fine. Hell, sir, you may even turn out to like this business."

One evening toward the end of their training in the desert, the SEALs deployed to one of the highway taverns near the Salton Sea for pizza and beer. They had congregated at several tables in the back near the pool table. Rawls, the platoon pool shark, was systematically thrashing his teammates in turn at eight ball. He prowled around the pool table with a familiarity that spoke of a misspent youth.

"Your turn, Mr. McConnell," said Rawls. "Let's see how good a shooter you are with a cue stick."

McConnell shrugged and grabbed a cue. The gallery was on his side but Rawls was too good for him, dispatching the eight ball while five of McConnell's balls were still on the table. McConnell again shrugged and returned to his seat.

"Well, who's next?" said Rawls, savoring his victory.

"I'll play pool with you sailor boy," said a tall, long-haired man in his early thirties who had just walked over from the crowd at the bar. He was dressed like a cowboy, but his designer jeans and the mother-of-pearl snaps on his western shirt said he wasn't a serious ranch hand. "And to make it interesting, let's play for a ten spot."

"Sure, why not," said Rawls, laying his bill next to that of the stranger's on the rail of the pool table.

The stranger paid a quarter for the balls and racked them tightly on the worn green felt. Rawls dropped two on the break and was cheered by the SEALs, who were now solidly behind him. But it was not a close game. The new player shot pool like McConnell shot tin cans. When his turn came, he ran the table, beating Rawls badly.

"Guess maybe I was a bit lucky there, sailor boy," said the man, smiling at several of his friends who had come over from the bar to watch. He was obviously hustling Rawls and enjoying it. He left the two ten-dollar bills on the table and turned to Rawls.

"How about it squid, double or nothing?"

"Y'know, you're one helluva pool shooter," Rawls replied as he concentrated on chalking the tip of his cue. The smile on his face was twisted slightly. "Yeah, that was a nice piece of pool shooting there, buddy. Real nice. You won the game all right, but I'll bet *you* double or nothing you don't win the postgame fight."

"The what?" said the stranger.

"Rawls, *no!*" shouted Chief Johnson, coming to his feet, but he was too late.

Rawls smoothly flipped the cue stick around and swung down on the man like a major-leaguer chasing a low slider, breaking the butt of the cue across his shins. The man howled in pain and reached for his shins as Rawls followed with a roundhouse punch to the side of his jaw, knocking him out cold. One of the stranger's friends from the other side of the table jumped to his defense. He was met by a hard, professionally thrown right hand from France that sent him to his knees and doubled him over like a Moslem at prayer. He looked up half-consciously as the blood seeped through the fingers of both hands from his broken nose. Three more of the opposition stepped up but they pulled back when the platoon closed ranks behind Rawls and France. There was a volley of overturned chairs, tables, and broken glass. True to their training, two SEALs broke out on either flank—one grabbed a chair and the other snatched up a beer bottle by the neck.

"Aw right, goddammit, *that's it!*" screamed the shrill voice of the tavern owner's wife as she charged along the battle line. She was a fat, hard, middle-aged desert rat who had performed this duty many times before and was afraid of nobody. Both sides drew back.

"You goddamn Navy guys get the hell out of here. Buford's callin' the po-leece and if you're not outta here in thirty seconds, we're pressin' charges. Just look at this place," she sobbed, ignoring the wounded patrons. "First that stunt last week and now this. You assholes are permanently eighty-sixed, so *don't come back*!" The SEALs scrambled out of the tavern like a bunch of junior high kids caught smoking in the boy's room. McConnell saw Rawls snatch the money from the pool table as they made for the door.

"Ja-sus Key-rist," boomed the voice of the harpy from inside the tavern. "Just look at this fuckin' place."

Chief Johnson got to the wheel of the stake truck and the rest of the platoon piled onto the bed. They bounced out of the parking lot and headed down the highway in the direction of the camp. The details of the encounter were immediately relived and embellished. Rawls and France basked in the glow of their triumph and nursed their sore right hands. The rest of them talked animatedly about what they would have done had the battle been more fully joined.

"I guess we showed those imitation rednecks a trick or two, huh, sir?" said Reed, sitting down next to McConnell. Tom Reed was the biggest Foxtrot SEAL. He was a local boy, having grown up in nearby El Cajon and played college football at San Diego State. He'd had a tryout with the Chargers and a few other NFL clubs. Ultimately he was too small to play defensive end in the pros, but he was just the right size for a SEAL M60 machine gunner. He was a handsome man with a soft voice that suggested an inner strength to match his physical dimensions.

"I guess we did," said McConnell. "Say Reed, what did that old gal mean by 'that stunt last week'?"

"Well, we were down there last Friday drinking, an' I guess we got a little shit-faced. Bono thought they were wateran' down our beer so he called 'em on it. They told him to go to hell, so he gets a case of the ass and decides to retaliate. He climbed up on the pool table and took a shit in the corner pocket. You otta seen him, sir, squattin' up there on the cushions like a fuckin' gook. Watson was laughin' so hard he peed his pants."

McConnell had to smile at the thought of the blocky little Italian perched on the table with his trousers around his ankles taking a dump.

"Were they really watering your beer, Reed?"

"Who the fuck knows, sir. We'd had about a dozen pitchers. If they were, they were doing us a favor."

The platoon broke desert camp, and was back on the Strand the following week. The deployment was three short weeks away. The only real training scheduled was a week of night operations with the border patrol. Each fire team was driven to a sector along the Mexican border where they would patrol the canyons and draws looking for illegals walking north. The SEALs carried most of their operational gear and ammunition load for training purposes, but the only weapons allowed were side arms carried by the fire team leaders. It was strictly sneak-and-peek training. When they spotted a border crossing, they would radio the border patrol to intercept and take action. For the team, it was good training. Their lives would depend on their ability to see and not be seen at night. For McConnell, it allowed him time with his point man. On point, Cribbs was the eyes and ears of the fire team, and made most of the tactical decisions in the field. The chief was right when he said they had a good one.

Harold Cribbs's face bore the scars of teenage acne that had gone untreated, and two of his lower teeth were missing. He was a small man with quick, ferretlike movements and an untrusting nature. Cribbs was from a small town in Kentucky and, like McConnell, had grown up hunting. Except that he had the concentration and purpose of someone who hunted for food rather than for sport. He wore VC-style black pajamas in the field, and carried an AK-47. He reasoned that if the Viet Cong saw him first, they might hesitate, thinking he was one of them, and allow him to get off the first round. Cribbs was a two-tour veteran and he claimed this masquerade had saved his life. McConnell felt comfortable walking behind him and they learned to communicate almost without speech or hand signals.

Their last night on the border, Cribbs signaled the squad to a halt and motioned McConnell forward. He pointed across a shallow ravine to where a line of dark forms threaded its way along the far slope. Cribbs joined his hands together, indicating he wanted to intercept them. McConnell nodded and Cribbs led them carefully down the side of the hill. After they crossed the ravine, Cribbs stopped abruptly. He drew his hand across his throat and pumped his right fist: *Ambush—right side*. The squad file of SEALs scurried into the dry scrub on the right side of the path they had been following. A moment later, a line of men speaking Spanish in low tones filed by, close enough for McConnell to touch them.

"Cribbs is phenomenal," McConnell later told Chief Johnson as they waited for the border patrol truck to pick them up. "He works the game better than my dog and I had a good one. I'm surprised that Mr. France didn't assign him to his own fire team."

"Well, sir, Mr. France likes Rawls to walk his point, and Rawls isn't bad. Cribbs worked with the lieutenant some before you came aboard, but I think he found Cribbs was a little too conservative."

Following the week of border work, most of the platoon members rotated out on leave prior to their departure. Only Lieutenant France, Chief Johnson, and the new guys stayed around the team area during the final weeks before deployment.

The last two weeks in San Diego were a pleasant hiatus for McConnell. He went into the team area for a few hours each day, but there was little for him to do. He assisted

France with the officer duties such as command briefings and message traffic. Chief Johnson attended to the manifests, equipment custody records, and the other paperwork required to get a SEAL platoon from San Diego, California, to Firebase Delta in the Republic of Vietnam. Sometimes Johnson would take him over to the Chief's Club for a sandwich and a beer. The more McConnell got to know his chief, the more he came to respect and depend on him. There was a mutual feeling of friendship and trust growing between them.

He spent most of his afternoons with France out at Mission Beach, where France had an apartment. They passed the time drinking beer, ogling the girls, and playing over-the-line softball. As if it were a part of his training, France took him on the local party circuit and to the Downwinds, as well as the other military club nights. The last few days floated by and McConnell allowed himself to fall into the easy party life of the beach crowd. At the Mission Beach watering holes, it was not that hard to find a lady to spend the night with.

The sun and fun of Southern California passed the time, but couldn't make McConnell forget that he was going off to war. There were always questions in his mind. The predeployment training had gone well, but were they really ready? Am I ready? He tried not to think about it, but the simple odds were that some of them might not come back. He tried to picture in his mind what it would be like. He mentally worked through different combat scenarios and what he would do—how he might react. He was afraid, but drew confidence from the veteran SEALs and from the universal soldier's armor—"Others may die, but it can't happen to me." It allowed him to control the fear. Apprehension, well spiced with excitement and anticipation, drove McConnell's thoughts on the eve of Foxtrot's deployment.

The Foxtrot SEALs trickled in from leave and the platoon was back up to strength. Chief Johnson gave most of the orders as they began their final equipment preparations. Tom Harper presented operational briefings on Firebase Delta and their future area of operation, or AO. Lieutenant Commander Green gave them a final commanding officer's briefing, wishing them good hunting and urging them to be careful.

The morning of their departure, Chief Johnson supervised the loading of the platoon's equipment and weapons aboard the aircraft. As Foxtrot Platoon milled about under the wing of the plane, the men's excitement masked most of their regret at leaving. They were dressed in their flat jungle greens, which would be their uniform for the duration of the deployment when they were not in the field. The only visible emotion was in the sad faces of the few red-eyed wives and girlfriends who accompanied their men to the plane. To McConnell, getting on the plane was a turning point, like when he first left home for college and then again to join the Navy.

"You look a little far away there, Mr. McConnell."

"I was just thinking, Chief. Looks like training's over and it's time to go and do it."

"Training's never over, sir, but it is time to go to work."

"Your wife here to see you off, Chief?"

"She gave that up after my third trip. It's just as well—she's not too good at good-byes and I have to see to the gear. Speaking of which, I better make a last check with the loadmaster. See you on board, sir." There was a melancholy air about the chief that was contagious and it made McConnell apprehensive.

There was little for McConnell to do but watch. He looked for the other new guys, but the chief had them busy with equipment. France was enjoying the attentions of one of the girls from the beach who clung fiercely to him. He suddenly felt very alone and apprehensive—that he was being carried forward by events over which he had no control. I wonder, he thought, if the other guys feel like this?

"You ready for this deployment, Mr. McConnell?"

"Yes, sir, Captain." Lieutenant Commander Green had quietly appeared at his elbow. He was shorter than McConnell but broader, his barrel chest just starting to thicken at the waist.

"I certainly hope so," he replied as if he weren't convinced. They watched for a few moments before Green spoke again. "You know, Mr. McConnell, a lot of people think this war is the ticket—promotions, medals—a chance to be a hero. That's bullshit. It's just a job—a damn tough job and dangerous, but nothing more.'' McConnell wasn't sure a response was required, so he said nothing. Then the older man turned abruptly to face him and offered his hand.

"Good luck, mister. You take care of those sailors and you listen to your chief."

"Aye, sir."

Green left him and soberly made the rounds, shaking each man's hand and wishing him a safe tour. They trooped aboard the old C-54 while the women cried, and the other SEALs who came to see them off gave their teammates a thumbs-up or a clandestine obscene gesture. The old transport taxied to the end of the runway and almost shook itself apart as the pilot ran up each engine prior to takeoff. The old girl then lumbered back down the runway and crawled into the air, turning west out over Point Loma, putting San Diego behind them. Foxtrot Platoon was officially away on deployment.

Chapter Five

FIREBASE DELTA

THE C-54 STRUGGLED up to its cruise altitude of 9,500 feet and McConnell, like the rest of the SEALs, traded his uniform for a set of blue team-issue sweats. Some of the men read and others slept. Rawls set up a poker game in the back of the plane using one of the platoon weapons boxes as a card table. McConnell had received a letter from his father the day before, but, in the confusion of the loadout and departure, had decided to save it for the flight. Now as they droned across the Pacific, McConnell fully reclined his seat and opened his father's letter.

Dear Son,

I hope this reaches you before you leave San Diego, but if not, I know the Navy is good about forwarding mail. Your mother's letters used to follow me across the Pacific. They were often late and sometimes they came in bunches, but they always seemed to find me.

Jimmy, this is a hard letter for me to write. There are some things I want to say to you and this seems like the best way. Perhaps we should have talked more when you were home last spring, but you were just beginning your Navy training and seemed so sure about an assignment to the underwater team. But that's only part of it. Some things are just easier to write than to talk about. When you were growing up, you used to ask me about my

Navy days aboard ship during the last war, or I should say about World War II. I probably made life on that destroyer sound like one big pleasure cruise with the exotic ports-of-call in the beautiful South Pacific. The war was a trying time for me and I guess, next to you and your mother, one of the few important events in my life. But aside from the adventure and travel, it was also war, and I never told you about that part of it. I think it is time that I did.

At first there were long transits and escort duty, but they were uneventful. We spent the long hours training and were constantly at general quarters, but we didn't fight the ship. All that changed at Guadalcanal. We finally got into combat, but even those wild night battles up the Slot were just noisy, high speed affairs, firing at invisible targets. I never did see the enemy. During daylight, the Jap aircraft pretty much left us alone and concentrated on the carriers and other large ships. We were doing our job, but I never felt it was enough. Maybe that's why I volunteered to ride on the landing craft and serve as liaison officer to the destroyers like mine who would help guide the landing craft to the beach.

My first landing was at Tarawa. After an incredible naval bombardment we loaded our Marines into the mike boats and headed for the beach. Those young boys were so confident and full of life. They were nervous and scared, but they couldn't wait for that bow ramp to drop so they could charge ashore. It went bad from the start. We were held off the beach in deep water by hidden offshore reefs, so many of them drowned under the weight of their equipment after they stepped off the ramp. I guess that's when the Navy decided they needed you frogmen. Those Marines that made it ashore took a fearful beating. I don't know how they did it, but those marvelous boys fought and held that beachhead. After the beach was secured, we were sent back in to ferry the wounded back out to the transports. Jim, those broken and maimed boys were so different than the ones we took ashore earlier that day. I'll never forget the carnage on that beach and the courage of those young Marines. Truk, Saipan, even Iwo Jima didn't seem quite so bad, but maybe I was used to it by then. After we took the Marines ashore and returned back out to sea, we were pretty much out of danger. But what I really dreaded was going back to pick up the wounded. Sometimes the blood would drain back along the deck to where I was in the coxswain's flat. There was nothing I could do but vector my boats to the nearest ship for offloading. Sometimes I would recognize one of the boys we'd taken ashore earlier and it would be that much more difficult. It's been a while, but I used to have nightmares about those landings. Never about the initial assault when we were getting shot at—just the faces of those wounded boys we took back off the beach. I guess that is the price I paid for being a volunteer.

Well, Son, it looks like you're the volunteer now, and your mother and I are anxiously waiting for you to come back. I know you are going to be a fine officer and that you will do your duty. Just please be careful. I'm not quite so sure I understand this war—it's a lot different from mine. But I know you believe in what you are doing, and your mom and I are behind you. We both love you very much.

I hope this rambling about a war fought before you were born doesn't upset you. They never told the officer candidates in my day what it would be like. They taught us how to march and salute and navigate, but they never prepared us for the real purpose of war. They never taught us that war is the business of killing people. I think I might have handled it better if I had some notion of what it was all about. I guess that's why I'm writing this letter; so you will have a better idea of what lies ahead, if that's possible. Maybe I needed to say this more than you needed to hear it, but I hope it helps you to prepare for your landings.

Get your work done and come home, Jim. Your mother sends her love as do I.

Dad

McConnell dropped the letter to his lap and closed his eyes, trying to picture a younger version of his father directing landing craft operations under fire. He found it hard to transform the affable, slightly overweight insurance man into anything but his dad, smiling across the dining room table or walking across a cornfield in the fall with a shotgun broken across his shoulder. Why didn't I know about this sooner? Growing up, he remembered the other kids bragging about what their fathers had done during the war. All McConnell could offer was that his dad had spent the war on a ship, sailing to and from exotic ports in the South Seas.

He reflected on his dad's comment that he, McConnell, believed in what he was doing. What *do* I believe in, he thought? We're supposedly on our way to fight the spread of communism, but is that really why I'm here? Or have I been so stupid and self-centered in trying to be someone special that I've just managed to stumble into the path of this war. Next time I see Dad, there'll be a lot more to talk about than duck hunting.

Three days and several islands later, Foxtrot's plane waddled into Saigon's Tan Son Nhut Air Base and taxied to a stop in a sandbagged revetment. The platoon quickly offloaded the equipment while the plane refueled, and then watched as it taxied back out to the main runway for takeoff. The aircrew preferred to stay overnight in the Philippines rather than Saigon. Lieutenant France went into the city to meet with the staff at the headquarters of the U.S. Naval Forces, Vietnam—NAVFORV—to report in and to officially receive the platoon's in-country assignment. He took Rawls with him. McConnell joined Chief Johnson with the gear and digested his first impressions of Vietnam. It as only midmorning and already the sun was fierce. It smelled like a sewer and was far warmer and more humid than a summer scorcher back in Mattoon. Military transports and F-4 fighter-bombers jockeyed for position on the taxiways, while GIs dressed in various mutations of the standard fatigue issue darted about the apron in jeeps and weapons carriers. The Vietnamese soldiers he saw were dressed in tailored tiger-stripe camouflage uniforms, in sharp contrast to the sloppy Americans.

"Hey, Joe, me numbah one!" said one of the VNs as he walked past McConnell. "You got-a smoke?"

Bono gave him a cigarette and he ambled off, grinning and waving.

"Chief, these guys any good, the Vietnamese, I mean?"

"Well, sir, some are and some aren't. A lot of guys don't think so, but when they're led properly, they're not bad. The trouble is, their officers have to buy their rank, so its lucky to find one who knows what the hell is going on. Their Marines are probably the best of the lot. I can tell you one thing, the success of our tour can depend on our Kit Carson Scouts."

The Kit Carson Scout program was set up for VC guerrillas who came over to the government side. The good ones were assigned to special American units as scouts, and they had proved themselves loyal to the SEALs. This was due partially to the prestige of serving with the Navy SEALs, and in no small part to the platoon commander having authorization to pay them healthy cash bonuses for operational success.

"You really think they're going to help us?"

"Most of them were VC for years before they *chieu-hoied* under the government amnesty program. Some of them now fight for the money and some really hate what the communists are doing to their country. If we're lucky, we'll get a couple of them that fight for both reasons. You get Cribbs and a good Kit working point and you can almost forget about booby traps."

"Yeah, Chief, but can you trust them?"

"It's their ass too, sir, and I personally know most of them or can find out about them. They'll be part of the fire team and we'll be damn glad to have them."

"You remember it being this hot last trip, Chief?"

"Not to worry, sir, the mosquitoes and the flies will soon take your mind off the heat."

"Mosquitoes?"

"Big enough to screw a turkey flat-footed, sir."

For the next two and a half hours McConnell, Chief Johnson, and the rest of Foxtrot Platoon sweltered in the heat waiting for Lieutenant France and Rawls. The fact that the men were left to bake on the tarmac bothered both

McConnell and Johnson, but neither said anything. Shortly after midday, a jeep came bounding across the tarmac with France driving and Rawls in the back with two Vietnamese girls. The passenger seat next to the driver was stacked with several cases of beer, and both France and Rawls were half drunk.

"Hey, Jimmy!" announced France, skidding to a stop. "The admiral sends his personal regards and his permission to go straight to Firebase Delta and make 'em dance. Do not pass go, do not collect any VD in Saigon. A Navy CH-46 will be here within the hour to take us down to our new home."

One of the girls was wearing Rawls's hat and sat very close to him rubbing the inside of his thigh, while the other began passing out beer to the rest of the men. Both were slender, doe-eyed creatures and both wore long close-fitting *ao dais*, slit well up the sides. Neither looked older than fourteen.

"I tried to get the lieutenant to hold us over for a few days, guys," said Rawls, "but he's anxious to get on with the war. The *mama-san* at the U and I Club sent these samples over so you can see what you're missing."

The platoon drank beer and Rawls fondled the girls until the chopper came to collect them. The girls wandered back toward town leaving the jeep parked on the apron, awash in empty beer cans.

"Hey, Dave, who's going to return that jeep?" McConnell asked as they finished loading the 46 and climbed aboard.

"Probably the MPs. Rawls stole it while I was having tea with the admiral."

Firebase Delta was about an hour and a half southwest of Saigon. They flew at 6,000 feet to stay above the small-arms fire before the pilot spiraled down toward a cleared area clinging to the north bank of a large river. Firebase Delta was a study in brown. The defoliated area around the base was just a shade lighter than the creamy milk chocolate of the Bhi Hap River. Even the things that should not have been brown—the patrol boats at the pier, the corrugated roofs on the buildings, the tents and the metal matting of the landing pad—were given a dunglike cast from the dust and the rust. From higher up the base had looked orderly. A barbed-wire perimeter enclosed sand-bag bunkers, mortar pits, and evenly spaced tents and buildings. The base seemed to have been initially planned with some overall design. But as the chopper bled off altitude and they got closer, scattered equipment boxes, crates, trash, fifty-five-gallon drums, pallets, and drying laundry spoiled any perception of neatness. The helo set down on the landing pad just inside the main compound, and the Foxtrot SEALs stepped out into the muggy late afternoon, typical of the lower Mekong Delta.

The empty 46 lifted into a hover and literally sand-blasted everything in the vicinity of the pad. Then the big helo banked out over the river, running over the water to gather speed for a rapid climb. The SEALs packed their equipment off the helipad and surveyed their new home. The kerosene smell of the chopper gave way to a low tide, river-swamp smell that competed with the noxious blend of diesel fuel and human excrement from the burning privy cans. The inmates moved about the base dressed in jungle boots, shorts, and T-shirts, some with head bands and some with ball caps. No one paid the new arrivals much attention except a seedy-looking young man in a tattered flight suit who told them to get their crap out of the area since he was expecting *his* gunships back any moment. An Army buck sergeant appeared and conferred with Chief Johnson, who then proceeded to herd the men and equipment into a plywood hut not far from the helipad. A rising *fump-fump-fump* announced the incoming helicopter gunships. McConnell spotted them as they dropped over the treeline across the river to the south, and came fast and low across the water toward him. A hundred meters from the pad they rocked back forty-five degrees, surrendering speed and altitude. In turn, they set down on the pad beside each other and continued to turn on the metal deck while they were attacked by a motley crew of men dragging ammunition cans and carrying rockets. One man dragged a long hose from a reel near the pad and fueled both machines. The other men stuffed rockets in the pods on either side of each Huey gunship and traded the full ammo cans for empties. Each pilot gave a thumbs-up to the man in the ragged flight suit who held both arms straight over his head, waving them in small circles, index fingers pointing skyward. When the other men had cleared the pad, he turned ninety degrees and dropped his arms to a horizontal position. First one gunship, then the other lifted and hesitated, then nosed over, gathering speed to return out over the river in the direction from which they had come. The whole evolution had lasted less than five minutes.

"First time you seen a hot re-arm, sir?" said the young man who had just directed the evolution. There was a faded second class petty officer's insignia on the left arm of his flight suit. He was sunburned and badly in need of a haircut. He looked to be no more than twenty years old. McConnell smiled and nodded to him.

"Petty Officer Rollins, Delta Seawolf Detachment, sir. You guys must be the new SEAL platoon."

"Nice to meet you, Rollins. I'm Ensign McConnell, Foxtrot Platoon. You sure turned them around in a hurry."

"That was nothin'. If you guys are out there in the shit, we can do it in half the time."

"Well, that's a comforting thought, Rollins. That a special service to Navy SEALs, or standard for any unit in contact?"

"Hey, Mr. McConnell, the Seawolves an' the SEALs got an understanding. You get into trouble and we come hot! If one of our birds goes down, you jump in and get us. The SEALs over at Bac Lieu saved our CO's ass a few months back and he's still buyin' you guys beer. Anyway, I got to go get set up in case the birds want another hot spin. Welcome to shit city, sir."

McConnell followed the rest of the platoon and stepped up into their hut, or hootch as they called it. The structure was suspended on posts some three feet in the air so there was ventilation under the floor. It was thirty feet wide across the front and some fifty feet long. The sides were plywood on the lower half and screened the rest of the way up. Open two-by-four trusses supported a corrugated steel roof. There was no wind and the sun on the metal roof made the building an oven. The front part of the interior was littered with several card tables and metal folding chairs. One front corner had the makings of a kitchen with a counter, sink, and an old refrigerator. The cabinets were fashioned out of used mortar round boxes—some had doors, some didn't. A tall narrow shipping crate attended by three stools served as a bar and delineated kitchen area from dining or lounge area. An unpainted plywood partition separated this living area from the sleeping quarters located in the rear of the hootch. The doorway built into the partition was garnished by a beaded curtain.

In this dormitory area, the SEALs unpacked their gear and the platoon boxes. The prison-style, two-tier bunks along the walls, complete with soiled mattresses, were separated by rusted, standard-issue upright metal lockers. Some of the men rigged the bunks with gray-white sheets and mosquito netting. There was a room framed into the corner with half-inch plywood. Inside the cubicle were two single bunks and two lockers; officer's country at Firebase Delta. McConnell noticed someone had tossed his gear on one bunk. France's gear was on the other.

"Well, Ensign, what do you think of your new quarters?"

"To tell the truth, Rawls, it's a little grim."

"Hell, sir, a few nights sitting out on ambush with the leeches and the rats and you'll dream about this place."

McConnell's fire team was aligned along one side of the open bay with France's team on the other. Bono, Watson, and Tex Barnett followed the lead of the veterans by putting loaded magazines in their weapons before doing anything else. Each man's web gear, complete with ammunition and grenades, was prepared and laid out at the foot of the bunks. The loaded weapons were hung on the wall by the head of each man's bed. The platoon could be armed and ready in a matter of seconds.

"How's it going, guys?" inquired McConnell as he wandered down the bunk room.

"Jes like a pig in shit, sir," replied Barnett. "An' Ah thought our barn back home got hot in July."

"Hey, Boss, when we gonna operate?" asked Bono.

"Yeah, sir," added Watson half seriously, "we gonna do some shootin' tonight?"

"Well, I wouldn't waste any time getting your gear set up, but it'll probably be a few days before we do it for real. I think the plan is to take some time to study the territory a bit before we turn you war dogs loose."

Reed just smiled and shook his head. He was seated on a lower bunk and busy packing rounds into the magazine and flextray of his M60. Cribbs was over in the corner talking to a couple of the Kit Carson Scouts. Like the Kits, he squatted on the floor with his rump on his heels, arms folded and resting on top of his knees. He produced a pack of cigarettes, offering one to each scout before he took one. McConnell had yet to see a Vietnamese without a cigarette in his mouth or in the process of lighting up. McConnell wandered back to the cubicle where France handed him a cold beer, which he emptied without taking the can from his lips.

"Well, Jim, I think we ought to climb into a fresh set of greens and pay a call on the base commander. We don't want to rush right over, but it'll look a little tacky if we wait too long."

"Come in, boys, come in." A tall, thin, white-headed man in starched fatigues came around the desk and pumped both their hands. "Colonel Frank Beard here." The colonel was a career man who would soon retire with thirty years of service. His was a dying breed in the U.S. Army. He was on his third war and still on his first marriage—too politically naive to have become a general, but a solid professional nonetheless. Firebase Delta was the latest in a succession of difficult but non-career-enhancing commands. "Welcome to Firebase Delta. I think your arrival makes our little family complete."

"How's that, sir?" inquired France.

"Well, let's see. I have a headquarters company, a base security element, a squadron of Navy Swift boats, part of the Vietnamese junk force, a rural pacification team, a sensor implant team, a PSYOPS group, a VN Ranger company, an artillery battery, a Navy Seawolf detachment, associated cooks, bottle washers, and camp followers, and now a Navy SEAL platoon. Sometimes I'm not sure whether we're suppose to kill 'em, spy on 'em or pacify 'em.''

"If it's okay with you, sir, we'll just kill 'em," France stated casually. "What kind of bad-guy activity do you have around here?"

The colonel eyed France critically, then began to pace behind his desk. "I'm afraid we don't have a lot of hard intelligence about the enemy. There's quite a bit of small unit VC activity. The boats get a bit of sniping and an occasional B-40 rocket. We get mortared about once a week. Nothing serious but it keeps us from a good night's sleep. The real activity is in the Nam Can forest. It's crawling with VC and there's company-size and larger NVA units moving in and out. We put a battalion in there and can't find anything. We put a company in and like as not it gets chewed up. A lot of it is mangrove swamp and most of the solid ground is covered with triple canopy. There are a few open areas and small rice paddies, but mostly mangrove. You could hide a division in there."

"They ever try to come inside the wire, sir?"

"Not yet. I think they know we can call in more helos and fixed-wing air than they want to deal with. They just harass us."

"So why are we here?"

"Show the flag. Keep up the notion of a government presence. Keep control of the river and the canals, at least during the daytime. Kill as many of 'em as we can. That's what you said you're here to do, isn't it, Lieutenant?"

"Uh, yes, sir. I hear our boat-support unit got here a few days ago. Any other support we can count on?"

"There's the Seawolf Det, of course. Since there's a lot of you Navy boys here, I can usually beg a slick helicopter from the Navy base at Binh Thuy. The Swift boats are always ready to give you a ride or help out, but they really don't like to get into the smaller canals where they can't maneuver. The last bunch of SEALs we had here went most places by sampan."

"Anything else we should know about, Colonel?"

"That's about it, boys. I know you call your own plays, but you're to keep me informed on what you're doing.

That means I want a personal briefing before you go into
the field. I've got a small tactical operations center I keep
manned twenty-four hours a day to direct traffic and man
a communications watch. Clear your operations with them.
And don't pull any of your crazy SEAL shit. I have enough
to worry about without a bunch of hooligans on my base.''

"Hey, sir," replied France, arms outstretched in a show
of innocence. "We're just here to fight a war." They again
shook hands with the colonel and left.

"Well, what do you think about the colonel?" said
McConnell as he and France walked back to the hootch.
It was almost dark and the perimeter security elements
were starting to put out parachute flares.

"Seems harmless enough. But he must have pissed
somebody off to get shit-canned to this asshole corner of
the war."

"Might not hurt to treat him a little better. It's his base,
and ultimately he controls us and our support assets."

"That's right. It's his base, but the base is here to support combat operations. As a practical matter, he really
works for us. We're the guys that're going out for the body
count. And if he doesn't see it that way, screw him."

That night the platoon straggled back from the chow
hall and congregated in the front of the hootch. Most of
the men were in the SEAL noncombat uniform—UDT
swim trunks, green T-shirt, and shower shoes. It was as
if they had been there a few months instead of a few hours.
There was a card game under way and someone had ap-
propriated a dart board. McConnell got a beer from the
reefer and put a mark by his name on the typed platoon
roster taped to the door. Rawls had already organized the
beer mess. Then he joined the other new guys at one of
the tables.

"Hi, Boss, grab a seat," said Bono. "You and Mr.
France get the colonel all squared away?"

"Oh, I think so. You guys all settled in?"

"It sure ain't the del Coronado, but it'll do," said Barnett. "When d'yuh think we'll go out on patrol?"

"Not for a few days, anyway. Mr. France wants to get
around the base and talk to the other combat and support
elements. Maybe some additional training."

"Mr. McConnell," said Watson, "you nervous about going out for the first time, I mean on combat operations?"

McConnell hesitated a moment, wanting to be careful in his response. "Yeah, I suppose I am, but maybe anxious is a better way to put it. We've worked hard and I think we're ready. So does the Chief. This is what we've trained for, and now we're going to get to do it."

"Well, I don't know if *I'm* ready," said Bono, "but I'm sure as hell ready to stop thinking about it and just do it."

"Amen to that," added Barnett.

A cluster of five beers were ushered onto the table by a huge pair of hands. Reed grabbed a chair and eased his large frame down between McConnell and Watson.

"I don't want it said that I failed to buy a round for my teammates on their first day in Vietnam." He put a hand on McConnell's shoulder and toasted them all. "Here's to us and fuck Ho Chi Minh."

During the next few days the Foxtrot SEALs settled into their new quarters and routine. Chief Johnson attended to the housekeeping details—chow, shower facilities, ammunition issue, etc. Rawls found a source of hard liquor and set up a thriving bar trade in the hootch. France and McConnell began making calls on the other units stationed on the base. The first stop was the Seawolf Detachment whose hootch was adjacent to the helipad. The aviators lived in relative luxury in that their hootch was air-conditioned.

"Evening, gentlemen, request permission to come aboard," announced France as he entered. "The air-conditioning is nice but how cold is the beer?"

"Hey, Dave, how's it going?" said a large, solid-looking man coming to his feet to grab France's hand. He had a ruddy complexion, dark red curly hair and a handlebar mustache. Like the three other pilots in the room, he was dressed in a well-used brown flight suit. "I knew we were getting a SEAL platoon but I never thought it'd be you. Can't stay away, huh?"

"Aw, there's nothing to do in San Diego but drink and

screw. I just couldn't wait to get back. How about yourself, Carl? You should have rotated back by now.''

"I was back in the States for a while but I had the chance to come back and take the Det here. It's a minor command but it'll look good come promotion time.''

"Promotion, my ass. You just wanted to get back here so you could strafe innocent civilians. But I'm glad as hell you're here. Carl, this is Jim McConnell, my number two. Jim, Carl Belding. Carl and I did a little lootin' and shootin' together on my last trip. Made 'em dance, right, Carl?''

"Dave did the looting, I did the shooting. Glad to meet you, Jim.''

Belding introduced them to the other pilots and then led them to a table with three very cold beers.

"Carl, what kind of action you got going around here? The colonel says the Nam Can's crawling with bad guys.''

"The colonel's right. About every third time we fly over there under two thousand feet we get shot at. Lately we've taken some fifty-one caliber fire. And you know I fear fifty-one cal like fleet sailors fear rust.''

"How about targets?''

"Occasionally we catch a sampan in the open and we've bailed out the Swift boats a few times. Sometimes we fly support for the Army, but mostly we just respond to being shot at. Hell, there's camps, probably whole villages in there. We can't see half the canals from the air in that dense canopy. That's why we're glad you guys are here. Maybe you can find us something to shoot at. I know the Ponies would love it if you could find them some targets.''

Belding was referring to the Navy OV-10 Bronco squadron in Binh Thuy, nicknamed "the Black Ponies.'' France continued to probe Belding. McConnell was impressed with the precision and depth of his questions and how well he listened. He knew his platoon commander was eager to get the platoon into the field, yet he was being very methodical in preparing for combat operations. He was persistent and meticulous. By the time they left the Seawolf hootch they had a lot better idea about the opposition they could encounter and a general feel for the disposition of the enemy in their area of operation.

The next stop was the boat-support unit. The SEAL platoons in Vietnam were assigned an element of Boat Support Unit One and SEAL support craft, depending on the requirements of their area. They walked out onto the pier to where two low silhouetted dark green craft were nested together. They were Medium SEAL Support Craft. France asked for the boat officer and a sailor in greasy blue coveralls nodded toward the stern of the nearest MSSC. They climbed aboard the thirty-six-foot craft and walked aft.

"Lieutenant Smith?" France called to the lower half of another dirty pair of coveralls draped over one of two large V-8s in the engine compartment.

"Who the hell wants to know?"

"Dave France, Foxtrot Platoon. You trying to fix that engine or hump it back to life?"

A lanky form with straight dark hair and a broad easy smile appeared clutching a crescent wrench. The man's face was smudged with grease and his arms were covered with it. He stood erect in a casual sort of way, and the strong jaw and high forehead suggested he was a man of breeding.

"Well, I'll be go to hell, if it isn't God's gift to hookers."

"How you doing, Smitty?" said France. "No need to get cleaned up just for us."

"That'll be the day," he replied. His Southern accent had a crispness to it that hinted of an Ivy League education. "I heard it was either going to be you or Fred Wilson that'd be bringing a platoon here. Then I heard Fred got shot so I figured on you."

"Well, somebody's gotta look after you. These crates going to run or do we have to swim for it?"

"Aw, they're worn-out pieces of shit, but we'll have them up on step and hummin' in a few days. How soon y'all gonna be ready to operate?"

"Probably in about a week, maybe less. Oh, Smitty, this is Jim McConnell. Jim, Lieutenant Junior Grade Robert J. Smith, the pride of Atlanta."

"My pleasure," said Smitty, extending a dirty hand.

"Jim, you look like a pretty decent fellow. Why are you hanging around with this lowlife?"

"Glad to meet you, Smitty," said McConnell. "Dave kind of grows on you after a while."

"You been out on the water yet?" said France, getting right to business.

"Not really. We've run a couple of klicks each way on the river to test engines and I was up one of the canals to fire weapons. There's a lot of indians out there, Dave. I hope y'all aren't going to get my ass shot off this trip."

"C'mon, Smitty, you're just a bus driver. We're the working stiffs."

"Yeah, I know all about that 'we drive—y'all do the work' stuff. This is a bad area, Dave. Those guys shoot B-40s like kids back home throw rocks."

"So I've heard. We'll probably be doing a lot of our traveling by sampan. Most of the time we'll only need you to get us to the launch point and stand by for any contingencies."

"You mean come an' bail your ass out if y'all bite off more than you can chew."

"That too. Do me a favor, Smitty—get a map of the AO and plot all the known VC water ambush sites and dates for the last year or so. Maybe we can figure out a pattern to their activity. The Wolves have a plot they keep where they've taken fire. Put that on our chart, too. And don't let any of the local VNs see it—not even our Kits. I don't want any leaks."

Smitty sent one of his sailors for beer, and the three of them talked about operations and some boat training for the SEALs. Soon the conversation dissolved into stories about the last tour, the Army nurses at Binh Thuy and the whorehouses in Saigon. Smitty had been with France for part of Victor Platoon's tour. His apparent society background didn't stop him from taking part in the pleasures of the Orient. McConnell found himself liking the affable boat officer and developing a respect for his knowledge of small boat and SEAL operations.

"You know, Jim," said France as they walked back up the dock, "we're damn lucky to have experienced guys like Belding and Smith to support us. It could mean the difference when the shit gets thick. And my friend, the shit can get thick in the Nam Can.''

"How come those guys are back here for a second tour? I thought pilots and line officers like Smitty only had to do one shot in-country.''

"They're back here 'cause it's the only war we got,'' said France with a laugh. "Hell, Smitty could be cooling his corporate heels in the Georgia National Guard if he wanted—his old man owns half of Atlanta. They're here for the same reason we are—they love it!''

"Oh, is *that* why we're here? I've been wondering about that.'' Cribbs met them as they approached the hootch.

"Boss, you got a minute?'' France left them and went off to find the junk force adviser.

"Sure, Cribbs, what's up?''

"I need you to meet our two scouts. This is sort of a formal presentation, so you might want to play along. Why don't you go on back to your room, I'll round 'em up.'' McConnell was seated on his bunk when Cribbs returned with the two Vietnamese. All three stood at attention. Cribbs rapped on the side of the cubicle since there was no door.

"Sir, I'd like to present our two scouts.''

"Very well, Petty Officer Cribbs,'' said McConnell as he stepped to the middle of the door and came to attention.

"Sir, this is Corporal Huyhn Khac Ngoc and Private Tran Van Con, reporting for duty.''

"Chao ong. Ong manh Gioi, Thieu Uy," they said in unison. The two VNs saluted as did Cribbs who stood with them. This little ceremony could have seemed comical, but McConnell could see it was important to them. The corporal, the one the SEALs called Billy, was a short, bandy-legged man in his mid-twenties, but who looked forty. One of his eyes was milky and those few teeth he still had were yellow from tobacco. He wore a dirty white T-shirt and baggy shorts that revealed the sores and scars on his legs. He had a perpetual smile and the stoic acceptance of a man who had been at war on one side or the other for the past ten years. Con was taller and a quiet, reserved boy of seventeen. He was handsome to the point of being almost pretty. He was dressed in black trousers

and a faded aloha shirt, a gift from the last group of SEALs he had worked for. He had been a VC regular for about three years and had come over to the government side some eight months ago. Con had grown up in a nearby village and knew the area well. He was the only one of the scouts that Chief Johnson did not know from a previous tour. McConnell returned their salute.

"Petty Officer Cribbs, please tell them we are glad to have them on our team and that I am honored to serve with them." Cribbs began a dissertation in broken Vietnamese. McConnell caught an occasional American word like *numbah one* and *okay.* Then Con made a short, serious speech while Billy smiled.

"Con says that they like American SEALs," translated Cribbs, "and that together we will kill many Viet Cong." McConnell could think of nothing to add to that, so he formally shook hands and saluted them again.

"Thanks, Boss," said Cribbs with a wink as he ushered the two scouts back to the front of the hootch.

During the next several days, Foxtrot Platoon made final preparation for combat operations. The two squads formed into their fire teams and patrolled the relatively friendly area within a thousand meters of the base. They spent time on Smitty's boats and practiced with the mounted M60s and fifty-caliber machine guns as well as the stern-mounted 7.62 mini-gun. The boats had thirty-caliber armor that could stop most small-arms fire, and they were fast with a lot of offensive firepower. But they were gasoline-powered, and a B-40 rocket could turn one into a fireball. Most of the time was spent practicing in sampans. At first it was a comedy with the sampans tipping over as the big Americans were unable to control them. But once the SEALs got the hang of balancing them properly and the knack of handling the long slender paddles, they were almost as good as the VNs. Three or four men in a sampan could glide along in total silence and at night they were almost invisible on the water.

Their instructors in the sampans were the four Kit Carson Scouts assigned to the platoon. They helped the SEALs master the flat, shallow draft boats, and taught them how to hold a paddle braced against one shoulder so they could paddle with one hand and hold a weapon with the other. The scouts had by now been assimilated into the fire team. They bunked in the platoon hootch, ate and drank with the SEALs, and for all purposes were a part of the platoon. The only hint of trouble came when it became obvious that the Kits were better-than-average card players. The SEALs in McConnell's fire team were soon given to kidding Con, trying to elicit one of his shy smiles, while Billy became the squad clown. Con worked with Cribbs at point and Billy usually stayed close to Chief Johnson or Bono. McConnell noticed that Con and Cribbs were spending a lot of their free time together, and Bono and Billy were always sneaking around and playing tricks on each other. The Kits knew some English phrases and Chief Johnson and Cribbs knew some Vietnamese, so communication was difficult but not impossible.

During those final few days of preparation, McConnell noticed a subtle change come over the Foxtrot SEALs. They seemed to drink a little more in the evenings, but they were more subdued. France continued to press for information about the AO and the enemy, meeting each Swift boat or Seawolf that came back from a mission. He paced about the base like a caged tiger. He began to hover over both fire teams and double-check responsibilities assigned to the Chief. Johnson pacified him, although McConnell could tell it grated on the Chief. Even Rawls changed—he seemed to soften. He was patient and considerate when the new men asked him questions, and he began to address McConnell as "Mr. McConnell" rather than "Hey, Ensign." Only the Chief seemed to have held a steady course since they arrived at the firebase.

"Mr. McConnell, I think Lieutenant France is going to stand the platoon up tomorrow."

"You think we're ready, Chief?"

"Well, you'd always like to have more time, but I think we'll have to learn the rest on the job. Really, sir, I think the fire team is as ready as it's going to get for now. It's time we went out an' earned our pay."

"How about the scouts?"

"The Kits are all right. Billy's a little drifty, but he's

been around the block a few times. He'll be okay when we go to work. Con is more serious than your average VN, but Cribbs says he's real sharp and that's good enough for me. And, Mr. McConnell?''

"Yes, Chief?"

"You're ready too, sir. You're a good patrol leader and you're going to do just fine.''

Chapter Six

FIRST CONTACT

"ALL RIGHT GUYS, we're operational," Lieutenant France told the platoon on the day that marked their first full week at Firebase Delta. "I sent off our stand-up message this morning so we are officially in business. As we begin operations, we'll try to have only one fire team in the field on patrol each night. The team that's not in the field will be on call. Unless it's really important, only one squad will be out at a time. We'll be working around the edge of the Nam Can to begin with. Until we can develop some intelligence for specific targeting, we'll do some careful patrolling in the area and set some trail and canal ambushes. Now I know the Nam Can forest has a reputation for being exclusive VC real estate, but we're going to change that. We're better than they are, and Charlie's going to know that there's a SEAL platoon in the area. That's it for Mr. McConnell's squad—my guys stick around. We're going out tonight. Warning order goes down in five minutes."

McConnell stayed for France's warning order, a preoperational briefing where the patrol leader defines the type of mission, time frames, and any special equipment or weapons that the men should have ready. They were doing an insertion off the Bhi Hap River and a foot patrol. It was a reconnaissance patrol, hoping to learn more about enemy movements. Since they needed more intelligence about the area, a priority for both teams would be to capture VC alive. Late that afternoon, France had his full patrol briefing, which McConnell and Chief Johnson attended. It was expected that the standby fire team leader or his assistant attend the other squad's patrol brief to learn the details of their mission. Should the team in the field get into trouble, it was important for the backup fire team to know as much as possible. After the briefing, McConnell went for a walk around the base. A strange feeling settled over him. The preparation and training for SEAL operations was over. McConnell had known for some time that eventually they would be in the field for real, but it had been easy to lose himself in preparing the deployment and enjoying the good life in San Diego. Now he realized that "tomorrow" was just that—twenty-four hours away. He'd be risking his life and the lives of his men. He wandered down onto the dock where Smitty was preparing one of his boats for France's mission. McConnell noticed a different attitude and sense of purpose with Smitty's men as they made final checks on radios and guns.

"Jim, you going out tonight?"

"Tomorrow night, Smitty. You all ready to go?"

"Pretty much so. My port engine is running a little warm at idle, but it'll be okay. Y'all look a little out of sorts there, Jim. Pre-op jitters?"

"Yeah, I guess so. I kind of wish we didn't have to wait another day to get our feet wet."

"I know what you mean. The waiting can be worse than the actual event."

"You seen much action, Smitty?"

"We were at Binh Tre for three months this tour and it wasn't too bad on the boats. Last year I was with Victor Platoon, and it seemed like we got shot at every other time we went out. Y'know, it sounds all wrong, but it isn't the actual getting shot at that's so difficult—it's the anticipation. It's wonderin' just where they might be waiting for you. But y'all will do okay, Jim. You got a good fire team, and I can tell your guys have a lot of confidence in you."

"Thanks, I appreciate your saying so. Just the same, it'll be good to get one behind me. Tell me something,

Smitty, how come you're over here for a second tour? You really didn't have to come back—why did you?''

"Same as everyone else—the near sexual gratification of my latent aggressive nature.''

"Huh?''

"Jim, I'll probably have to work for my old man for the rest of my life when I get out. So while I'm in the Nav, I might as well be here where I can run my own show, even if it does get a little hairy. I didn't think I'd ever want to come back—not after the last trip. But sitting around at the boat unit in Coronado while your buddies are over here runnin' the rivers—well, it wasn't as easy as I thought it would be. Even for a good-lookin' dude like me.''

The voice of one of Smith's crewmen interrupted the momentary silence: "Hey, Mr. Smith, the power supply to the mini-gun is on the fritz again.''

"Aw shit. Excuse me, I gotta check this out.''

"Take care, Smitty, and have a good op.''

"You bet. See y'all tomorrow night.''

France and his men left with Smitty on the boat just after dark and returned just after first light—tired, wet, muddy, and having made no contact. McConnell watched them pull into the dock and then he began to plan for his operation that evening. Late that morning he gathered his fire team and gave them their warning order.

"We'll be doing a canal ambush from sampans,'' he began as he lifted the night cover of his wristwatch and glanced at the luminous dial. "The patrol brief will be at sixteen hundred, and we'll leave the pier at twenty-one hundred. Mr. Smith will have us to the embarkation point by twenty-one fifty. It should take us about forty-five minutes to get into the sampans and paddle to the ambush site. We'll use three boats. Con, Cribbs, and Barnett will sit one, two, and three in the first boat. Myself, Reed, and Watson will follow in the second. Billy, the Chief, and Bono will bring up the rear. Light ammo load and concussion grenades. Bono, you're the primary prisoner handler—Barnett, you have primary illumination with your 203 launcher—Chief, you back him up with pop-flares. I'll carry the radio as usual. Watson, you carry extra M60 ammo. Water only and life jackets. We should be back in time for breakfast—earlier, if we make contact. Any questions?" There were none but no one made a move to leave. "Chief, have three seaworthy sampans ready to go. You and I will brief the Kits at fifteen-thirty. Cribbs, you better sit in on that one, too. That's it, guys, see you at sixteen-hundred."

The men drifted off to prepare their equipment and weapons. At sixteen hundred the squad, together with France, Rawls, Smitty, and one of the Seawolf pilots, were again seated in the front of the platoon hootch.

"Again, we leave the dock twenty-one hundred," McConnell began. "Be on board the number-two boat no later than twenty-fifty. Reed, Barnett, and Watson will man the boat M60s and port fifty caliber. Cribbs, Billy, and Con will tend the sampans, one on either side and one towed astern. We'll do no more than six knots to the launch point. I'll load first, then Cribbs's boat, then the Chief. At my signal, Cribbs will lead off down the canal. We'll have a slight current helping us in and again bringing us home. There will be a sliver of a moon so let's keep about a ten-meter interval to maintain visual contact."

McConnell paused to tack a map of the AO to the sleeping area partition and grabbed a fly swatter for a pointer. Rawls used the break to step over to the reefer and get himself a beer. No one else moved.

"We'll go west on the Bhi Hap and then turn south down this canal. About one hundred meters inside the mouth of the canal, Mr. Smith will nose into the east bank and we'll get into the sampans. Then we'll continue down the canal and turn west at this dogleg here. Our primary ambush site will be the north side of the canal where our canal is joined by this smaller canal coming in from the south. We should have a good field of fire from this position on the top of the T formed by the two canals. Cribbs will be responsible for anything coming in from the west to our right and the Chief will look for traffic from the east to our left. Reed and I will concentrate on anything coming from the small canal in front of us to the south. The kill zone will be directly in front of Reed.

"Let's keep about five meters between sampans at the

ambush site. I'll set up first. Cribbs, you and the Chief pick up my signal line and take your position on the flanks. Initiation will be on my command or my first round. Barnett has illumination on contact and Watson has security responsibility to the rear. If the bad guys aren't out, we'll break ambush about zero four-thirty and head back to the boat. Cribbs will lead us out. Our primary frequency is 27.1 on the PRC 77; 36.1 is the secondary. Our call sign is 'Jakeleg 27' and the boat is 'Southern Belle.' Emergency visual is a red star cluster from a pencil flare. Coming home, visual authentication by flashing penlight is November-November answered by Alpha-Alpha. Cribbs, the Chief, and myself all have hooded strobes to spot for the Seawolves or the Ponies should we need them. Emergency rendezvous point will be the inside or northwest bank of the dogleg on the main canal.''

McConnell paused to look down his briefing notes to see if he had omitted anything, then glanced around at the small group. ''Remember our standard procedures, and think about what you'll do if we get hit. If we're ambushed, and you're in the tracers or you get straight-on muzzle flashes, get into the water. If you're away from the point of fire, start getting some rounds out. Let's think about what we're doing out there, guys.'' McConnell paused to make brief eye contact with each man. ''Chief?''

''Sir, I think you've covered it,'' said Johnson, rising to his feet. ''This is a good fire team. I'm real happy with where we are, but like Mr. McConnell said, we're playing for keeps. Concentrate on the small things. Be smooth and deliberate in the sampans. Use your night-vision techniques. We're a lot better than they are if we pay attention and work together. And I'll have anybody's ass who falls asleep on ambush.''

''That's it, men. Be ready to go and be on time.'' McConnell rolled up his map and was just leaving to brief Colonel Beard when Rawls came up to him and held out his hand. ''Good luck to you, sir. You guys are gonna do just fine.'

McConnell shook his hand and eyed him closely, looking for some trace of sarcasm. The smile was there, but he could detect nothing but sincerity in Rawls's face.

"Thanks, Rawls, I appreciate that." McConnell stepped past him and left the hootch in search of the colonel.

After the evening meal, McConnell made a final check of his gear and began to dress for the operation, knowing that this time the ritual of gearing up was for real. He changed into blue jeans and jungle boots, and shivered at the touch of the cool rubber bladder of the life vest on his chest and back. The vest, which resembled one from a three-piece suit, made him look like a gang member in *West Side Story.* The long-sleeved camouflage jungle shirt changed that. He tucked in the shirt and banded the smoke and concussion grenades to the thick leather belt supporting his jeans. Next came the mesh multipocketed vest that would hold the balance of his operational gear. Most conspicuous were the four long pockets on his chest that held his spare Stoner ammunition. Each pocket held fifty rounds of linked ammo. He carried a loaded drum of one hundred fifty rounds on the weapon and would reload by feeding each of the fifty-round bandoleers directly into the breach of the weapon.

The balance of the load—medical kit, pop-flares, knife, strobe light, penlight, and canteen—were secured to the front or sides of the vest. He made a final check of the radio and adjusted the straps so it rode squarely in the middle of his back. He then covered his face, hands, and neck with dark green and loam camouflage paint. Instead of a hat, McConnell wore a headband he had made from a section of an olive-drab towel. He had soaked the material with insect repellent and it did a reasonably good job of keeping the mosquitoes away from his face. After a final check and inventory of his equipment, McConnell took his Stoner rifle from the pegs by his bunk. He adjusted the strap so the weapon hung just above his waist, yet would easily swing up to firing position. He checked to verify that the bolt was forward on an empty chamber. The Stoner fired with the bolt in the rear or cocked position. He would not jack the bolt back until he was in the sampan.

"Oh, Lordy," he said aloud as he turned to leave for the boat, "here she goes."

* * *

There was just enough light from the moon to distinguish the tree line from the sky, but not enough to pick up the shoreline. The trip down the river was like walking down a long dark hallway. He could sense that there were walls but he could not touch them. The muffled burble of the engines sounded to him like a roar and he was sure it could be heard for miles. McConnell stood with Smitty, forward and just behind the coxswain. Occasionally Smitty would put his face to the radar scope hood and then study his compactly folded map with his red penlight.

"We're on course and dead on schedule," he announced in a low voice. "We should pick up the mouth of the canal in about fifteen minutes. When y'all are in position, give me a radio check on the hour. I like to know you haven't fallen asleep and it gives us on the boat something to look forward to."

"Will do," McConnell replied. "If I don't want to talk I'll break squelch three times and you answer the same." He liked Smitty. The man had a quiet, unassuming competence that was very reassuring. A good boat support officer, McConnell concluded, was like a good waiter. He has to think ahead and anticipate the next move. He has to be patient, adaptable, and responsive. He very seldom gets credit when things go well but inattention to his duty can spoil everything. In SEAL operations, a bad call by a boat officer could mean disaster, and the SEAL operators would hold him fully responsible. Smitty picked up the handset of the boat radio.

"Home Plate, this is Southern Belle, we are at Point Alpha, over."

"Roger, Southern Belle, Point Alpha, out."

The tall boat officer then looked around and addressed the men in a low conversational voice. "Look sharp now, we'll be leaving the river soon. About ten minutes to sampan launch. Everyone stay put until I find a good spot on the bank."

The coxswain throttled back to a slow idle and turned left down the canal. Five minutes later Smitty nosed the craft into the left side of the canal. The boat slid onto the mud bank and cut its engines. They sat there in deafening silence for another five minutes, everyone alert for any sign of enemy activity.

"Ready, Chief?" McConnell whispered.

"Aye, sir."

"Cribbs, let's do it."

Getting nine heavily armed men over the side of a boat with twenty-four inches of freeboard into sampans with four inches of freeboard in near total darkness is a feat. The well-practiced evolution was relatively quiet, but McConnell flinched at every sound. He was quite relieved when the little flotilla left the parent craft and filed down the canal. There was a muffled volley of metallic clattering as the SEALs chambered rounds and armed their weapons.

"Jakeleg 27, this is Southern Belle, radio check, over."

"Southern Belle—27, roger, over."

"Roger, 27, good hunting—break—Home Plate, Home Plate, this is Southern Belle, my ducklings are away, over."

"We copy, Southern Belle, your ducklings away, out."

Pushed by a half-knot current, the fire team in the three sampans slipped deeper into the Nam Can like shadows passing across the moon. Except for the soft lapping of the paddles, McConnell and his team moved in total silence. The boats to his front and rear were scarcely definable dark lumps on the water. For the first time McConnell experienced the eerie feeling of moving undetected through enemy territory. It was much like a teenager coming home late and trying to sneak up to his room without waking his parents. He was finally "in the field" and it was tense and exciting business. They made the dogleg to the right and passed close to the inside bank, Cribbs knowing that a potential ambush probably would come from the outside of the bend where the attackers would have an unobstructed view in both directions on the canal.

McConnell sensed they were approaching their ambush site as he noticed the lead sampan moving slower. The adjoining canal that marked their ambush site was almost abeam to the left before McConnell picked it up. The lead boat held water midcanal while McConnell guided his craft to the right bank, in among the low brush. The other two sampans came alongside, each taking an end of the signal line, and moved out bow and stern from McConnell's boat to take their positions. McConnell felt the weight in his boat shift as Reed and Watson settled into a comfortable position—comfortable as you could get sitting cross-legged on a cold wet board. There were some faint metal-on-metal sounds as Reed positioned his M60 and ammunition feed tray.

"Southern Belle—27, in position, over."

"Roger, 27, out."

Waiting patiently for something to come along to shoot at wasn't entirely new to McConnell. At first, he was startled by each new ripple in the water to his front or rustle in the foliage behind him. Gradually, he cataloged the night jungle and river sounds, and his subconscious began to filter them out. This was not unlike sitting in a lakeside duck blind back in Illinois. It was warmer and a little less comfortable but much the same. Only this time, the game he hunted were other men, and that made it an entirely new experience. The night wore on and the canal in front of them remained empty. Occasionally McConnell could hear the faint, muffled scraping as one of the other boats bailed water. He periodically traded "You okay?—I'm okay" messages on the signal line, and he checked in with Smitty hourly. Finally the luminous dial of his watch showed it to be half past four. McConnell signaled the others to prepare to leave. He heard movement from the other two boats and he felt Reed and Watson shifting in his own craft. One of them stifled a yawn and somebody farted.

"Southern Belle—27, leaving position, over."

"Roger, 27, leaving position, out."

Cribbs's sampan left the bank first, wheeling around and leading the little group back out the way they had come. McConnell was no less alert on the way out. If a canal sentry had seen them go in, they were sure to get hit on the way out. But the paddle back was as uneventful as the trip in. As they approached the section of the canal where they had taken to the sampans, McConnell called Smitty and requested a visual signal. He saw the faint red dot, just ahead and to the right—*dah-dit, dah-dit*. He responded—

dit-dah, *dit-dah*—with his own penlight, and Cribbs led them toward Smitty's signal. McConnell almost bumped into the boat before he saw it. This again made him aware of just how hard it is to see on the water at night, and just how invisible they really were in the sampans.

Disembarkation from the sampans was only just slightly more clamorous than the loading. They were on the river moving easterly back toward the firebase as the sun came up. Smitty had several thermoses of hot coffee for the trip home, which were most welcome. The inactivity and the dampness had chilled them to the bone. When they reached the base, they left the Kits to tend the sampans and filed into the front of the hootch for a debrief. McConnell went quickly through his post-operation checklist. Most of the items were not applicable, as they had made no contact.

"I think we did a good job out there tonight. There just weren't any indians on our canal, or at least none that we saw. On the negative side we were a lot quieter at the beginning of the operation than at the end. We've got to play the game all the way and not let up at the end. Keep that in mind on the next one. Any questions?"

"Just a comment, sir," said Chief Johnson, rising to his feet. "Mr. McConnell's dead right, men. We've got to concentrate and work at it all the way. We're never more at risk than when we're coming back the same way we went in, or when we're getting in and out of the sampans. Now this may not mean much, but this was a damn good patrol. Yeah, I know we went huntin', and we didn't get anything. But our discipline was good and we hit our checkpoints on time. We operated according to the plan. I've been with fire teams that couldn't do as well halfway through the tour. If Charlie had come down that canal we'd have drug his dick in the dirt. Keep concentrating on the small things and stay alert. We'll get our share of kills and live to brag about it." The Chief glanced at his watch. "Chow goes down in fifteen minutes. Nobody eats or sleeps until his weapon is cleaned and his gear is set up. When's our next warning order, sir?"

"The other squad's going out tonight so we'll be on standby at nineteen hundred. Next warning order is at

fourteen hundred tomorrow afternoon for tomorrow night's
Op.''

"Then unless Mr. McConnell has anything else, you're
on your own time."

McConnell pulled the Chief aside after the men had left.
"Chief, you really think we did that well out there?"

Johnson seemed offended at first but then smiled. "Mr.
McConnell, they really aren't doing too bad. You led well
and they followed well. Don't you think I'd say so if I
thought differently?"

The dark face paint accented the lines across his forehead. "Sorry, Chief. I just want to make sure we do it
right. I don't want to make any mistakes out there."

"If I think something is wrong with the fire team," said
Johnson as he put his hand on McConnell's shoulder, "including you, sir, you'll be the first to know." His smile
was a broad grin, causing McConnell to squirm self-
consciously."Let's shower and get some chow. Then you
better get some sleep, sir. You look like hell."

McConnell headed for his room and for the first time,
he was aware of how tired he was. He had been up about
twenty-four hours, and the tension and fatigue were beginning to take their toll. He hadn't realized how much
the responsibility of a patrol and the constant anticipation
of "what if" could translate into physical exhaustion. He
cleaned up his gear and grabbed a quick shower. He sat
down on his bunk to put on his boots, which was the last
thing he remembered until Lieutenant France woke him
up early that afternoon.

The fire teams fell into alternating nights in the field,
sometimes in sampans, sometimes on foot patrols. Several
mornings later, France's team came into the hootch yelling, pounding tables, and opening beer. They had been
on a sampan patrol and managed a dawn ambush of four
VC on the water.

"Jesus, those bastards never knew what hit 'em!"

"That one dude musta had fifteen holes in him!"

"An' the dumb-shit in the bow of their boat was tryin'
to stop the bullets with his hands. *Troi oi! Troi oi!*"

France settled them down and hurried through his debrief. "Okay then, that's two KIAs and two probables."

"No way, sir! Those other two had to be blown away. They just sunk, that's all."

"Maybe," said France, "but we're doing it like the Marines. It has to be F-O-H."

"FOH?" whispered McConnell to Chief Johnson.

"Foot on head, sir. You have to make sure their heart stops."

"Now, I don't want to be too critical," continued France, "but we sent close to two hundred and fifty rounds after those four guys and we probably got hits with less than ten percent. We have to improve that. I know those two probables are feeding the crabs now, but they don't count unless they're confirmed. Otherwise, good job, guys. The first one's always the hardest."

McConnell questioned France and Rawls about the details of the operation. There was a lot of animated talk and laughing as McConnell's fire team provided an audience for the victors. McConnell finally broke away and headed for the chow hall, thinking about his team's patrol that evening.

Now that France's fire team had made contact, when will we see action? And how will I measure up? I can't let the pressure get to me. I've got to be patient and do my job—concentrate on the small things, like the Chief says, and everything else will take care of itself.

"Listen up, guys," began McConnell, pointing to the map. "We're walking tonight. The boat will insert us here on this canal. Then we'll patrol across this piece of ground looking for a major trail and a good ambush site. After the hit or zero four hundred, whichever comes first, we'll come back to the canal and meet the boat here, about three hundred meters east of the insertion point." Details of the mission, patrol assignments, communications plan, and special procedures filled out the patrol briefing, and the fire team split up to make their final equipment checks. The missions were not to the point of normal routine, but doing things for the third and fourth time made them a lot smoother in the preparation as well as the execution in the field.

"Good luck, Jim," France called as he was heading for the boat. "Make 'em dance."

The SEAL support craft nosed into the bank and grounded itself. Smitty shut down the engines and they sat in silence, listening for something that was not a jungle or river sound. First Con and Cribbs, then the rest of the fire team in turn slid over the bow and into the bush. They set up a semicircle perimeter in front of the boat and again waited and listened.

"Sweetheart, this is Altar Boy, we are moving, over."

"Roger, Altar Boy, good hunting, out."

They moved cautiously across the scrub brush and into the denser foliage. The fire team pushed through mangrove trees and nipa palm until Con picked up a lightly traveled trail heading in the direction of their travel. McConnell allowed Cribbs, based on Con and Billy's advice, to take the team down a trail while on patrol. The ability to move quietly and quickly sometimes offset the safer but noisier crashing through unbroken trail. Forty-five minutes of walking brought them to the major trail they were looking for. After a short conference with Con and Cribbs, McConnell elected to turn left along the new route to look for an ambush site. The new path was worn and obviously well traveled. It wound along a large irrigation ditch through thigh-level elephant grass and an occasional clump of bamboo. It was relatively open country for the Nam Can. There was good visibility except where the overhang from a periodic palm tree hid sections of the trail from the half moon. They moved very cautiously, pausing to listen every thirty to forty yards. On one such stop, McConnell was startled as Cribbs wheeled to a crouch and took three quick steps back in his direction.

"Patrol—four, maybe more!" he whispered, then melted into the grass on the left side of the trail. McConnell paused for a second, then signaled to Watson, who was five meters behind him: "*Hasty ambush! Left side!*"

Just like they had done it in practice so many times

before, the message rippled down the column, and the SEALs moved five to seven meters off the trail and took up positions. McConnell's heart raced as he took his Stoner off safe and strained to see up the trail from his concealed position. He heard them before he saw them. There was the singsong staccato of Vietnamese and the clatter of loosely slung equipment. The trail in front of McConnell was softly washed by the moon, and the open area created by the irrigation ditch made a perfect backdrop. The first man was carrying his rifle with both hands at waist level, while the second had his weapon across his shoulder, holding the end of the barrel in one hand with the stock draped behind the back of his neck. He caught a glimpse of the sweeping curve of the banana clip in the AK-47. The Stoner slowly came up to his shoulder in firing position as he looked to his left up the trail for more VC. These first two belonged to Chief Johnson at the rear of the fire team. The third man passed, also armed, but there was something different about four and five. Recognition flashed and McConnell knew the first one was a prisoner, walking with his head down and his arms close to his sides. Number five had a rifle carried on his hip, pointing down and toward the man to his front. Number six, also carrying a rifle, seemed to be the last one. This was all too easy, thought McConnell, like some orchestrated training exercise. Nonetheless, his first tracer took the man behind the prisoner with a quartering shot in the small of his back and spun him to his right so he was facing his attackers. The second tracer caught him on the left shoulder spinning him back. Four quick rounds between the tracers walked across his rib cage, causing him to vibrate as the rounds slammed into him. McConnell knew he was dead or dying as he swung the Stoner to the last man and squeezed. Number six was already jerking from the impact of rounds from Cribbs's AK-47 and their combined fire made him twitch like a disco dancer under a strobe light. McConnell was aware of the automatic weapons and tracers to his right as he forced himself to look up the trail for more VC.

Whoosh—pop! A parachute flare appeared over the irrigation ditch behind the trail. McConnell whistled twice signaling the fire team to advance on a skirmish line. The SEALs approached the trail cautiously. There was a burst of fire to McConnell's right, and the SEALs froze in anticipation until Chief Johnson called, "Clear on this end, sir!"

"Perimeter security! Chief, take Cribbs and the Kits and check them out. I want to be out of here real quick." McConnell wandered down the line to look at the damage. The VC were pretty well torn up, although two were still alive. One was moaning softly. The other clawed the ground and gurgled as he tried to breathe while his lungs filled up with blood. McConnell instantly knew the sound. He had lung-shot a deer once and it made exactly the same sound. Only he had quickly killed the fallen deer to end its suffering. The pop-flare went out as the four perimeter SEALs took up security positions around the VC-littered section of trail. The prisoner was surprisingly unhurt. Watson and Reed, immediately to McConnell's right on the firing line, had recognized him as a POW and had concentrated their fire on the VC walking in front of the prisoner. Reed's M60 had taken the top and side of the enemy's head off. The prisoner had no idea what was happening. At first McConnell thought he was hit but he was just too terrified to stand up. He just lay in the middle of the trail in a fetal position and cried.

"He'll be okay, sir," said the Chief. "I'll have Billy walk with him on the way out." McConnell dropped to one knee and unslung the radio to extend the whip antenna while Cribbs and the Kits searched the bodies and collected their weapons.

"Sweetheart, Sweetheart, this is Altar Boy, over."

"Roger, Altar Boy, you are weak but readable, over."

"Sweetheart, we are hot—repeat, we are hot. Leaving position and heading for home, how copy, over."

"Roger, you are hot. Do you require assistance, over?"

"Negative at this time. ETA your posit forty minutes, over."

"Roger, ETA forty minutes, out."

The Chief came up and squatted beside McConnell. "We're all finished here, sir. One of them's still breathing but he's had it."

"Right, Chief," said McConnell, slinging the radio on his back. "Send the point guys up here and call in the security." At Johnson's signal they formed up and McConnell sent Cribbs back up the trail leading the fire team out. They soon picked up a path heading in the direction of their pickup point. The team cleared the area at a good clip, but then settled into their normal, more cautious patrol pace. It was not until they were well into the return trek that McConnell mentally began to review the details of their first combat action. No more than five minutes had elapsed from the time they first saw the VC until they cleared the area, but it seemed much longer. He still couldn't believe the VC patrol had been such easy prey. Several competing emotions buffeted McConnell as he tried to focus his attention on the return to the boat. He was elated that they had successfully come through their first combat action. It was a textbook ambush, made sweeter in that it had been a hasty, trailside set up. They had taken a captive of the VC who might provide some useful intelligence. But in reality, McConnell knew that the VC had never had a chance. Basically we just murdered five men who never knew what hit them. As France would put it, we "made 'em dance." Now he understood why the instructors at San Clemente had referred to ambush training as "practice premeditated murder." I should feel something, McConnell told himself. I just killed a man, maybe two, and I'm responsible for the execution of them all. Execution—was that what it was? Somehow, even this perception, however convoluted, did not seem to bother him, nor did it appreciably reduce his sense of accomplishment. In many ways, it was another successful hunt. If he was troubled at all, it was by that very lack of feeling at having just killed five men. Preoccupied with these thoughts, he nearly bumped into Cribbs, who had paused on the trail in front of him.

"The canal is just up ahead, Boss, and Con thinks we're close to the pickup point."

McConnell called the boat and began the extraction procedure. It was still dark when they pulled up to the dock. France, who had been monitoring the radio traffic, was waiting for them.

"Understand you did some damage out there, Ensign," he said, shaking McConnell's hand. "Finally got that Stoner broken in right."

"Cribbs saw them well ahead of us and made the right call. The fire team did a super job. We just blew them away!" He was still excited and realized he was talking faster than normal.

"I see you snatched one of them. I'll get Rawls to have a little chat with him and see if he can be encouraged to be cooperative."

"I don't think he's a VC, Dave. He was their prisoner before he was ours."

"All the better. It shouldn't take much to get him to roll over on those bastards. Nice work, Jim."

Most of the base was still asleep except for the night security force and the watch. It was a boisterous group that made its way up from the boat toward the hootch. McConnell found Cribbs walking with Con and parted them, placing a hand on the shoulder of each man.

"Harold, thanks for what you did back there. I was hoping the first one would go well, and you made it easy for me. It was a perfect call. And thank you, Con—*Cam on ong*. You and Billy numbah one."

"You bary welcome, *Thieu Uy.*" The young man beamed.

"Glad we could do it for you, Boss. Helpin' a new platoon officer break his cherry is almost as good as helpin' a young broad break hers." McConnell guessed that the rough-hewn Cribbs was probably more successful breaking in platoon officers than converting virgins, but he said nothing. For his part, Cribbs was glad that McConnell had taken the time to thank Con. Some platoon officers took the scouts for granted.

The fire team trooped into the hootch and began passing out beer, shaking them and spraying each other with foam as they opened the cans. McConnell was surprised when Colonel Beard stepped into the hootch and asked to sit in on his post-op debriefing.

"Happy to have you, sir. Can I get you a beer?"

"You're not going to squirt me with it, are you, mister?"

"Oh, no, sir, we don't do that to colonels."

McConnell accepted the colonel's congratulations and Beard accepted a beer, taking a seat along the wall of the hootch. McConnell settled his men down and methodically went through his post-op debriefing checklist. When he was finished, he paused to look around at the dirty clothes and smiling, sweat-stained blackened faces. They looked like the cast in an Al Jolson musical. The tension release, blended with a high from the successful operation, made McConnell feel euphoric but strange.

"We did a good job out there tonight. I'm very proud of all of you. It was the point guys that set us up so well, so the credit goes to Con and Cribbs for this one. Let's hope they're all this easy and this one-sided. That's it, men—you got the rest of the night off."

The fire team milled around drinking beer and retelling accounts of the action. It was a scene from the winner's locker room. France played the proud older brother, and Colonel Beard gave him a fatherly grip on the shoulder as he departed. Chief Johnson came up to him and formally shook his hand.

"They could have made a training film out of that one, sir. You did a nice job."

"Thanks, Chief. Knowing you were right there was a big help. I still can't believe how sloppy those guys were."

"Well, I'm afraid they won't all be like that, but we can sure enjoy it when they are. I told you we're better than they are. Say, you all right, sir?"

"I couldn't be better. I'm just so glad to have this behind us, the first one and all. I guess I'm just a little wound up. I think I'll take a shower and try to get out my after-action report before breakfast."

McConnell came down the steps of the hootch wrapped in a towel and carrying a beer. His camouflage-blacked face and hands were in sharp contrast to his white torso, like a nude coal miner after a day underground. He was headed for the shower when he noticed Watson sitting by the hootch on a pile of sandbags.

"Watson, what are you doing out here?" McConnell walked over and sat down beside him.

"Oh, just trying to settle down a little. That was some patrol, huh, Boss?"

"Sure was. I hope every time we make contact it goes like that." After a moment he added, "I appreciate your contribution to the fire team and supporting Reed with the M60. I know he likes working with you."

"Thanks, sir."

"Watson, you okay?"

"I'm fine. I was just thinking about our hit tonight—kind of playing it back in my mind. Y'know those guys we dusted were most of them younger than me and I'm the youngest guy in the platoon. They must really believe in what they're doin' to be out there at night with guys like us sneakin' around. Christ, we really shredded 'em. I was makin' hits on that one guy, and then Reed hosed him with the '60. His head exploded like a fuckin' melon. I went to check him out and he had brains all over his shirt, like someone had spilled cream of mushroom soup on him." He laughed self-consciously. "I guess that's called blowing their brains out."

McConnell thought about this. He had never before considered how dangerous it was to be a Viet Cong. "Better him than us," McConnell offered. "I think maybe I know how you feel. Killing five guys sure is different than shooting silhouette targets out in the desert, isn't it?"

"You got that right, Boss."

"I guess when you scrape all the bullshit away, this is what being a SEAL is all about. It's killing people, and it's our team against theirs. I can't say that it's going to get any easier out there. I'm just lucky to have guys like you and Reed and the Chief on my team." They sat for a few moments in silence. "Hell, Watson, maybe guys like you and me should have been pilots or gone into the artillery. Then we could drop bombs or lob shells and never have to see what happens on the other end."

"We'll do that next tour, Boss."

"Next tour for sure. Well, I better get into the shower. You ought to give it some consideration, too—the shower, I mean. You're getting a little gamey." McConnell got to his feet. "You all right there, teammate?"

"Hey, Boss, the only easy day was yesterday." And as McConnell headed off, "Thanks for the chat, sir."

"You bet, Watson, see you at breakfast."

McConnell stood under the shower for fifteen minutes and allowed the hot water to leech some of the tension out of him. He thought about the operation, about Watson and about the men they had slain. He wasn't so sure that they had escaped their first combat action without casualties after all.

Chapter Seven

PARAKEET OPERATIONS

THE FLUSH OF McConnell's first operational success faded into the demands of planning future operations. Once back into the field, the cold reality of "what if" quickly gave some perspective to their victory. This was not a business that allowed you to rest on your laurels.

The prisoner they had rescued from the VC did not prove to be the willing and cooperative informant they'd hoped for. In fact, he gave the impression that he would rather have been a prisoner of the VC than a guest of the Americans. Chief Johnson questioned him, the Kits tried to befriend him, Rawls threatened him, and France tried to bribe him. Foxtrot Platoon may have freed his body, but the VC still held his soul. It seems he was a prominent man in his village, and the VC had taken him prisoner as punishment for some minor offense. If they were going to kill him, they would have done so in the village as an example to others. When he was taken prisoner, he knew he was probably not going to be killed. Now when he returned to his village, he felt the VC would most surely come to take revenge, and probably his life, for the work McConnell and his fire team had done on the squad that had originally captured him. A few days later, Rawls sought out the two platoon officers in the mess hall.

"Morning, sir—morning, Mr. McConnell. Mind if I join you?"

"Morning, Rawls," said France as his leading petty officer sat down next to him. McConnell, sitting across from both, nodded. Rawls never seemed to eat, but frequently stopped by the chow hall for a cup of coffee.

"Sir, I been thinking. Why don't we turn loose of that dude Mr. McConnell brought in a few days ago?"

"Let him go?" replied McConnell.

"Why do that?" said France. "He's scared shitless that the VC will come back and kill him."

"Yeah, I know," leered Rawls, "and to make sure, let's take him home in one of our boats. Let the villagers see him with us. We could even drop off a couple bags of rice and some medical supplies. The Rural Pacification Team pricks are always hot for that shit."

"But you're making sure they're going to come for him," said McConnell.

"Like flies to the garbage, sir. There's only one way to that village from the Nam Can—the Binh Loc Canal. We set up on that canal and we can probably make some money."

"Rawls, you should have been a gangster," said France with a big smile.

"But they're still going to get him," persisted McConnell. "We're not going to be on that canal forever."

"Who gives a shit, sir?" replied Rawls without rancor. "The guy's history anyway."

Four nights later by the luck of the alternate draw, France's fire team took out the probable VC assassination squad scoring four kills, two probables, and capturing one. It was some two weeks after that when a passing fisherman reported that the VC finally had come to the village and killed their reluctant former captive—along with his wife and three children. McConnell was horrified when he heard this.

"Dave, we as good as killed that poor bastard!"

"Wrong, Jim. He was dead when you pulled him alive from the VC squad you cut down. We just made the VC pay a little higher price for his life."

"But what about his wife and kids!"

"What about them? You think we should back off because Charlie kills women and children like the San Diego cops give out speeding tickets? Look, Jim, we're here to kill VC—that's our job—we're in the depopulation business. We get paid for it. Happiness is a hot machine-gun barrel, and all that shit. When possible, we want to do that job and not get our asses shot off. That dude you brought in gave us a chance to improve our odds, and we had to take it. I'm sorry about his family, but life's cheap in this country.''

McConnell didn't like this, but he had to accept it. Six months earlier this kind of reasoning would have been unthinkable to him. But despite serious reservations about the morality of their tactics, he was beginning to nurture a smoldering dislike for the VC. And he was forced to admit to himself that it was getting easier for him to go out and hunt them. It was coming to that—he was hunting again.

After the hit near the village on the Binh Loc Canal, they went back to sampan ambushes and foot patrols in and around the Nam Can forest. This was becoming increasingly dangerous as the VC now knew they were in the area. The Kits were especially nervous about going back night after night. Nonetheless both fire teams conducted successful ambushes and Foxtrot Platoon continued to roll. And with operational success and confidence, they ventured deeper into the Nam Can forest.

The following week, McConnell was leading his team on a foot patrol not far from where they had made their first contact. The squad was in their normal patrol order and working their way down a main trail looking for an ambush site. McConnell was about to turn the patrol around. They were getting quite deep into enemy territory and at the limits of effective communication with the boat. Then he heard a hollow metallic click to his left. It took but a fraction of a second to mentally question:

Now, that's a familiar sound, what is it? and to answer himself with a cold stab of terror: *That's the safety catch of an AK-47!*

McConnell was left-handed so the barrel of his Stoner was trained to the right side of the trail. In mortal fear, he spun to his left and dropped to one knee coming to a firing position. Midway through his pirouette, Cribbs opened up on full automatic fire. Outgoing red tracers were soon being crossed with incoming green ones. Bullets ripped past McConnell to his right and over his head as the Stoner answered in eight- to ten-round bursts with very little interval. Cribbs and Con to his front had gone silent, but Watson, who was directly behind him, had begun to fire. McConnell worked the enemy ambush site right to left and back again. A muzzle flash winked at him and he bracketed it with tracers.

He felt the bolt of his weapon fall home on an empty chamber and he dropped to the ground on his side, fumbling for a bandoleer of ammunition. He heard the *pop-pop-pop* of an AK-47 on rapid single-fire as Cribbs came back on line with a fresh magazine. He had his reload in place and was ready to shoot, when he became aware that the volume of fire to his left was becoming louder. Peeking over the grass along the edge of the trail, he saw red tracers in front of him were moving left to right and there was no mistaking the sound of Reed's M60 as the biggest dog in this fight. He, along with the trailing members of the fire team, had flanked the enemy position, bending the squad file into an L shape. Four of them, led by Reed, were assaulting their would-be ambushers from the left flank.

McConnell resumed firing in three- to five-round bursts, directing his fire ahead of the advancing line of his teammates. There had been no return fire since the SEALs had flanked the enemy position. Their fire became more disciplined as McConnell and the others from the front of the file joined the flankers and moved through the VC ambush site. Moonlight glanced off a moving shadow fleeing up the trail. McConnell snapped off a five-round burst with a single tracer burying itself into the man's back as he went down. McConnell called for a defensive perimeter.

"Gimme a count!"

"Cribbs and Con here."

"Watson, okay!"

"Yo, Reed."

"Tex here!"

"Johnson."

"Bono and Billy okay!"

McConnell could hardly believe that nobody was down. God, that was close! Another few steps and the whole fire team would have been in the kill zone of the VC ambush. Only the noise of the safety catch, and their collective reflex to suppress fire and to flank the VC ambush, had saved them. Training! Thank God for our training. The thought of what might have been, nearly made McConnell throw up. He was shaking badly and could barely hold the radio handset as he called the boat.

Smitty acknowledged that they had been in contact and put the Seawolves on standby. They were not only compromised and deep in the Nam Can, they had expended a terrific amount of ammunition in the exchange. McConnell stepped over to the VC position as the SEALs were finishing a hasty search of the bodies. There were seven of them in a line just behind a stand of nipa palm and they were much too close together. The beam of his penlight revealed just how mangled the corpses and the near-dead were, like automobile victims in a don't-drink-and-drive film. And again, the gurgling. This time he did vomit.

"You okay, Boss?" said a dark form dropping to one knee beside him and placing a hand on his elbow to steady him.

"Thanks, Cribb—I'll be fine. I just can't believe how bad those guys got chewed up."

"Yeah, ain't it great? While those assholes were shooting at you and me, Reed turned their flank and got 'em all in a row. That '60's shit hot. Then the Chief and Barnett ripped 'em with canister rounds from their 203s. By the way, sir, don't touch any of 'em. I rigged two of 'em with grenades."

Another dark form appeared. "Sir, Reed's down to fifty rounds and everyone else is below half. We have to avoid contact on the way out."

"Thanks, Chief. Cribbs, take us out of here and keep off the trails as much as possible."

They were well into the trip back before McConnell felt the weakness in his knees leave him, but the taste of puke in his nose and mouth was with him all the way home.

The body count indicated that it was another successful operation, but it was a very subdued fire team that arrived back at Firebase Delta. France, Rawls, and several others were on the dock for their return. Word was relayed that they had been in trouble. Like consoling family members, they moved among the new arrivals, handling equipment and talking quietly. France took the radio off McConnell's back and walked with him up the dock.

"Got a little hairy tonight, huh, buddy?"

"Sweet Jesus, Dave, I almost lost my whole fire team! That was an ambush team and they were waiting for us!"

"Take it easy, Jim—"

"Take it easy, my ass. They almost had us. If we keep this up every night, it's just a matter of time before one of us gets rolled up."

Later that morning France and Rawls sat by themselves in the front of the hootch having a beer. McConnell's team was sleeping, physically and emotionally drained from the previous night's action. McConnell himself and several of the others had knocked back multiple shots of whiskey from a bottle Chief Johnson had produced for the post-op debriefing.

"I was talking with Cribbs and Reed," began Rawls, "and the ensign wasn't just shitting you—they almost got rolled up."

"Yeah, I know. I think that one even scared the Chief. Reed said he'd never have been able to advance on their flank if McConnell hadn't hung tough in there. He was in the kill zone. Lucky for all of 'em he reacted the way he did. Johnson claimed he pinned them down so well they didn't know Reed and the others were on their flank until it was too late."

"He sure can shoot, I'll give him that. And he's got balls, all right."

"You ever been in a kill zone, Rawls?"

"I was with Billy Denard and Al Riggio when they bought it. It ain't fun, I can tell you that. How's McConnell handling it?"

"He's pretty shook, but who wouldn't be? Y'know, I think it bothers him more that he led his men into an ambush, than that the indians almost dusted him."

"Think they were too far back into the boonies?"

"Maybe. McConnell's right though, we can't keep going back there like we have been. This kind of thing was overdue. I think I'll go have a chat with my favorite colonel."

France didn't take his fire team into the field that evening. Instead, he gathered the whole platoon together in the hootch. There was a collective sigh of relief at the break in the routine.

"Okay, listen up. We're going to make a few changes in our operations. I think Mr. McConnell's walk in the forest last night shows they're starting to take us seriously. The good colonel has managed to get us a Navy slick out of Binh Thuy and we're gonna have it all to ourselves for the next few weeks. We can't totally ignore the Nam Can, but with a bird at our disposal, we can range into the open country to the north and do some parakeet operations."

At the mention of parakeet operations, a cheer burst from the group. Parakeet ops were far and away the SEAL favorite. And there was the prospect of not going back night after night into the Nam Can forest.

"Now pay attention. I'm catching the mail bird out tomorrow morning for Binh Thuy to brief the slick pilots. I should be back in a day or so with the helo. Chief, I want you and Rawls to work on the targeting. Send the Kits on a few days' leave and see what they can dig up. Jim, I want you to thoroughly brief the Seawolves. I don't think Carl and his boys have ever flown parakeet ops. Try to schedule some practice time for later this week. Smitty will continue to run the river at night. By now, the indians and their spies are probably keying on the boats. We'll be going back there and we don't want them to know exactly when. And since we're officially taking the night off, will one of you guys pass me a beer? Gentlemen, the drinking lamp is lit."

It took the platoon until about one-thirty in the morning to drink all the beer in the reefer. They were not loud or rowdy except for the hoots and cheers when Reed and Rawls squared off for a K-bar throwing contest. Most of them just got quietly shit-faced before crawling off to their racks and passing out.

McConnell saw France off on the courier helicopter midmorning and stepped into the Seawolf hootch. He sat down with Carl Belding and the other three pilots over coffee to talk about the upcoming operations. They too were excited and looking for an operational change of pace.

"Parakeet operations are nothing more than hit-and-run with helicopters," said McConnell. "The first thing we do is target a building or hootch where we think the VC may be hiding or have hidden supplies. We've got some leads from a VC France captured, and the Kits are out looking for some other potential targets. When we've identified a target hootch, we plot it on the map and if possible we have you guys fly by and check the location so you can find it again."

"Won't that tip them off?" asked one of the pilots.

"We hope not—and not if you maintain a steady course and stay high, like you were on a routine transit flight just passing by. At this stage of the game we know where the target is and hopefully what it is. When the slick gets here, we'll strip off the doors and get it rigged as an insertion helo. The slick can hold a full fire team with four guys in each door. We go in on the deck, downwind from the target. And I mean on the deck, with the slick pilot just lifting the nose of the bird over the treelines and rice dikes. Now, our pilot can't really navigate when he's this low. That's where you guys come in. One gunship trails about a half mile behind at fifteen hundred feet, the second farther back and higher. You give the slick pilot course corrections—come left, come right—that sort of thing, and ranges to the target."

"But won't they hear us coming?" asked Carl.

"That's the reason you make the approach from downwind. When we were training back in the States, one fire team would sit in one of our practice hootches while the other team did helo assaults using this technique. Unless the pilot came in too high, we couldn't hear a thing until the slick flared for a landing. And then it sounded like a hurricane coming down.''

"So we guide the slick to the target. The slick lands and you crazies attack the hootch, right?''

"Almost. We just need the slick to get down to six to ten feet off the deck and slow to about five knots. We bail out and the slick clears off as soon as he can. The gunships roll in and cover him off the target. Then you hang around for fire missions and to cover the slick when he comes back to extract us. The Chief said it really helps to confuse the VC if you guys stay in a low weave around the target and make dry firing runs.''

"The Chief probably also figures it might draw some fire away from you.''

"Matter of fact, he did mention that, but I wasn't going to bring it up.''

"When do we start?''

"As soon as Lieutenant France gets back with the slick. He went to Binh Thuy hoping to find a pilot with some experience with parakeet ops. Then he wanted a day or two for rehearsal. There's a couple of abandoned hootches near a semifriendly village just up the river. The Kits said it would be okay to use them for practice. Oh, one more thing. When we're operational, we should probably have the Ponies on standby just as a contingency.''

"You mean just in case you jump in on a battalion of indians.''

"Hey, Carl, you said you were looking for some targets, didn't you?''

"Find some yes, but not be one. This ought to be interesting. Tell Dave we'll be ready when you are.''

France arrived the next day with the slick Huey and they immediately began to get the new helicopter ready. They removed the large, sliding passenger compartment doors as well as the pilots' doors. The canvas seats and other equipment that served the helo's normal functions of ferrying personnel and cargo around the Delta were removed. Both pilots and the single crewman were fitted with additional body armor. The senior pilot was an ex-

Seawolf driver and had flown gunships in trail for parakeet ops, but this was his first turn as a slick pilot.

"Jim, this is Sam Benjamin. Sam's consented to be our chauffeur for the next few weeks."

"Nice to meet you, Jim. Call me Benny. Dave tells me you been busy out there in indian country."

"We sure have, Benny, but we've kind of worn out our welcome in the Nam Can. I'm looking forward to the flight operations."

"So am I. It's been my experience that if the targeting's right and we can surprise 'em, it's a lotta fun. If not, we get nothing or we step into the *ka-ka.*" Benny was a New Yorker—short, dark, intense, and Jewish. He had fine, thinning black hair and a short dense beard. A surprisingly thin mustache separated a squat, round nose from his thick, full lips. McConnell thought he looked more like a delicatessan manager than a helicopter pilot.

The next two days of training went well. The pilots perfected the required low-lead/high-trail technique, and worked out communication and navigation procedures. The SEALs used the time to refine their tactics. The helo would come in low and fast, and flare out close to the objective. The SEALs leaped to the ground, running to their assigned positions in the assault formation as they closed on the target hootch. The addition of the Kits to the fire team allowed Reed, with the M60, and Barnett to act as flankers while Con, Cribbs, and Billy charged directly into the hootch. Watson and Bono remained on either side of the door to provide covering fire. McConnell positioned himself directly in front, radio handset in one hand and Stoner in the other. Chief Johnson took a position behind McConnell, acting as rear security. It was fast, noisy and exciting.

The hairiest part of the practice sessions for the SEALs was the ride into the target. Benny was an exceptional pilot, and he pushed the aircraft to the limits of its capability. McConnell found it thrilling to skim a few feet over the rice paddies and treetops at eighty-five miles per hour. But it was next to terrifying when Benny stood the chopper on its side for a last-minute course correction and when he flared back to "break" the machine to a hover so they could jump out. The first part of the run would be low and steady, but the last ten seconds would usually be violent, stomach-wrenching evolutions with the target hootch invariably appearing just in front of the slick. By the end of the second day, both aviators and SEALs were ready for the real thing.

McConnell's team drew the first operation. It was a suspected VC ammunition and equipment cache. Billy brought in the information on the target and its location from "a friend" who wished to be paid for it. The word was out that the SEALs had "boo-coo piasters" for this kind of information. The material stored at this location was reportedly due to be picked up by the VC that evening, so a strike that day was required. The warning order and mission briefing were given in the morning for an early afternoon operation. The target was just off the juncture of two canals known well to the Seawolf pilots, and Carl felt they could easily vector Benny to the target hootch. There was an atmosphere of anticipation and excitement not unlike a group of schoolboys waiting for their first trip on the *big* roller coaster.

McConnell noticed the change in his men as they prepared themselves for the mission. They were probably no safer than going out at night on foot patrol or in the sampans, but it was just easier to be less afraid in the daylight. And it was faster. If all went well they would be on the ground no longer than five or ten minutes. That seemed a lot better than an extended period of "what ifs." It was easier, McConnell admitted to himself, to be brave for a few tense, wild moments than to muster the courage required to put yourself at lesser risk on a long dark night patrol.

"Gentlemen, shall we begin?" said Benny as he completed his preflight check and climbed into the pilot's seat. The SEALs and their two scouts boarded, four seated in each side door—legs hanging outside. McConnell knelt between the two pilots, clutching his radio handset. The slick lifted off, followed by the two Seawolf gunships, and headed northeast. The formation skirted the objective, arriving at a point some seven miles downwind and to the southeast of the target.

"Caretaker, this is Seawolf Leader, your course to target is two niner zero, ready when you are, over."

"Leader, this is Caretaker, roger two niner zero. Commencing run to target, out."

The slick dropped down to about twenty feet above the ground and began streaking across the rice paddies. The SEALs in the doors kept an eye on McConnell for hand signals as they raced to the target.

"Caretaker—Leader. Come left five degrees—four kilometers to target."

"Roger, Leader, left five degrees, four klicks to target." McConnell relayed distance to target, holding up four fingers. Benny dropped the slick down to an altitude of fifteen feet, and the ground became a blur.

"Caretaker, left five, two klicks."

"Roger left five, two klicks."

"Right ten, Caretaker, one klick."

"Roger right ten, one klick."

"Five hundred, dead ahead."

"Five hun—target in sight. Tally-ho! Tally-ho!"

The lone hootch was perched in a small packed dirt clearing some twenty meters from a canal of the same width. A well-used path ran along the canal in both directions. There were clumps of bamboo on one side of the hootch and a small grove of banana trees on the other. Low brush and elephant grass skirted the back of the hootch for some forty meters before giving way to a broken mosaic of small rice paddies.

The SEALs and the two Kits were now standing on the skids while remaining firmly clamped to the side of the aircraft with both hands, bracing for any last-minute course changes and the rapid deceleration at the target. Benny skidded the slick across the canal, almost standing it on its tail. The rotor blades screamed in full collective as they clawed air down and ahead of the aircraft, creating waves of spray from the canal, then dust from the clearing. He slightly overshot the intended insertion point, bringing the slick to a stop almost on top of the hootch and blowing off half of the palm-frond roof. The SEALs tumbled out and scrambled to their assault positions. The empty helo cleared off over the banana trees and down the canal as

the two Seawolves whistled overhead. Reed and Barnett
sprinted to either side of the hootch and slid into place
like base runners on a double steal. McConnell made eye
contact with Cribbs and nodded. The wily point man
bolted through the door followed by Con and Billy. Watson and Bono stepped up to cover them. From inside the
hootch there erupted a volley of Vietnamese, arguing and
screaming. This held McConnell's attention until Barnett
began to fire from the left flank.

"Two guys out back, Boss! One's down—the other's
gone!"

"Tomboy, this is Seawolf Leader. Got a man running
west of your posit. Request release, over."

"Leader—Tomboy, you are released, go get him." One
of the Seawolves began to fly a low, tight circle behind the
hootch, affording his door gunner a good field of fire.

Billy emerged from the hootch leading three women and
a surly, ten-year-old boy. All had been bound at the wrists
with nylon snap-tie handcuffs. They were an undernour-
ished, ragged-looking lot. Billy made them kneel in a row
in front of the hootch. One of the women began wailing
loudly until Billy viciously slapped her across the mouth
with the back of his hand.

"They're dirty, Boss," reported Cribbs. "All kinds of
shit in there."

"Chief, take Cribbs and Con and search the place and
have Billy watch these people. Watson, you and Bono go
with Barnett and check that indian he hit out back. Don't
lose eye contact with Reed."

"Tomboy—Seawolf Leader, your runner is KIA. How
are you doing down there, over."

"All secure here, Leader, we'll be ready to go in about
five minutes—you copy, Caretaker?"

"Caretaker, I copy, out."

"Seawolf Leader, roger, out."

A few moments later Chief Johnson signaled him to the
hootch. McConnell moved inside and surveyed the interior, well lighted by the gaping holes in the roof. There
were a dozen or so rifles and two AK-47s along with several hundred rounds of ammunition. Metal pans were
stacked like pie plates in one corner near about forty

pounds of plastic explosives. The hootch was a claymore mine factory as well as an armory. Con and Cribbs were busy stripping the bolts out of the rifles. They would break the stocks and throw the barrels into the canal.

"What about the rest of this shit, Chief?"

"We'll throw the claymore pans in the canal and keep the AKs. The rest will burn. Sir, since we got two loads if we're taking the prisoners, we really ought to do a stay-behind." In a stay-behind ambush, only some of the SEALs would extract by helo. The rest would hide near the target to wait for the VC to come back.

"Who goes?"

"Send Bono, Barnett, Con, and Billy with the VNs. Five of us can handle it."

McConnell considered this for a moment, then keyed his radio. "Caretaker—Tomboy. I have eight pax for you and request a raincheck, over."

"Roger, Tomboy, eight pax and a raincheck. Be there in thirty seconds, over."

"Tomboy, roger, out."

McConnell called in the fire team and tossed a smoke grenade by the canal in front of the hootch where he wanted Benny to land. He quickly issued instructions and followed the four SEALs, who were part of the stay-behind, into the stand of bamboo near the hootch. Their movement was masked by the smoke from the signal grenade and the dust created by the prop wash of the incoming slick. The two Seawolves crossed overhead one more time before following the slick over the horizon. Benny was making for the firebase at maximum speed to unload and return, while the two gunships took station orbiting downwind out of sight. McConnell and his men burrowed into the bamboo and elephant grass, and waited quietly in the silent wake of the departed helos. They didn't have to wait long. Fifteen minutes after the choppers were gone, two men approached from along the canal, one of them armed. They paused to wait for a third man, also carrying a rifle, to join them. The three cautiously approached the hootch, and came to within fifteen meters of the SEALs' position.

McConnell signaled to the Chief to tell them to surrender. Johnson shook his head. McConnell repeated to signal.

"Sir, no way," whispered Johnson.

"Do it!" hissed McConnell.

"Lai day! Lai day!"

All three broke for the cover toward the rear of the hootch. They didn't have far to go, but the SEALs cut them down before they made half the distance. They had finished searching the bodies and were in a defensive position with the Seawolves overhead when Benny returned with the slick. They then set the hootch on fire and called for extraction. The five SEALs were back at the fire base barely forty-five minutes after they had left. Chief Johnson walked with McConnell on the way back to the hootch.

"Sir, did you really think those guys would *chieu hoi* or did you do that to justify shooting them?" Johnson could be annoyingly straightforward and he was clearly angry.

McConnell stopped and looked at the Chief. "I'm not sure," he said honestly. "I knew they couldn't get away if they made a run for it. I also knew they probably wouldn't give up. I guess I figured it wouldn't hurt to try."

"It didn't this time, but that was a dangerous thing you did back there. Begging the ensign's pardon, sir, but perhaps you should get a few more combat patrols behind you before you ignore my advice in the field." There was a tense silence between them before Johnson continued. "The odds, sir. Always play the odds in our favor. You try to be decent and fair out there, and you cut our odds. One of us might get killed—maybe you. The only time I ever saw one of them drop his weapon and surrender, it was a trap." Johnson continued on to the hootch leaving his officer standing in the road. It was one of the few times Johnson had been short with him. It was also the first time he had gone against Johnson's advice in the field, and the first time he had done anything except try to kill an armed VC.

Over the next week and a half they flitted around the lower Delta and met with periodic success. Even when they came up empty, the action was fast-paced and exhilarating.

"This is better'n sex," declared Tex Barnett. "Two lootin', two shootin', an' two takin' pictures. We gotta try this at one of them drive-in banks in San Diego. We'll be down the road 'fore the fuzz knows what's goin' down."

They still did an occasional sampan ambush or foot patrol at night, but their time and energies were taken with the planning and execution of the parakeet ops. Things were running smoothly and the body count rose steadily.

McConnell's team was up for a mission, and they were going after a suspected VC resupply point. The target hootch was in a rice paddy area some forty meters from a heavily wooded area. There were three hootches altogether, a large one and two smaller ones on a built-up, mud-packed area surrounded by paddies. Benny approached the hootch from the west, away from the tree line and put the fire team out some twenty meters from the large target hootch. Those on the right side of the aircraft jumped to a rice dike and began running for the target. Those on the left side dropped into a paddy and followed close behind, splashing through the calf-deep water. McConnell, having his choice, elected the dry side and took a position near the door of the target hootch. Their set up was very quick. Con, Billy, and Cribbs popped through the door of the larger hootch just after the slick had peeled away. The two smaller hootches were on the other side of the larger one, away from their insertion point. Reed covered them on the right flank while Barnett stood in a paddy to the left with a field of fire that covered the back of the three hootches. McConnell was vaguely aware that there were no cooking fires, nor were there any people around. Then Con and Billy burst out through the door with Cribbs close behind them.

"Grenade!" yelled Cribbs as he dove to the ground not far from McConnell's feet. McConnell just got himself flat on the hard-packed mud when there was a large *krump-sssssh* as the grenade exploded. The fragments blew through the stick and grass structure and whistled over his head. The walls of the hootch blew out and the roof dropped to the floor. Then a roar from the tree line announced a B-40 rocket that took out one of the smaller hootches completely. McConnell fumbled with the radio handset while trying to stay low and see what was going on. For the first time, he clearly heard the distinctive snap of enemy bullets as the shock wave announced their close passing. The Seawolves had seen the explosions and had traced the B-40's exhaust trail to the tree line. They began an attack weave, one bird flying straight in on a rocket attack while the other, rolling off the target, covered him with his door gunner. They laid their fire into the tree line closest to the SEALs' position. The SEALs were also firing into the tree line, but it was apparent that the enemy was well dug in. Another B-40 round leveled the remaining hootch.

"Seawolf Leader—Little Boy, over!"

"Go, Little Boy."

"Carl, give me a good strong run to cover our movement. We will fall back to the rice dike west of our current posit, over."

"Roger, Little Boy, stand by."

McConnell shouted instructions to the fire team while they waited on the Seawolves. Both gunships rolled in on the enemy position and effectively suppressed their fire. The SEALs scrambled to relative safety, having put a rice dike between them and the enemy. A head count revealed everyone had made it, but Reed had taken some shrapnel in his side from the B-40.

"What do you think, Chief?"

"We're gonna have to break contact and get away from that tree line, sir. No way that slick can get us here."

"How's Reed?"

"He'll be fine until we get back. So will you."

"Me?" McConnell caught Johnson staring at him. He instinctively brought his hand up to his neck and it came away bloody. He had felt a stinging on his neck during the exchange, but had assumed it was a hot shell casing from his Stoner. He'd been burned by them before. This was something else.

"Seawolf Leader, we're going to break farther east to the next dike, can you cover, over?"

"One more pass, Little Boy—we're almost dry, over."

It's going to take more than their one pass to break this one, McConnell thought, and I don't want to stick around here without air cover while the Seawolves rearm. He was running low on options when a new player joined the game.

"Little Boy, this is Black Pony Section One Five, do you have some traffic for us, over?"

"Roger that, Black Pony One Five! Where are you, over?"

"Near your posit at angels seven. Can you mark your target, over?"

"One Five, this is Seawolf Leader, we will mark on our next pass, then it's all yours. Do you see me, over?"

"Leader—One Five, that's a roger. I've got you my five o'clock low. Go ahead in and we'll follow you."

The Seawolves with their 2.75-inch rockets and machine-gun fire could only temporarily suppress the enemy fire. The Black Ponies carried five-inch Zuni rockets and the OV-10 was a highly accurate launching platform. The tree line erupted as the Zunis slammed into the VC position like boxcars, and the enemy did not come out between the Pony's firing runs to engage the SEALs. Nonetheless, McConnell and his men leap-frogged away from the tree line, half of them firing from the cover of a rice dike while the other half splashed across a paddy to the next dike. After four of these maneuvers, they took up a normal patrol to a position where the slick could safely extract them. When Benny finally got to them, they barely had two hundred rounds between them.

The guys must be getting used to this crap, thought McConnell as he savored the euphoria that always came right after they escaped danger. He held a gauze pad to his neck by hunching his shoulder so he could use both hands to load a bandoleer of ammunition into the drum of his Stoner—just in case. Bono was teasing Billy, while Watson lit two cigarettes and gave one to Con. Cribbs and Barnett were arguing over who was going to give Reed a shot of morphine, ignoring Reed, who made it clear nobody was giving him a shot of anything unless it was Jack Daniel's. The laughs and horseplay were a good sign, but they couldn't hide the fact that it had been another close one. McConnell asked Johnson for a cigarette.

"Didn't know you smoked, sir," said the Chief after he gave him a light. "You gonna be okay?"

"No problem, Chief, but you might rock me a little before we land to break the suction my asshole has taken on this seat."

Chapter Eight

THE HOLIDAYS

THE DISPENSARY AT Firebase Delta was a small one-room affair equipped to handle routine sick-call duties and prepare casualties for evacuation to the Army surgical hospital in Binh Thuy. Major Bill Stinson, a balding surgeon in his mid-thirties with circular, granny-style glasses, was the base medical officer. His rumpled fatigue trousers and tight-fitting olive green T-shirt accented his pearlike physique. Stinson's manner was gruff when he treated casualties, acting like a cranky old man who'd found kids playing on his well-manicured lawn. But everyone knew it was an act. Stinson had no use for the war and it genuinely frustrated him to see young men hurt in the fighting. Reed lay on his side on top of the treatment table while Stinson inspected and poked at the wound. McConnell sat off to one side on a stool.

"When are you going to learn to call ahead when you have a man hit? I could have met the chopper on the pad."

"Didn't think it was that big of a deal, Doc," said Reed, which did little to assuage McConnell's guilt at not having radioed ahead. Not to mention that he'd let Reed stop by the hootch for a beer before coming to the dispensary.

"It's nothing serious, but you're going to have to go up to the surgical unit in Binh Thuy and have that shrapnel dug out. Looks like there may be several pieces in there.

And depending on how much digging they have to do, they may keep you for a few days.''

"You're shitting me, Doc. Can't you just fix me here? I mean, what's the big deal?"

"That shrapnel has to come out or you stand a good chance of some serious infection."

"Boss, you gonna let him do this?"

"You bet I am. The war will be here when you get back. Take a few days off—it's almost Christmas, anyway."

Watson packed a kit for Reed while Doc Stinson dressed the wound on McConnell's neck. It was a clean gash, from a piece of shrapnel having grazed him as it passed by. Reed was mortally embarrassed when Stinson made him submit to being carried on a litter to the helipad, and he became almost angry when Cribbs, wearing a jungle shirt backwards with the collar turned up, followed behind the stretcher-bearers reading the Twenty-third Psalm from an old Bible. The fire team had now been bloodied.

"Well, it's time for the annual VC resupply stand-down," announced France the next morning when he came back from the daily commander's briefing. "As of midnight tonight there will be a holiday truce. The North Vietnamese have convinced those idiots in Saigon to agree to cease all offensive military activity until after New Year's. The truce is for ten days this time, so Charlie must really be low on supplies."

The veterans knew that while the U.S. and South Vietnamese forces stood down during these truce periods, the VC and the North Vietnamese would use the opportunity to move men and material. There was much grousing by the SEALs about the "chicken-shit VC tactics," but there was little force behind it. They were like barroom brawlers saying "Let me at him," fully expecting their friends to hold them back. It was a legal opportunity to stay out of the field. France decided that Foxtrot Platoon would split the truce period in half with one fire team off for five days over Christmas and the other off for New Year's. McConnell's team won the toss and elected to quit the war for Christmas. The rules of the truce still allowed for defensive actions, and ambushes were interpreted by the

SEALs as defensive actions. The fire team remaining at Firebase Delta would set up on major traffic points supported by the boats and if Charlie was out moving at night, they would defend against him.

The following morning, McConnell and his men mustered on the helipad waiting for the courier helo to Binh Thuy. Billy and Con had been given the five days off and had already left the base. Both were Buddhists but they would go home for the Christian holiday. The rest of the fire team had the high spirits of a bunch of ten-year-olds waiting on the bus for summer camp. They looked like a squad of mercenaries, dressed in their flat jungle greens—each with an overnight bag in one hand and an automatic weapon in the other. Barnett sported an Australian bush hat and Cribbs wore a silk camouflage ascot. The boys were going to town for the holidays. Town, in this case, was the Navy base at Binh Thuy, situated on the Mekong River. Nearby Can Tho offered most of the sinful pleasures of Saigon but on a much smaller scale. They landed at the base just before midday and checked into the transit barracks. With some reluctance, McConnell allowed his Stoner to be checked in at the barracks armory.

"Sir, why don't you join me at the Chief's Club for a sandwich and a beer? Only decent place to eat on the whole base."

"Sounds great, Chief." After a short walk, they entered a converted World War II–type quonset hut that served as the CPO mess. The dining area was dark and air-conditioned. They took a table in the corner with a plastic checkered tablecloth while an unseen phonograph played a Frank Sinatra ballad from the fifties. The Navy's chief petty officers were of another generation than their junior officers. The sandwich was worthy of a high-quality urban Stateside deli.

"Well, sir, we're almost halfway through the tour. What do you think of it so far?"

The Vietnamese waitress brought them another beer and McConnell exchanged his empty bottle for a full one. He took a pack of cigarettes from his blouse pocket, shaking one free for the Chief before taking one himself.

"Hell, I don't know. It's been a day at a time since we arrived at the firebase. What do you think, Chief—are we getting the job done?"

"We're having a good tour, sir. Except for that ambush we almost walked into, we've pretty much taken it to them." The mention of that near-disaster made Mc-Connell's stomach churn. "But I should tell you that it's not going to get any easier. The Nam Can is important to the VC and they're not stupid. The more we operate there, the more they'll try to second guess our operations and nail us."

"I know that, Chief. I also know that Mr. France wants to run up the body count. When you think we're going to the well a little too often, you let me know, okay?"

"You can count on that, sir. Mr. France is a good man, but sometimes he doesn't balance the risk with the reward." Johnson hesitated, then added, "Mr. McConnell, you're doing a fine job with the fire team. And the other new guys are shaping up real well. We take it a step at a time and we'll be back on the Strand before we know it."

"Thanks, Chief, and thanks for all your help. Doesn't it get a little old, breaking in new guys like me?"

"The VC do most of the breaking in. You been at the game long enough to know it's preparation and concentration, and a little bit of luck."

"Rifles and radios, huh, Chief?"

"That's it, sir, rifles and radios."

"What are you going to do for five whole days without the platoon to look after?"

"I been coming here on and off for the last four years, so I got a few friends in the area. How about yourself, sir?"

"I'm going to forget all about warning orders and mission planning and the Nam Can forest. I'll probably drink too much and sleep about twelve hours a day."

"Well, if you find yourself in need of some tension release, look up Cribbs at the U and I Club out in town. He'll see that you get officer-quality comfort at enlisted men's prices."

"The U and I Club. Wasn't that the name of the place that France and Rawls stopped by in Saigon?"

"There's one in every town, sir, just like there's a Texas Bar and a Tiajuana Bar. Probably a franchise."

"Thanks, Chief. If I feel myself getting a little tense, I just might do that."

They finished their beer and walked over to the hospital to visit Reed. The U.S. Army Third Surgical Hospital had become a social focal point for SEAL platoon officers. Their men were all-too-frequent guests there, and the Army nurses were the only source of round-eyed women in the Delta.

The hospital reminded McConnell that Christmas was just two days away. Colored lights rimmed the door to Reed's ward and paper Santas and reindeer littered the chalk-white prefab walls. McConnell and Chief Johnson arrived to find Reed surrounded by the rest of the fire team. Barnett was pouring him a drink from a pocket flask, using a paper pill cup as a shot glass. Bono sat on the end of Reed's bed with a stethoscope listening to his own heart. Watson was at the foot of the hospital bed spinning the crank handles, causing both Reed and Bono to move up and down at odd angels. Cribbs had found a Santa Claus hat and beard and was ho-ho-ho-ing around the ward. Next to Reed were two other SEALs. One had a gunshot wound in his shoulder that was not serious but would send him home. The other had lost one leg just below the knee. Both were enjoying the entertainment provided by the Foxtrot SEALs.

"How's it going, Reed?" inquired McConnell.

"Easy day, Boss. I'll be out of here in no time. They scraped on me for about an hour yesterday, and they come and change the bandage just about every time I drift off to sleep. The doc says it has to heal right." Reed rolled over and showed McConnell a wound on his right "lovehandle," between his rib cage and hip, that was some four inches across. It reminded McConnell of raw hamburger and was painted with disinfectant like a light coating of mustard.

"Don't let him shit you, sir," said Watson. "He's got terminal gonorrhea and he's trying to pass it off as a war wound.'' Watson was now seated on a chair by Reed's bed and seemed to be the only serious visitor.

"Looks like a busy place," said McConnell as he surveyed the ward that held some twenty patients.

"You know, sir," said Reed, "except for Tom an' Frankie an' me, everyone else here either got hit by a jeep or drank the local water or is on drugs. There's a couple of Army guys at the other end who got shot down in a helo. It ain't the VC that filled this ward."

McConnell turned to the bed next to Reed's. "How're you doing? I'm Ensign Jim McConnell from Foxtrot Platoon."

"Howdy, sir. Frank Bosley, Delta Platoon at Dong Tam." He extended his hand and his grip was unusually strong. "Reed says you guys have been busy."

"Pretty much so. They treating you all right?" asked McConnell uncomfortably. What do you say to a twenty-one-year old who has just lost a leg? he thought.

"They've been terrific. I leave on the medivac flight for Yokosuka tomorrow, then on to Balboa Hospital in San Diego. I was hot to get back to the Strand but this ain't what I had in mind. Reed says you're a good guy to work for, sir."

"Reed just *thinks* he works for me," said McConnell loud enough for Reed to hear. "Senior Chief Johnson makes it look that way so I'll feel important."

"They going to issue you a leg when you get back to Balboa?" asked Johnson, coming to McConnell's rescue. He knew how to talk to broken SEALs.

"That's what they say. Hell, I just bought a new Mustang with four on the floor. Can you drive a clutch with a wooden leg, Chief?"

"You won't have any problem with the car. Just stay out of any ass-kicking contests until you get some practice with it."

"Right, Chief. Hang on a second—Captain! Oh, Captain! Could you please fix my pillows? I'm having a terrible time with them."

McConnell and Chief Johnson stepped aside for a fatigue-clad Army nurse. She was fairly tall and wore no makeup or jewelry except for small gold earrings. Her light hair was efficiently pulled behind her head in a short ponytail. She had a narrow turned-up nose with a dusting of freckles, giving her a girl-next-door look. She attended Bosley with a blend of patience, resignation, and humor.

"Sailor, I think we've been through this drill a few too many times today."

"Oh, yes, ma'am, but only you can make me feel really comfortable."

"I'm sure, but I have a lot of other work to do besides fluffing your pillows. Excuse me, Lieutenant, do these clowns belong to you?"

"Uh, yes, ma'am, they do. And it's Ensign, not Lieutenant."

"Whatever. Have them hold it down or they'll have to leave."

"Hey, it's Christmas."

"Hey, it's a war. Hold it down or they leave, okay?"

"Yes, ma'am." She gave McConnell a tired but not unfriendly smile and moved on down the ward. Her fatigues had to be tailored because she fit them a little too well. McConnell stared after her, wondering just how she'd look in nonregulation attire. She was the first round-eyed woman he'd seen in three months.

Later that evening McConnell found himself at the Binh Thuy officer's club drinking gin and tonics. The troops had headed for town, and Chief Johnson had retired to the CPO club with another platoon chief. It had been several months since McConnell had drunk hard liquor, and it was doing a number on him. The officer's club was a modified Butler building that had been dressed up inside with dark paneling and cream-colored acoustic tile. McConnell was perched on a barstool, leaning on the bar that bisected one end of the large, narrow room. He looked through the blue cigarette haze that hovered over the tables of drinkers to an overly decorated fake Christmas tree standing sentrylike by the door at the opposite end of the room. Bobby Helms wailed out "Jingle Bell Rock" from a battered jukebox along the wall. Air conditioners in each of the six inset windows ran wide open. The tables were full and new arrivals were starting to crowd around the bar. The club catered to a mixed bag of officers, mostly Army and

Navy with an occasional Marine and Air Force type thrown in. All were in one form of uniform or another—fatigues, jungle greens like McConnell, or flight suits. All of them were drinking hard.

"Well, I'll be dipped in shit. If it isn't Jimmy McConnell of Foxtrot Platoon." McConnell turned around and was greeted by Benny, grinning ear to ear with a drink in each hand. "Drinkin' alone ain't healthy—c'mon over and join us. We got a table in the corner." Without waiting for an answer, he turned and headed through the crowd. McConnell collected his drink and cigarettes from the bar and followed.

Nine of them crowded around a table for four—six in flight suits and two Army nurses. The table was a forest of glasses. One of them had just finished a raunchy story and the men roared while the two nurses smiled and pretended to be embarrassed.

"Hey, gang, this is Jimmy McConnell, one of the SEALs I been ferrying around the lower Delta the last few weeks. We gave 'em hell, didn't we, Jim?"

"If you buy the bullshit Benny's been handing out," said one of the pilots, "he snatched you from the jaws of death on a regular basis down there." McConnell knew firsthand that Benny was an exceptional pilot, and he had in fact, extracted them from several difficult situations. But it was an unwritten rule that all pilots bragged about their flying skills while their fellow pilots put them down.

"At least twice a day," said McConnell, playing along, "sometimes three or four times."

"There you have it," Benny said, beaming. "I was down there with my ass on the line while you lounge lizards were up here guzzling tax-free booze and preying on poor helpless nurses like Betty and Pam here." The other pilots protested loudly. Not about preying on nurses, but about dodging the war, citing recent examples of personal valor in combat actions. Benny finally quieted them down and introduced McConnell around. One of the nurses said that she had seen McConnell at the hospital and commented on the antics of his men.

"By the way, Jim, you ought to buy Mike Quinlan there

a beer. Mike was the section leader of the two Black Ponies who covered us on your last extraction.''

''Mike,'' said McConnell, raising his glass in a toast, ''you can drink on me the whole night. That was a nice piece of work. We couldn't have moved if you guys hadn't come along.''

''Thanks—glad to be of service. It's nice to know we were able to help. Most of the time we load ordnance into an area and get no feedback or damage assessment.''

''Nothing against the Seawolves,'' said McConnell diplomatically, ''but those Zuni rockets are terrific. Once you guys hit that tree line I don't think we took any more fire.'' With this comment, he unwittingly redrew a familiar battle line, because half of the pilots were Seawolves and the other half were Black Ponies. This was well-plowed turf: which was more effective—the close support of the helicopter gunships or the heavier armament of the higher flying fixed-wing OV-10s? Both camps tried to draw McConnell to their side of the debate. He parried these attempts by buying both sides more drinks. At fifteen cents a drink, it was no problem. The two nurses feigned interest, but they couldn't care less and had heard it all before anyway. McConnell arrived back at the table with another round of drinks and found Bosley's nurse sitting in his chair.

''I'm sorry, Ensign, I didn't mean to take your seat.'' She started to get up, but McConnell waved her down and went off to find another chair. He managed to wedge the new seat next to her as he rejoined the group.

''Hi, I'm Jim McConnell. I hope we didn't give you a hard time today.''

''Glad to meet you. I'm Connie Thompson. No, it wasn't so bad. I just wish you guys wouldn't bring liquor into the ward.'' McConnell tried to act surprised but Nurse Thompson just smiled and shook her head. There was something very compelling about this girl. He was especially taken by her wide-set blue eyes that lit up when she laughed. A slight overbite enhanced her smile and added a solid warmth to her face. The evening wore on and the club became louder and more crowded. Christmas carols broke out periodically at some of the tables and around the bar. McConnell noticed that Connie sipped one drink for most of the evening but she smoked one cigarette after the other. He was getting a little dizzy from the gin, and realized that if he didn't get something to eat, he was going to be in real trouble.

"Connie, I've got to get some food in me. Is there someplace to eat close by?"

"There's a PX cafeteria by the hospital that's probably open. It's not that great but that's probably your only choice. You want some company?"

"Boy, would I," said McConnell as they got up to leave. Their departure was met by a round of hoots from around the table and a lewd remark from Benny.

They walked from the cool, loud, congested atmosphere of the club into the heavy, humid Delta night air. Nurse Thompson had been on McConnell's mind since that afternoon and he was glad to be alone with her. She was not beautiful in the conventional sense and she would have turned few heads back in Southern California. But there was a strength and natural grace about her, and a hardy femininity that could not be smothered by the uniform. The cafeteria—the stainless-steel room as Connie called it—was nearly empty. A burger, fries, and a milk shake helped to dilute the effect of the alcohol on McConnell. Connie had a dish of ice cream. When they had finished, he went back and got coffee for both of them while she lit another cigarette. They quickly ran out of back-home talk, and the conversation turned to the war. Connie had been in-country for about nine months and had another three to finish her tour.

"I'd even thought about extending. We practice some good medicine here, and the thought of emptying bed pans at Walter Reed doesn't really thrill me. But it's starting to wear me down."

"How so?" prompted McConnell. She was from Boston and McConnell was enchanted by her accent.

"Well, for one thing, watching the guys that come through here and how they deal with being a casualty can be a bummer. The bad ones have to face being disfigured or crippled for life. Those with slight wounds, like your man Reed, have to lie around and think about going back into combat. I used to think the ones who were not disabled, but wounded just bad enough to be sent home, were the lucky ones. But many of them are dragging around so much macho baggage, they think they're running out on their buddies. Deep inside, they're glad to be getting the hell out, but they're on a real guilt trip. It's a lose-lose situation. I used to be able to deal with it, but it's starting to get to me. Just getting tired, I guess. Hey, I'm sorry to be going on like this. It must sound a little silly to you.''

McConnell could see that Connie's genuine care for the men in her wards probably made her a good nurse, but it also caused her a great deal of pain. "No, it doesn't sound silly at all,'' he replied. "I guess I never really thought about it. I suppose I should have. It seems the day-to-day business of operations doesn't leave room for much else. My guys seem to be handling it okay.''

"Jim, you may know how to sneak around the jungle and all that, but you don't know squat about wounded men. Take that kid Bosley. You probably think he's going to be one of those optimistic heroes who'll overcome his loss with cheerful determination and unfailing good humor?''

"Well, he's a tough kid,'' said McConnell defensively. "I think he's got a good attitude and—''

"Horseshit. He's tough around you because you guys carry a double load of macho baggage. I'm the one who sees them crying at night. Guys like Bosley have no one to turn to. In a lot of ways, you're his family, and you expect him to grin and bear it. Sometimes I wonder about you guys.''

"What can I say? We don't get a lot of sensitivity training at SEAL school.''

"Well, maybe you should. Tell me something, are we winning the war here in the Delta? Are we really making a difference in the war against communism?''

"I honest to God don't know, Connie,'' McConnell replied. She had taken on a cold, hard veneer since they started talking about casualties and the war. She was asking him questions he had thought about and probably should be concerned with, but they were almost irrelevant to his day-to-day work. "The Viet Cong own most of the real estate, at least they do in the lower Delta. We've made them a little more careful about how they move around, especially at night near Firebase Delta, but they still move. I know we're a very small part of the war, but from what I've seen, we're just harassing them. I can't say that we're winning.''

"How can you continue to fight if you don't think we're making progress—that there's an end in sight?''

"Well, I never really think about an end to the war—just the next operation.''

"I've been here for the better part of a year, and it seems to me this war is a way of life. The government controls the cities and the VC control the rural areas. We get a steady supply of wounded GIs, and everybody gets drunk at night and tells war stories. It's got to mean something.''

"I don't know what to tell you, Connie, I really don't. I'm here to run SEAL operations and get my men safely through the tour. It may not be right, but I don't think much about the course of the war—whether we're winning or losing. I do know the VC are a nasty bunch, and they kill innocent people on purpose. If we don't win here, there's going to be a real bloodbath.''

"Well, I think the bleeding done on both sides since we've been over here adds up to the same thing. You SEALs have had your share. I've had up to eight or ten of you in the ward at one time. How many of you are there over here?''

"Five, sometimes six platoons—about eighty or so of us in the field.''

"And it seems two or three of you get killed every month—sometimes more.'' She rolled her cigarette on the edge of the ashtray, making a shallow cone of the ash, and looked at McConnell. "Jim, you're three months into your tour—how many VC have you killed?''

"Connie, why?''

"How many?''

McConnell looked straight at his coffee cup and answered in a low voice. "My fire team has accounted for twenty-four confirmed enemy KIAs.''

"Not your team—*you*. How many men have *you* killed?"

He felt his cheeks flush in anger as he looked up and measured her. "Seven."

"Do you keep tally sheets, Ensign? Do you carve notches on the handle of your gun to keep score?"

"Now just a goddamn minute! Killing people, even some dirtbag VC who's trying to kill you, is part of the game here. And the body count? It's like having a baby, Connie—it's hard *not* to keep score. No, I don't carve notches on my gun!"

Connie retreated a bit at the strength of McConnell's reaction. "There was an officer here from one of the other SEAL platoons last week, and the sonovabitch had notches carved on his shotgun."

"Big deal! The jet jockeys shoot down a MiG and they stencil a kill on the side of their plane. Five kills and you're an ace. They put your picture in *Stars & Stripes*. You're a fucking hero. What's the difference!" McConnell suddenly realized that he was almost shouting, and the few others in the cafeteria were staring at them.

He leaned back and stared at the stained plywood ceiling. Taking a deep breath, he exhaled heavily and continued in a soft voice, "Sometimes I don't know how I got here. It was my own doing—I volunteered. I wanted to be someone special—to be in the teams. I don't really give a damn about this war or this country. Maybe I should have quit when I got to SEAL team, but I can't walk away from it now. My men depend on me—I'm responsible for them. It's my platoon's job and my fire team's job, and it's my job to kill VC. That's what we do. That's . . . ."

He saw that her hand holding the cigarette was shaking, and when he looked closely at her face, he saw the two streams running down her cheeks. She looked up at him, her large blue eyes shining and full. She wasn't weeping or sobbing, but each time she blinked, more tears were forced into the two rivulets.

"Would you mind walking me to my room?"

"Yeah, sure—hey, I'm sorry, honest. I didn't mean to go at you like that." McConnell stumbled to his feet and led her out of the cafeteria. Walking back to the hospital, he put his arm around her shoulders. She drew his hand to her face and he felt the tears on her cheek with the back of his hand. The touch of her smooth moist skin sent a charge of electricity through him. When they arrived at her room she opened the door and led him inside. "Connie, I really am sorry. I just—well—I was out of line. I had no right to talk to you like that."

She turned and put her arms around his waist, and her head on his shoulder. They were both quiet for a moment. "No, Jim, I'm the one who should apologize. I'm always looking for someone to blame for this damn war. You're a good man, Jim McConnell, and you're the last person I should blame."

"Truce?"

"Truce."

She kissed him lightly on the lips, then led him to the single bunk in the corner of the sparsely furnished room. They undressed in silence and made love—quietly at first, almost tentatively—then harshly, with a sense of urgency, as if their passion was a perishable thing to be used quickly or lost forever. Finally exhausted, they held each other in a deep, dreamless sleep and did not awake until the middle of Christmas Eve morning.

McConnell had a leisurely lunch at the mess hall, nursing a hangover and a very warm feeling inside. He didn't know if it was the girl or the circumstance, but he had never experienced such a combination of passion and tenderness. Just thinking about her and last night made him feel good all over. Connie had gone to her shift at the hospital, promising to see him at the club that evening. He had nothing better to do so he wandered around the base and out the gate toward Can Tho. He climbed into one of the old Citroen taxicabs.

"Where go, *Thieu Uy*?"

"U and I Club, *papa-san.*"

"U and I Crub, okay!"

The ride into Can Tho took about ten minutes. The city had a French village look to it but most of the one- and two-story buildings were in a state of decline. The broad avenues were dirty and commercial. The cab pulled up in

front of frame-and-stucco storefronts. McConnell handed
the driver a wad of *piasters* and got out.

"You numbah one Joe—I make you bery special deal!"
The man tried to drag McConnell into a store with racks
of clothes on the sidewalk.

"Some other time," said McConnell as he walked
across the street to the U and I Club. A brightly painted
sign hung over the door, boasting of beautiful ladies and
real American liquor. The old man who was seated by the
door leaped to his feet as McConnell approached, escorting him inside as if the American officer was his own
procurement. Two bar girls spotted him and hurried over
to escort him to a stool. They were young, pretty, painted,
and wore very short skirts.

"Ah, welcome, *Thieu Uy*. You come-a sit ober here.
You bery welcome our crub," said the one on his left.
The other one held his arm and noticed the cover on his
watch, then looked at the cloth jump wings on his blouse.

"Ah lookit, he Naa-vee-see-al. Big watch, kay-bah
knife, bum fuck!" Both girls covered their mouths and
laughed.

McConnell ordered a beer and looked around. It was
smaller than he had imagined. He sat alone at a long,
elegant mahogany bar that bisected the front portion of a
dark, narrow room. Soda fountain–type stools lined one
side of the bar while a large mirror with an ornate back
bar adorned the opposite wall. Past the bar, the room gave
way to tables along one wall and padded booths along the
other. A doorway with a velvet curtain segregated the bar
from the rest of the club. The dark green linoleum that
had been laid over a concrete floor was dirty and chipped.
The ceiling may have once been elegant but now served
as a backdrop for a light olive green silk parachute with
its apex fitted around an ornate chandelier in the center of
the room. A smell of stale beer and open sewage perme-
ated the club. An elderly woman with the look of authority
brought him a warm bottle of San Migele and two glasses
of tea for the girls. McConnell paid for all three while one
of the girls poured his beer.

"Hey, Cribbs, look-it—could that be the Boss?" Barnett had just walked in with a Vietnamese girl half his

height under each arm. Cribbs was right behind him with
his arms full of packages.

"Mr. McConnell, glad you could make it out into
town." He handed the packages to the woman behind the
bar and they exchanged a few words in Vietnamese. She
looked sharply at McConnell, then set a cold beer on the bar
in exchange for his warm one.

"Say, Boss," said Cribbs warily, "we're not being recalled, are we?"

"Nope. I just thought I'd come out and see how you
guys are doing. I see you're playing Santa Claus."

"Just a few things from the base. It goes a long way
here." And on the black market, thought McConnell, but
he said nothing. They sat at a table in the back and the
bar girls crowded around. The *mama-san* brought another
beer for him and one for Barnett, and waved her hands
when McConnell tried to pay. She brought a scotch and
water for Cribbs and treated him with a respect that bor-
dered on reverence.

"Well, whadda yuh think of the Yew an' Ah, Boss—
great place, huh?"

"We've sure drunk beer in worse places, Tex."

"Amen tuh that."

"I see you got two of those sweet things. One of them
not enough?" The two girls still clung to either side of the
lanky Texan.

"Aw, they're jes' little ones, sir. Takes 'bout two of
'em to make one regular-size gal from back home. Right,
darlin's?" He squeezed them and they both giggled.

The three Americans talked in English and the girls
talked in Vietnamese. Cribbs dropped in and out of both
conversations. They were on their third beer when Watson
and Bono walked in, both carrying packages. They set
their bags on the bar and joined the others. More girls and
beer arrived at the table.

"We just left Reed," said Watson. "They're gonna release him this afternoon so he'll be here tonight. How
about you, sir—Christmas Eve at the U and I? We got all
kinds of booze and fancy eats."

McConnell wavered. He liked these men and wanted to

stay—they were his friends. He also had a feeling it was going to be a wild time at the U and I Crub that night.

"Sorry, guys, maybe tomorrow. I got to be someplace tonight."

"Round-eye?" said Cribbs with a smile.

"Yeah, a round-eye," he admitted.

"Officers!" said Cribbs as he rolled his eyes. "You invite them to a banquet and they opt out for a cheese sandwich."

McConnell finished his beer and rose to leave.

"Merry Christmas, Boss," said Bono.

"Same to you, Bones, and to all you guys—Merry Christmas."

"You too, sir, have a good one."

"Take care, sir."

As he turned to leave, an absolutely gorgeous girl that *had* to be Miss Vietnam came out from the back and sat down next to Cribbs. The wily point man gave him a wink and McConnell tossed him a casual salute. Cribbs probably wasn't the answer to an American girl's prayer, but he did all right here. For all I know, thought McConnell, he could be the mayor of Can Tho. The bright sunlight was in sharp contrast to the dark interior of the bar. He pulled the bill of his cap low on his forehead and began to look for a cab.

McConnell arrived back at the club by six o'clock and ordered a sandwich and beer. He watched the same crowd gather as the previous night while he started on his second beer.

"What say there, buddy," said Benny as he dropped into the seat next to McConnell. "Merry Christmas, and all that shit."

"Hey, Benny, how's it going?"

"Not bad, not bad. Say, I remember you leaving with Captain Connie last night, but I don't remember you coming back. You're not fraternizing with senior officers are you, boy?"

"Just got a bite to eat and walked her home," replied McConnell.

"Uh-huh, you just walked her home?"

"That's right, no big deal." Then, to change the subject, "What goes on here tonight, it being Christmas Eve and all?"

"Same as any other night—get hammered. Probably be less fighting and more singing."

"It's a crazy war, Benny."

"You're telling me. I almost get my ass shot off during Hanukkah flying parakeet ops for you guys, and here I am getting potted with a bunch of *goyim* on Christmas Eve. My mom'd shit if she could see her little boy now."

"Benny, what are you doing here? I mean, in Vietnam? Do you think we should be involved over here?"

The blocky pilot squared around and faced him. "Pretty heavy questions there, Ensign Jim. You got me at a disadvantage 'cause I'm still sober, which is not going to last all that long. My bottom line is I love to fly. I also think Ho Chi Minh sucks, but that's a side issue. Why the other hundred thousand or so round-eyes are here, I couldn't say. And I'm not sure I really give a shit." He chugged his martini and wiped his mouth with the back of his hand. "But I'll tell you one thing, Jim, Lawrence of Arabia was right."

"Lawrence of Arabia?"

Benny, lifting his empty glass, looked across it into the blue haze cloud hanging over the bar:

"It is better that they do it imperfectly,
Than you do it perfectly,
For it is their country and their war,
And your time here is limited."

"Sir Lawrence was probably an insufferable prick, but he knew what he was talking about. It was true with his wogs and it'll probably be true with our gooks. The VC and the North'll wear us down until we get tired and go home."

"Are you saying we're losing?"

"I'm saying I don't think we can win. In the end it'll be the same thing."

McConnell wanted to talk about this, but he saw Connie come through the door. He was out of his seat immedi-

ately to escort her to the table, but she was accosted by
two other officers and led to an old upright piano that had
been pushed against the wall by the jukebox. She immediately began to bang out the tunes, alternating Christmas
carols with requests from those gathered nearby. Mc-
Connell fought his way through the crowd and hoisted his
beer on top of the piano.

This was a different Connie Thompson than the one he'd
met the night before. She laughed while she played, and
she played very well. An Army doctor with a sensational
baritone voice sat beside her on the bench and led the
singing. She played the old favorites with a great deal of
flourish and showmanship. On jazz numbers she would
dangle a cigarette from the corner of her mouth, hunch
her shoulders and toss her head from side to side like Ray
Charles. She played to the crowd and they loved her. She
was radiant. The mostly male gallery crowded around and
cheered. McConnell watched with total admiration and a
little jealousy. He ordered another beer and held his ground
at the end of the piano. When he finally attracted her attention between songs, she motioned him to her.

"Why don't you save me a seat at our table," she whispered as he leaned close, "and if you don't have quite so
much to drink, tonight might be even more fun than last
night."

McConnell met her eyes and laughed, knowing he was
blushing. He made his way back to join Benny. The group
at his table had gotten into the spirit of things, drinking
hard and singing. McConnell had begun to drink the Coke
he had ordered when Benny placed a large hairy hand on
his shoulder and inclined his head toward him in a con-
spiratorial manner.

"Y'know, Jim, some women will tell you they like a
sober, caring lover. But when it comes right down to it,
it's that all-night, champagne hard-on that really puts a
smile on their face."

McConnell sputtered and nearly choked on his drink.
"Now goddammit, Benny, you got it all wrong." He tried
to play dumb; but the more he did so, the louder Benny
laughed, holding his sides while tears trickled out of the
corners of his eyes and found their way into his dense

beard. Soon McConnell gave up and joined him, and both of them were rolling in their chairs with uncontrolled laughter. Their hilarity was contagious, feeding on itself. It finally subsided, leaving them both exhausted. McConnell couldn't remember when he had laughed like that.

Connie finally joined them some fifteen minutes later. She wedged a seat between them and signaled for the waitress.

"Hi, guys, what's up!" McConnell caught Benny's eye and they both again convulsed into laughter.

"What's going on here? Did I say something wrong?" The waitress arrived to take her order. "I'll have a stinger," she told the girl, "and I think you better get my friend here a beer. The Coke doesn't seem to agree with him." This comment by Connie set them off again.

"Honestly, what *is* the problem with you two? I think I'll go to the lady's room. Maybe you'll be settled down by the time I get back—if I come back."

"No, Connie, wait—" McConnell tried to stop her but was again racked with laughter.

Connie rejoined them at their table and, like most of the others near them, settled into a steady pace of hard drinking. They went around the table, each telling where they had been and what they were doing last Christmas. There was a living room fireplace in a Minnesota snowstorm and a midnight Mass in Atlanta. Another had found the Christmas spirit fighting for last-minute presents at Macy's. Benny surprised them all by announcing that he had been sitting at this very table exactly one year ago.

"I rotate back the end of February after eighteen months in this paradise," he said, "with a terminal case of prickly heat and a corner on the air-medal market."

"Twelve's the normal tour," offered one of the pilots. "Why the extension?"

" 'Cause peace-time flying sucks."

No one commented on that one, although an extension of a combat tour was unthinkable to most of them. Several Vietnamese bar maids circulated among the crowd, carrying trays loaded with tumblers of egg nog, cold and well fortified. The senior officer, a bird-colonel Army surgeon, called everyone to their feet and led them in "Silent

Night'' and ''God Bless America.'' He then quietly set his glass on the bar and walked out. Connie held McConnell's hand under the table and gave him a sad, warm smile. The mood was rapidly shifting to melancholy when Connie's baritone friend arrived at the table and suggested a round of caroling at the hospital wards. They collectively leaped at this idea and were soon making their way to the hospital, everyone again flush with the Christmas spirit.

Their reception on the wards ranged from applause to tears. A few of the ambulatory patients joined them and their number had nearly doubled by the time they finished. McConnell's family Christmas had been the standard close-knit WASP affair, with midnight service, relatives, and lots of presents. This was so very different and, in many ways, so much more like Christmas. The atmosphere was charged with warmth and emotion. Something magical seemed to pass between carolers and casualties— a tightly woven fabric of closeness that he had never experienced before. His identification with these strangers and the affection he felt for them made the feelings for his family back in Mattoon seem inadequate by comparison. Chance and circumstance now had made these people his family. The comradeship fashioned by this alien and dangerous country so far from home bound them tightly this Christmas Eve.

McConnell savored this avalanche of warm, good-clear-through feelings, squeezing Connie's hand as they exchanged me-too glances. As McConnell told himself that it didn't get any better than this, he was saddened by the thought that maybe it never would. Future Christmases would have this one as a benchmark. It would be a tough act to follow.

He and Connie walked back to her room with their arms around each other, neither wanting to break the spell by talking. In her room they closed the door softly behind them.

''Merry Christmas, Jim McConnell.''

''Merry Christmas, Connie.''

For a long time they just held each other. Then, as if by some unspoken cue, they began to squeeze each other fiercely. This finally gave way to a sweet, controlled passion that became yet one more wonder for McConnell to contemplate on his first Christmas away from home.

It was a tired and ragged but largely contented fire team that gathered at the Binh Thuy helipad in preparation for the trip back to Firebase Delta. the prospect of going back to the war was not a happy one, but they were resigned to the task. They had spent all their energy and money having a good time in the allotted five days, and there was no place else for them to go. All but Chief Johnson and McConnell had spent their waking hours at the U and I Club. The Chief spent most of his time at the CPO club. It was suspected he had a thing going with one of the *mama-sans* out in town, but he never talked about it. McConnell was the last to arrive.

"Reed, my man," said Cribbs, "isn't that our ensign in the company of your nurse?"

"Sure is. I heard he was getting after her."

"I wonder if the Boss got into her pants?" said Watson.

"Hard to say," replied Reed. "Tom pinched her tit in the ward one day, and she clobbered him with a bedpan."

"Well, I hope she fucked him," offered Bono. "The Boss needed something to get his mind off operations."

"She's awful skinny and she got no boobs," said Barnett. "Ah like 'em with a little mo' meat on 'em."

"Why'd a guy want to screw an Army nurse when the price of pussy out in town is so reasonable?"

"Officers don't screw, they copulate."

"All right, wise guys, knock it off," said Chief Johnson as the two approached the group. McConnell introduced Connie around, and the men made a polite, collective fuss over her while the helicopter crew completed their pre-flight. Then Chief Johnson ordered them aboard.

"What a nice bunch of guys," said Connie. "I can see why you care for them so much."

"Uh-huh," replied McConnell nervously, noting that the troops were being just a little too nice. "They're a good bunch all right."

"Well, Ensign, take care, please write, be careful, and all of that crap."

"You bet I will. If we get a break, I'll try to hitch a ride up here to see you."

"Any time, sailor, only I don't want to see you in here on a medivac chopper."

They looked at each other for a moment and then she kissed him quickly on the mouth and walked away. He stared after her for a few seconds before he picked up his kit bag and Stoner rifle, and followed his men to the waiting helicopter.

Chapter Nine

TRAN VAN CASH

THE HUEY SPIRALED down to Firebase Delta and the fire team was back home. Lieutenant France and his team were lined up and ready to board the chopper as McConnell's men filed off. They had a few moments together while the aircraft refueled. France briefed McConnell on operational matters, while the troops exchanged information about hot spots in Can Tho.

"Things have been pretty quiet, but then we didn't go too far from home. Just up the river four or five klicks. Smitty and the boat would watch the river on radar and we'd duck a few hundred meters up a side canal."

"Anything moving out there?"

"Smitty took after a radar blip, but it was a false return or the VC made it ashore. Like I said, we didn't stray too far from home, and I don't want you getting too far from the base either, not without a backup. It's a chicken-shit way to run a war, but you can't fight city hall. If you catch them on the water moving supplies, make 'em dance."

"Enjoy yourself in Binh Thuy, Dave. We'll be careful here."

"Happy New Year, Jim."

"Same to you. See you in a week."

France and his men swarmed aboard the helo and were gone. McConnell and the others walked back to the hootch

and slowly began to check over their operational gear.
McConnell checked in with the Seawolves and with Smitty
down on the boat. He paid a quick call on Colonel Beard,
where he received another lecture on being careful and a
caution about violating the conditions of the cease-fire.
Chief Johnson intercepted him on the way back to the
hootch.

"Mr. McConnell, I was talking with Rawls and he
thinks that the movement of the boat may be tipping off
the VC. The Kits think so, too." Con and Billy had been
waiting for them when they got back to the hootch. "Why
don't we try sending the boat up the Bhi Hap in one
direction while we go the other way in sampans? As long
as we stay on the river, or not too far off it, we can do it
safely. Who knows, we might get lucky."

The next night the fire team took to the river in Smitty's boat with the sampans in tow. They proceeded a few
klicks west of the base before Smitty brought the boat to
a slow idle and the SEALs carefully lowered themselves
over the side and into the sampans. The three small craft
then reversed their course and headed back toward the
base while Smitty continued west. The Bhi Hap was in
full flood behind them so they made good time. Within
fifteen minutes, they slid quietly along the southern bank
of the river opposite the base and continued in an easterly
direction.

"Big Brother, this is Peter Pan. Passing Home Plate,
over."

"Roger, Peter Pan. Copy you five-by, stay in touch,
over."

"Peter Pan, roger out."

An hour later they reached a small canal just east of a
quasi-friendly village that was situated on the north side
of the Bhi Hap. The canal joined the river from the south.
McConnell turned to the right into the canal and directed
the ambush setup on the east bank, just south of the entrance to the river where the mud spit formed by the
canal–river juncture gave way to covering foliage. A
three-quarter moon was just on the rise behind them,
affording visibility of the canal to the front and the river

off to their right. The terrain behind was relatively open with little danger of ambush, but McConnell still directed claymore mines to be put out in a defensive perimeter to their rear. They then settled in to wait out the night.

Sitting on ambush, relatively motionless for several hours, gave McConnell time to reflect. He thought about the ease with which he and the others had dropped back into an operational posture. It was their first operation in more than a week, but it seemed like they had been out of the field for no more than a day. His senses and being were immediately buried in the practice of his trade. The dirty sweat-stale smell of his web gear and jungle shirt was almost comforting. The familiar sting and pungent aroma of the insect repellent in his camouflage face paint competed with the reassuring metallic smell of the gun oil on his weapon. He felt like an armadillo, encased in his radio, ammunition belts, and grenades; like a human turret looking out over the barrel of the Stoner rifle. Since they had taken to the sampans, he automatically began using his night vision techniques—never looking directly at what he wanted to see, but scanning to either side for an irregular shape or a telltale movement. His head continually moved in twenty- to thirty-degree increments, pausing to methodically search a segment of the bank or water, then moving on to the next sector. McConnell had returned to the workplace. And returning with him, like another member of the squad, was the fear. Fear of making a mistake, fear of being ambushed. He had come too close to disaster to believe it could never happen to him. Their close call in the Nam Can forest some weeks back had made him near-paranoid about being ambushed. He was playing the "what if" game again. What if the VC saw them enter the canal and were waiting for him to come out? What if they get inside the perimeter and hit them from behind? He had to play the game because he was in command, and ultimately he was responsible. But the what if game fed the fear.

He was forced to look at the work they did as a game. A deadly serious one, but a game nonetheless. How do we get them and not let them get us? All traditional mo-

ralities of right, wrong, truth, justice, and fairness were
challenged by the winning of this game.

McConnell did his best to concentrate on the canal,
but sitting there on ambush with nothing to do but watch
and wait, he could not keep Connie from creeping into
his thoughts. The idea of not knowing when he would
see her again made him feel terribly alone. He had almost confided in her about his fears and the terrible responsibility he felt when he was in the field, but he
couldn't bring himself to do so. She might have thought
him foolish or less than brave. A lot of guys were having
to put their butts on the line, and he was just one more.
And she might ask more questions about why he was
fighting and his personal commitment to the war. More
than that, he was afraid to do anything to disturb what
they had going between them.

These musings were brought up short by an urgent tug
on the signal line. He searched down the canal and in a
moment he saw the outline of a large sampan with four
people in it. He took the Stoner off safe and leaned toward
Watson in the center of his sampan.

"Get a flare up when I fire," he whispered. Since there
was a cease-fire, he signaled Cribbs to have Con hail the
sampan when it was directly in front of them.

"Ngu'ong lai! Ngu'ong lai! Lai day!"

Muzzle flashes winked from the front of the sampan
and were immediately answered by the concentrated fire
of the SEALs on full automatic fire. The hapless sampan
became a pyrotechnic magnet, absorbing the converging
streams of bright red tracers from the bank. Someone
listening from the village across the river might have
thought the few shots he heard were a signal to start up
a half dozen chain saws. But the villagers on this river
knew different. McConnell called a cease-fire as the riflemen quickly changed magazines. Watson's pop-flare
revealed a bullet-riddled sampan settling into the water
with at least two inert figures in it.

"Grenades in the water!" ordered McConnell. "Cribbs,
check 'em out!" Concussion grenades would kill or stun
anyone who managed to get over the side before the SEALs
opened fire.

"Fire in the hole" echoed across the canal and three splashes appeared around the drifting sampan.

Whump-whump! Whump!

Mini-geysers bracketed the battered hulk as Cribbs in the point sampan paddled out into the canal. Chief Johnson's boat drifted away from the bank to cover them.

"Big Brother, this is Peter Pan, we are hot, over."

"Roger, Peter Pan—I copy you hot. ETA your posit ten minutes, over."

"Roger, ten minutes, out."

McConnell watched Cribbs's sampan carefully circle their quarry, which by now floated semi-submerged with only the bow and stern rising above the surface. He noted with satisfaction that Watson and Reed had turned to face the back shore, which was now their area of responsibility. The pop-flare died as Cribbs's sampan made its way back to the shore. The little craft had a strange look to it, moving awkwardly and riding low in the stern. Then McConnell realized that the first two were paddling, while the third man lay back over the stern dragging an inert form.

"Hey, Boss!" Cribbs hissed across the short piece of water between them. "We got a live one."

They made the recovery easily as Smitty brought the boat into the bank near the ambush site. The captured VC was beginning to moan, but he was still unconscious. Barnett handcuffed him and put a piece of tape across his mouth before handing him up to the boat crew. They took in the claymores and tied the sampans in a line astern. Smitty had taken them halfway home when Chief Johnson came up to where McConnell was standing in the coxswain's flat.

"Sir, we got something special here. This guy's got a pistol on him and a document case strapped to his chest. The Kits are pretty excited. They say he's a big honcho."

They arrived back at the firebase just before dawn and took the prisoner to the holding area, a concrete slab with chain-link walls and roof. He was semiconscious by this time, although highly disoriented. The only visible sign of injury was a trickle of blood out of one of his ears.

McConnell assumed that he had gone over the side of his sampan when the challenge was issued. The concussion grenades had blown out his eardrums, but had otherwise only stunned him. Chief Johnson left Billy with him and sent for Doc Stinson. Johnson knew there would be little time for medical attention once the Provincial Interrogation Center detachment, or PIC Det, got to him. The nearest PIC was located in Binh Thuy, but the firebase had a local representative. The document case was turned over to the base PIC man for analysis, and the fire team headed for the showers and to breakfast. Later that morning Chief Johnson caught McConnell as he was finishing his after-action report.

"Sir, I just came from the G-2 office where they were going over the documents our man was carrying. The *Trung Uy* who heads the PIC Det is pretty sharp. He and the Army G-2 think the guy we got last night is province level or possibly a COSVN level cadre."

"COSVN level?"

"Central Office of Vietnam. The highest level in the VCI or Viet Cong Infrastructure. Sir, it's like one of them capturing a U.S. senator."

McConnell was elated at the news but did his best to be cool. "Pretty good night's work, huh, Chief?"

"Good night's work! Sir, in five tours, I've managed to take down a few district-level cadre. Last year Whiskey Platoon killed a VCI province chief. Nobody's ever captured a COSVN cadre."

"So they really think this guy is a biggie?"

"They're sending a special chopper for him this afternoon."

"Well, it was a lucky hit. And it was your idea to double back in the sampans, so you get the credit for this one. Where is he now?"

"They're keeping him under guard in the back room of the G-2 hootch until the chopper gets here. You'd think they were holding Uncle Ho."

"Good job, Chief. Now, unless there's something pressing—like the VC are coming through the wire—I'm going to crash." Ten minutes later he was sound asleep, even as the heat of the midday sun took the temperature in the hootch well up over one hundred degrees.

The following day a report from the Provincial Interrogation Center confirmed that they had captured a COSVN-level cadre. The report further indicated they would keep the platoon advised of any operational intelligence derived from the ongoing interrogation. France and the rest of the platoon arrived back at the firebase that evening.

"Christ, Jimbo, I leave you alone for a few days and you go out and capture a top dog VCI. You trying to make me look bad or something?" Through the bonhomie, McConnell detected that France was half serious and more than a little jealous.

"You go fishing in the right place and sometimes a big one will jump into the boat. Tell Rawls the tip about the boat was the key. We caught them moving downriver when they thought we were upriver. Nice to have you back, Dave."

"Everybody in Binh Thuy is talking about it. We'd have stayed another two days, but I thought I'd get the other squad back here and ready to go if the Interrogation Center comes up with any hot leads."

McConnell could imagine just how popular this decision to come back early had been with the guys in the other fire team. "Think he'll talk?"

"He will if he has any toenails left. Those VNs at the PIC could get your mother to confess that she's a virgin."

The information that was extracted from the captured VCI cadre allowed the platoon to launch a lucrative series of operations. Their recent capture had been a senior finance and resupply chief. He was persuaded to disclose the location of several arms caches and the names of several province and district level VCI cadre. The SEALs liked the arms caches because of the souvenir potential, but they were usually booby-trapped. The Kits could find most of the traps and they often took along an Army explosive ordnance disposal specialist for good measure. McConnell's squad had burst in on the hootch of a district recruiting chief and killed him as he ran out the back of his dwelling trying to escape. This was the highest and best use of the SEAL fire teams—responding to intelligence on specific targets.

Most of the time the VC felt secure in areas under their control and were complacent. No American or South Vietnamese army unit could move undetected at night like the SEAL units guided by the Kit Carson Scouts. Both fire teams were successful in the wake of this intelligence bonanza, but McConnell's team continued to fare better, and maintained bragging rights in the SEAL hootch. McConnell could tell this chaffed at France, but was partially offset by the overall success of *his* platoon. However, it noticeably rankled Rawls.

The operational plum that had eluded the platoon was the taking of a province level VC finance cadre whose name had been obtained from their talkative friend at the Interrogation Center. Finance cadre were at the top of the list of potential targets. As the tax collectors of the Viet Cong infrastructure, finance cadre were the least popular with the villagers and performed a most vital function in the VCI organization.

There was also the prospect of booty. One of the other platoons had recently killed a district level finance type and had found a few gold rings on him. The rumor mill had it that he had a lot more gold and South Vietnamese currency on him, and that the members of the SEAL platoon who got him were the richer for it. Given the poverty in the lower Delta, McConnell knew there was probably no serious money involved. But the idea of robbing from the VC was so very appealing to the SEALs that there was always more than a passing interest in VC tax collectors. Cribbs began calling this particular one Tran Van Cash, and it caught on with the rest of the platoon.

France's fire team had been unsuccessful on two different occasions in catching Tran Van Cash on a trail ambush. They knew from the intelligence reports that Cash lived in a small village in the northern part of the operating area, some twenty kilometers from the base. They even knew the location of his family's hootch, but an assault on the village or even a surprise parakeet operation was unlikely to succeed. The man was constantly on the move, and infrequently visited his home village. Their quarry had to know by now that he was a target. So would the local VC forces assigned to protect him, and they would be taking extra precautions. There was always the danger that the VC would use him to decoy the SEALs into a trap.

France had sent the Kits individually into neighboring villages to gather intelligence, but they couldn't come up with an informant who could predict where Tran Van Cash would be at a given time. One night France and his fire team made a night patrol that took them near their man's village. The purpose was to grab a farmer on the way out to his fields in the early morning and interrogate him. If Cash was in the village, he would call for Seawolves for cover and assault the VCI man's hootch. They arrived back at the base midmorning, having patrolled out to a main canal and been extracted by boat. They had captured their farmer, but Tran Van Cash was not there. McConnell felt the pursuit of Cash was becoming a little too intense and therefore dangerous. He said as much to France when he returned from the mission.

"Jimbo, they didn't even know we were there. On top of that, we know the money man will be there day after tomorrow, so we can plan a hit on him."

"How about the farmer?"

"We had to bring him out with us. The village will just think he was grabbed by the VC and pressed into service. We'll turn him loose after the operation."

"Look, Dave, I'm not sure I like this. You know that going back to the same place more than once is bad news. It seems like we're taking too many chances." What he meant was that France was taking too many chances.

"Hey, you got your VC biggie—let me have a shot at mine. I got an idea how we can get this guy. Come on into the hootch and I'll show you on the map."

France outlined on the map how he planned to get Tran Van Cash. His village was a small one on a secondary canal surrounded by rice patties. There was a wooded area about five hundred meters from the village also bordering the canal. Tran Van Cash, according to their informant, would be staying the night at his home village. He was to leave the following day, probably on the main trail leading away from the village on the side opposite the canal. France proposed taking the whole platoon in along the canal in sampans. They would hide the sampans in the wooded area and patrol on foot the short distance to the village. McConnell's fire team would set up outside the village near the canal and serve as a security element. They would also be in a position to attack should Tran Van Cash try to leave by the canal. France's fire team would set an ambush on the trail. The plan called for both fire teams to be in position before dawn and wait for their target to make the first move. If Cash failed to appear by midmorning, France's team would enter the village with McConnell and his men providing cover. France thought he could get a slick helo to stand by in case they needed emergency extraction. Otherwise they would go back down the canal by sampan with the Seawolves covering them until they got to Smitty and the boats.

"Well, what do you think?"

"I'm not sure. Do you really think this guy's worth the risk?" McConnell was buying time. He wanted to think about this and talk it over with Chief Johnson. Most of the risk was being shouldered by France and his team, so he felt a little sheepish about hesitating to endorse the plan.

"Jim, this guy's a province level VCI money man. We bag him along with your COSVN level cadre, and we will have totally fucked the VC IRS in An Xieun Province."

"Okay, Dave. But let me run it past the Chief first."

"Attaboy, but don't let Johnson talk you out of it. He can be an old woman sometimes. I'll get to work on the slick. You let Smitty know we'll need to have two boats ready."

To McConnell's surprise, the Chief shrugged his shoulders, and if he was opposed to the idea, he didn't let it show.

"Maybe it'll work. One thing's certain, the lieutenant

and Rawls are dead set on getting this guy. Our acting as
a security element will make it a little easier for them,
and I don't see that we're hanging it out too far.''

"I'm still a little goosey about going back to the same
place a second time, and I don't like being out in the
daytime in sampans.''

The Chief smiled at McConnell, like a scholarly cleric
would at a young acolyte who had just correctly recited a
difficult passage of scripture. "I'm not sure I like it much
either, sir, but they'll go with or without us. We probably
ought to tag along and back their play.'' So Foxtrot Platoon began to plan the details of their operation against
Tran Van Cash.

A Navy slick helicopter landed late the following day.
McConnell was impressed that France could get one on
such short notice, but the platoon had been very produc-
tive recently and they were getting a lot of cooperation
from Navy Binh Thuy. The two boats, each with a fire
team, left just after sundown. They had a long trip ahead
of them if they were to be in position by first light. The
trip in was an easy one for McConnell with France's fire
team as the point element. France was in the first of
Smitty's two boats on the long transit from the firebase
and led the line of sampans as they made the final paddle
in.

The moon was high and about half full—somewhat
dangerous, but easier to control the movement of a full
platoon. When they reached the wooded area near the
village, they established a security perimeter while the
rest of the platoon drug the sampans out of the canal and
hid them. France led the platoon to the position Mc-
Connell was to take, then took his fire team off in the
direction of the trail to the village. McConnell surveyed
the area. They were crouched behind a rice dike that was
one side of an irrigation ditch with another four-foot dike
just across the intervening ditch behind them and away
from the village. He noted with satisfaction that from this
position he could easily cover the canal and side of the
village facing him. He could also see the trail where
France and his team would be waiting. The saw grass on

both dikes was knee high and provided excellent concealment. McConnell placed his men along the dike facing the village and two men on the dike across the ditch as rear security.

"Hey, Chief," whispered McConnell, pausing beside Johnson, "Rawls and the Lieutenant seemed awful sure there would be no one out to work the paddies today. I hope they're right."

"They both been acting like they swallowed a canary the past few days. Maybe they know something."

"Great position, huh, Chief?"

"It'd take a company to dig us out of here. Let's hope there *isn't* one in that vill."

McConnell took his place along the dike and waited for dawn.

"Blueboy Two, this is Blueboy One. We're in position, over."

"Blueboy One, this is Two. Roger, we're standing by. It's your show, Dave, over."

"Blueboy One, roger out."

Dawn passed into morning and there was very little movement from the village. McConnell's mind began to race. Why was there so little activity? Was this a trap? Perhaps this was some kind of religious holiday and the villagers were not moving about. At eight o'clock, McConnell heard chanting, almost a wailing from within the village and soon there emerged a procession out onto the main trail. It was led by a middle-aged peasant and followed by two young men in black pajamas carrying a litter with a shrouded body. There were flowers draped across the litter and the young men, as if to guard their precious cargo, had rifles slung on their backs, barrels pointed down in deference to the deceased. A small procession of villagers followed the litter-bearers.

"I'll be damned," whispered McConnell to himself, "it's a funeral procession."

It happened very quickly. The trailing litter-bearer shouted something and dropped his end of the litter. The white bundle slid down the incline and rolled off the trail. He reached for his weapon, his elbow behind his head like he was trying to scratch the middle of his back. Concentrated fire from at least two automatic weapons ejected him from his place in the procession. The first porter just stood there and was killed on the spot. His face absorbed a solid burst of fire that unhinged one side of his jaw. He went to his knees, then fell backward onto the empty litter, his hands still grasping the two poles. The leader of the beleaguered procession began running up the trail while the villagers fled back to their homes, confused and terrified. McConnell heard Rawls shout, "Stop! *Dung lai,*" before a stream of tracers walked up the running man's back and pitched him forward onto the trail. Two SEALs raced up the trail after the fallen leader while France's Kits broke cover and quickly searched the litter-bearers.

"Jimmy, we're going into the vill and search his hootch. Get the Wolves up and sing out if you see anything, over."

"Roger, Dave, and watch your ass—we can't shoot while you're in there." France acknowledged and McConnell quickly snapped up the buggy whip antenna he had rigged earlier.

"John Henry, John Henry, this is Blueboy, over!"

"Roger, Blueboy, you are very weak but readable, do you copy, over."

"I copy, John Henry, we are hot—I repeat, we are hot. We need our friends, Priority three, over."

"This is John Henry. Copy you hot, Blueboy. Friends turning on a Priority three. ETA your posit fifteen minutes, over."

"Roger, one five minutes. Blueboy, out."

McConnell watched while France and his men quickly moved into the village on a skirmish line. The little hamlet swallowed them up and in a few minutes he heard some shouting and a scuffle. The Seawolves were overhead by the time France and his fire team reappeared. Their number had grown by one as they acquired a prisoner who was bound and blindfolded. He carried himself with some dignity, and McConnell assumed he was the village chief.

"Blueboy Two, this is One, over."

"Go ahead, One."

"You want to do a stay-behind? You might catch a support squad coming back here."

McConnell considered this for a moment. It made sense but he didn't like it. "Negative, One, we'll cover you until you're in the water, then we're out of here."

"Roger, Two."

France's fire team patrolled past their position and headed for the sampans. Once they were under way, McConnell's team followed. McConnell didn't like this. It was daylight and they were in a bad area. Nonetheless, they reached Smitty and the boats without incident. The Seawolves stayed with them until the two mother craft were back out on the Bhi Hap before they made a last low pass across the water and headed for home. McConnell finally began to relax and was joined by Chief Johnson in the coxswain's flat as they headed for the firebase.

"That was a strange setup, Chief. How did they know our man was going to be leading that funeral procession?"

"You still don't know, do you, sir?"

"Know what?" said McConnell, squaring around to face his Chief.

"I didn't know either. I suspected it, but I wasn't sure until I had a talk with Rawls. The stiff in the funeral—that was Tran Van Cash's wife. When those guys were here a few nights ago, they slipped into the vill and killed her. That's why they knew to set up on the funeral."

"You gotta be shitting me, Chief." But McConnell had only to look at Johnson to know he was serious. He turned and walked to the stern of the boat. He stood there for a while, watching the sampans dance in the boat's wake. It all added up, and it was the logical result of France's ambition and Rawls's cunning. The farmer they had brought out would have been branded as a traitor who did the killing and fled. They were right to take McConnell's squad in behind them, he admitted. If it had been a trap, they would have needed a security element to cover their withdrawal. But any shred of admiration for the ingenuity of the operation was overshadowed by the fact they had murdered the man's wife, knowing a good Buddhist could not stay away from the funeral of a spouse. Tran Van Cash probably figured that the nice-guy Americans would be incapable of orchestrating such a heinous chain of events, but he was wrong—dead wrong.

"You okay, sir?"

"Yeah, I'm okay, but that's the last time this fire team is going to be used as a condom when Rawls and Mr. France want to go out fucking. You get any more suspicions, you let me know—is that clear?"

"Aye, aye, sir."

For the next several days, McConnell kept to himself and, except for operational necessities, had little contact with the members of his fire team or the rest of the platoon. Several congratulatory messages had come in from up the chain of command regarding the elimination of Tran Van Cash. Foxtrot Platoon was becoming known as the hottest platoon in-country, but this only seemed to add to his depression. Some of his fire team speculated that their officer was in love, but most concluded that he was sulking about the conduct of the Cash operation. Late one evening he was reading *Stars and Stripes* on his bunk when France came in. He had a beer in each hand and handed one to McConnell. He dragged a folding chair away from the wall and sat down facing McConnell.

"Okay, Jim, what's wrong?"

"I think you know what's wrong."

"I probably do, but why don't you tell me anyway."

"For starters, Dave, I think the Tran Van Cash op stinks. First of all, to kill his wife and set up on the funeral was more than just wrong—it was murder. You did this and then you lied to me. I took my team in there not knowing the full story. Dave, I feel dirty and I feel betrayed."

"Okay, Ensign, I think I see where you're coming from. Now I want you to listen and listen hard. Taking out that guy's wife was probably the only way that we could get him. And we've since learned from the village chief we brought out that Cash's wife was VCI cadre, too. She was a card-carrying VC, Jim, just like her old man. These people are committed. They're not like us where the men go off to fight and the wife and kids sit at home on the sidelines. It would be very unusual for a guy at that level not to have his wife involved."

"You didn't know that before you killed her."

"No, I didn't. And it would have made no difference if she were clean. I wanted to get the sonuvabitch, and it was my call. That's why I didn't tell you the whole story. If this turns out wrong, or the press gets a hold of it and blows it up—it was my decision and mine alone. You won't have to say 'I was just following orders' if this thing gets nasty. You didn't know because I didn't tell you." McConnell felt some of his anger subside as he realized that France had tried to protect him.

"Dave, you know I probably wouldn't have gone if I had known."

"Maybe. Maybe that's another reason I didn't tell you. I needed you to cover us in case it was a trap. And there's nobody else I'd want covering me than you. You're good out there Jim, real good. And you're a decent guy. But don't tell me you'd have sat on your moral ass back here at the fire base, knowing I might really need your help." McConnell considered this and again he knew France had saved him from a difficult decision. He said nothing for a few moments while the Platoon Commander watched him and finished his beer.

"Okay, Dave, but I want your promise that good or bad, you'll level with me in the future."

"You got it." France got up to leave and paused at the door. "I'm not asking that you abandon your principles, but you have to see the VC for what they are. They have no reservations about murder, torture, extortion, or any other means to get their way. They're a rotten bunch of cock-suckers and they deserve to die. If we play by Queen's

Rules against these thugs, we're gonna come out second best.''

"But for Christ's sake, we don't want to be like them."

"No, but I didn't come over here to lose the game. We may not win the war, but this platoon is going to score some points." McConnell had nothing to offer so he said nothing. He still didn't agree with France, but he envied him his strong hatred of the enemy. It had to make the job easier. "By the way, I was going to send Rawls out on the chopper to Binh Thuy with the documents we took from Cash's hootch. Things are pretty slow right now, so why don't you do it? You could stay overnight and be back on the next day's mail run. Think you could do with an overnight in Binh Thuy?"

McConnell shook his head and smiled. "You win again, Dave."

Late that next morning McConnell arrived at Binh Thuy. He dropped off the document package at the PIC and headed for the hospital where he learned that Captain Connie Thompson had been transferred back to the States two days earlier. He was on his second scotch at the club when one of the nurses came up to him.

"I took Connie up to Saigon and saw her off," she said in an accusing tone. "She told me to mail this to you, but since you're here I can deliver it in person." She turned and hurried out of the bar while he opened the letter.

Dearest Jim,

I am writing this from the passenger terminal at Ton Son Nhut airbase. There's a C-141 scheduled out of here for Travis AFB, and I should be out of here in a few hours. I have orders to Madigan Army Hospital in Tacoma, Washington, and will report there after a month's leave. As you read this I'll probably be back in Boston.

My hasty exit from Vietnam was not the bravest thing I've ever done—very un-SEAL-like I'm sure. A few days after you left I began having some problems. There were several mornings I just couldn't get out of bed. It was like I weighed a thousand pounds. There was nothing physically wrong, I guess, but to get a drink of water took everything I had. The chief surgeon called it "extreme fatigue" and moved up my rotation date. I think a civilian doctor would have called it a breakdown of sorts. Whatever, I'm due for a "comprehensive examination" when I come back off leave. I can't wait to get home to see my parents. I do feel much better now that I'm really leaving, but a little ashamed. I guess in some ways, I too am running out on my buddies.

And you, Ensign, are certainly one of my buddies. I think I really care for you, Jim. I'd like to tell you that I do, but with my current frame of reference, I just don't know. My ability to care and feel and to love have been terribly distorted by this damn war. Emotional trauma the Army calls it. Jim, I just couldn't take it anymore.

I do know that you were so refreshing to be with. Maybe it's because you can do your job and keep your feelings out of it. You're different from the others, Jim. Everyone talked about how good you were in the field, but you. Maybe I hung around with the pilots too much, and they tended to blow their own horns a lot. I guess what I'm trying to say is that I don't really know how I feel about you or us or much else for that matter. I do know I have to get this war thing out of my system before I can be sure of anything. So where does that leave us? Tacoma is only a thousand miles or so north of San Diego, and you'll have some leave available when you get back in a few months, right? I do want to see you again and I hope you won't hold it against me for sneaking off like this.

Your friends say you're a good SEAL, Jim, but take extra-special care for me. I would like to have seen you again, but I truly think I was more than due for rotation.

See you back in The World.

Connie

He carefully folded the letter and placed it in the shirt pocket of his jungle greens.

"Jimbo my lad, back so soon." Benny, dressed in a dirty flight suit with large wet circles under the armpits, eased himself onto the next stool.

"Just in town on business for a day. Hoped to see Connie but no luck."

"That a 'Dear Jim' letter you just put away?"

"No, it wasn't," replied McConnell. Benny always seemed to be able to read him. "At least I don't think it was."

"You like her, Jimbo."

"I think so."

"Wanna do her a favor?"

"Sure."

"Stay alive."

"Stay alive?"

"Yeah, stay alive—as in, don't get dead. A few months after she came in-country she had a thing going with a Seawolf pilot. She coulda had me but she fell for my wingman. We were on a support mission over near Song Ong Doc. Fred's bird was hit by small-arms fire. His copilot brought the chopper back, and she was on duty when they brought him in. He held on for a few days, but there was never any hope he'd make it. Then there was this Special Forces captain last summer. He was a VN adviser at a firebase over near Ha Tien. A real John Wayne type and not a bad guy for a Green Beanie. He was in here to get some shrapnel dug out. They saw each other for a few days and then he buys the farm a week later in a rocket attack. Luck of the draw, I guess, but it'd do you and her both some good if you'd stay out of a body bag."

McConnell remained silent for a moment, digesting

what Benny had just told him. "She never said anything about it."

"Well, no shit, Sherlock," sighed Benny. "What's she supposed to say? 'Last two guys I fooled around with got smoked, so please be careful'? Bartender! How about getting me and this rocket scientist here a couple scotches, and make them doubles."

So McConnell and the burley helicopter pilot began serious work on two world-class hangovers.

Chapter Ten

THE COMPANY

THE PLATOON HAD about two and a half months left in the tour. Close enough for "when I get back" to be creeping into conversation, but still far enough in the future for the Foxtrot SEALs to realize they had plenty of war available to them. Following the Tran Van Cash affair, the two fire teams met with only moderate success. McConnell's group was becoming more cautious in the planning and execution of their operations. They were like a team with a comfortable lead in the third quarter. They played the game no less hard, but took fewer chances. While he was taking a more conservative approach to the missions, McConnell sensed that France was still pressing hard for operational success.

The VC operating in the area were now well aware of the SEAL activity, and they were far more wary than they had been when the platoon first arrived. This tended to lower the probability of a successful operation and increase the risk. There were reports that the VC had patrols and ambush teams out looking for them. Through all this, McConnell was becoming emotionally hardened to the task of leading combat patrols. The prospect of going home was still too distant for him to permit himself to think about. The day-to-day responsibility prevented him from looking past the next mission. But he was acquiring an appreciation for the second- and third-tour SEALs and a renewed awe of Chief Johnson, who would be completing his sixth.

When possible, the fire teams would react to intelligence brought in by informants or captured VC. This information allowed the selective targeting that had produced much of their operational success. Such information was not always available so they were often forced to go on patrol and set ambushes at night, trying to avoid a telltale pattern to their activity. On one such night patrol well north of the firebase, McConnell was leading his fire team back to the boat for pickup just as dawn was breaking. The first light was beginning to make amorphus gray forms of the moving line of SEALs and gave some definition and depth to the foliage. They were moving through an old rubber plantation. The fire team followed a path through the short saw grass, weaving among the orderly rows of scarred and neglected trees. They were in squad file and moving easily, gradually opening the intervals between them as the light grew stronger. McConnell searched his assigned sectors, straight ahead and to the left. Suddenly he felt, as much as heard, Watson, who was directly behind him, make a sudden move accompanied by a faint click as his M16 came off safe.

"Ambush right!" he cried as he fired into a tall stand of grass some ten meters from the trail. McConnell quickly picked up a dim form moving away from them and put it down with a quick burst. Reed and Barnett, just behind Watson and closest to the ambush site, opened fire. McConnell could find no more targets and there was no return fire, so he called for a cease-fire.

"Point element assault!" he yelled. Cribbs, Con, and Watson joined him on a skirmish line. Each fired short bursts or single rounds as they advanced on the enemy position. The rest of the fire team held position to cover them from counterattack.

"Oh, Jesus, no!" yelled Watson, who got there first. "Cease fire! Cease fire!"

McConnell joined him to find a young Vietnamese woman and her two daughters lying in the grass. All three were well shot, but one of the small girls was moaning. Cribbs approached them from the flank.

"Young kid up the way. He's had it."

They stood there for a few seconds staring at the three still forms. The moaning was becoming weaker, but the sound was still deafening. McConnell wanted to sit down and cry, but he knew that he didn't have that luxury.

"Defensive perimeter," he ordered. "Chief, get up here!" The SEALs moved quickly to take up positions in a rough circle around the three victims. Watson did not move.

"Jesus, Boss, I thought they were VC—they were on line . . ."

McConnell started to reply when Chief Johnson arrived.

"You on perimeter, Watson?"

"Yeah, Chief, but I—"

"No buts, sailor—move it." Watson started to reply, then moved off to his perimeter position. Johnson and Cribbs quickly checked the woman and the two children while McConnell radioed in. The woman and one of the girls were dead. The second child was breathing in uneven gasps and the moaning had almost stopped. She had been shot many times.

"She got a chance, Chief?"

"I doubt it—she's cut up pretty good. Sir, we got to move."

"I know. Give her some morphine and we'll clear out." Johnson quickly dug into one of his pouches and produced a small tube with a needle on it. The young girl made no reaction as he plunged it into her thigh.

"Squad file. Cribbs, point us out of here," McConnell called in a low voice. Cribbs and Con resumed the march down the trail and the others moved to follow.

"Hey, Boss, we just gonna leave 'em?" said Watson, falling in behind McConnell.

"They've had it, Watson. And there's nothing we can do anyway."

"But, sir, that one kid, she's still alive."

"Watson, that's it! We're on patrol and there's nothing we can do. Now do your job!" McConnell immediately felt bad for Watson as he turned his back on him and followed Cribbs up the trail. But that feeling was pushed aside by the immediate concern of getting the fire team

safely out of the area and back to the base. If there's a VC
unit in the area, where will they try to intercept us? Should
I shift to an alternate pickup point? We aren't too far from
the main canal. Has the shooting alerted a VC rocket team
and put Smitty's boat in danger?

The fire team had gathered in the front of the hootch
late that morning for the patrol debrief. McConnell was
thankful that neither France nor any of the rest of the platoon was there. He asked Smitty to skip the post-op meeting, and the boat officer, sensing there had been a problem
on the patrol, had not asked any questions. McConnell
laid his Stoner on his bunk and stripped off his web gear,
dropping it on the floor. He sat down on the ammo crate
he used as a night stand to collect himself before the debriefing. He had thought little about what had happened
at the rubber plantation until they were out of the field.
Since then he had thought about nothing else. He wanted
to be outraged and angry. He wanted to grieve for the
three poor souls they had killed and the little girl they left
to die. But strangely, the feeling wouldn't come—and that
really bothered him. He knew this was an accident in the
high-stakes, dangerous game they played, but accident or
not, he should feel something. They had just wiped out
an entire family! He made his way to the front of the
hootch, an emptiness inside him. The fire team waited
quietly there for him.

"Okay, officially we made no contact on this patrol.
What happened this morning couldn't be helped, but I
don't want the hassle and red tape that goes with reporting
that we killed some civilians. Nobody up the chain of
command wants it either, but there'll be an investigation
if I report it." McConnell, who had been standing with
Chief Johnson while he spoke, walked over and sat down
with the rest of the men.

"Now let's think about what happened. First of all, if
that had been a VC ambush squad, they'd have kicked our
ass. That is, they would have if Watson hadn't seen them.
Con, Cribbs, and I all missed them, but Watson didn't.
We've got to be more alert. We didn't come over here to
shoot women and kids but, shitty as it is, I'd rather have

this happen than have one of you hesitate and get half of us killed. The Rules of Engagement say that if we can't see they're armed, we're supposed to challenge them before we shoot, right? We don't have the luxury of always going by the rules. Not if we want to go home alive. That may not be by the book, but it's the way I want it done . . . Watson?''

"Yessir." He sat with his elbows on his knees looking down.

"If those had been four VC this morning, your reaction would have saved our asses, and everyone here would be trying to buy you a drink. You did the right thing out there. Okay?''

"Yessir," Watson repeated, still looking down at the floor.

"That's it. Mr. France and his team will be in the field tonight. We'll be back on the job tomorrow night.'' McConnell rose and headed back to his bunk. The rest of the group began to stir around the hootch. Cribbs slapped Watson on the back as he went to the reefer for a beer.

"You may have fired first, Watson, but you probably didn't kill anybody. Everyone knows what a shitty shot you are. Reed and I probably did the damage.''

"I'd agree with you," said Reed, "but the Boss was shooting, and we know he doesn't waste bullets.''

"Yuh know, the Boss is aw-fuckin' right," said Tex Barnett. "Most officers would go by the book an' put our ass on the line by yellin' *'Lah day—Lah day'* ever time we see a gook out there.''

"Civilians ought to know better than being out in a free-fire zone at night," added Bono.

"Yeah, but we can still get in trouble for shooting civilians," said Reed.

"No you can't," said Chief Johnson.

"Why not?" said Reed and Cribbs together.

"Don't you understand what Mr. McConnell said? He *ordered* you to disregard the Rules of Engagement. When in doubt, shoot first. He made a point of doing that, so if anything is ever said, we're off the hook. We're following his direct order—he's taking full responsibility.''

"Why would he do that, Chief?" asked Bono.

Johnson sighed in an exaggerated show of patience. "Because he's a good officer and he looks after his men."

Later that evening McConnell was sitting on his bunk in the hootch reworking the backpack harness that carried his radio. The SEALs were always modifying or working with their equipment and weapons, trying to find a better way to carry their gear or a faster way to reload. France had just left for a night patrol, and the rest of McConnell's team was asleep. He was about to turn in when Carl Belding rapped softly at the doorframe of his cubicle. McConnell looked up from his work as Belding dropped onto France's bunk. He was wearing his ever-present dirty flight suit. He looked tired and the dark red tips of his handlebar mustache dropped parenthetically around his mouth. As McConnell put the radio aside, he noticed that the pilot had two glasses in one hand while the other balanced a bottle of Johnny Walker Black on his thigh.

"Evening, Carl. What brings you slumming to the SEAL hootch?"

"Bad news, my friend. Bad news."

"What's wrong, Carl?" Was it France or Smitty? They hadn't been gone that long!

"Benny's dead, Jim. He bought the farm up near Chau Duc. He'd been overdue since yesterday from a routine transit flight." McConnell was stunned. He flashed on images of Benny holding forth at the club in Binh Thuy or smiling from behind his lip microphone in the seat of his chopper.

"You sure?"

"They found them this morning. His bird crashed in some dense canopy a few klicks off the Mekong River. Charlie had already been there and stripped the bodies and the chopper. The three of them were in shallow graves near the crash. The copilot and crewman hadn't been in-country more than three weeks."

McConnell started to speak but couldn't. The thought of Benny's broken body being recovered from wet, clinging Delta mud sent a shudder through him. He had caused death, but this was the first time someone close to him had been killed. The war abruptly took on a different meaning. It had just claimed someone he knew and cared for. A wave of nausea swept over him as Belding handed him a tumbler of scotch.

"Did they get out?" McConnell asked hoarsely as the liquor seared his throat.

"I don't think so. They didn't burn, though. It looked like Benny was in auto-rotation and tried to drop it in tail first. They just went in too hard. He was one of the best and I'll bet he fought it all the way in."

"When was he due to go home?"

"Exactly eight days and a wake-up."

"Carl, if Israel is full of guys like Benny, those Arabs don't have a chance."

"You got that right." A moment of silence passed between them. "Warm scotch doesn't cut it, Jim—we need some ice."

McConnell and Belding retired to a table at the front of the hootch and charged their glasses with ice and more scotch. They talked about Benny, and about the war and going home and more about Benny. Chief Johnson found both of them slumped over the table at dawn. He put his platoon officer to bed and then woke the pilot. It wasn't like Mr. McConnell to drink when they were the on-call fire team. He was beginning to worry about him.

The two fire teams began ranging with greater frequency into the areas to the north and east of Firebase Delta. They still worked the Nam Can forest, but the specter of VC ambush teams and the dense foliage that made air support difficult caused them to avoid the area unless they had specific intelligence on a solid target. When working north of the base, they would typically go in by boat at night and patrol on foot to the target to be in position for a dawn strike. The Seawolves or the Black Ponies were usually available to escort them and the boat back to a safe area the next day. Such was the case one morning after an unsuccessful attempt to ambush a VCI proselytizing cadre. They were returning to the pickup point and wanted to be out of the field as soon as possible. It had rained most of the night, and the day broke with a high overcast, promising not to be too warm but very humid. They had been walking for about an hour and Con estimated another thirty minutes on the trail to the pickup point. They were wet and tired, and anxious to finish logging another combat patrol, even though they had nothing to show for it.

The trail they were following wound in a southerly direction through a sparsely wooded area. Trees of any size had been taken long ago and the new growth had to compete with the low scrub and nipa palm. Cribbs and Con carefully skirted the rice fields they came to and avoided the occasional hootches they encountered. As always, when moving in hostile territory, it was a compromise between trying to move quickly and yet be as careful as possible. They were traveling at their normal daylight patrol interval of five to seven meters. McConnell could clearly see both Con and Cribbs moving in front of him. The trail was about to take them into a tree line when both men froze in a low, alert crouch. McConnell stopped and signaled the rest of the squad to a halt.

He watched his two point men carefully. They were motionless and intense, like two pointers, and he knew they had seen something they didn't like. Then Con dived off the trail into the tall grass, and a wide-eyed Cribbs gave him a frantic *many bad guys coming* signal and did the same. McConnell signaled *hasty ambush, right side* to Watson. The word was passed back, and the squad fell off to the right of the trail like a row of dominos. McConnell's heart began to race with anticipation. Cribbs seldom got excited like this in the field.

McConnell waited and in a few moments he saw the reason for Cribbs's concern. One, two, three, make it four NVA soldiers were cautiously making their way toward them on the trail. All were dressed in the dung-colored field uniforms of the North Vietnamese Army and carried AK-47 rifles. All but the first man were wearing the jungle pith-type helmets and carried field packs. These were not regional VC guerrillas. They were Ho Chi Minh's varsity troops, and they moved down the trail like professional soldiers. McConnell was thankful that his point men had seen them first, and he hoped they would pass without spotting them. He took his Stoner off safe and hunkered lower into the grass as they passed. McConnell covered them as they moved away from his position, and was ready when they made their move.

The last member of the file saw one of the SEALs in hiding and shouted a warning. He turned to his left and leveled his weapon, but that was as far as he got. McConnell had an excellent angle and the line of four NVA appeared over his long barrel like they were walking shoulder to shoulder. They were no more than fifteen meters away. Their interval was too close and they all tried to turn and shoot from a standing position. His first rounds caught the last man between the shoulder blades. His second shot, a fifteen-round burst, took the other three, although most of the fire team would later say that it was all one long burst. At least two other SEALs also took them under fire. The result was a thorough chewing of the four NVA troopers. Weapons, helmets, loose equipment, and limbs flailed as they vibrated from the impact of the rounds and fell to the ground.

"Perimeter!" yelled McConnell as he raced to the fallen men. He did not have to look back down the trail to know Cribbs and Con would be covering him. He arrived there just ahead of Chief Johnson and was greeted by the usual moaning and gurgling of the near dead. It was amazing, thought McConnell, how many times you could hole one of these guys and they refused to die. And sometimes it took only one round.

"Get the Wolves up quick, sir," said Johnson. "These guys probably aren't alone." McConnell reached Smitty and requested air support while Johnson and Bono made a quick check of the bodies.

"Hey, Bones," called Reed from the perimeter, "one of them dude's got a pistol. Grab it for me."

"Leave it, Bono!" cut in Johnson. "Sir, I don't like this, we gotta—"

The Chief was cut short by some yelling in Vietnamese from the tree line just ahead of them. Then a whistle sounded and a burst of automatic weapon fire came from their flank to the left of the trail. The incoming rounds

were high but the snapping sound could be clearly heard
as they passed overhead.

"Rear security point out and leapfrog!" yelled Mc-
Connell. Chief Johnson and Bono bolted back up the trail
in retreat, closely followed by Billy, Barnett, and Reed.
McConnell noted Watson's position to his right as he
looked for the enemy to his front. He then moved quickly
to the cover of some low brush some five meters to the
left of the trail. An NVA soldier darted toward them across
an open area near the trail. Several automatic weapons
opened up from the tree line to cover him. McConnell
raised his weapon, but the man's feet ran out from under
him while his upper torso stopped like he was clotheslined
about the neck. *Good shooting* Cribbs, thought Mc-
Connell. The AK-47 had tremendous stopping power at
close range and, next to McConnell, Cribbs was the best
shot on the fire team.

"Yo! On the point!" came a yell from the Chief,
some forty meters behind them. McConnell whistled
and the point element began to fall back. Con and
Cribbs came ripping past him while he and Watson fired
two- and three-round bursts sparingly to cover them.
When they had passed, he signaled Watson to move out
behind them. Watson started up the trail and McConnell
moved to follow, when the young rifleman abruptly slid
to a stop on his knees and pointed his M16 right at
McConnell.

For a crazy fraction of a second, McConnell thought
Watson was going to shoot him. As the rounds tore past
him, a quick, cold fear replaced his confusion. He leaped
away from Watson's line of fire and came around shooting.
Watson had knocked one of them down and he stitched
another NVA soldier across the chest. Two others dove for
cover in the tall grass. If Watson hadn't picked them up,
they would have killed both SEALs.

"Go!" shouted McConnell and he followed Watson up
the trail on a dead run. He saw Chief Johnson on one side
of the trail and noted that Reed had the M60 in a well-
concealed position on the other. Watson followed Con and
Cribbs to the next setup while McConnell paused with the
rear element.

"Whadda you think, Chief?" he gasped.

"Infantry company. That was their point element we rolled up. We gotta break contact, sir. They pin us down and flank us, and it's all over."

"I'll whistle, Chief."

"Get those fucking birds up, sir. We're gonna need 'em."

"Right, Chief," called McConnell as he ran down the trail. It was the first time he remembered hearing Chief Johnson swear, and he did not find it reassuring. Cribbs had selected the site for their leg of the leapfrog and he pointed where he wanted McConnell to be. It was his call. McConnell whistled to Chief Johnson, signaling that they were in position, just as a brisk exchange began between the Chief's group and the oncoming NVA.

"Ghost Rider, this is Whiskey Two Seven, you got my birds, over?"

"About thirty minutes, Two Seven—they have other traffic."

"Ghost Rider, I'm Priority Two and I need help. Please expedite, over."

"Roger, Two Seven, wait, out."

Smitty called back with a twenty-minute Seawolf ETA as Barnett led the Chief's element past their position. They leapfrogged three more times, but were unable to break contact. The skill of the SEALs made it costly for the NVA chasing them, but the flankers—first on one side, then the other—kept pace and threatened to surround them. They could keep this up as long as they didn't run out of ammunition or a SEAL didn't get hit. McConnell fought to control the growing lump of fear in his stomach, which was especially bad as he waited for Chief Johnson's element to break away and pull back through his position in the retreat. "What if" and where were those goddamn Seawolves! On the next leg, McConnell ran out of the cover of the wooded area and into a field of rice paddies.

Chief Johnson and his four men had taken a position across the first paddy behind the cover of a rice dike, some thirty meters into the open area. McConnell followed Cribbs and the other two splashing across the first paddy.

They scrambled over the dike and into the next paddy as they made for the second rice dike. Johnson and his men were in good position to cover them, but they needed to open the distance between themselves and the woods. The NVA would hesitate to follow them out into the open where they would be vulnerable to air strikes. McConnell dove over the second dike to temporary safety just behind Cribbs, Con, and Watson.

"Oh, Jesus, I'm hit, Boss! I'm hit!" McConnell jumped past Con to Watson's side. He pushed the wounded man's hands away from his thigh and ripped his trousers with his K-bar. The round had grazed him and just sliced through the muscle on the outside of his thigh. There was a lot of blood, but it was not serious and, hopefully, not disabling. He needed Watson and they didn't have much time.

"Watson, listen to me!" Getting no response, he grabbed him by the front of his shirt and shook him, "Goddammit, listen to me!" Watson looked up from his wounded leg at McConnell.

"Sir?"

"It's gonna hurt, but it's gonna be okay! We gotta cover the others, and I need you on line—can you do it?"

"I can do it, Boss." And with that he rolled over and recovered his weapon. He changed magazines, then took a position on the dike.

McConnell saw that Con and Cribbs were in position as he whistled to Chief Johnson. Time was working against them because an increasing number of the NVA were coming to the edge of the rice field and taking firing positions. Two geysers erupted bracketing Johnson's element and their protective dike. The water and mud absorbed most of the force of the hand grenades, but hastened the need for them to fall back. McConnell and his group began to return fire. He noted with satisfaction that Watson had laid out his 40mm grenades. Small-arms fire might keep their heads down, but the air bursts of the forty mike-mike detonating in the trees over their heads could inflict some casualties.

When the point element began firing, Chief Johnson made his move, sending Reed, Bono, and Billy running across the open paddy to McConnell's dike. While they ran, Johnson and Barnett began throwing grenades into the trees. This was a gutsy call by the Chief, thought McConnell. It would take more time, but fewer men running left more men to provide cover. The three sprinters were two thirds of the way across the forty-meter patty when Bono pitched forward facedown in the ankle-deep water. Reed and Billy reached the dike some fifteen meters down from McConnell and dove over the four-foot earthen barrier to safety.

"Boss! Help me, Boss!" McConnell peeked over the dike and saw his fallen man. He was some ten meters from the dike in front of Reed's position. He was now on his back in the ankle-deep water and his left leg was bent at an odd angle at the knee. The NVA fire was becoming intense, and he knew the odds of sending a man after Bono were not good.

"Ray, can you hear me!"

"Yes, sir."

"Can you move at all?" No response. "Can you move, Bones?"

"I'm sorry, Boss. My legs won't move!" McConnell again looked over the dike. Bono was up on one elbow, trying to push himself along with his arms. The side of his face, his nose, and one ear were packed with mud. There were splashes in the water around him from the incoming rounds.

"Bono!"

"Sir?"

"Get down and don't move! Stay as low as you can and we'll get some help, okay?"

"Mr. McConnell, don't leave me!"

"No way, Bones. We'll have you out of there in a minute. Just keep down!" He looked again at Bono, now flat on his back like he was floating in a swimming pool. He tilted his head back at McConnell and raised his hand from the water in a thumbs-up sign.

Oh sweet Jesus, thought McConnell as he slid down behind the dike. We're fucked. We're totally fucked! How am I going to get the Chief and Barnett across that rice patty? The NVA will make a try for us soon. I can't leave

Bono—he's counting on me. But I'll probably lose a man if I send one back for him. He sat there for a moment in complete despair, almost in tears. He might have remained that way indefinitely had not a very sweet sound reached his ears. It was faint but steadily growing louder. It was the unmistakable rhythmic *fump-fump-fump* of inbound helicopters.

"Seawolf! Seawolf! This is Whiskey Two Seven, how copy, over!"

"Roger, Two Seven, this is Seawolf Leader. Read you loud and clear, over." McConnell slumped against the dike, tenderly cradling the handset in gratitude as if it, by itself, had brought him deliverance.

"Boss!" yelled Reed. "The Chief's puttin' out smoke." McConnell came out of his reverie and snatched a look over the dike. Johnson had popped smoke grenades on either side of his position. There was no breeze so the thick red smoke seemed to hover around the canisters on top of the Chief's rice dike and spilled over into the paddies on either side. McConnell ducked his head just as an enemy round spattered mud on the top of the dike. More of the NVA were digging in along the edge of the rice field, and their riflemen were looking for them.

"Seawolf Leader, this is Whiskey Two Seven. I need help Priority One—I say again, Priority One. You see us yet, over?" This was McConnell's first Priority One. It meant that the team on the ground had been wounded or would immediately sustain casualties unless they received help. Both were true in this case.

"Negative, Two Seven—mark your position, over." McConnell fumbled with his pencil flare launcher and on the second try sent the small double red cluster skyward.

"Okay, Two Seven, we have you. What can we do, over?"

"Seawolf Leader, you have my smoke, over?"

"Roger, Two Seven, red smoke."

"Okay, Leader, give me everything you have on one run. Target is the edge of woods along rice paddy, one-eight-zero and thirty meters from my smoke, over."

"Roger, Two Seven, one-eight-zero, thirty meters from red smoke. All ordnance, one run, over."

"That's a roger, Carl. Give us a good one—they're really on our ass."

"You got it, Two Seven—break, Seawolf Trail, you copy, over?"

"I copy, Leader. We'll follow and cover you. Trail, out." McConnell watched the two gunships bank around to the east seeking a position to begin their firing runs.

"Reed! Get ready to cover them!" The big machine gunner looked down the dike toward McConnell and nodded. Cribbs and Watson put in fresh magazines.

"How many grenades you got left, Watson?"

"Six, Boss."

"Keep 'em in the trees behind the Chief."

"Yes, sir."

"You okay, buddy?"

"Hurts like hell, but you can count on me." McConnell gripped his shoulder as he scuttled past him to a new position on the dike. He peered over the mud barrier and quickly saw that the Chief and Barnett were still pressed against their dike. A rippling *whoosh-whoosh-whoosh-whoosh* announced the beginning of the lead gunship's firing run. McConnell joined the other SEALs shooting into the woods. As the rockets tore into the NVA position, Chief Johnson and Barnett began their dash across the rice paddy to their comrades. Johnson carried both men's weapons while Barnett ran ahead for Bono. The Texan's long strides marked an even succession of splashes toward the downed SEAL like a line of tracers. The shorter Johnson churned along not far behind. Barnett grabbed Bono by the front of the shirt with both hands in midstride and kept running. Both men and the inert Bono scrambled over the dike just as the rockets from the trail Seawolf hit the enemy positions. At least for the moment, the fire team was safe.

The two elements of McConnell's fire team regrouped behind the security of the second rice dike. The Seawolves had no more rockets but they maintained a high orbit as the door gunners took the NVA positions under fire. Cribbs put a field dressing on Watson while Reed and Chief Johnson tended Bono.

"We need a dust-off, sir," called Johnson, "and soon!"

"Right, Chief. How you fixed for ammo?"

"Four 40mm grenades and Reed has about thirty rounds. The rest of us maybe fifty each." The true professional, thought McConnell. Probably the first thing he did when he came over the dike was to get a bullet count and redistribute ammunition. Cribbs, Watson, and himself had less than a hundred rounds between them and no grenades. The Kits had no ammo left. Even Chief Johnson's threats could not make them learn fire discipline. It was full automatic fire each time they replaced a new magazine. They had probably been empty before the fire team reached the rice paddies.

"Seawolf Leader, this is Two Seven. I need a dust off and a slick, over."

"Roger, Two Seven. Neither one available right now, but Black Ponies will be on station in zero five minutes. My wingman and I will take you out in two lifts, over."

"Thanks, Leader. Please expedite as my wounded critical. Two Seven, out." McConnell briefed his men on the extraction by the Seawolves. Chief Johnson would take Bono and his group out on the first lift. McConnell began to think that the worst was behind them when the first mortar round arrived. It landed in the middle of the rice paddy behind them and showered them with water and mud. This meant that their NVA infantry company had a heavy weapons platoon with field mortars.

"Carl, we got a problem here. They're ranging us with mortar fire, over."

"I copy, Two Seven. Our friends should be here any time." Another mortar round took out a section of the dike fifteen meters on the other side of Chief Johnson. It would take several more rounds to tamp the base plate of the mortar into the ground before the NVA could accurately spot the fall of the shot onto the SEALs' position. McConnell thought they were doing a pretty good job with their initial salvos.

"Whiskey Two Seven, this is Black Pony Zero Three,

over." McConnell grabbed the handset as he saw the section of inbound OV-10s off in the distance. They looked like little black X's.

"Black Pony, this is Two Seven, do you see us, over?"

"Negative, Two Seven, we have the gunships but not you. Request you pop smoke, over." McConnell tossed two purple smoke grenades on either side of the SEALs' position.

"Smoke out, Black Pony."

"Roger your purple smoke, Two Seven. What's your traffic, over?" McConnell gave the Ponies instructions for their firing run and ensured that the Seawolves were in position to come in and extract them. When the Ponies began their firing run, Belding would send his wingman in for half the fire team while he provided cover with his door gunner.

"Two Seven, this is Pony Zero Three Lead rolling in."

"Roger, Pony Lead, continue." The OV-10s didn't really make a firing run in the traditional sense. They flew over the target at four thousand feet, rolled upside down, and pulled through to a near vertical dive. It was from this stable, one o'clock position they sent their Zuni rockets into the trees near the rice field. The *whoosh* of the incoming rockets was complemented by the beating of rotor blades as the first Seawolf came in for extraction. He came in low from the north and popped up to fifty feet at the last possible second, dropping the tail of the helo almost into the paddy as he braked to a hover behind the SEALs' dike. Belding in the second bird came in a little higher and to one side, crabbing slightly to give his door gunner a field of fire. Barnett carried Bono to the chopper and handed him up to a crewman who jerked him aboard by the collar of his jungle shirt. Then he, Reed, Billy, and Chief Johnson in turn vaulted into the crowded cabin of the Huey. Billy slipped and fell, straddling the skid as the helo rolled half on its side and cleared off back to the north. He might have fallen farther had not Reed grabbed him by his web harness and hoisted him back into the retreating bird. McConnell scarcely heard the rattling of the Seawolf door gunners or the impact of the Zunis as the SEALs expended the last of their ammunition in covering the extraction.

"Fifty-one cal! I got fifty-one cal fire!" The voice of Carl Belding's wingman flying the trail Seawolf reflected all the terror that Seawolf pilots had for fifty-one caliber ground fire. It was deadly to the fragile, low-flying helos. They had been very lucky to have made the first half of the extraction and not lost one or both gunships.

"I copy, Trail, I copy—are you hit, over?" Belding's voice was that of a parent trying to calm an excited child.

"Negative, Leader! They fired under us as we pulled off the extraction, over."

"Understood, Trail—break. Whiskey Two Seven, how're you doing, over?"

McConnell knew what Belding had to say when he keyed his handset. It would be suicide to come back for them with the fifty-one waiting. "We're dry, Leader, and we got more incoming mortars. Any bright ideas, Carl?"

"Negative, Two Seven. We'll hang around for a while and look for an opening, over."

McConnell huddled against the dike and braced himself as a mortar round dropped on the other side of it, harmlessly but very close. Watson and Con stared at him, waiting for him to tell them what to do. Cribbs drew his 9mm pistol and chambered a round. He met McConnell's eyes and shrugged—he would take it as it came. Inside McConnell, fear, like a terminal case of heartburn, mounted as he searched for a way out. They could work their way along the dike but he was sure the NVA would soon have men on the flanks. Their best bet was probably to run for it. It was a terrifyingly long way to the next dike, waiting for a bullet to crash into your spine. And he wasn't sure Watson could run. Oh God, what am I gonna do?

"Seawolf Leader, this is Pony Zero Three. I have a section of fast movers with eight five-hundred-pounders each. Will that solve your problem, over?"

"Roger, Zero Three, it might work. Our guys are pretty

close so they'll have to lay those eggs just right. You copy, Two Seven?''

"It's our best shot, Carl," replied McConnell. "Bring on the artillery." McConnell tossed out his last smoke grenade and instructed the other three men to dig in as the jets made their run. McConnell caught a glimpse of the two F-4 Phantoms as they rolled in on the enemy position. He was surprised how low they were. He heard the aircraft roar over and for a fraction of a second, he thought nothing was going to happen. Then the five-hundred-pound drag bombs marched along the edge of the rice field. *Boom-boom-boom*-BOOM-BOOM-BOOM-*boom-boom!* Each detonation was like a punch in the kidneys. McConnell heard the beat of an incoming helicopter along with the roar of the second F-4 before his string of bombs hit. He looked up and saw Belding's chopper walking on its tail across the paddy. The bird leveled in a hover a few meters from them and they scrambled aboard. There was no second gunship flying cover. If the fifty-one was still operating, Belding wasn't going to risk his wingman. McConnell, from his prone position in the helo, felt the pitch and acceleration of the metal deck against his face as the gunship clawed its way back across the rice paddies and out of danger. He held his breath, waiting for the big fifty-one caliber slugs to tear into the machine, but they extracted without being fired on. When he opened his eyes, he saw a smeared, bright red blood trail across the floor of the chopper. At the end of the red streak was a smiling SEAL named Watson. Part of the grimace was from the pain, but mostly it was the genuine smile of a nineteen-year-old boy who just realized he was not going to die.

McConnell propped himself up against the rear bulkhead of the cabin. The sudden release from the tension and fear left him with a familiar euphoric, seminauseous feeling. He had lost the handset to his radio in the mad scramble to board the helicopter, and it now trailed behind him at the end of its spring-coiled phone cord. Cribbs picked up the handset and keyed the transmit button.

"Hey, Mr. Belding?" The pilot turned in his seat to

look back at Cribbs. "You want me to come up there and give you a blow-job right now, or you wanna wait 'til we get back to the base?"

Cribbs couldn't know that his remark was being amplified and retransmitted across the Delta. Back at the firebase, a huge cheer went up from the crowd gathered around the command post loudspeaker, where half the base anxiously listened for word of the trapped SEALs.

Chapter Eleven

STANDING DOWN

IT HAD BEEN two days since their escape from the rice field. Cribbs called it the immaculate extraction. The fire team was two men short and badly shaken. Watson and Bono had been medivaced to Binh Thuy shortly after their rescue from the NVA company—or what was left of the company. An ARVN battalion had made a sweep of the area the next day and found the shallow graves of some twenty of the enemy. There were equipment and blood trails, indicating many wounded. A regular NVA company was too disciplined to leave equipment and some of their dead behind unless they were very badly mauled.

The report from the Third Surgical Hospital was that Watson would mend, but he would be out of the field for as long as three weeks. Bono was far more serious and had already been air-lifted to the Yokosuka Naval Hospital. He had taken a round in his right rear cheek, and the bullet had lodged in his pelvis after doing some damage to the socket of his right leg. A "hitter in the shitter," as he described it to Watson prior to his being flown to Japan. It was the kind of wound that would take a while to determine the extent of the injury and the extent, if any, of permanent damage. McConnell had talked with Watson by radiophone, and he had reported that Bono was in good spirits but a lot of pain.

McConnell had removed the fire team from operational

status for a week—they were standing down. This decision had not been well received by his platoon commander.

"Jim, I know you had a rough time and you guys need a few days off, but a whole week?"

"It was more than just a rough day at the office. I have two men wounded, one seriously. We were lucky they didn't roll all of us up."

"Yeah, I know, but you gotta climb back on that horse— the sooner the better. You know, we only have about six more weeks of uptime on the deployment."

"Look, Dave, my guys have pulled their weight on this deployment. Unless that's a direct order—no, even if it *is* a direct order, we're not going out until I think we're ready, and right now, I say it's a week."

"We got a job to do, Ensign."

"And we also got to look out for these guys. How many VC scalps are you willing to trade for one of our men?"

France had backed off, but his constant push for operational results and KIAs was getting to McConnell. Part of it, he admitted to himself, was his own fear. Every time he thought about going back to the field, he felt the same paralyzing, burning lump in his stomach that he had felt when he was huddled with his men against that rice dike— when he felt that they had no chance of getting out. If he allowed the thought to persist, he would begin to sweat and start shaking. Chief Johnson was solidly behind him on this decision, but McConnell suspected that it was more in deference to his need for a break than for the rest of the men. What preyed on McConnell's mind was not so much that he was afraid, but that he had almost allowed the fear to consume him. He knew he had lost it for a moment in the rice paddies, unable to think or move. He had just managed to overcome it in time and do his job. Now he was haunted by the prospect that the next time he might freeze up completely.

The only positive aspect of this recent brush with death was the superb performance of his men. He felt a glow of pride as he recalled just how great they had been. The veterans had been sturdy, solid professionals during the running firefight, and the new guys were nothing short of heroic. Watson's courage after he had been wounded and

Bono's grit as he lay helpless in that rice patty were heroic beyond anything McConnell could have imagined from his frog school classmates. And Barnett—he always seemed to be at the right place and do the right thing. He was ashamed that he had been so consumed by fear while they had performed with such valor.

McConnell remembered seeing the movie *The Bridges of Toko-ri* when he was in high school. At the end of the movie, an admiral talking about the bravery of his carrier pilots said, "Where do we find such men?" McConnell felt much the same way about his SEALs. Where do these guys come from? Where do they find the courage to follow me, time after time, into this muddy and dangerous mangrove wilderness? Why did they do it—why did they volunteer? You didn't have to be a draft dodger to avoid the shooting part of this war. They could all be safely aboard ship, probably well away from the Tonkin Gulf and Vietnam. These men weren't superpatriots and none of them had a commitment to the freedom of South Vietnam. He contemplated this as he lay on his bunk waiting for mail call, moving as little as possible in deference to the heat of the afternoon.

"Mail call! Hey, gang, looks like th' Boss got a letter from that foxy Army nurse. Here yuh go, sir." Barnett made his way out of the cubicle and began passing out mail to the rest of the platoon. Connie had written him from home and a couple of times from her new assignment in Tacoma. She had remained home for only a week before reporting back for duty. Her letter from Boston indicated that while she was glad to be home, she had difficulty relating to her parents and civilian friends. Being back in uniform at an Army hospital had been "comfortable but a little depressing." McConnell reclined on his bunk, and began to read Connie's letter.

My Dear Jim,

I am writing you from the intensive-care ward here at Madigan Hospital. Since I am senior and the old lady of the shift, I spend most of my time in the supervisor's office. I have a whole flock of second lieutenants, so there is very little real work for me to do. They all think I'm special because I've been "over there." I tell them that medicine is medicine and it's not all that different, but we all know it's not the same. When I make rounds, I see some of these kids in here with shrapnel and bullet wounds, and I feel like I'm right back there. Sometimes I have to step outside and see my breath in the cold winter air to break the feeling.

I heard about Benny and I'm so sorry. Jim, I know how much you liked him. We all did, but it must have been especially hard on you. That dear sweet bozo was a very special person. Somehow I was not surprised. I remember the other pilots saying he flew hard and very close to the edge. Whenever someone I know gets hurt of killed over there, a part of me is wounded or dies with them. Dear God, will it never end?

I have something to tell you and it's not an easy thing to say. I'd considered waiting until you get back in a few months, but you deserve my honesty. And it would hurt us both if you didn't hear this from me. Jim, I'm seeing someone here, and more than that, I think it's serious. He's a physician—actually, a patient. Bob was at a field hospital up in I-Corps for a year and saw casualties from the main force fighting right after Tet. He's a very caring and sensitive man, and what he saw there scarred him deeply. He's been unable to practice medicine since. We began having long talks about the war and our feelings about it. I've been able to help him and he's been good for me. Bob really needs me, Jim, and right now, that's very important to me—it's what I need. I hope you can understand this—the needing, I mean. You're such a strong person and I know it must be difficult for you to relate to this. I also know there should be better common ground for a relationship than a shared trauma from Vietnam, but I only feel really at peace when I'm with him. Jim, I think about you daily, and I pray for your safe return. A part of me is with you. I'm sorry it can't be more than that and I hope you'll forgive me.

I can't think of anything else to say. I guess these few lines have taken all the courage and emotional reserve

I have for the moment. I have one last favor to ask of you—please don't write to me until you get back. It's weak and silly on my part, but I just can't handle mail from Vietnam anymore, not even from you.

I know you will take care of your men, but please take care of yourself. This war doesn't deserve any more victims, least of all a good person like you. My thoughts are with you.

Your friend,

Connie

He read the letter again and then carefully folded it, placing it in his stationery box.

She doesn't think I need her, thought McConnell. Christ Almighty! Do I have to be some sort of casualty to need her? Now she's fallen for some doctor who saw a few shrapnel wounds and went screwy.

McConnell got to his feet and looked out the window of the small room. Two Vietnamese women squatted in the dust between the hootches, arguing and swatting flies. The initial shock of Connie's letter wore off and he reflected on their time together. Why didn't I tell her how important she is to me—that in my own way, I do need her? But I have responsibilities, and goddammit, I just can't let up. I have to lead these men. I simply can't afford the luxury of being weak or soft—or, he conceded, maybe even needed. I'm scared out there—I'm scared and I want to go home. But I can't go home, until Foxtrot Platoon goes home.

He pulled on a T-shirt and slid into his shower shoes, then headed out of the hootch and into the humid afternoon heat. Vietnamese and Americans alike moved slowly around the base, but only the Americans sweated. McConnell walked around the base perimeter, occasionally pausing to chat with men who were lounging on top of bunkers or in the mortar pits. A few of the more ambitious filled sandbags. McConnell was well known around the base and treated with respect. Eventually he found himself down on the dock. He hoped and half expected to find

Smitty there, but the two SEAL boats rested quietly at their moorings. He was about to walk back to the hootch when he saw a familiar shape at the end of the dock. The man was fishing with his back to McConnell, but he had seen too much of that backside not to recognize Cribbs.

"Catching anything?" said McConnell, easing himself down on an ammo box not far from where Cribbs sat with his feet hanging over the dock with his ankles in the water.

"Hi, Boss! Had a couple of bites, but nothin' to show for it. If I really wanted some fish I'd take a sampan out with some DuPont lures." Cribbs was referring to hand grenades taped to blocks of C-4 explosives. Dropped in the water near the mouth of a canal, they could bring up twenty or thirty stunned fish per shot. Vietnamese with access to American bases took a lot of fish like this. "I used to fish a lot at home, and it's kinda relaxin'." McConnell reached over and helped himself to one of Cribbs's cigarettes.

"You going back to Kentucky when you get home, Harold?"

"No way, sir. There's nothing back there for me."

"Isn't your family still there?"

"Oh, they're there all right, and that's one of the reasons I ain't goin' back. Y'see, Boss, I come from a real poor county there. It wasn't kinfolk an' corn squeezin's an' fiddle music like you see in the movies. My old lady was a righteous Southern Baptist and my old man was a drunk. We lived on welfare and they fought a lot. The Navy was my ticket out of there."

"Why the teams? There's a lot easier ways to make a living than this."

"Right on, sir. Makes you wonder, especially after that last one. Y'know, I was on a destroyer for a year. Every time I turned around my division officer had me on report, and the chief did nothing but drink coffee and talk about the old Navy. Besides that, I got seasick."

"You, seasick?"

"I felt like shit just sitting at the pier. Anyway, I put in for the teams. Training was a pain in the ass, but I like SEAL team. I walk a good point, and I don't have to take shit off nobody."

"You do walk a good point. I feel real comfortable with you out front."

"To tell the truth, Con does most of the work. We play this little game—who can move the quietest and who sees something first. Con's the best gook I ever worked with, and he's a helluva nice kid. Y'know sir, sometimes I get on better with Orientals than I do with Americans." Cribbs wound in his line to check the bait and deftly cast back out into the shallows toward the shore. "Say, Boss?"

"Yeah?"

"I'm here 'cause I got to do my hitch, and I'm not sure there's much on the outside for me. Why are you here, sir?"

McConnell looked out across the mud-brown water to where the broad Bhi Hap River made a slight dogleg to the left some half mile to the east of the base. Why am I here? I don't know myself, so how can I tell him?

"Well, to tell you the truth, I don't know. It wasn't like I made a decision to come here, to Firebase Delta. It seems like I made a series of decisions that eventually led me here. A year ago if someone said, 'Hey, buddy, you want to run SEAL operations in Vietnam?' I'd have said he was crazy. I barely knew what a SEAL was. Now I'm not so sure *I'm* not the one who's crazy. To be honest, I really don't know why I'm here, except to get the job done and get us back home in one piece. Sure seems like there ought to be a better reason."

"Sir, you can take it from me and the other guys in the fire team, that's a damn good reason."

"It'll have to do for now, but I'd sure like to think that we're accomplishing something—that we're making a difference."

"C'mon, Boss, we're the pros. We do it 'cause nobody else can. Leave that moral shit for the politicians and the do-gooders."

"Maybe you're right, Harold," said McConnell as he rose to walk back down the dock.

"Sir?"

"Yeah?"

"You did a nice job of getting us out of that last mess. For a while there, I thought it was gonna get a little hairy."

"Going to get a little hairy!''

"And that was a nice touch, sir, letting those guys think they almost had us, then calling in those fast-movers with the five-hundred-pounders.''

McConnell caught the twinkle in his point man's eye.

"Think I got a bite here, Boss,'' said Cribbs, fighting the small rod like it was a deep-sea fishing rig. "Yep, I definitely got a live one here.''

McConnell walked slowly back up the dock, smiling to himself and grateful for Cribbs's support and approval. Where did he get such men?

The next few days passed slowly for McConnell. One of the Seawolves had to fly to Binh Thuy to pick up some parts, so he had a chance to see Watson for a few minutes. He was doing well and it appeared that he would be back with the platoon in about ten days. McConnell found Binh Thuy heavy with the memories of Connie and Benny, and he was glad to get back to the firebase.

He arrived back at the hootch that evening just as France and his men were gearing up for a night patrol. Later on, after they had gone, he was sitting in the front of the hootch reading a two-week-old *Time* magazine. The rest of his men had gone to the movie, which was shown up against the wall of the chow hall. McConnell noticed that *Time* gave just about equal coverage to the conduct of the war here and the protest against the war back home.

"How about some coffee, sir?'' Chief Johnson sat down across from him, a Styrofoam cup in each hand.

"Thanks, Chief.'' It had become a frequent but un-scheduled ritual that when the other team was out and the rest of the men were at the movie, the two of them drank coffee and talked.

"I've been talking with Rawls, and it looks like we'll get Doc Young until Watson gets back.'' Their fire team would operate with one of France's men while Watson was gone, so both teams would work one-man-short. Then, with Watson back, McConnell would be a man short for the balance of the tour.

"You think he'll fit into our team okay?''

"The Doc's a solid guy, sir. Don't let the fact that he's

a diving dick-smith fool you. He'll hold his own when the going gets tough.'' The Navy assigned a medical corpsman to SEAL platoons on deployment. They went to diving school for scuba qualifications and jump school, and they trained with the SEALs prior to going to Vietnam, but they did not go through basic UDT/SEAL training. Technically they were not SEAL operators. The Geneva Convention and the Navy considered them to be noncombatants, but the platoon officers considered them another rifle barrel in the fire team. The corpsmen, for the most part, were superb operators. And sometimes these non-SEAL-trained SEALs were guilty of exceptional heroism under fire during combat operations.

''How does the Doc feel about being shuttled off to our fire team?''

''Between you and me, sir, I don't think he minds it too much. Even though we've been in a couple of scrapes, we don't hang it out as much as Lieutenant France's team. Everyone knows you lead a good patrol.''

''I told Mr. France that we might be standing down for a few more days. How are the rest of the guys doing?''

''They're okay and I think they're ready to go back out, but we're not ready until you are.''

''I'd like to begin with one or two easy ones—get back into the flow and break Doc into the squad. You have any ideas, Chief?''

''Well, sir, Cribbs and I were talking with the Kits and we haven't done much work south of the base.'' McConnell and Chief Johnson had begun the planning that would take them back into the field the following night.

Chapter Twelve

FRANCE'S GAMBLE

"ALL RIGHT, GUYS, listen up. We're going to start working in the area south of the base. We haven't spent too much time there since we've been here, and there hasn't been a lot of reported activity in this area. But we do know that the VC feel pretty secure there, and they consider it kind of a rear services area. We'll leave in the boat just after dark and go east on the Bhi Hap—then we'll patrol south and set a canal ambush on the east–west canal that's about four klicks south of the river."

McConnell went through the details of a very well prepared patrol briefing. In some ways it was like he was dong it for the first time, and he experienced the same first-time jitters he had felt last October. But these jitters were grounded in the knowledge of just how dangerous it could be, and the terrible responsibility that went with his job. He sensed the men were watching him closely, looking for some sign of uncertainty or weakness. He felt like he had to prove himself again. Toward the end of the briefing, he was rushing to finish, wanting to hurry and get it over with.

"That's it, gentlemen—be on the boat at twenty-one thirty." McConnell rolled up the briefing map while the men milled around the front of the hootch, talking about the upcoming operation. He left the hootch to find the colonel so he could brief him on their plans.

"Hey, Mr. McConnell." Doc Young followed him out of the hootch and McConnell turned to wait for him.

"Yeah, Doc, what is it?"

"Well, sir, I just wanted to say that I appreciate the opportunity to be in your fire team and work with you guys, and uh, well, I'll do a good job for you—I won't let you down." Aside from Chief Johnson and Rawls, Doc Young was the only other senior enlisted man in the platoon. He was a medium-built, sandy-haired six-footer, quiet and extremely intelligent. The rest of the men kidded him because he read the classics, rather than the crotch-novels that circulated through the platoon. Doc Young wore glasses, the clear-framed Navy-issue type with a black elastic band that held them tight to his face.

"Thanks, Doc. I appreciate your volunteering to work with us. We're lucky to get a good man like you."

"Sir, I wasn't the only volunteer, but I guess Mr. France thought I was the most expendable."

Not the only volunteer, thought McConnell, well how about that. "You're on our team now, Doc, and I'm damn glad to have you."

"Thanks, Boss. I'll sure do my best."

McConnell headed across the base in the direction of Colonel Beard's office. Young's admission and vote of confidence was like a shot of oxygen to an asthmatic. He was relieved to think that he still held the men's confidence and trust, but he began to feel the pressure of keeping his fear under control so he would not betray that trust.

Gearing up for the operation was a strange experience. Each piece of equipment he carried was designed to kill someone or signal for help because someone was about to kill him. The chillingly familiar feel and smell of his web gear and ammunition load ignited the burning lump in his stomach. When he took the Stoner rifle down from its peg on the wall, it almost felt like a foreign object in his hand. As he fed the linked belt into the feed tray and closed the top cover, he was beginning to sweat. Christ, thought McConnell, this is your forty-fifth combat operation and it's an easy one. Get a hold of yourself!

"Hey, Mr. McConnell," came a voice from the front of the hootch, "you about ready, sir?"

"Yeah. Yeah, be right there." He slipped on his headband and slung the radio onto his back. Then he slipped his head under the strap of his weapon and headed toward the door. He ducked through the partition door into the front of the hootch and found his fire team in full battle dress and camouflage, all lined up and standing at attention.

"What's going on here, Chief?" said McConnell cautiously. He wasn't sure whether it was a joke or a mutiny.

"I thought the lieutenant would like to inspect his men before we went into the field."

"No really, what's going . . . what did you say?"

"Sir, I thought the lieutenant would want to inspect his men."

"What's this lieutenant stuff, Chief?"

"You've been kind of busy, sir, and you probably missed the message from the Strand. Congratulations, Lieutenant junior grade McConnell." Johnson stepped forward and shook his hand and the rest of the fire team broke ranks and followed him. Lieutenant France, Rawls, and the rest of the platoon filed through the front door and joined the receiving line. McConnell was caught totally off guard, mumbling thanks and blushing under his black face paint. He had totally forgotten that the Navy automatically turned ensigns in Vietnam into junior grade lieutenants after a year of service.

"Okay, men, let's get down to the boat," said Johnson. "I'm sure the new Jay-Gee would like to buy us a drink, which he owes us, but it'll have to wait 'til we get back."

McConnell led his men down to the dock, where Smitty had him formally piped aboard while his crew served as side boys. The lump of fear was still there, but there was now a small, but most welcome, kernel of confidence growing alongside it. The operation went off on schedule and according to plan. They made no contact and were back at the dock just after sunrise.

"Glad to have that one behind us, Chief," said McConnell as they walked back to the hootch.

"Just like riding a bicycle, sir. You never really forget how."

* * *

The fire team conducted three operations over the next week. On the last one they caught a VC squad carelessly walking down a trail just before dawn, and they killed them to a man. That afternoon, when McConnell could no longer sleep due to the heat, he got up and found Watson sitting in the front of the hootch.

"Welcome back, stranger. Couldn't take having those nurses fuss over you any longer?"

"Hi, Boss. I tried to stretch it out but they finally threw me out. I hear you guys made some money last night."

"They were a real careless bunch, walking down the trail like they were on a grade school outing. It was pretty easy pickings. How's the leg?"

"Not bad, sir. I got a whole stack of extra dressings and Doc Stinson is supposed to see me daily for a while. They told me not to get it wet for another week, but really, I'm ready to operate. By the way, congratulations on making Jay-Gee."

"Thanks, Watson. I don't want to be chicken-shit about this, but you go back in the field when Doc Stinson says you can—no arguments."

"Whatever you say, Boss. Speaking of docs, I hear Doc Young's been filling in. How's he been doing?"

"The Doc's done a great job for us, but he's just a pinch hitter. I'm real glad to have you back on the team." McConnell reached over and gave him a good hard squeeze on the shoulder and the young man beamed. "And, Rick, that was a nice job you did back there in that rice field. You got hurt and you still hung in there. Thanks. I don't think we could've got out of that one without your work with the grenade launcher."

"I almost froze up, sir. But it won't happen again—you can count on me."

"I know that. We were classmates in hack-it school, remember?"

Periodically, one of the fire team members would stumble out of the sleeping bay, and the homecoming would be replayed. Lieutenant France's team was standing down that night so the platoon celebrated his return. It was also a Thirty-Day Party. Foxtrot Platoon had one month left in the tour.

* * *

Three days later they were back at work on a canal ambush. This time the operation was a boat/SEAL ambush setup. Smitty's boat would insert the SEALs on a canal bank, then idle or drift a hundred meters down the canal and take up a position on the opposite side of the same canal. If the SEALs made a hit, the boat could be there to support them. If the boat made the hit, the SEALs were in position for a stay-behind or could easily be taken out. McConnell usually stayed on the boat for these ambushes. It allowed his petty officers an opportunity to lead a patrol while he could remain close by and in constant radio communication.

This time they moved down a series of secondary canals southeast of the base. Tonight, Reed would be leading the SEAL element. Smitty nosed the boat into the bank and the big SEAL sent Cribbs and the two Kits over the bow first. Then he, Barnett, and Doc Young followed. Watson was not yet cleared for fieldwork, but he managed to get on board the MSSC. He manned one of the mounted machine guns, along with Chief Johnson. Smitty eased away from the bank and idled on one engine down the canal.

"Uncle Charlie, this is Linebacker, over."

"Roger, Linebacker, over."

"We have a setup, Uncle Charlie. Let us know when you are in position, over."

"Roger, Linebacker, out."

Smitty found a piece of the opposite bank with some overhanging vegetation that provided good cover for the boat. The foliage would also help muffle any inadvertent noise that escaped from the boat. McConnell called Reed and notified the base that they were in place. Then began the long vigil, waiting for some unlucky VC patrol to come paddling down their canal. They were relatively secure once they were in place. The danger was in the insertion and especially in the extraction. No bad guys appeared that night, so about four in the morning, McConnell decided to call it a night.

"Linebacker, this is Uncle Charlie. Are you ready for pickup, over?"

"Roger, Uncle Charlie, nothing moving here. Ready when you are."

"Understood, Linebacker, we'll be there in one zero minutes, over."

"Roger, one zero minutes, Linebacker out."

Smitty got under way and eased back up the canal toward the SEALs' position.

"Linebacker—Uncle Charlie. How about a light, over."

"Wilco, Uncle Charlie."

McConnell spotted the *alpha-alpha* of Reed's penlight, as did Smitty, and the boat moved guardedly toward that section of the bank. Johnson, Watson, and the rest of the boat crew manned their weapons as they prepared for extraction.

"Hold off, Uncle Charlie, we got something here!"

Smitty cut the engines and they slowly drifted in front of the SEAL position. Oh no, thought McConnell, they're going to make contact and we're sitting ducks. We can't fire since we don't know exactly where they are. He heard a round of metallic clicks as the boat gunners took off their safeties. "Steady now," he whispered to those around him. There was a lot of tension on the boat.

"Linebacker," he whispered into the handset, "report!"

"Stand by, Uncle Charlie."

The burning lump of fear exploded in his stomach and the "what if" scenarios raced through his mind. It was Reed's call and he could do nothing but wait and back his next move. Dear God, Reed, play it safe and get yourself out of there! The seconds dragged by—then he heard crashing in the brush on the shore. McConnell cupped both hands behind his ears to hear better. The crashing continued for almost a minute. Then he heard muffled cursing. "Shit! . . . Goddammit! . . . Aw, fuck!" And then a very clearly spoken "Son-of-a-bitch!" followed by silence.

"Uncle Charlie, this is Linebacker, ready for pickup, over."

"Roger, give us a light, Linebacker."

Smitty picked up Reed's light and made for the canal bank. After a very tense extraction, they began working their way back up the canal toward the Bhi Hap and home. When they were back on the river and running on step for the base, McConnell began to relax. But the tension and worry had left him with a burning pain in his gut. He made a note to pack some Rolaids in his web gear. He left Smitty in the coxswain's station and started back to find Reed, but was intercepted by Chief Johnson.

"Sir, why don't you wait until we get back to talk to Reed."

"What's wrong, Chief? Are they okay?"

"They're fine. Cribbs is a little scraped up, and I understand Barnett has a few scratches." Johnson was being uncharacteristically evasive and that too puzzled McConnell. "Just the same, sir, I'd wait until we get back to get the full story from both Reed and Cribbs."

"Okay, Chief. We'll be home in a few minutes anyway." Something wasn't right. But McConnell was satisfied that his fire team was intact, and his curiosity was pushed aside momentarily by an overwhelming feeling of relief. When they got back to the hootch, he sent the others to the showers while he sat down with Reed, Cribbs, and Chief Johnson. Cribbs's hands were cut up and there was a nasty scrape on his cheek and nose, like he had fallen off a bicycle on a gravel road. Normally, the first thing both he and Reed did after an operation was get a beer, and neither had made a move for the reefer. Something was definitely wrong.

"All right, let's have it."

"Well, sir," began Reed, "we had a good position along the canal, and there was a trail some five meters off the canal behind us." He made very little eye contact with McConnell as he spoke. "We set up so three of us watched the canal and the other three watched the trail. It was a good setup, Boss, but there just wasn't anything moving on the canal or the trail. Then when you were coming to get us and I showed you the light, this huge lizard comes walking down the trail.

"A what!"

"A lizard. You ought to have seen the bastard," said Reed, warming to the story. "He musta been six feet long and—"

"A six-foot-long lizard!"

"Well, maybe only five feet, but he was huge, like one of those things you see in *National Geographic*. So we tried to capture it."

"All that crashing in the brush—you were wrestling with a lizard?"

"It was my fault, Boss," said Cribbs. "I thought if we could catch it and bring it back to the base, it'd make an all-time pet. I just didn't think he would be so hard to handle. I tackled him first and he was beating the shit out of me. Then Barnett jumped in, but dammit, sir, he whipped us both."

"You mean to say that right there in the middle of indian country, during an extraction, you tried to make a *hoi chanh* out of a giant fucking lizard!" McConnell was on his feet now and he was shouting.

"Yes sir," answered the two guilty parties together, both staring at the floor.

"And you placed the fire team and the boat crew at risk so you could stroll around the base with a world's-record lizard on a goddamn leash!"

Silence.

"Reed, you were in charge—how could you allow this? And Cribbs, you ought to know better. If a VC squad had come down that trail, the only thing that would have saved your ass is they might have been laughing too hard to shoot you!"

Again, silence.

McConnell walked around the table and stood with his back to them, looking out the front door. Shit! His two best men had just done something incredibly stupid. He liked and needed both of these men. They were the heart of his fire team. How could they have been so irresponsible? He wasn't sure what made him angrier—that they had abused the responsibility he had given them, or that they had put him through the ringer when he thought they were in trouble. He walked back over and sat down.

"Okay, you guys," he began in a calm, measured voice. "You fucked up and I'm disappointed in you. I gave you a job to do and you let me down. Look, we've been through too much together for me to keep you after school, or come up with some kind of chicken-shit punishment. You men are the best operators in the platoon. The Chief and I depend on you, and the younger guys look up to you. I can't have this kind of crap going on in the field.

"How would you live with yourself if your screwing around out there had cost the life of one of your teammates?" He paused for a moment. Neither man spoke or moved. "There's VC and NVA out there that want kill us—we can't make it easy on them because we're stupid. Now, I want this thing behind us. You give me your word this was a onetime, dumb-shit move, and I don't want to ever mention it again." McConnell stood up and looked at them.

"Okay, Reed?"

"Okay, sir."

"Cribbs?"

"Okay, sir."

"Fair enough, Chief?"

"Yes, sir."

"Then that's it. Reed, see that Doc Stinson checks out your men. That reptile might be poisonous."

"Aye, aye, sir."

McConnell headed for the showers, exhausted by the emotional strain of the operation and the strain of having to chew on two of his best men. He was still angry, but he had to permit himself a quiet smile as he pictured this hapless lizard being jumped by two SEALs—then thrashing both of them. He wondered just how effective his little speech had been.

Over the next few days, the great lizard snatch became a well-known secret, and there was some discreet kidding at the expense of Reed and Cribbs. Then one night, after something not so discreet was said, Reed slammed Rawls up against the wall of the hootch and promised him that if he ever said another word about it, he would rip off his head and shit down his throat. Neither officer nor the Chief intervened, and no one ever mentioned it again.

Once again Colonel Beard was able to get a Navy slick helicopter from Binh Thuy dedicated to the platoon's use. Not only did the prospect of parakeet ops appeal to the two fire teams, but the nature of the quick helo strikes made for limited time in the field and regular daytime hours. The platoon was starting to draw in its mental and physical reserves, and the parakeet operations were less demanding, if no less dangerous. The fire teams again ranged into the open rice patties to the north and east of the base. The first day each team ran an operation and neither was successful in making a hit. Lieutenant France's team overran an empty hootch, while McConnell and his men could find no trace of the weapons they thought were hidden in a farmer's rice bin. That evening one of France's Kits brought in some information on the possible location of a tax collector. Since they often traveled at night and laid up to sleep during the day, they decided to hit the suspected hootch in early afternoon. One of the Seawolves made a high overflight early that morning and located the target hootch. It was known to be a bad area with a lot of indians, but it was a chance to get another tax collector.

McConnell and Chief Johnson attended the patrol briefing late that morning and prepared to stand by if the other team needed help. Unless something went wrong, it was a day off and one less day until the end of the tour. They were now counting them down.

"I hope they have good intelligence on that money man, because that's a pretty bad area," said the Chief.

"Mr. France seems to think they have a good shot at it," replied McConnell. "They're due for a big one— maybe they'll get him."

Chief Johnson and Cribbs joined McConnell at the helipad to see the other fire team off. There was the typical nervous, carnivallike atmosphere that accompanied the launching of a parakeet op. The slick, loaded with waving, black-faced SEALs, followed the Seawolves out across the river and made a sweeping turn back to the north.

"I'll be glad when they're back from this one," said Cribbs. "The Kits were pretty goosey about it."

"Our Kits or theirs?"

"All of them."

"Don't worry," replied McConnell. "Mr. France knows we're too short to hang it out too far."

"I hope so, Boss."

* * *

Less than twenty minutes later McConnell heard inbound helicopters and headed for the helipad. He arrived just as the slick touched down. The SEALs crowded off the helo, and the pilot shut it down while the two Seawolves landed on the other side of the pad.

"That was a quick trip, Dave. What happened?"

"We took some small-arms fire on the way in, and the pilot aborted. He wanted to come back and check the damage." The slick's blades were slowing to a stop while the two pilots and their crewmen were crawling around under the helo.

"Were you getting a lot of fire?"

"Nah, just one round that I felt. Probably some farmer with an SKS got off a lucky shot." The Chief and Cribbs arrived and waited off to the side.

"Doesn't look like a serious problem," said the slick pilot who joined them. He had removed his helmet and gloves, but he was still sweating. "We took a round in the belly and it lodged in one of the floor supports. Jesus, I hate getting shot at."

"Right, hang on for a second, okay?" France went over and pulled Rawls aside for a conference while McConnell and the slick pilot were joined by Carl and his wingman. The three pilots began talking with their hands, replaying the details of the flight. A few minutes later they were rejoined by France.

"Let's go back, only this time, can you come in from the west?"

"Well, yeah, I suppose so. Whadda you think, Carl?"

"We can guide you in from the west, no sweat. Your bird up?"

"We can fly. Hey, Dave, you sure you want to go back there? I mean like we weren't quite to the target and they put a round in us."

"One slope in a rice field with a rifle. Besides, we're coming in from the other side."

"Okay, Dave, but I want those gunships a little tighter on my ass. Carl?"

"We'll get you on line to the target, then close it up tight on final."

"You get me in there," said the slick pilot, "and I'll get them on the ground. Dave, give me a few minutes to top off on fuel and we'll get turning."

McConnell was stunned. He couldn't believe what he was hearing. You can stay behind, but you never go back. He caught France before he rejoined his fire team.

"Dave."

"Yo, Jimmy."

"You think this is a good idea, going back to the same place?"

"It's a chance at a money man, and I don't think they'll expect us to come right back."

"Hey, look, you're pushing it. You're compromised and you've lost the element of surprise. What if they're waiting for you?"

"If there were some main force activity there, they'd have hit us with more than a single round. I tell you, Jim, the last thing they'll expect is for us to come right back."

"I hope you're right, Dave, because you're betting your ass on it."

France rejoined his men and they huddled for an impromptu briefing on the edge of the pad. McConnell still couldn't believe they were going back in.

"What's going on, sir?"

"They're going back in, Chief."

"Alternate target?"

"Same target, Chief."

"Sir, that's not good."

"I know, but Mr. France wants that money man." They watched as the SEALs reboarded the slick. The aircraft lifted off and followed the Seawolves back out over the river.

"Chief, go down to the operations shack and monitor the radio traffic. Cribbs, get the team together, and have them saddle up and stand by. I think those guys will be okay, but we better be ready just in case." McConnell went to the SEAL hootch and quickly changed into blue jeans, T-shirt, and jungle boots. He slung his web gear and radio over his shoulder, grabbed the Stoner and headed back to the helipad. He piled his equipment on the edge of the pad and stepped into the Seawolf hootch. They had a receiver there so he could listen to the traffic between the Seawolves and the slick. He joined two off-duty pilots who were glued to the set. The three helos were on their final run to the target.

"Target right ten degrees, five hundred meters, Carrier Pigeon."

"Roger, Seawolf Leader, target in sight. Here we go!"

"Close it up, Seawolf Trail—on final."

"Roger, Leader, I've got you covered."

"This is Carrier Pigeon, my chicks are on the ground."

"Roger, Pigeon, chicks on the ground."

McConnell was beginning to sweat as he followed the flow of the operation from the speaker, even though the hootch was air-conditioned. At least they were safely on the ground. He was amazed at how much emotion and feeling could be transmitted by voice. He could hear the turbine whine in the background and almost smell the burnt kerosene odor of the helo's jet exhaust. Mentally, McConnell was running across a rice paddy with an automatic weapon and looking for targets.

"Troops are standing by, Boss. How're they doing?"

"Thanks, Harold. They're on the ground but no word yet." McConnell had no more than turned away from Cribbs when the speaker crackled.

"Leader, this is Seawolf Trail. They got a man down!"

"Roger, Trail—I'm breaking left to cover. Can you see where it's coming from, over."

"Negative, Leader, but there're some bunkers zero-nine-zero from their LZ, over."

"Roger, Trail, I'm rolling in now—break—you copy, Pigeon?"

"I copy, Leader. I can't see anything and I can't raise them."

A man down! Oh God, thought McConnell, don't let this be happening! He sat in agony as he listened to the gunships roll in, clear and cover each other on firing runs. He could hear the helos calling to the men on the ground, and while he would not have been able to hear their transmissions, he could tell from the repeated calls that there was no response.

". . . see another man down, Trail, what's your station time . . ."

". . . small-arms fire from that village every time I get close, Leader . . ."

Sweet Jesus, they're in deep shit and their radio's down. Why, Dave? Why did you have to go back!? McConnell was almost sick with fear. He grabbed the land line to the operations hootch and yelled for Chief Johnson.

"Chief, they're in big trouble. Get the Ponies up and—"

"I tried. The Ponies are committed up north, so I—"

"Any fixed wing in the area, Chief? We gotta—"

"Sir, be quiet and listen!" The Chief paused and so did his officer. "The colonel found a section of Army Cobra gunships at Can Tho that can be there in about thirty minutes. I caught the courier helo at Bac Lieu, and they'll be on their way as soon as they refuel, ETA fifteen minutes. Have the Seawolf personnel standing by to rig the courier bird for an insertion. We can be up there to help them when the Cobras get on station." McConnell took a deep breath to calm himself.

"Good work, Chief."

"Right, sir. See you on the pad."

The pilots said they would notify him of any news that came over the gunship circuit, so McConnell stepped outside into the bright sunlight. The heat reflected in waves off the metal Mars-matting of the helipad. He put on his jungle shirt and checked his weapons load and the radio before strapping them on. Chief Johnson joined them, and McConnell gathered his fire team in a football-like huddle for quick briefing. If they were lucky, the Seawolves could stay on station long enough to vector their chopper into position to support the crippled fire team. The courier helo arrived and had barely touched down as Seawolf ground crews attacked it, removing doors and equipment so it could serve its new mission. Colonel Beard came striding up to the group as the courier helo was ready to go. McConnell stepped out to meet him.

"You going in after them, Jim?"

"I don't really have a choice, sir. We have men down and no radio communication."

"I understand," the tall Army man replied, "but don't let this thing get out of hand."

"Sir?"

"Don't let the VC use your men that're down as bait to lure you and the others into a killing zone. Be smart about it."

"Aye, aye, sir." He turned to go follow his men to the helo.

"Here," yelled the colonel over the noise of the helo, "take this!" He handed McConnell a small knapsack with a shoulder strap as he ran for the waiting chopper. As soon as he was aboard, the aircraft lifted off and headed north.

The slick circled high over the area while Carl Belding in the lead Seawolf briefed McConnell and the courier pilot by radio on the situation below. The SEALs on the ground had inserted in a dry rice paddy just outside a small village of some ten hootches. They had immediately come under fire and were forced back to a tree line away from the village. Two of them were down in the open field while the others were still pinned down in the tree line. McConnell directed his pilot to land them a hundred meters down the tree line on the side away from the village. They would try to work their way toward the other SEALs from there.

"Seawolf Leader, this is Jakeleg, can you cover on insertion, over?"

"My wingman and I can support you with our door gunners, but that's all we have left, Jakeleg. Army Cobras ETA ten minutes, over."

McConnell thought about it but decided not to wait. The guys down on the ground needed help now. "We'll go in now, Leader—do what you can. The courier will wait around for the Cobras while you go home for a hot turn-around, over."

"Roger, Jakeleg, and good luck. Keep your head down until we get back. Seawolf Leader, out."

McConnell slipped on the intercom headset and briefed his pilot on where he wanted to land and how to make the approach. The man in the left seat nodded and began a long sweeping descent to the west of the village where he would make a low approach to the LZ. McConnell shouted instructions across the noisy interior of the helo's cabin to his men, as the SEALs prepared for the insertion.

The fire team scrambled off the slick and ran into the tree line. The helo cleared off while the two gunships crisscrossed their position while the door gunners expended the last of their ammunition. Then the Seawolves, along with Lieutenant France's slick, headed south for fuel and ammunition. After the noise and activity of a helicopter insertion, he was always surprised at how quiet it was and how alone he felt when they got on the ground. The men had automatically gone into squad file order along the tree line. McConnell worked his way back to Chief Johnson.

"What do you make of it, Chief?"

"Hard to tell. Doesn't look like main force activity, or we'd have taken fire on the way in. I'd say it's a well-placed machine gun or snipers—maybe both. Cribbs is just going to have to feel his way."

The fire team began to work their way up to the tree line toward the rest of the platoon. There was no firing from the SEALs or the VC ahead of them. They were some twenty meters from the other team, who were huddled in the foliage, when the first rounds began slicing through the nipa palm above their heads.

Snipers!

Moving slower and much lower, they closed on the other fire team. McConnell was met by a scared and much relieved Doc Young.

"What's the deal, Doc. Where's France?"

"Am I ever glad to see you, Boss! The lieutenant's down and I think he's dead. So is Rawls. We were halfway across that field when they opened up on us. No automatic weapons, just snipers. There's at least two of them. Every time we try to move, they hit us!"

"Easy, Doc. What happened?"

"We were pulling back for the tree line and Mr. France went down. Morales and one of the Kits also got hit. Trung's not too bad, but Morales took a round through the shoulder and I had to give him morphine. Rawls went back for the lieutenant. We tried to cover him but he didn't have a chance. They hit him before he could get near the lieutenant. We did our best, but we didn't even know where they were. I'm sorry, sir.''

"Not your fault, Doc. Get back on the line and take care of your wounded.''

McConnell crouched in the tree line and considered his options. Up until now, events had carried him forward and he had few decisions to make. Now he had to come up with a plan to get France and Rawls out of that field and not lose any more men. Lose men! He was trying not to think of them as men. The ones who could function were riflemen, and those who were down would take a rifleman off line to attend to them. But when he peered through the foliage and saw France and Rawls facedown in the mud of the dry patty, that resolve left him. Rawls was only twenty meters away and France some ten meters farther. He could see the side of Rawls's head and it looked like there was some blood coming out of his ear. France's face was buried in the mud. The square box of the radio had ridden up off his shoulder, but he could see little else. The scattered hootches of the village were on the far edge of the field. Two men dead and for what? He knew what would have to be done, and the thought of it terrorized him. A bullet snapped through the foliage just above his head and he wriggled back into the relative safety of the tree line. Chief Johnson crouched-hopped over to his position.

"How do you want to handle this, sir?''

"It's probably not a good idea to wait until dark.''

"That'd help with the snipers, but there's going to be a lot of indians here by nightfall. We got to get out of here now.''

"You see where the sniper fire is coming from?''

"Chances are one or more of those hootches has a bunker in it. The area around the village is pretty open so I would guess they're in spider holes on either side of the vill. That money man must have been there, because these guys are good—real good.''

"How's the other team?''

"Morales is not good and he can't walk. Trung was hit in the leg and Billy's with him. Doc and the other three are okay, and they have about half of their ammunition load. They're all pretty scared, sir, but they'll do their job.''

"Okay, Chief, here's the way we'll do this. We'll have the Cobras hit the village and the two Seawolves work either side of it. Put the M60s on either flank so they won't be shooting over France and Rawls. Tell them to look for muzzle flashes. Have the grenadiers put out forty mike-mike as fast as they can into the vill and to either side." McConnell hesitated as he made his hardest decision. "Cribbs will be in charge of the recovery team. I'll send Barnett and Oakley with him. We'll get France and Rawls back here and then work back along the tree line for an extraction." He couldn't yet bring himself to say "the bodies." "That sound okay, Chief?"

"It's our best shot, sir. It's awfully open out there. I have a few smokes but we could use more."

McConnell almost smiled as he tossed the colonel's knapsack over to Johnson. It was filled with smoke grenades.

"Have a couple of the better arms standing by when I give the word. We'll get the smokes out just before the gunships start their runs."

"You got it, sir." Johnson began working his way along the line, briefing the men and passing out the smoke grenades. The Army Cobras soon arrived overhead, and the Seawolves were just a few minutes behind. McConnell raised them on the radio and told them what he wanted. He then found Cribbs, and called Barnett and Oakley over to him.

"Get out there and get back just as quick as you can. Drag them by the collar, stay low, and keep moving. You're going to have everything we got covering you. Okay, guys?"

"We'll get the job done, Boss," said Cribbs. He was carrying only his AK-47. The other two had shed their weapons and ammunition load to move faster. Barnett gave him a thumbs-up and Oakley barely nodded. Oakley was a big kid, almost as big as Reed and a good athlete. McConnell was counting on him to lug France back to the tree line. He's scared, thought McConnell, but who isn't?

"Chief, get the smoke out," yelled McConnell. He then called Carl, who was coordinating the four gunships and told him to begin their firing runs. The eight or ten smoke grenades scattered around the two fallen men began to produce a dense, multicolored fog. There was a slight breeze that carried it away from them toward the enemy. Then the village erupted as the Cobras' first rockets hit. They also sprayed the area with their 7.62mm nose-mounted mini-guns. It was a great show, but questionably effective if the VC were well bunkered.

"Cribbs! Go!" shouted McConnell as the SEALs along the line picked up the firing pace. Cribbs and Barnett raced out of the tree line into the field, but Oakley didn't move.

"Oakley, go!"

"Sir, I can't, I—" His mouth was open but no more words came out. He was frozen.

McConnell stripped off the radio and was ready to plunge after his two men when Doc Young broke from the tree line and into the cloud of smoke. McConnell quickly recovered his Stoner and began firing. He thought he saw a muzzle flash, winking at them from the left of the village and he shifted to take it under fire. The smoke and the noise of the rockets and the helos made for a real battle scene. All this for a couple of well-placed snipers, thought McConnell. Soon three crouched forms, struggling with two loads between them, came out of the smoke toward them. McConnell held his breath until they reached the safety of the tree line. They made it! Sweet Jesus, they're safe! Now for the relatively easy part of getting back to the extraction point. His elation was blunted when he saw the two gray, dirty inert forms that had been France and Rawls. Doc Young quickly checked both men for a pulse before looking up at McConnell and shaking his head.

"Thanks, Doc. Barnett, Cribbs—nice work out there." McConnell looked at the line of men crouched against the tree line. Foxtrot was now his platoon, and he had to get them out of there. He turned to find the Chief and saw him grimly motioning to him from their right flank along the tree line. He crouch-crawled over there, leaving Cribbs to ready the two corpses for movement.

"Chief?" There was a look to Johnson he had never

seen before. He put his hand on McConnell's shoulder and squeezed—something he had never done before.

"You better come over here. It's Reed."

What he saw when he moved around behind his Chief almost stopped his heart. Watson was holding Reed like a little girl holds a big doll. Tears flowed down both of Watson's cheeks making vertical flesh-colored lines in his dark face paint. McConnell moved beside them, knowing Reed was dead but hoping it was not so. A sniper round had hit him between the nose and cheekbone and opened up the back of his head like melon. The muzzle flash of the short-barreled M60 had been a beacon for the enemy snipers. His face looked peaceful enough except for the small entry hole and fully dilated eyes, but his brains were all over the front of Watson's shirt.

"They weren't worth it, sir," Watson accused him in a soft voice. "Even alive, they weren't."

"I know."

"Then why the fuck are we here?" For the first time Watson looked right at him. McConnell just shook his head.

"Because they'd have come for us." For a moment, neither man was able to speak, and a strange, sad communion passed between the three of them, blocking out everything else.

God help me, thought McConnell, if they can get Reed, they can get us all.

"Sir, we have to move."

"I know, Chief. Send Barnett and Doc back to help Watson."

"I'll take him back myself!"

"I know you will, Rick, but let the Doc wrap his head and Barnett can carry your gear."

McConnell worked his way back along the line. Every eye was on him. He had never felt so scared and alone, but he could allow none of it to show. McConnell recovered his radio and gave the gunships their extraction plan. Slowly but steadily, the platoon, dragging three inert forms and the semiconscious Morales, worked their way back along the tree line to the LZ and called for extraction. The dead and wounded, plus Watson and Doc Young, went out

on the first lift. McConnell and the rest of his platoon
followed on the second.

Both slicks touched down at the same time. Doc Stinson
quickly looked at the dead and moved on to the wounded.
Morales was lucky that the bullet had not tumbled, passing
through and exiting cleanly. The morphine was wearing
off, and he was in a great deal of pain. Trung, one of
France's Kits, had a bullet wound in his calf. He stoically
accepted the pain and limped along without complaint.
Stinson sent them with one of his medics on the courier
helo back to Binh Thuy. Then he turned to the dead.

He tended to them right there on the pad, carefully ex-
amining their wounds and filling out forms. McConnell
watched them die again as they were slipped into the rub-
berized vinyl body bags. There was a finality in the low
growl of the heavy zipper that drew up to the head of the
bag and sealed them within.

How tragic, mused McConnell—they came here as sailors and they're leaving in olive-drab, Army issue body
bags.

Stinson tagged the bags and handed McConnell a folder
of paperwork.

"Get a receipt for them in Binh Thuy. They've been
known to lose them up there." McConnell was startled at
the callousness of Stinson's remark, but he had only to
glance into the doctor's eyes to see that they were full of
compassion. "And get them there as soon as you can. For
the family's sake, they should be refrigerated as soon as
possible."

"Hey, McConnell," said the slick pilot coming over to
them at the edge of the pad. "I'd like to leave as soon as
we refuel. Any passengers?" McConnell looked at Watson.

"Two. Myself and this man."

"I'd like to go, too, sir. They were my team leader and
LPO," said Doc Young.

"Make it three," said McConnell.

"Three it is," said the pilot, "and I'm sorry about your
buddies."

* * *

The flight to Binh Thuy took just over an hour. It seemed like an eternity. When Bono was hit, it had taken something from McConnell's spirit, but the loss of Reed had cost him a part of his soul. The big man lay on the floor of the helo in front of him. His legs were across McConnell's feet and he didn't want to move them, somehow thinking it might disturb Reed. McConnell had never really seen dead men before. When his grandfather died, he had only looked to be resting in his casket, like he was taking a nap. He had seen dead Viet Cong, but they were the enemy—they were fallen game. The three battered, muddy, bloody corpses he had taken out of the field that day were a part of him. France and Rawls had been his teammates. But Reed was his friend and his responsibility. A man must have a soul, he thought, because there was such a difference in Reed, the steady, easygoing man he had come to treasure over the past eight months, and the pale, broken form he became in death. The Reed that Watson had clung to so fiercely in the tree line was gone. God, I miss him already.

"Excuse me, big guy," McConnell said aloud as he shifted his feet over to the other side of Reed's corpse.

The sergeant in charge of the morgue in Binh Thuy was efficient in handling paperwork, while maintaining an air of patience and solemnity that would have done credit to a civilian funeral home director. These were not the first men who brought him their dead friends, and he was very professional about it. But in a civilian mortuary, you didn't have to help drag the deceased out of the back of a weapons carrier and place them on the cold concrete floor of a refrigerated Butler building.

"Christ, I thought we had a tough job," said Watson as they left. "How'd you like to be a nine-to-fiver there?"

"Takes all kinds to run a war," said Doc Young. "Safer maybe, but no thanks."

"Where to from here, sir?" said Watson. He still had a distant, disbelieving look to him.

"I think I'd like to buy you gentlemen a drink," said McConnell as he steered them to the officer's club.

They took a seat in the corner at a table for four. They

piled their web gear on the extra chair and leaned their rifles against the wall. The Vietnamese waitress brought them a round of beer and quickly retreated from the table. From around the room, they drew polite glances and open stares. Many of the patrons felt they were almost "on the front line" because Binh Thuy was so remote from the big bases near Saigon or Da Nang. But they had only to look at the three drinking quietly in the corner to know that they personally were very far from the action. The three SEALs looked like hobo chimney sweeps in their mud-caked jungle wear and blackened faces. The sulfurous odor from the smoke grenades blended with their own stale sweat and the dried blood of their comrades. They smelled like combat.

"Excuse me, gentlemen, but this is an officer's club and I thought you might consider—"

"It's a pleasure to meet you, Colonel," said McConnell, rising to his feet and offering the man a dirty hand. The senior officer hesitated, then took it. "I'm Lieutenant junior grade Jim McConnell, Foxtrot Platoon Commander, SEAL Team One. This is Ensign Young and Warrant Officer Watson."

"I see," replied the colonel doubtfully. "Well, we try to maintain a certain standard here and—"

"I understand, Colonel. Look, sir, we're transients and we just had one son-of-a-bitch of a day. We'll just have a few quiet beers and then we'll be on our way." There was a coldness and finality in McConnell's voice that was not lost on the colonel.

"Very well, men. Carry on." He walked back over to the bar where he was met by the club manager, a senior NCO.

"What shall I do, sir?" he said to the colonel, glancing across the room at the three invaders.

"Buy them a round on the house," he said with a shrug, "but keep an eye on them."

McConnell, Watson, and Young drank beer for the next four hours and did what families and friends do when they bury their loved ones. They retold the funny stories and exploits of the deceased, and tried to get through the sober, reflective lulls in the conversation. They laughed a lot, cried a little, and they mourned. The beer had taken the heaviest toll on Watson and he had to be supported by his two teammates when they moved to leave. The club was full, but there was a buffer of empty tables around the three warriors. The room fell silent except for the clatter of their web gear and weapons as the two SEALs helped their comrade through the door.

McConnell himself was feeling no pain, but he was jerked sober when he thought about he future. Tomorrow he had to go back to Firebase Delta and pull his platoon together.

Chapter Thirteen

KILO PLATOON

THE HELO CROSSED the river and gently rocked back to a hover before coming to a rest on the Firebase Delta landing pad. McConnell was not particularly glad to be back, but he was glad to be off the helicopter—he didn't want to admit it, but he was becoming afraid of them. On combat operations, there were more compelling things to fear, but on the transit flights, when they were cruising along at five thousand feet and he had the time to think, he had begun to develop "what if" scenarios for when the copter crashed. It was noon when they touched down at Firebase Delta. Colonel Beard was waiting when they landed.

"Glad to have you back, Lieutenant."

"Thank you, sir."

"I know it's been a tough trip, but could you please come over to my office for a few minutes?"

"No problem, sir. Watson, tell the Chief I'll be wanting to talk with him as soon as I finish with the colonel." McConnell followed Beard while Watson and Doc Young headed off toward the SEAL hootch. Colonel Beard's office was neat, almost spartan. There was an absence of military memorabilia that was usually found in the office of a senior officer. The older man motioned him to a chair by the side of his desk while he moved around behind it.

He settled into a beat-up leather swivel chair like a cowboy would ease into his saddle.

"Jim, I received a message yesterday that your relief will be leaving the States in ten days. A Lieutenant Bohannon with your Kilo Platoon. They should be here in about two weeks. In the meantime, I need you to stay in the field. I know it'll be hard for you to go back out after what you've been through, but we need to keep the pressure on the VC."

"I'm not sure we have enough men for a standby fire team. We can go out, but I can't get too far back in the bush without a backup. And to be honest, sir, I'm not sure how combat-ready my men are right now."

"I know you'll need some time to regroup. Let me know when you're ready to stand up. As for a backup squad, there's an Australian Special Air Service group attached to division up in Three Corps. They'll have a fire team here in a day or so, and they can stay until the new platoon is in the field." The colonel hesitated, then added, "How're you doing, Jim?"

"Okay, I guess. We lost three good men." Three, thought McConnell, but it was Reed, the big man with the easy grin—cradling his M60 like it was a toy—that stood out in his mind. After a moment he continued, "This shouldn't have happened, sir. There was no reason to go back there after they took fire on the first time in."

"I know, son. I felt the same way. I probably should have stopped them, but it was a field commander's call. And that's as it should be, I suppose. I know I used to resent it when the man behind the desk played patrol-leader-in-the-sky and tried to call my number in the field. You think Lieutenant France would have listened?"

"No, sir," replied McConnell, meeting the Colonel's eye. "He wanted that money man." Both men were quiet for a moment.

"You did a good job of getting your platoon out of there," said the colonel getting to his feet. "I'm truly sorry for your losses." McConnell moved to leave, but stopped at the door.

"Colonel?"

"Yes, Jim."

"How did you know I'd need those smoke grenades?"

Colonel Beard leaned over his desk, supporting his lanky frame on straight thin brown arms. He rested on his knuckles, head down, like a sprinter at the starting line—then looked up at McConnell.

"In Korea, I was a new second lieutenant, just commissioned out of the ranks. I let part of my platoon get separated and pinned down. It was a rifle platoon—about thirty men. I had no supporting arms. I took a squad to relieve them and we got cut up pretty bad. I lost half my platoon to North Korean snipers that day. If I'd had some smoke, I could have saved a lot of those men."

The Chief was ready for him and handed him a hot cup of coffee. McConnell sat down across from Johnson at a card table in the front of the hootch. I'll bet a lot of the U.S. Navy is run like this, thought McConnell, or it should be. When things get tough, the officer and his chief petty officer sit down over coffee.

"How are the men, Chief?" said McConnell, getting right to the point.

"They're doing surprisingly well, sir. They're scared and still pretty shook. I think everyone knew something like this was going to happen. We've been pressing pretty hard, especially Mr. France's team." What Johnson said made sense. Being safe and alive when others had been killed or wounded was somehow invigorating, even if it was a less than noble thought. There was a sense of "the big one finally happened and I'm still alive," and McConnell was not immune to this feeling.

"Our relief has been ordered in and they'll be here in two weeks or so."

"Mr. Bohannon is a good man. He was with Bravo Platoon in the Rung Sat last year."

"Chief, how come everything I think is current information is old news to you?"

"Just part of my job, sir. And what the message traffic didn't say is that the Kilo Platoon chief is Chief Kanaka, so we should have a smooth turnover. I think you know

Kanaka, don't you, sir?" McConnell watched Johnson for a knowing smile or wink, but detected neither. "Kanaka and I have been corresponding for the past month," Johnson continued. "Platoon turnover is serious business and I like to stay ahead of the game." McConnell just smiled and shook his head. He would never get used to Johnson's ability to anticipate, nor the British-like, offhanded manner in which he regarded this near-clairvoyant capability as normal routine.

"Chief, we still have to operate for a few weeks. I assume you know about the SAS."

"Yes, sir. I worked with the Special Air Service on my third tour. The Aussies are real pros."

"Do they work like us?"

"Not exactly. They're normally used for long-range patrols and try to avoid contact. They're good in a firefight, although their mission is mostly reconnaissance. They like to work with us because we go out looking for it."

"That may be so, Chief, but we're going to be looking for it very carefully for the next two weeks."

The two men talked for about an hour, planning the reorganization of the platoon and integration of the SAS men when they arrived. It was agreed that McConnell would take over what was left of France's fire team, and Chief Johnson would lead the other team. They would use the SAS troopers as augmentees.

"Sir, I had a talk with Oakley and he's pretty shook up about what happened yesterday. He thinks he's a coward for having froze up like that."

"What do you think, Chief?"

"Watching his platoon officer and LPO die were more than he could handle right then. I don't think it'll happen again, but he's worried about what the other guys think."

"And what do they think?"

"They think he froze up, but they're not being as hard on him as he's being on himself."

"We need every man we have left, including Oakley. I'll have a talk with him."

"Thanks. Oh, one more thing, sir, I've packed out Reed's and Rawls's gear to send out on the courier helo tomorrow morning. It's already down at the pad. I figured you'd want to take care of Mr. France's things. And the sooner the better. It's not good for their gear to be around the hootch.''

McConnell left Johnson and headed back to his cubicle. On the way back he saw Watson sitting at the foot of his bunk with Reed's M60 taken apart and laid out on a clean towel. He was carefully oiling each piece and reassembling the weapon. There were several rows of 7.62 linked ball ammo stacked on another towel, ready for loading. The backpack magazine and flex-feed tray stood by awaiting final assembly. McConnell knew Watson should be hung over, but there was a calm intensity in his face that hid all signs of his drinking the night before.

"You okay there, Rick?"

"I'll be ready to go when you are." McConnell walked over and looked down at Watson as he deftly snapped the pieces in place. He worked the bolt back a few times, allowing the heavy recoil spring to carry it home with a loud metallic clatter. The machine gun seemed almost as big as he was, but McConnell knew he could handle it. He had watched as Reed had taken Watson to the edge of the base, and put him through live-fire drills. You can't replace a man like Reed, but Watson would be a better-than-adequate M60 man.

"I know you'll do the job, teammate—I'm counting on it." McConnell clamped him on the shoulder and wandered back over to his cubicle in the corner of the sleeping area. It was now his alone. He knew he should get right to France's things, but he managed to put it off long enough to take a shower and clean up his equipment, which was still dirty from the day before. Packing France's gear turned out to be a quick task because he was remarkably neat. Must be that Naval Academy training, thought McConnell. He stuffed the contents of France's locker into his parachute bag, mostly boots, field gear, and greens. McConnell felt awkward and almost ceremonious as he gathered his dead platoon commander's shaving gear and packed his dop kit.

The last thing he came to was a cigar box full of letters.

McConnell glanced through them, noticing that several were from girls in San Diego. He wondered about France's wife, or ex-wife. There was also a small, neat stack of envelopes, all postmarked Syracuse, New York. Mc-Connell wondered what France's parents were like, and how they had taken the news that their son was dead. They would probably have been notified by now. McConnell drew a picture in his mind of two naval officers—one a chaplain, the other the escort officer—standing on the porch of the France home. Spring would be coming to upstate New York, but not for Mr. and Mrs. France, who had just learned their son was somewhere over the Pacific, stretched out in the cold bay of a C-141 jet transport.

At least you get a good ride back home, Dave. Not like the crates we'll have to ride back on—but the price of your first-class ticket was your life.

McConnell shuddered as he thought of those two somber officers standing on *his* front porch. I've got to pull myself together, he thought. I've got to stay sharp for another two weeks and keep my seat on that ancient, piston-driven junker reserved for live SEALs.

"Cribbs!"

"Yes sir."

"Grab somebody and haul this stuff down to the helipad and get it manifested for tomorrow's courier run."

"Aye aye, sir."

McConnell stretched out on his rack and closed his eyes. He had already sweated through his T-shirt, but he was too tired to get up and take it off. It would be an hour, maybe two before evening chow went down—time enough for a few winks. He had just drifted off to sleep. Only for a few moments, but long enough for the ghosts of France, Rawls, and Reed to make an appearance.

"Boss, wake up!"

"Huh . . . wha . . ."

"Boss, snap out of it—wake up!"

"Dammit, Cribbs, what is it?"

"We gotta move, Boss. There's a Seawolf down!"

McConnell was seated on his bunk, arms straight out to either side to hold himself upright, before Cribbs's message sank in—Seawolf down! "Not again," he said quietly. "God, not again."

"How's that, Boss?"

"Where's the Chief?" replied McConnell, coming more fully awake.

"He's down on the dock. I sent Barnett after him." Cribbs was already strapping on his web gear and grenades.

"What do we have for a slick?"

"They're all up-country. The one gunship is covering the downed bird until the Wolves from Son-on-Doc get on station to relieve him. Then he'll be back here to get us."

We'll be lucky to get five guys in a gunship, thought McConnell. Christ, could we use a slick! Chief Johnson joined them as McConnell began putting on his combat gear.

"How do you want to do this, sir?"

McConnell paused for a moment. It was hard to formulate a plan with so many unknowns.

"Chief, you stay here with the extra men and try to get a slick here as soon as possible. I'll take the first group in." He looked past Cribbs and Johnson to the rest of the platoon that had assembled just outside his door. To a man, they had an expectant look on their faces, like he was choosing up sides for a game in the schoolyard, and nobody wanted to be picked last. "Cribbs you're on point. Doc Young, there may be some wounded so I'll need you. Watson, you're the M60 man." Then he saw a large man behind the others, seated on his bunk with his elbows on his knees and looking down at the floor.

"Oakley, saddle up! You'll be going with me." The big SEAL stared at him briefly with a puzzled look on his face, then he moved for his equipment.

The SEALs straggled over to the helipad as a lone Seawolf landed. Carl Belding leapt out of the pilot's seat and trotted over to McConnell and the other SEALs. The ground crew began refueling and rearming his helo. McConnell produced an acetate-covered map and they gathered around it.

"We took some fifty-one cal fire here," began Belding, shouting over the sound of the turning helo, "and Mike managed to clear the area before his engine quit. They went into the trees about here, right on the edge of the Nam Can.''

"Anyone hurt?''

"The copilot has a broken wrist—one of the door gunners has a broken collarbone and maybe some internal injuries. They're all cut up and bruised. They were lucky—Mike had to drop it through the trees.''

"Radio?''

"Good so far, although the range is only about half a mile. They've managed to move about two hundred yards away from the crash site to here.'' McConnell could see no landing zones close to the downed bird.

"Okay, guys, listen up. We'll have to rappel in through the canopy. We'll secure the area and get the downed crew ready to move out as quickly as possible. The sooner we get there and clear out of the area the better. That crashed helo is going to attract a lot of attention. There's a semi-cleared area right here, about four klicks from the crash site. We'll try to get there before dark for an extraction. Carl?''

"Yeah.''

"I'm going to need my scout. Can you leave a door gunner behind?'' Belding hesitated before nodding. "Cribbs, get Con saddled up and let's get ready to go down the rope.'' McConnell didn't ask if there were any questions—there wasn't time. It was four-thirty and daylight was working against them for an extraction by helo before nightfall. Chief Johnson approached him as he took a six-foot length of half-inch nylon line from his web gear and tied a Swiss seat around his waist and crotch.

"You going to be okay on this one, sir?''

"I don't have much choice, Chief," he replied while he placed the snap-link on the ropes where they crossed just below his navel.

"Be careful, sir, it could be a setup. I've seen the VC use a downed pilot as bait.''

"I'll be careful, Chief, and if I smell a rat, we'll back off. If that slick gets here, get them ready for an extraction and you better break out the McGuire rigs just in case.''

The ground crew finished shackling the rappeling line

to the ceiling of the cramped gunship cabin and the large
coil was tied to the floor. Con and Cribbs leaped abroad
on the run as they lifted off. Once airborne, there was
nothing for McConnell to do but think about the mission
they'd been dealt. It would be a difficult and dangerous
insertion. There were unarmed and wounded men on the
ground, they had limited air cover, and they were right in
the middle of indian country. Various disaster scenarios
flashed through his mind and the familiar lump in his
stomach began to burn. He leaned forward between the
two pilots, looking out through the vibrating Plexiglas
windshield. It was a beautiful Delta afternoon without a
cloud in the sky. The dense Nam Can forest below them
looked like a rumpled emerald carpet with the texture of
cauliflower.

"We're about two minutes out," yelled Belding over
the turbine noise. "Mike said he'll send a star cluster up
to mark his position."

"I'll go down alone first," replied McConnell. "Don't
send the others down until I give the word." Belding gave
him a thumbs-up and began his descent. McConnell
shouted final instructions to his men and took two turns
around his snap-link with the rappeling line. He saw a red
roman candle–like flare rise from the lush green canopy.
Belding banked the helo toward the signal and came to a
hover some thirty feet over the trees. Two other Seawolf
gunships orbited nearby. McConnell threw the coiled line
out over the chopper's skid and leaped out of the helo. He
allowed himself to fall as fast as possible down the line,
knowing he'd be safer on the ground. He crashed through
layers of leaves, limbs, and brush before he arrived on the
muddy ground. It was very dark compared to the bright
world above, and he strained to see into the gloom and
shadows.

"Over here!"

McConnell whirled as his Stoner automatically came to
the firing position, and he almost shot a man standing not
ten feet away in a tattered flight suit. He quickly looked
around and moved to the man. It was Mike Rowney, the
pilot of the downed bird and Belding's wingman.

"Boy, am I glad to see you, y'know, we—"

"Seen any VC?" said McConnell, cutting him short.

"Not a one. We cleared the crash site and moved as—"

"Get your crew ready to move out and do nothing unless I tell you to." McConnell continued to search the brush and trees while he radioed to the hovering Seawolf. Ten seconds later Watson led the first of the SEALs down the line. They came down very quickly with the exception of Con, who came down last, almost shinnying down the rope. McConnell placed them out on perimeter, and sent Doc Young to the flight crew to look after the wounded. He then vectored the helos off to the south of the crash site as a diversion. They listened in silence for a few minutes but heard nothing.

"You ready to move, Doc?"

"Yes sir. Three of them can walk, but we'll have to carry the gunner. I had to dope him up to keep him quiet—he's in a lotta pain."

"Get 'em ready to move, and I'll send Oakley over to give you a hand." Then, turning to Rowney, "You do exactly what the Doc tells you to do. He's in charge of you and your crew now, understand?" The pilot nodded. McConnell gave him a forced smile and a quick thumbs-up. He signaled for Cribbs and Con to join him, and unfolded the map he carried tucked in one of his ammo pouches.

"Tell Con to make for this clearing, and that I'll walk point with him. I want you to bring up the rear in case they come up from behind." Cribbs conferred with the scout, and Con moved off cautiously in a northerly direction with McConnell behind him. Oakley shouldered the unconscious flyer, and they fell into a file behind McConnell, with Watson and Cribbs bringing up the rear.

They moved quickly along the forest floor and were making good time. McConnell was beginning to relax as he concentrated on the woods in front of him and the back of his point man. McConnell marveled at how he could drop Con off anywhere in the province, and he would know exactly where he was. They had been on the trail for about an hour. At this pace, they would make the clearing with daylight to spare. Then Cribbs sent a danger signal up from the rear. McConnell kept the others moving while he quickly worked his way back to Cribbs. As rear security, he had been waiting and listening in the brush for two to three minutes at a time, then jogging up the trail to catch up with the patrol.

"What do you have?" whispered McConnell as he knelt beside him.

"About seventy meters back, a VC platoon and they know we're just ahead of them."

"How many?"

"Twelve, maybe fifteen."

McConnell had only two options—run or fight, and he knew running would probably only postpone the fight.

"What do you think?"

"Let's fucking take 'em."

Easier said than done, thought McConnell, but I don't really have much choice. The canopy was still too thick for the Seawolf gunships to be of any help.

"We'll pick up the pace and set up at the first ambush site we come to. I'll send the Doc ahead with the fly-boys, so the five of us will have to handle it. Keep an eye out for them back here."

McConnell caught up with the others and briefed them as he worked his way back up to Con. They soon came to a stand of nipa palm, just to the left of their route. McConnell directed the SEALs to set up and sent Doc Young ahead with the flight crew. The nipa palm afforded them concealment but very little cover. McConnell would have preferred a better site, but did not have the time to look for one. There wasn't even time to put out claymores—it would be a shoot-out with automatic weapons. The five ambushers were not in place more than two minutes before the first pair of black pajamas filtered out of the trees, followed closely by the rest of the enemy file. They were moving quickly and, to McConnell's satisfaction, the VC were again too close together. A strange calmness came over him as he took the Stoner off safe and gauged just how far he was going to let their point man move abreast of them before he killed him. He was positioned on the left side of the SEAL line and was responsible for the first man.

You mother-fuckers, he thought, are going to pay for killing Reed.

It was the first time he had felt this cold rage before a firefight. He moved slowly to a kneeling position by the side of the nipa palm to get a better field of fire. He trembled slightly, aware that he couldn't wait to begin shooting.

When he took the first enemy soldier, the barrel of his Stoner was no more than two meters from him. He went for a head shot and the man's face literally exploded. Then quickly and methodically he began working down the file as four other rifles opened up on full automatic fire. Tracers crisscrossed through the file, while the scrambling VC tried to shoulder their weapons or hide from the devastating fire. He saw two of them hurled backward as they were dragged off the trail by Watson's M60 rounds. McConnell and Watson picked up the firing while the other three changed magazines. Then he signaled for them to assault. They moved forward on a skirmish line, firing in short bursts to conserve ammunition, but still maintaining fire superiority. They fired into the forms on the ground as well, to make sure they stayed down. McConnell was totally lost in the killing. It was a near orgasmic experience, the long vibrating Stoner barrel ejaculating tracers. Then the bolt of his Stoner fell on a round cocked sideways in the breach. He dropped to one knee to clear the jam. As he did this, a black-clad figure not ten feet in front of him stepped from behind a tree and took aim on him. McConnell looked into the muzzle of the AK-47 assault rifle, and knew he was a dead man. His eyes never left his executioner while his hands fought to clear the weapon. Then the AK jumped from the VC's hands as he was hammered against the tree by automatic fire. McConnell saw Oakley on his right move in front to cover him while continuing to fire and move forward. He cleared the Stoner and rejoined the firing line, but the rage was gone. They moved through the VC column and set a perimeter while Con and Cribbs quickly checked the bodies and placed grenades under some of them with the pins pulled. Con fired twice into one of the prostrate forms. Some of the VC may have escaped but not many. Quickly they collected the enemy weapons and discarded them as they moved to rejoin the others. Five minutes after they had opened fire, they were back in a file and making for the extraction point. At least for a while, they were safe from pursuit.

McConnell tried to focus on the trail ahead and not think about how close he had come to dying, but it was not possible. It was like he had been an observer of the drama, and in his mind's eye, he saw both himself and the VC—he fumbling with the jammed Stoner and the enemy soldier so close he could not miss. Why did the man hesitate? Was he out of ammunition? It happened so slowly when he mentally replayed it. The ever-present fear was now matched with a growing feeling of acceptance—that it was either your turn, or it wasn't. This was in direct conflict with his rational side which mandated that he alone was responsible for controlling these events and the safety of his men. I can't give in to this, he told himself—I *am* responsible and I *do* have control! The short tropical dusk was almost upon them when they reached the clearing.

It was a clearing of sorts in that there was not the dense canopy that was typical of so much of the Nam Can forest. But the tall brush, bamboo, and young mangrove trees would make it impossible to land a helicopter. The jungle grows faster than maps are updated.

"Seawolf One Five, Seawolf One Five, this is Jakeleg Two Seven, Over."

"Roger, Two Seven, this is Seawolf One Five Leader. What is your traffic, over?"

"Roger, Leader, we are at the Lima Zulu, but it is fouled, repeat the LZ is fouled. Do you have a slick, over?"

"Negative, Jakeleg. We have one escorted gunship with McGuire rigs, over."

"Understood, Leader. Wait, out."

That meant that Carl's gunship, escorted by the Seawolf Det from Son-on-Doc, was the only asset available to get them out of the field. He would never be able to take them all out, but he could at least free himself of the flyers, and that would greatly improve the chances for the rest of them.

They had no alternative but to walk out. He took out his map and called Cribbs and Con over.

"We're here and it's about nine klicks down to the Bhi Hap. Can Con get us there by dawn?" After a short conversation with the scout, Cribbs turned back to McConnell.

"He can do it, but he says we should make the extraction before it gets light. There's gonna be a lot of indians out looking for us."

"What's new?" replied McConnell. "We'll send the flight crew out by McGuire rig. I'll help Doc Young with the hookups; you and the other three set up in a wide perimeter. As soon as that helo leaves, we haul ass."

Cribbs nodded and moved off with Con to brief Watson and Oakley. McConnell called for extraction and got the aviators ready to go. The fact that one of them was unconscious would make it difficult but not impossible.

A McGuire rig was nothing more than a long rope with a snap-link at the end of it and a rope loop tied just above the snap-link. The snap-link was tied to a man's Swiss seat and the loop placed under his arms and around his body for additional safety. The lines were attached to a lifting point on the underbelly of the helo. As many as five men could be safely lifted by a gunship and carried in this manner. It was a scary and uncomfortable ride, dangling some two hundred feet below the helo, but there was no way to winch them aboard. The ten-minute ride back to the base would be most unpleasant for the four crewmen, but they would then be safe.

"Seawolf Leader, this is Jakeleg Two Seven. I have four pax ready for McGuire rig, over."

"Roger, Jakeleg, but hurry. I can't hover without a horizon and it's fading fast. Can you give a light, over?"

"Roger, look for my light, Jakeleg out."

When he heard the beat of rotor blades, he pointed a hooded strobe light with a red filter toward the incoming helos. The strobe lights they carried were directional so there was little chance of their being spotted by the VC, and were easily seen from the air. Belding authenticated his red light and brought the gunship to a high hover over their position. He and Doc Young quickly secured the four men to the ends of the McGuire rig lines. They placed the injured man in the middle of the other three, and tied them all together so they would not swing independently and bump into each other when airborne.

"Thanks, Jim, and good luck to you guys," said Mike Rowney as he was secured to the line.

"Right, Mike," said McConnell, "just make sure my message with our pickup time and coordinates gets to Lieutenant Smith." He signaled to the helo, and the clump of men were hoisted into the fading light. They hesitated for a moment in space, then disappeared eastward over the horizon. Young handed McConnell a pack that had come down with the McGuire rigs. It contained sandwiches, Cokes, and ammunition, and was the unmistakable hand-iwork of a senior chief petty officer who anticipated.

The six of them quickly cleared the area, moving east-ward before turning south. After about a half hour on the trail, they stopped to eat and redistribute ammunition. McConnell and the other SEALs took their little yellow dexidrene pills to stay alert. It would be another ten hours before they would be out of the field and able to rest. McConnell began to feel better once they again started moving. The pills helped, but it was more than that. It was dark and he had Con and Cribbs working point in front of him. Considering how vulnerable they had been for the past few hours, it was almost comfortable.

The stay-awake pill was just starting to wear off when they arrived back at the dock the following morning. It had been a long walk and a tense extraction. They had seen only one VC patrol, and managed to avoid it. Once aboard the boat and safely in the middle of the river, a concerned Lieutenant Smith handed him a cup of coffee.

"Aren't y'all a little short for this bullshit?"

"No problem, Smitty. When we get back to the base I'm going to sleep until my relief arrives."

But there was one more evolution ahead of him. When he stepped onto the dock, there was a delegation of men in flight suits with several bottles of champagne. Carl Belding thrust a glass into his hand and charged it.

"Thanks, Jimmy," said Belding over a raised glass.

"We appreciate what you did." A grateful Mike Rowney shook his hand.

"How's your door gunner, Mike?"

"Not good, but he's alive. We sent him and my copilot out on the slick about a half hour ago. I can't tell you how glad I was to see you come down that rope, Jim."

"You guys have saved our ass enough times," said McConnell, draining his glass. "About time we were able to do something for you."

"Glad to have you back, sir," said Chief Johnson as he took McConnell's web gear from his shoulders, "although it is a little late in the tour for these unscheduled walks in the woods."

"Let's hope it's the last one, Chief," replied McConnell as they walked up the dock. "The sandwiches hit the spot, but I'm glad we didn't need the bullets." The champagne and the lingering effects of the dexidrene combined to give him a good buzz, but he knew he would crash hard in just a very short time. As they walked up the dock to the shore, he noticed a group of men in light brown field camouflage uniforms. Each man had a Belgian-made F.A.L. rifle slung over his shoulder—a distinctive weapon with a long barrel protruding from the bottom of the forestock. They were a tanned and weather-beaten lot.

"You gentlemen must be the SAS squad I was promised."

"Too right, sir," said a lean, sandy-haired man in his late twenties. He casually saluted with the palm of his hand forward in the British fashion. "I'm Sergeant Brownyer from the Second SAS Squadron—I'm the senior noncom."

"Glad to have you here, Sergeant. Chief Johnson will make you comfortable and show you around. We'll get together later on today after you're settled."

"Thank you, Lieutenant. We heard about your mission last night. Good on you, sir."

There was another reception at the hootch. They had been through too much the previous day to celebrate, but the dark mood was broken. There were genuine smiles and quiet congratulations. The rest of the platoon joined the returnees in a cold beer as McConnell settled them down for a debriefing.

"This is going to be real short. For a quick reaction drill, you guys did an outstanding job. Things got a little hairy out there, but Cribbs and Con once again kept us out of trouble. Doc, you did a super job of managing the flight crew, and Watson must have got half of that VC platoon with his M60. And Oakley." He paused as he met the big man's eyes. "If you hadn't been there standing tall when my Stoner jammed, this platoon would have lost another officer. Thank you.

"Now that the Aussies are here, we'll be going back to regular operations, but not until the six of us who were out last night get some sleep. The platoon will stand down until tomorrow night at the earliest. Chief?"

"Nothing here, sir. We'll be ready to go when you and the others are rested up."

McConnell slept for ten hours and spent the next evening drinking coffee and talking with Chief Johnson. Sergeant Brownyer joined them and they made the fire team assignments. They were like three major-league coaches setting the batting lineup for the big game. Brownyer was on his second tour and most of his men were veterans. He and two of his men would join Chief Johnson while the other three SAS men would be integrated into McConnell's fire team. McConnell was back in bed by midnight and slept until late morning.

The two fire teams alternated in the field for the next ten days. In keeping with McConnell's instructions, they were conservative operations and did not challenge the VC in their most secure areas. Johnson made contact twice and McConnell only once. Late one morning he was sitting at the bar in the hootch smoking a cigarette, when his attention was taken by the sound of an incoming helo. It was not the sound of a Huey, but the heavy rotor-beat of a much bigger ship. McConnell glanced around the room. He saw that the sound was well marked by other SEALs in the hootch. They all quietly got up and filed down to the helipad.

The SEALs who walked down the ramp of the CH-46

in their greens had a different look to them from the ones
who waited at the edge of the pad. McConnell's men wore
a collection of green T-shirts, shorts, and shower shoes.
In spite of the casual dress, they looked old and tired compared to the new arrivals. McConnell walked over to the
tall Navy lieutenant and held out his hand.

"Welcome to Firebase Delta. I'm Jim McConnell."

"Hello, Jim. I'm Ron Bohannon and this is Kilo Platoon. You guys about ready to go home?" Bohannon had
a broad easy smile, dark hair, and a thick black mustache.
His deep-set eyes were protected by heavy eyebrows that
nearly ran together in the middle of his forehead.

"Ron, if you're ready to run SEAL operations in the
Nam Can, we're ready to go home."

Bohannon laughed and shook his head. "We won't hold
you up too long, but I'll need your help to get acquainted
with the AO." Then, in a quieter voice, "Jim, I'm sorry
about Dave France and the others. They were good men."

McConnell nodded his thanks and grabbed one handle
of Bohannon's parachute gear bag. The two officers headed
for the hootch with the load swung between them. Mc-
Connell's men helped the new arrivals unload the weapon
boxes from the big helo under the dual supervision of
Chiefs Johnson and Kanaka. Kanaka, Bohannon told
McConnell, was Kilo's second-in-command. Team One
was short of officers and not all the platoons could deploy
with two. Bohannon went on to say that Kilo had only one
man who was not a second-tour SEAL. Team One now
considered Firebase Delta as the most dangerous assignment in-country so it drew the most experienced platoon.

Bohannon moved in with McConnell, and the rest of
Kilo Platoon took temporary quarters in the hootch next
door. The kitchen-lounge area in the front of the Foxtrot
hootch remained the activity center for all the SEALs.
Neither McConnell nor Johnson was scheduled to go out
that night so the two platoons drank beer half the night.
McConnell's men got caught up on news from the Strand
and Bohannon's men learned about the Nam Can forest.
After the troops had turned in, Johnson put on a pot of
coffee. The two chiefs and their officers sat down to talk

business. They were joined by Smitty and Sergeant Brownyer.

"Okay, Jim, what do you have in mind?" began Bohannon.

"Chief Johnson and I will continue to operate just like we have been. We'll begin to drop off a few of our men and add yours as we go. We can start with the Aussies. It looks like Sergeant Brownyer and his men are going to be here for a while, and they want to start to operate as a separate squad. They'll clear their operations with me until you relieve me. Then you'll have three fire teams to work with."

"Sounds great. Unless you see it differently, my point man and I will go out with you on the next patrol, and Chief Kanaka and his point will go with Chief Johnson. We'll work it up from there." They discussed other aspects of the turnover. Smitty proposed a training schedule for the men to spend time on the boats and learn the waterways. His relief wasn't due for another three months so the new platoon would have his experience to draw upon. A few of the platoon weapons would pass from Foxtrot to Kilo. The Kits were also a pass-down item. The platoons would come and go, but the word *tour* had no meaning for Con, Billy, and the others. Their status was somewhere between that of a foster child and an indentured servant. They would pass from platoon to platoon and do their work until they grew old or were killed.

The next few days were busy ones. In the daytime, McConnell and Johnson showed their reliefs around the base, and tried to pass on what they had learned over the last six months. McConnell noted that Bohannon asked many of the same questions France had on their arrival. At night, they went into the field. McConnell found that the Kilo SEALs were well prepared and that Bohannon and his men knew their way around the jungle. It must be the training, thought McConnell. They think just like we do out on patrol. One afternoon five days after Kilo's arrival, he caught Bohannon in the front of the hootch.

"Ron, I was talking with Cribbs and Con, and they recommend we go south of the base tonight. We haven't been down there in a while and we might catch something moving on the canals.''

"Good idea, Jim, but it's not 'we' anymore.''

"What do you mean.''

"I stood Kilo up this morning. You're out of it.''

McConnell was completely taken by surprise. He knew Bohannon would soon take over, but he thought that he would set his own relief date. An uncontrolled feeling of relief was held in check by the indignation at not being consulted. Bohannon took two beers out of the reefer and handed one to McConnell.

"Don't I have a say in this?''

"No, this one is my decision.'' He continued in a softer voice: "You've done it all as a first-tour SEAL. You've taken your licks in the field and you've established yourself as a first-class operator. But there's one thing you aren't going to do this trip; you're not going out there knowing it's your last operation. It's not so easy a thing as you might think—your last combat operation.'' McConnell thought about it for a moment and he knew Bohannon was right.

"What made you do it this way?''

"My first platoon commander did it for me. Since Dave France isn't here, I'll do it for him. You're down, Jim, and congratulations,'' he said, raising his glass. "You made it—you're a first-tour SEAL.''

McConnell didn't let it show but a little something inside of him let go, and it made him feel light-headed. He sat down and took a long pull on his beer.

"And to get you out of here so you're not under foot, the 46 will be here tomorrow afternoon to take you and your platoon to Saigon. The freedom bird leaves the day after tomorrow, you lucky sonuvabitch.'' Bohannon was now grinning broadly and he held out his hand. McConnell flushed and noticed his own hand was shaking slightly. The tall lieutenant gripped McConnell's hand with both of his own, and looked him right in the eye. He knew exactly what was going on inside McConnell.

"Well, I better leave you to pack. I have to go down and talk to Smitty about our operation tonight. See you later, Jim.''

"Uh, sure, Ron. Where're you going, anyway?"

"Sorry, partner. I can't discuss operational shit with you noncombatants. See you at chow." He laughed and headed out the door.

McConnell finished his beer in one swallow and walked back to his cubicle. He started to pack, but then stopped and sat on his bunk.

It was over.

It was really over.

The tears were spilling over his cheeks before he knew he was actually crying. He sat there for a few moments, confused and unable to focus his thoughts. Then he rolled on his side facing the wall with his knees drawn up near his chest, and was asleep in a matter of minutes.

That night the Foxtrot SEALs gathered in the front of the hootch for their last night at Firebase Delta. It was a bittersweet gathering. They toasted each other for having made it through the tour, but the excitement of finally leaving was dampened by the knowledge that fourteen of them had arrived together and only nine were manifested on the flight home. France, Rawls, and Reed were dead. Morales would be okay, but Bono might be a cripple. Five of the nine who remained had Purple Hearts. It had been a very costly six months. It could have been worse, McConnell told himself, but he knew it could also have been a lot better.

"All packed up and ready to go?" said Colonel Beard as he sat down beside McConnell.

"Evening, sir," he replied. "I didn't even see you come in. We'll box up the weapons and field gear tomorrow. The rest of it goes into a parachute bag and that's a five-minute evolution."

"That's a soldier's life, Jim—put everything you own in your pack." Then the older man reached over and placed his hand on top of McConnell's shoulder. "Son, you may not hear much of this when you get back, but thanks for what you did over here. I'm not going to bullshit you, and tell you that your operations changed the course of the war. You're a professional officer—you do your job and you draw your pay. But you have my respect and gratitude."

"Thank you, sir. I appreciate that. I think Lieutenant Bohannon and his platoon are going to do a good job for you. By the way, Colonel, when do you rotate back to the States?"

"Another sixty days if they can find what they call 'a suitable replacement.' Which means someone who'll take the job."

"Where will you go next, Colonel?"

"I'm goin' fishin'. There's a stream in the Ozarks that's got a ten-pound rainbow trout with my name on it." He rose from the table, offering McConnell his hand. "Enjoy your last night ashore, sailor. I'll see you at the helipad tomorrow." He made the rounds shaking each man's hand and left.

As the evening wore on, a parade of base inmates came by to say good-bye to the departing SEALs. The Seawolf personnel were especially conspicuous. Carl Belding still had thirty days left to complete his tour. McConnell felt like he was abandoning Belding and the others. The war was its own entity, but the people like Carl and Colonel Beard and Smitty had become very special to him. Nurse Thompson would call this the "running-out-on-your-buddies syndrome" that afflicts the male warrior species. He really wished Smitty was there, but he was out that night with Bohannon.

"Where are the other SEALs, Chief? I thought Kanaka and his team would be here."

"It's not their party, and they'll probably stay away. How'd you like to sit around and drink with a bunch of guys going home, knowing you had a full tour in front of you? They're the on-call fire team anyway. The Aussies are going out at first light. Get you another beer, sir?"

"No thanks, Chief. I have a little duty to perform and now is as good a time as any. Why don't you get the troops together and pass around some glasses? I'll be right back."

McConnell slipped through the beaded curtain and soon returned from his quarters with a bottle of fifteen-year-old scotch in each hand. The SEALs gathered around the table while McConnell opened a bottle and poured a generous measure in each man's glass.

"Hey, Boss, where'd you get the high-priced booze?" asked Watson.

"Mr. France left it for us."

The men stood in silence while McConnell poured himself a shot.

"Gentlemen, to the Foxtrot SEALs who aren't with us tonight—God bless 'em."

"God bless 'em!"

McConnell opened the other bottle and recharged their glasses. Then he raised his own to the men in front of him.

"Now here's to you men. Thank you for your sacrifice, your courage, and your friendship. It's been an honor to serve with you." He drained his glass and set it on the table.

"We'd like to drink one to you, sir," said Cribbs, stepping forward. "This tour was no fucking cakewalk. Thanks for being there for us. Here's to you, Boss."

"To the Boss!"

"Right on!"

"Fuckin'-A!"

The warmth and goodwill of those around him made peace with the ghosts of those not there, at least for the time being. The tour had exacted a price from each of them, but being safe, alive, and going home was a powerful tonic. The mood of the group took a festive but mellow turn as other end-of-tour bottles stashed around the hootch were broken out. McConnell migrated around the room, spending a few minutes with each man. Watson, the perennial short-hitter, was babbling incoherently to Barnett, who listened patiently. Cribbs and Doc Young sat across from each other at the bar with a bottle and two shot glasses between them. The Doc was trying to help Cribbs analyze his true feelings about his parents. McConnell approached a big SEAL at the end of the bar.

"Thanks for having confidence in me, Boss," said Oakley as he shook his hand.

"Thank you for being there when I needed you," replied McConnell. They moved on to small talk and what each planned to do when he got home. Oakley had saved McConnell's life and to an extent, McConnell had saved his. They would probably not speak of it again, but that bond would always be there. McConnell joined Chief Johnson at the table. It was one of the few times McConnell had seen the Chief take more than just one or two drinks.

"How's it going there, Senior Chief? You ready to go home?"

"You bet I am, sir, and congratulations again—you did a fine job this tour."

"Thanks for saying so, Chief, but you were there every step of the way. A boot platoon officer couldn't have had a better platoon chief." They drank to each other and watched the other SEALs with a paternal satisfaction.

"Sir?"

"Yeah, Chief?"

"Did Mr. France really leave that expensive scotch for us?"

McConnell reached into the breast pocket of his greens and fished out a folded piece of paper that he handed to Johnson. It was tattered on one edge where it had been torn from a spiral notebook. Johnson unfolded it and read:

Jim,

If you're reading this, then I probably didn't make it to the end of the tour. You're now the platoon commander of Foxtrot Platoon, and I'm counting on you to take the guys home. I know we didn't always see things the same way, but you're a good man and I know you'll do the job. Just remember that we're fighting a war, so you can't always be Mister Nice Guy. And give Rawls a chance. He's a little rough around the edges, but he'll stand by you.

The scotch is for the end-of-tour party so don't go drinking it ahead of time. When you do finish the tour,

have one for me. And remember, don't cut those VC
sons-of-bitches any slack—make the fuckers dance.

Dave

"Mr. France was right about Rawls."

"How's that, Chief?"

"He was right that Rawls would stand by you—he sure
stood by Mr. France. Rawls wasn't stupid. He probably
knew it was suicide to go across that paddy after Mr.
France. But he went anyway."

Johnson carefully folded the letter up and handed it back
to McConnell. Then he quietly poured them both another
drink.

The next morning was a busy one as the Foxtrot SEALs
cleared out of their hootch and stacked their gear bags and
weapons boxes on the helipad. McConnell had a late
breakfast with Smitty, who had just returned with Bohannon's fire team. He'd miss Smitty and both felt awkward
at saying good-bye. They shook hands and promised to
have their next beer together in San Diego. McConnell
grabbed his parachute bag and headed for the helipad.

"Here, let me give you a han' wi' dat, sir."

"Chief petty officers don't carry officers' bags, do
they?"

"Not often, but I make 'ception dis time, sir," said the
ever-smiling Kanaka. They slung the bag between them as
they walked to the pad.

"Good to be back in the team after the training unit,
Chief?"

"Not so bad, sir. We got a pretty good platoon. But I
can tell one t'ing. If had my twenty in, I'd be on Kauai
right now."

"Chief Kanaka," said McConnell as they dropped the
bag on the metal matting, "you'd trade your M60 for a
ukulele?"

"You bet you ass I would, sir. Have a nice trip home,
Meesta McConnell. You deserve it."

"Thank you, Chief. And you have a safe tour."

* * *

The Foxtrot SEALs sat on their gear bags and waited for the helicopter. McConnell felt out of place in a pressed green uniform and naked without his Stoner. Soon the big bird came spiraling down out of the sky.

"Okay, you guys, that chopper will want to be out of here in five minutes and so will we," said Chief Johnson. "Let's hustle that gear aboard."

The big CH-46 landed, covering everything with a new layer of dust. The ramp opened and the SEALs quickly loaded the platoon gear. As McConnell started for the helo, he saw Carl Belding and the colonel standing by the Seawolf hootch. They both came to attention and saluted. McConnell paused to return their salute, then grabbed his bag and hurried aboard.

Chapter Fourteen

MIKE PLATOON

McCONNELL AWOKE slowly from a very deep, and for the first time in a long while, dreamless sleep. Things were different—they were soft. He opened his eyes and examined his surroundings. The bed coverings were pastel and sweet, not the harsh, yellow-white military-issue linen that smelled like bleach. A down comforter floated on top of him. The cheery, flowered wallpaper was broken by window casements dressed in lace curtains. I'm sure as hell not in my hootch at Firebase Delta, mused McConnell as he pushed himself upright in the large double bed. This place is all female. Then he remembered Amy Brown and the Downwinds. Her presence was confirmed by singing and the smell of bacon coming from the hall. She had brought him home, fed him, and taken him to bed. He had had a lot to drink, but he remembered her being nothing short of fantastic. He found himself hoping he had given a good account of himself as well.

"Well, Jimmy, did you finally decide to wake up?" He glanced at his watch, noting that it was after nine.

"Morning. Sorry to be such a slob. Have you been up long?"

"An hour or so," she said, sitting on the edge of the bed. "You were sleeping so soundly I decided not to wake you. Hungry?" She looked even better than she had last night.

"For breakfast or for you?"

"Breakfast will be on in fifteen minutes, sailor," she laughed, tossing him a folded towel and washcloth. "The shower is down the hall, and there's aspirin in the cabinet if you feel the need."

The bath was even more feminine than the bedroom. There was lots of lavender and numerous short cylindrical containers. The shower nozzle looked like a telephone on the end of a hose and he could find nothing but round perfumed cakes of soap. After the shower, he joined her at the breakfast bar that separated the kitchen from a small living room. She fixed him a man's breakfast—bacon, eggs over easy, hash browns whole-cut from potatoes, and dark toast. Then she cleared away the dishes and poured them both another cup of coffee. McConnell felt wonderful.

"Amy, last night was terrific, and the breakfast was terrific. You're terrific."

"You're not so terrible yourself, fellah. What's on your schedule? Do they give you time off when you come back from Vietnam?"

"I've got some paperwork to finish up today. Then I'll probably put in for some leave to go home to see the folks. Let my dad take me down to the legion hall and show me off." He laughed but knew it would be close to the truth, even though he sensed both his dad and mom had been close to tears when he phoned from Hawaii to tell them he was out of it.

"I see the guys from the teams around and they're always talking about Vietnam. They say you were in a very difficult place. If you don't mind me asking, what was it like?" McConnell looked at her closely.

"You really want to know?"

"Back at Northwestern, half the campus protested against the war and the other half didn't care. Out here, half the people are in the military and the other half don't care. The country is so divided. I'd like to understand what's going on over there."

She was beginning to sound like Connie. If the women were in charge, he thought, there probably wouldn't be a war. How do I tell someone like her, in this neat, well-appointed apartment, about the fear and the mangrove and the "what if"? How can I describe what I've been through to someone like her? A part of him wanted her to know what it was like; to really understand what it took out of him—out of all of them—to be in combat, but he wasn't sure it was possible. The old adage "You had to be there" flashed through his mind. She honestly wants to know what it was like in Vietnam, but I'm not sure I can put it into words she'll understand.

"Vietnam is everything San Diego isn't. It was hot, humid, dirty, and dangerous. One of the men I was responsible for, a very good man, was killed and another seriously wounded. Two other men in the platoon were killed. I guess the worst for me was that I had to constantly make hard decisions." He paused, trying to bring it into focus. "I lived with the constant fear of making a wrong decision—one that would get my men hurt. We killed over a hundred and twenty VC, and they killed three of us. Somebody up the line probably thinks that's terrific, but those three guys weren't numbers—they were my teammates. I'll be twenty-three next month. I'm tired of being scared and I'm tired of being responsible."

She reached over and placed her hand on top of his. He saw the pain in her face that must have been a reflection of his own. He did not want to involve her in this, and he felt very self-conscious in discussing it. Maybe he was a little jealous of his feelings, even selfish.

It took me a full combat tour to feel this way, he thought—I'm not ready to share it just yet.

"Hey, look, we can talk about this if you want, but I've had enough Vietnam for a while. I really like the idea of not being there."

"That's okay, but if you want to talk about it, I'm here and I am interested."

"Do you have to go to work, or do you have the day off?" he said to change the subject.

"I have a flight this afternoon so I'm free until then. When do you have to go back to Coronado?"

"I've got to be at the team area by one o'clock."

"Well, we could go for a walk in Balboa Park or we can just sort of hang around here."

"I've had my share of walking in the woods for a while. Let's just sort of hang around here."

"Whatever you say, sailor," she replied as he took her hand and led her back to the bedroom.

McConnell carefully pinned the two single silver bars to the open collar of his khaki uniform. He had bought them in the PX in Saigon, but had yet to dress officially as a lieutenant (junior grade). He had not bothered to change the brown cloth ensign bars that were sewn on his jungle greens, the greens that remained in a pile in the corner where he discarded them last Friday. The sterile BOQ room was in sharp contrast to Amy's apartment. He'd just had time to shave and change before going over to the SEAL Team One compound. He felt like a real naval officer in the tropical khaki uniform and visored combination cap. He and Amy had made plans for next weekend, and he felt almost like a college kid again as he put the MG's top down for the short drive over to the team area. The gate guard at the Team One compound waved him through, and he swung the little car into the row of parking places reserved for platoon commanders. It was a place of honor, and he felt a conscious surge of pride as he got out of the car. He walked through the entryway and returned the salute of the quarterdeck watch.

"Afternoon, Mr. McConnell."

"Welcome back, sir."

"Afternoon, sir."

Again McConnell was treated with the respect of a returning warrior. He returned the greetings and salutes as he made his way across the Team One grinder to the connex box assigned to Foxtrot Platoon. There he found Cribbs, Oakley, and Watson unloading weapons and platoon equipment. All equipment, especially the weapons, had to be inventoried and turned in.

"Have a good weekend, guys?"

"Hey, Boss."

"H'lo, sir."

"Yeah, we had a good weekend—as good as you can have in Tiajuana," said Watson. "Paid good money to watch a floor show with fat naked women and farm animals.''

"I don't know, sir," said Cribbs. "You expose these turkeys to a little culture and they get crude. I'm tellin' you, it was gin-u-wine art.''

"Speaking of exposure, sir, we almost spent the night in the slammer 'cause your point man was walking around the Long Bar with his dong hanging out.''

"Ain't that what we're fighting for, Boss," offered Cribbs, "the right of the individual to freely express himself?''

"Don't listen to him, Boss," said Watson. "If Oakley hadn't sweet-talked the shore patrol, you'd have had to muster us in the brig.'' Somehow McConnell felt more at ease listening to Watson and Cribbs carry on, than he had the whole weekend.

"Uh, where is everyone, anyway?''

"Barnett is over at the armory," said Oakley. "Most everyone else is off on leave.''

"How about the Chief?''

"He went over to the operations office about fifteen minutes ago.''

"How's the gear coming?''

"No sweat, sir. We'll have everything squared away and checked back in by the time liberty call goes down.''

I'll bet you will, thought McConnell as he walked back across the grinder to the operations office. The office was empty except for the ops yeoman who was busily pounding the typewriter.

"Have you seen Senior Chief Johnson?''

"Huh—oh, afternoon, sir. Chief Johnson was here about ten minutes ago, but he left.''

"Where's Mr. Harper?''

"He's out on a beach run. He should be back in about a half hour.'' McConnell walked over and looked out the window across the grinder to see if he could see anything of the Chief. "Mr. McConnell?''

"What is it?''

"Sir, I think you better check out the status board.''

"What?''

"The status board, sir.''

He stepped over to the large board hanging on the wall. It looked much as it had back on that first day when he arrived at SEAL team, but the platoons and names were different. Across the top were the recent returnees: Delta, Echo, and Foxtrot, with *tour complete* written diagonally across the platoon rosters. He winced as he saw the lines drawn through the names of France, Rawls, and Reed. Bono and Morales's names merely had asterisks by them. Then there were the deployed platoons: Golf, Hotel, India, Juliette, and Kilo. And the platoons in pre-deployment training: Lima and Mike . . .

McConnell's stare froze on Mike Platoon:

Deployment:	Unassigned
Platoon Cdr:	Lt(jg) McConnell
Asst Plt Cdr:	Ens. Newell
Plt CPO:	HTCS Johnson
LPO:	BM1 Crabbtree
Corpsman:	HM2 Thomas
	BM2 Cribbs
	BM3 Watson
	QM3 Barnett
	BT3 Boyhan
	AT3 Horst
	RD3 Parrott
	Three to be assigned

Deployment ETD: 10 August 69

Subconsciously he had always known he'd probably have to go back, but he had effectively suppressed the idea. It was like dying—something you don't want to think about until you're at least forty. Maybe the war would end or he'd get assigned to UDT. Maybe he'd live forever. The tenth of August. That was just four months away. McConnell slumped into the chair near the status board.

"Shit."

"Beg pardon, sir?"

"I said, shit!"

"Aye, sir."

McConnell sat there for five minutes staring at the board. When he closed his eyes, he was back moving through the mangrove at first light, and he could almost smell the soggy decay of the swamp, feel the mud clinging to his boots. When he opened his eyes he saw Mike Platoon—10 August. He slowly got up and walked down the hall. He knocked on the door and opened it.

"Captain, can I see you for a moment?"

"Sure, Jim—come on in. Close the door if you like." Lieutenant Commander Green was seated behind his desk. He looked up at McConnell over half-frame reading glasses that looked small and frivolous on his handsome, well-lined face. He removed the glasses and leaned forward on his elbows, giving McConnell his full attention.

"Sir, it's about the deployment of Mike Platoon. We just got back! It's not right."

"I know. And I wouldn't be sending you back so soon if I had an alternative. The fact is I don't. General Abrams wants six Team One platoons in Vietnam and we're lucky to stand up five. We aren't getting that many officers through training and the UDT teams need men, too. I don't like this, but I have no choice." Green got up and walked over to the window, turning his back on McConnell. "Jim, you're one of the good ones, like Tom Bohannon who relieved you. You deserve better, but the only reward I can give you for being good is a quick turnaround. The same for your enlisted."

"Captain, there's over thirty officers assigned to Team One."

"I know. Fifteen are deployed with the in-country platoons or on advisory tours. Eight are in school or on predeployment status, like you. I have six who are due to get out of the Navy in the next few months. And there are a few who just can't cut it. I can't deploy officers who can't lead in combat. The men deserve better than that." Green turned around and looked at him. "Jim, there's two hundred and twenty some men assigned to Team One, but when it comes right down to it, the six or eight officers who can take platoons over there and run combat operations are the men I have to rely on. Officers like you who have proved yourselves and the platoon chiefs are the men I count on to get the job done."

"I'm not sure I'm one of those, Captain."

"Well, I think you are and I'm the boss here. You weren't six months ago, but I'm pretty sure you are now. When you young officers come out of training, we know you're tough. But it takes a combat deployment to see if you can hack it under fire. That's why we try to send a new officer with a veteran." McConnell just stood there looking at Green. He wanted a way out, but his commanding officer was not giving him one. As if reading his mind, Green continued, "If you don't want to go back, I can't force you. You volunteered in, and you can volunteer out. But your name stays on the board unless you request a transfer back to the fleet." McConnell digested this for a moment. In other words, he thought, I have to ring the bell.

"I understand. If it comes to that, I'll let you know." He shrugged and turned for the door. "Thanks for your time, sir."

"Any time. And thank you again for bringing that platoon back."

McConnell stood in the hall outside Green's office for a few moments, hands on his hips. He was trapped again. But it was far more terrifying this time. When he first came to SEAL team he had not known—really known—about Vietnam and combat deployments. He was fresh out of training, and flush with the adventure of it all. Now there were no illusions. Living with that knowledge over the next four months would be as bad as going back. He walked out across the grinder and ran into Oakley.

"Have you seen Chief Johnson?"

"About fifteen minutes ago, sir. He was headed out behind the paraloft."

"Thanks, Oakley."

"Mr. McConnell?"

"Yes."

"Sir, we saw the board—I mean, about Mike Platoon being formed. I got another year to do on this hitch, and I'm sure to be assigned to another platoon. If I have to go back, I'd like to go with you and the other guys."

"Okay, Oakley, I'll let you know." McConnell again began to feel like an involuntary volunteer.

The paraloft anchored the seaward end of the SEAL

team compound and rose some five stories above the sand. It was the last structure between the team area and the beach. McConnell walked across the blacktop and into the sandy area behind the paraloft where he found his chief. Johnson was sitting on the ground with his back up against the building, looking out across the water. His starched fatigue cap rode uncharacteristically on the back of his head, and his forearms rested on the tops of his knees, hands hanging down between his legs. McConnell quietly sat down beside him and assumed the same position.

"Afternoon, Senior Chief."

"Afternoon, sir."

They were silent for several minutes before the older man spoke with a quiet resignation.

"I don't know if I have another tour in me, sir. I mean, it's not like I haven't done some time on deployment. I was in the Run Sat twice. I've been with the PRUs on an advisory tour and I been in the lower Delta three times. And I'll tell you, sir, none of them was easy, but this last one was a sonuvabitch." He hesitated, then added, "I just don't know if I can do it again."

"I'm not so sure I can either. You've put in your time on SEAL deployments, Chief, and I'm sure there's a billet for you at the training unit or in UDT. You want me to talk to the Captain?"

"No, sir. I'm a SEAL team chief. If I figure I can't do the job, I'll retire. I got my twenty done and then some." It's the fucking bell, thought McConnell. It's still there, even for a man like Johnson.

Again the two sat in silence, each lost in his own thoughts about the past and what might be ahead.

"Chief, I'm going to have to make that deployment. It's going to be a tough one without a good platoon chief." Johnson picked up a small rock and pitched it toward the Pacific. Then he pulled the fatigue cap down over his eyes.

"Well, they can't send us back to Firebase Delta—we're too short on the turnaround."

"We could get assigned to one of those pacified areas, like up around Vung Tau."

"Right sir, and Ho Chi Minh and all the VC could *chieu hoi* next week."

They sat for a while longer before McConnell got to his feet and brushed the sand from the seat of his khaki trousers.

"Oakley says he wants to go with us."

"I think we should take him. Crabbtree just came over from UDT Twelve. He's never made a SEAL tour, but I think he has the makings of a good LPO. The others are kids out of training, but we'll work on them."

"Thanks, Chief."

"I wouldn't go back with anybody else, sir."

"Maybe not, Chief, but thanks anyway."

McConnell walked back across the grinder, thinking about the chief and his new platoon. He didn't see the stocky young officer approach him from the side.

"Mister McConnell?"

"Yeah."

"Sir, I'm Ensign Newell."

"So?"

"Sir, I'm assigned to Mike Platoon. I'm your assistant platoon commander."

"What's your name?"

"Ensign Newell, sir."

"No, your first name."

"It's uh, Gary, sir."

"Gary, from now on you call me 'Jim.' We got a busy four months ahead of us before we deploy. Let's go over to the ops office and get some coffee."